What the Duke Wants

Agents of Change, Book 1

Amy Quinton

D1608123

Amy Quinton

England, 1814: *Upstanding duke desperately seeks accident-prone wife from trade…*

She is from trade. He is a duke and a spy with a name to restore and a mystery to solve.

Miss Grace (ha!) Radclyffe is an oftentimes hilariously clumsy 20-year-old orphan biding her time living with her uncle until she is old enough to come into her small inheritance. Much to her aunt's chagrin:

She isn't:

- Reserved—not with her *shocking!* tendency to befriend the servants…
- Sophisticated—highly overrated if one cannot run around barefoot outside…
- Graceful—she once flung her dinner into a duke's face…by accident, of course.

But she is:

- Practical—owning a fashion house is in her future, unless someone foils her plans…
- In love…maybe…perhaps…possibly…

The Duke of Stonebridge is a man with a tragic past. His father died mysteriously when he was twelve years old amid speculation suggesting that the old duke was '*involved*' with another man. He must restore his family name, but on the eve of his engagement to the perfect debutante, he meets his betrothed's cousin, and his world is turned inside out… No matter:

He is always:

- Logical—men who follow their hearts and not their heads are foolish…
- Reserved—his private life is nobody's business but his own…

And he isn't:

- Impulsive—it always leads to trouble…
- Charming—that's his best friend, the Marquess of Dansbury's, area of expertise…
- In love…maybe…perhaps…possibly…

Can he have what he wants and remain respectable? Can she trust him to be the man she needs?

Dedication

To my mother-in-law, Hilary Quinton, for the many months listening to me talk about plot points, for reading and rereading work outside your preferred genre, and for your advice. I've picked up your brains from the porch floor and will hold on to them for you until your next visit to the States.

And to my friends and family for your support and encouragement.

Acknowledgements

I would like to thank Jessica Cale for the wonderful cover art. I would also like to thank Joanne Soper-Cook and Terri Schaefer for the editorial work.

Thank you!

Prologue

Eton College…
September 1798…

Thirteen-year-old Ambrose Langtry, 10th Duke of Stonebridge, touched his fingers to his lips as the taste of blood flooded his mouth. He had been walking across School Yard, minding his own business, when the fist appeared out of nowhere, striking him square in the mouth. The force of it knocked him to the ground; his books scattered across the cobbles, loosened papers swirled away with the wind.

He felt around for his split lip. *Ouch.* Yea, it was split, it stung. And to make matters worse, he was sprawled on his arse where any boy walking by could see. Still, he sat there, bemoaning his bruised tail bone as he poked around inside his mouth with his tongue, searching for loosened teeth. *Phew.* They all appeared to be intact.

A shadow fell over him, blocking the meager morning sun. Despite his disadvantaged position upon terra firma, he halted his personal inspection, looked up, and locked eyes with the boy standing over him, presumably the boy attached to said fist.

Ambrose arranged his face into his fiercest scowl while noting that the bully had brought along a friend. Typical. They always did attack in pairs. He was scared, but these tyrants definitely didn't need to know that. Oh, and his tongue smarted; he must have bitten it.

"Say, what do we have here? Looks like we have a first year who thinks he can look his betters in the eye?"

The boy was huge and a House Captain: one of a thousand thugs charged with meting out 'discipline'. They always seemed to be everywhere you didn't want them to be. Like ants.

"Do you know who we are, boy?"

The hammer-fisted giant smirked at his crony: another typical pimple-faced fourth year who, despite missing a surprising amount of teeth, grinned and stared daggers at Ambrose while punching his fist into his hand—definitely a bully.

A third assailant pushed his way between the other two.

"Well, well, well, if it isn't the Duke of Stonebridge," mocked the new arrival. The other two blockheads chuckled their contempt.

Lord Richard Middlebury. Ugh.

"I'd suggest we birch him now, but he might like having us pull his trousers down…Like father, like son, eh, Stonebridge?"

The boys sniggered again, then began to argue amongst themselves as they fought to decide how best to handle the 'situation'. Idiots, the lot of them. Middlebury probably'd be considered the 'brains' if one had to decide such a thing. That wasn't saying much.

He was unsurprised by their taunts. Vile rumors about his family spilled from everyone's lips since Father died. They said Father had been riding in his carriage with another man, a bare-arsed-naked-as-the-day-he-was-born other man. They said the pair of them had been cavorting at a molly house the whole night through. They said a God awful lot of things.

Bollocks. All of it.

It had been a year, yet the pain was ever present. Not a sore-tooth type of ache, but a throbbing-twinge-in-the-chest, knife-to-the-gut kind of ache. Excruciating. Agonizing.

Unbearable. Sometimes, he forgot. In fact, he scarcely thought on the scandal anymore. Yeah, he lied sometimes, too.

His three tormentors, fleetingly forgotten, drew his attention back to the moment at hand. They had come to an accord. Great.

"Is it true, little Ambrose? Would you like us to pull your trousers down?"

They sniggered again. All three of them, the loudmouthed boors. He tried to ignore them as he stood and brushed the dirt from his trousers. They allowed him to gain his feet and restore his garments without incident. Which was odd. And a bit alarming.

Father had not been prone to violence, and he, normally, was the same. Why this time was different, he didn't know, but for some reason, today the pain would not be denied, and with a strength he never suspected he possessed, he unexpectedly retaliated.

He bared a full year of built-up emotions through his arms and legs as he swung, kicked and bit at everything within reach. He saw red, and his eyes burned from the tears that threatened to fall. He blinked rapidly; a recent habit, for the tears were always hiding just beneath the surface. He became a mythical berserker, all but blinded by his anguish and no longer in control of his body. His hands ached from the repeated impact of fist to flesh. He didn't stop. He ignored his conscience. He wouldn't stop.

Occasionally, a word pierced his emotional storm: Bastard. He punched someone's face. Suicide. He kicked someone's shin. Weak. He elbowed someone's nose. Sodomy. He kneed someone's gut.

They were only words all jumbled together and fuzzy, but too reminiscent of past hecklings. The rage drove him indefinitely before silence pricked his awareness. His mind struggled to make sense of the disquiet while his fists continued to fly.

Then he heard a sound; one so soft, he might have imagined it, yet so compelling it seized his attention through his haze of anger:

"Ambrose..."

He ceased his attack, and with wild eyes, searched the crowd for its source, but he felt sluggish, as if he moved about in slow motion, his arms and head burdened with heavy weights. The pain in his knuckles was a distant throb. His bottom lip felt swollen and fat as he absentmindedly tongued his bloody split. Reluctantly, he let go his desperate search.

A mob of students had gathered to gawk, yet he heard nothing. Time crawled, yet it was over in minutes. He caught sight of a peculiar fluttering out the corner of his eye, and he twisted to get a better look. It was a bloody cravat flapping about in the breeze. He started to become further aware of his surroundings.

He was on his knees, straddling Middlebury, his hands squeezing the boy's neck. And the blood...it was everywhere. He looked about with increased anxiety, as reality— and with it panic—crept in. On reflex, he released his hold on Middlebury, whose head hit the cobbles with a wet, sickening thud. His other tormentors lay motionless nearby, as life reverted to full speed and the silence was shattered.

What have I done?

Cool air blew through the school yard, raising goose bumps across his clammy, overheated skin. An occasional gasp or whispered comment tickled his ears. He caught sight of onlookers eyeing him with disgust before turning their backs. Some help they were. The air smelled fresh and crisp and cold in his nose and birds chirped in nearby trees as if today were just an ordinary autumn day, oblivious to the humans and their discord. It was surreal. One of the boys moaned, but not Middlebury. Ambrose took this all in on a glance, his senses now hyper aware. And he was ashamed.

He had just reached down to check Middlebury's injuries, when he was jerked to his feet and spun about to face Head Master Smith.

Ah, bloody hell, I'm in deep shite now.

Head Master Smith was tall and gaunt, but impeccably dressed in unrelieved black from his boots to his cravat. Even his hair was black. By contrast, his skin was so pale as to appear luminescent, the whiteness only marred by prominent blue veins at his temples. He resembled death. Or what Ambrose thought death would look like if it took human form.

Ambrose trembled with frayed nerves, chilled to the bone at the sight, and his heart leapt in his chest. *God, please don't let them notice.* He thrust aside wild thoughts of every possible sentence he might face. At least he tried to. An eternity passed while he waited; thirty years at the very least. He would be an old man by the end, decrepit and scarred. Head Master would probably look the same. Preserved.

Ambrose was held in place by a guard, his arms clamped behind his back and his head held steady by his hair. The. Entire. Time. His scalp stung and had lost numerous strands of hair in the process while he waited. A few were caught in his guard's waistcoat. He was forced by this position to stare into Head Master's emotionless grey eyes. It was unnecessary, for he did not intend to look away. He wanted Head Master to believe he wasn't afraid. He wasn't afraid. At all. Surely.

No words were spoken before Head Master broke eye contact. It was all so anticlimactic. He nodded once at his guard before walking away without a word.

In response, the guard released his hair minus a few more strands, but not his arms. He was shoved forward down the path toward the Block, and he stumbled, often, over the uneven cobbles, his legs unsteady and fatigued. At the very last minute, before they turned out of sight, he looked back, but the throng had closed in, surrounding the fallen boys. He could see nothing but the dark jackets and hats of his fellow students, black marks in a landscape of green and blue and stone. He turned back around and plodded on to meet his fate.

The wind ruffled his remaining hair. Huh. He had lost his hat at some point during the melee. And with that thought, a memory surfaced: Father had just gifted him with his first hat, a bicorne. He was six years old, or thereabouts. He marched about the house and grounds all afternoon showing it off and brandishing a wooden sword. That evening, he sat with Father on an old bench under a grand English oak and talked about what it meant to be a gentleman. He had sworn never to forget.

Had he been alive to witness today's events, Father would have been disappointed and ashamed. His actions today had not been what Father would have considered appropriate behavior for a gentleman, surely, and that bothered him more than any of the suggestive taunts from earlier. *Ah, God…Father, I'm so, so sorry.* It was at that precise moment when Ambrose, recently named Duke of Stonebridge with no small amount of means at his disposal, realized…no, vowed…he would do everything in his power to clear the Stonebridge name, his family's name, of scandal.

Chapter 1

Beckett House…
Amberley, West Sussex…
Country Home of the Earl and Countess of Swindon…
25th April, 1814…

"What are we going to do about her, George? If she ruins everything for our Beatryce with her common…"

Grace Radclyffe, the twenty-year-old niece of the Earl and Countess of Swindon, leaned back against the wall, raised her eyes to the ceiling, and blew out her breath in relief as the shrill sounds of her aunt's remaining words were cut off by the closing of the study door. Thankfully, her uncle's response was indiscernible, his answering voice muffled by the paneled walls.

Grace had been on her way outside when Aunt Mary had come barreling down the stairs in high dudgeon. Grace had quickly dashed into an alcove beneath the stairs to avoid a confrontation. She had simply planned to wait for Aunt Mary to pass before continuing on her way outside and was surprised — well, perhaps not surprised as much as…caught unprepared…by her aunt's reproving words.

Grace's eyes watered as she fought for control over her emotions. She refused to cry, but it was never easy to know you were the unpleasant topic of a conversation, and there was no doubt that Grace was the 'her' to which her aunt referred. Who else could it be?

Grace pressed further into a corner of the alcove in an attempt to remain unseen whilst she pulled herself together. All around her, the staff hustled anxiously about their tasks as they frantically prepared for the arrival of the Duke of Stonebridge, one of a dozen guests expected to arrive today for a week-long house party. She could smell the familiar odors of lemon and oil as a maid set about cleaning the nearby stair rail.

"Miss Grace…"

Grace surreptitiously swiped at her eyes before peering around the corner to see the upstairs maid, Janet, standing there, her brow furrowed with concern.

One of the few joys of Beckett House, her aunt and uncle's house and Grace's home for the past year, was the staff, all of whom were welcoming and pleasant despite their employer's haughty airs. It horrified Aunt Mary to know how friendly Grace was with the staff, knowing them all by name and enough about their families to ask of them in conversation. Aunt Mary put the behavior down to Grace's father and his lowly beginnings.

Grace shook her head to prevent Janet from saying anything more. She was simply too upset to engage in conversation. However, to reassure the maid of her continued friendship, Grace lightly laid her hand upon Janet's arm and gave her a tender squeeze and a friendly smile before hurrying off toward the rear of the house and the French doors that led out to the back garden.

Normally, Grace maintained quite a sunny disposition and even now refused to allow her aunt's bitter prejudice to bring her down, but in order to regain her composure, she needed to get out of the house…

Now, twenty minutes later, Grace sighed with contentment as she sat on an old wooden dock with her skirts hitched above her knees, dangling her feet in the cool, clear water. The dock jutted out over a large lake situated in a clearing deep in the woods behind the rear gardens of Beckett House; thus she was obscured from view of the house and she could relax and enjoy some privacy.

She closed her eyes and tilted her face to the sky, the feeling of warmth from the sun at her back inviting her to unwind. Her bonnet lay beside her with her hair pins cradled in its bowl, the adornments all but forgotten as she rolled her head back and forth and allowed the sun to caress her face. Her loosened brown hair just grazed the flare of her hips with the movement. She inhaled deeply, for the air was cool and refreshing.

On her exhale, Grace leaned forward and looked down, staring meditatively at the water. She was content to simply watch its movement as it swirled about one foot where she rotated it in a figure eight pattern just beneath the surface.

Her thoughts drifted to her situation. Her parents were dead a year now and she was living at the mercy of her Aunt Mary and Uncle George, the Countess and Earl of Swindon, until she reached her twenty-first birthday which, thankfully, was only a few short months away.

In actuality, neither the earl nor the countess was her blood relation. Her real aunt was the earl's first wife, Florence Swindon. Florence and Grace's mother, Leanne, had been sisters, both born of a Baron. However, whilst Aunt Florence had married the Earl of Swindon, George Beckett, Grace's mother had remained in Oxford and married a man in trade, a local bookshop owner named John Radclyffe.

Grace barely remembered Aunt Florence, but her impression was that of a rather friendly, shy woman whom Grace did not often see, probably due to the earl and his prejudices against people in trade. Aunt Florence and Uncle George had one daughter, Beatryce, when Grace was three. Unfortunately, Aunt Florence died during the birth of her second child a few years later (the child also passed), and then nearly a year to the day afterwards, the earl married his second wife: Mary Swindon nee Wristwaithe.

Aunt Mary was an altogether different sort: outspoken and pretentious. She and Uncle George had three children together—again, all girls; though as expected, Grace did not know her cousins well since the Radclyffes were rarely invited to Beckett House, and certainly Uncle George and Aunt Mary did not deign to visit them in Oxford.

Now, Grace lived at Beckett House with her four cousins under the guardianship of her Aunt Mary and Uncle George. Though they were passively cruel to her, for they looked down upon her because her father had been in trade, they did their duty, if only just, and kept her housed and fed because, like it or not, she was (unfortunately to their mind) considered a relative even if not actually related by blood. Grace supposed she should be thankful to the earl and countess for taking her in when she was so distantly related. Alas, those feelings of appreciation escaped her at the moment…

"Grace. There you are."

Grace was jolted from her thoughts as the youngest of her cousins, Adelaide, came skipping down the dock toward her. Grace took a moment to smile at the young girl who, at the age of six, was full of life and energy. As usual, Adelaide was dressed in a play frock sans shoes, a bad habit she seemed to have picked up of late from following Grace about the garden.

"Good morning, Addie. What are you about this morning?"

Adelaide looked about furtively before responding, "Shhhh. I've come here to hide out from Mama and my nurse. They want me to put on my new dress and shoes and plait my hair, and I won't have it. How can I play all strung up like a May Pole?"

"Besides," she continued, "Mama is too busy calming Beatryce to notice my absence right now."

Grace inwardly cringed at the mention of Beatryce. Beatryce was the oldest of Uncle George's four children, and at eighteen, was out in society. Grace could not imagine

Beatryce walking the grounds with her head uncovered, let alone dangling her feet in the water. Beatryce was spoiled and vain, and always unsatisfied.

"Did Beatryce really throw the dancing slippers out the window?" asked Adelaide after a moment.

"No, Adelaide, she didn't, not really. She just felt like it. I'm sure she is just nervous about the duke's arrival this afternoon and is not acting her usual self…"

Grace cringed at the small white lie, and eyed Adelaide to see if she had swallowed it. It wasn't her place to speak ill of Adelaide's sister, so the lie seemed justified in this instance. Just this morning Beatryce had thrown a tantrum when she discovered Aunt Mary had allowed Grace to borrow an old pair of Beatryce's dancing slippers, and had tossed them out the window rather than forfeit them to Grace. Never mind that Beatryce had at least ten pairs of dancing slippers, while Grace had none.

What made matters worse was Aunt Mary had provided Grace with an old dress of Beatryce's as well, which was out of fashion and not at all flattering to her slim stature, but based on Beatryce's hysterics this morning, anyone would have thought Aunt Mary had presented Grace with the Royal Diamonds instead. Not to mention that the dress's pale shade of lavender did nothing for either of their complexions, thus, she couldn't imagine Beatryce wearing it out in polite society anyway.

Unfortunately, there was no help for it. Grace didn't have anything appropriate to wear for this week's events without borrowing from Beatryce, who was of a size.

One might think Beatryce would feel some sort of connection with Grace, having both lost their mother and being true cousins, but alas, Beatryce seemed quite content with her situation and her disdain for her lesser relative.

Beatryce's half-sisters Hetty (sixteen) and Sylvia (twelve) were quite shy by comparison. In truth, Hetty was attending a boarded finishing school and was not often around so Grace still did not know her well. Sylvia was quiet and strictly obedient to her mother and governess; thus, Grace rarely saw her except at a distance — probably by Aunt Mary's intention.

Adelaide, however, the youngest at six, was a force all her own. She was always running from her nurse, and from the day Grace arrived to live at Beckett House, had sought Grace out daily — much to her mother's vexation.

"Well, that is understandable, I guess. I didn't think Beatryce would be so silly over a pair of old dancing shoes. She has at least a dozen…"

"Yes, that would be silly, indeed."

Adelaide thoughtfully paused a moment more before chattering happily on about something completely unrelated: bugs (or was that ribbons with bugs?), as was her wont. Grace was relieved the girl hadn't pushed to further discuss Beatryce's behavior of late, and with the pressure of the upcoming house party, she couldn't help but allow her thoughts to drift, somewhat oblivious to her cousin's innocent babble.

For the most part, Aunt Mary and Uncle George left Grace alone and managed to avoid drawing society's attention toward their unwanted guest. They never took her with them to parties; nor did they take her to London whenever they made the trip. This was a mutually agreeable decision as Grace had no desire to come under the scrutiny of high society — the ton — and her aunt and uncle had no desire to acknowledge so close an association with trade or to risk some other embarrassment by their wayward ward.

Today, however, they had no choice, for society demanded they throw a house party to announce the engagement of their daughter, Beatryce, to the Duke of Stonebridge; hence all the lunacy over His Grace's imminent arrival. Grace didn't think the couple was officially engaged yet, but a proposal and formal announcement were expected, and several key guests were invited to stay the week to witness what was sure to be *the* event of the season.

Much to the chagrin of her aunt and uncle, all of this meant Grace had to be introduced to society after all. They couldn't very well send her away (there wasn't anyone to send her to) nor could they hide her in the attic whilst the guests were about— though Grace had caught her aunt looking at her oddly a time or two over the past week and was sure the thought had crossed her aunt's mind.

For the past month, Aunt Mary had fretted daily over Grace's upcoming introduction to society at this week's house party, though not just because of Grace's shocking family history in trade. No, there was also the wee matter of Grace's proclivity for accidental mishaps (she was downright clumsy) and her (shocking!) tendency to befriend the servants who, of course, all loved her in return, that had Aunt Mary dreaming nightmares over the possible scandals that could ensue.

Grace sighed as she told herself it was best not to dwell on such maudlin thoughts. She was never one to pity herself or her situation and she was happy, truly happy— though mayhap, in secret (and only rarely at that), she allowed herself to dream…Perhaps she'd envision a handsome, kind man coming to rescue her and carry her away from her reality and into a life of which she could only imagine…It was a brief indulgence—this dream—for she was confident enough in herself to know she would make do just fine with her own resources…and she knew her circumstances could be much, much worse.

Aaah, but sometimes it was nice to daydream…to picture someone else with whom she could at least share the burdens and joys of life.

"Grace, are you listening to me?"

Grace started as she realized she had been daydreaming and had long stopped attending to Adelaide's chatter.

"I am truly sorry, Addie, I let my mind wander away from me again."

"It's all right, Grace. I asked if you think the duke will like having me for a sister." Adelaide bowed her head shyly and fidgeted with the hem of her dress, such that Grace was startled by the uncharacteristically timid behavior.

Impulsively, Grace leaned over to hug Adelaide and said, "Oh, Addie, how could he not? You're everything a person could ask for in a sister, truly. Why would you think otherwise? Have you met His Grace? Has he been impolite or rude to you in any way?"

"No, not at all…It's just that everyone is acting all strange. I keep trying to imagine what His Grace might think of all of us—and our home…"

Beckett House was rather large to Grace's way of thinking, for prior to this, she had only ever lived with her parents in their small home above their bookstore in Oxford. She supposed Beatryce's duke might own a much larger house in any one of his numerous estates across the country, thus Beckett House might be considered modest by comparison.

Grace looked thoughtfully at Adelaide a moment before responding. "Addie, first of all, I should hope that His Grace wouldn't judge anyone by the size and lavishness of their home for it's a person's character that truly matters…and if he does consider the value of your possessions as a way of determining your worth as a person, then I think he is not worthy of your consideration in return—even if he does become your brother-in-law."

"Well, Mama and Papa must think it is important to impress His Grace with their things. They've even taken a guest room so the duke can have their rooms whilst he is here."

Grace thought it was quite funny that her aunt and uncle had done this and to hear them complain (albeit furtively) about having to share a room with each other (gasp!) to provide the duke with three rooms for his own personal use. She knew they had done so simply on account of his standing and the fact that he was planning to marry Beatryce, but really, couldn't the duke manage one single week with less? Was he so pompous and fickle that he would break off the engagement over something as silly as the number of rooms available to him for his weeklong stay? If so, she might actually pity Beatryce her chosen fiancé, but then she realized, knowing Beatryce, she and the duke might actually be quite alike in their preferences if this were so.

Mindful not to betray her internal thoughts, Grace said, "I think perhaps your mother and father do not want to take any chances that His Grace might be offended during his stay. It is too important to them and your sister that he is happy during this visit."

Grace paused to give Adelaide a moment to think about that, then added gently, "In light of that sentiment, dear, I think it best if you head back to the house and allow your nurse to truss you up in your finery. It will only be for a short time and you do want to make a good impression when you meet His Grace for the first time."

"But you said…"

Grace laughed. Adelaide was a clever child.

"I know, I know—he shouldn't be impressed by how expensively turned out you are, but you also don't want him to see your bare feet and dirt smudged knees and get the wrong notion, now do you? You rather do look like a stray waif at present…though an adorable one, to be sure."

"Well, I don't want him to think I'm not open to play, either. What if he thinks I'm too stuffy, all dolled up, and not at'all a fine candidate for a sister?"

Grace chuckled. "I think that His Grace will see the playfulness in your eyes when he looks at you and he will remember what it was like to be six years old. I think you'll do fine, dear."

Adelaide let out a loud sigh of resignation. Oh, how simple life was at six…

"Aaaaaall riiiiiight, IIIIII'll go…"

Grace watched Adelaide reluctantly rise and brush at the dirt on her knees. Adelaide looked at Grace a moment then asked, "Aren't you coming, too?"

"Oh, Addie, I'll be along shortly. Please, don't let me hold you back. You race on ahead before your mother sends the footmen out looking for you. She won't be pleased if she has to pull them from their duties to go looking for you, not now of all times, will she?"

Adelaide's eyes widened at the thought, and she immediately dashed off toward the path leading back to Beckett House, all the while yelling back, "You are right. I'll see you back at the house, Grace."

Grace laughed at the sight. Adelaide was a charming and precocious child…and right. It was time she headed back to the house and the reality within, though at the moment, she felt a near overwhelming urge to spend the entire day hiding out amongst the shrubbery instead.

Grace gathered her shoes, stockings, and bonnet, her pins still held within, and stood, holding her skirts high to allow the breeze to dry her legs before making her way back up the path to Beckett House. She knew she had to go through with it, the party and all it encompassed, though she didn't like it. She reminded herself it was only until her twenty-first birthday, and then she would be free to enact her own plans for the future. Until then, she could manage what was required to save her relatives from unnecessary embarrassment.

Grace sought out the sun and was surprised to note how long she had been sitting there, and with a renewed sense of urgency began to make her way home. She pulled her hair up in a loose topknot as she went and secured it haphazardly with her pins, just enough to hold until she could get back inside the house.

Along with her shoes, Grace still held her bonnet in hand even though her aunt would have an apoplexy if she got too much sun on her face and broke out in freckles, not to mention walking about barefoot. Grace chuckled at the subsequent 'scandal' this might cause amongst the guests. She thought about what her aunt would say if she wasn't able to get back to her rooms unseen; in addition to everything else, she was dressed in her most tattered morning dress, one she only used for mucking about in the garden when no one else was around.

A few minutes later, Grace came out of the woods, shoes and bonnet still in hand, and the full expanse of Beckett House and its surrounding gardens came into view. She stopped for just a moment to appreciate the sight of the manor home standing stoically before her with its plain, rough stone façade. It was quite inviting, in her opinion, though it seemed oddly placed amidst the manicured lawns and hedgerows her aunt obsessed over so keenly. The formal gardens were not quite to Grace's taste; her tastes ran more to the rough, untamed beauty of the area by the lake, which actually seemed to better match the house's architecture than its own gardens.

Grace shook off her woolgathering and picked up her pace; she had been gone for far too long. She was just walking down a slight rise at the edge of the formal gardens, not paying particular attention to where she was stepping, when she hit a patch of mud and slipped.

Her arms flailed about wildly as she tried, unsuccessfully, to remain upright—but, alas, therein lay the jest...She was Grace—not graceful.

"Oh, fiddlesticks," she said aloud, as she found herself spun around and on her backside in a rather large puddle of mud.

How could she have missed that?

Grace landed so hard she was fairly oozing mud from her crown to her toes. Already, she could feel the telltale signs of liquid earth soaking into the back of her dress.

Grace closed her eyes to offer up a wishful prayer that no one was about the gardens to witness her mucky mishap. Then she took a deep breath and calmed herself by considering that the guests, including His Grace, were not expected until much later. She was likely in luck.

Grace was just contemplating the best route back inside the house without alerting anyone else of her — misfortune — when a monogrammed handkerchief suddenly appeared over her shoulder.

Chapter 2

The Bull and Thistle Inn…
The evening before…

Crash…

Breaking glass followed by raised voices and boisterous laughter disturbed the tenuous peace at the Bull and Thistle Inn—the only inn and tavern in the small village near Amberley in West Sussex. It was a nightmare for anyone planning to attempt something as mundane as sleep.

Ambrose Philip Langtry, 10th Duke of Stonebridge, gritted his teeth in annoyance as he stripped out of his travelling clothes. He was weary and needed sleep. It was going to be a long night.

"Bryans, we're leaving at first light. I don't care how early we arrive at Beckett House; it will be preferable to remaining here any longer than absolutely necessary," he told his valet. The inn was a rowdy place and he would die a happy man if he never saw its rotting façade again.

"Yes, Your Grace. Shall I call the guard and have everyone clapped in irons, then?" responded Bryans, audaciously, yet with a somber face. He had been with the duke a long time and had grown somewhat impertinent over the years.

"I am in no mood for your cheek this evening," he told Bryans with all seriousness. With a stern look and a raised brow, he dared the man to continue his insolence. But Bryans just ignored him and continued about his duties. The man had some nerve.

Both men almost missed the knock on the door due to all the noise coming from downstairs, despite the racket being muffled through two floors of guest rooms. The duke pulled his dressing gown tight as Bryans answered the door.

Stonebridge nearly groaned out loud as Bryans revealed, once again, the innkeeper's now familiar face in the open doorway. Instead, he gritted his teeth and waited patiently to hear the innkeeper out.

"Aaah, Your Grace, I'm righ' sorry for the racket below and though' I should check if'n you needed ought…and I brough' some of me own 'ouse brandy to 'elp you sett'l in for the nigh'." The innkeeper grinned widely as he brought in a tray with his offering, revealing gaping holes where several teeth should have been.

The duke would be dying of thirst before he had any more of that swill the innkeeper called brandy. Of course, he didn't say that out loud, but the poor plant in the corner would probably be dead by morning.

"Thank you for your generosity. We're fine and just retiring for the night. Good evening." Stonebridge nodded his head toward the door to make his wishes clear: he was ready to retire without further disturbance. The curt dismissal was so short as to be rude, but Stonebridge couldn't find it in himself to care. The innkeeper and his wife had stopped by his privately reserved dining room eighteen times during dinner, and now his patience was at an end.

"Righ' then, I'll be off, but don't 'esitate to ring if'n you need anythin' at'all…" The innkeeper backed out of the room, scraping and bowing the entire way. It was almost comical, especially as he nearly ran his arse into the door frame on his way out.

Stonebridge detested the overzealous show of deference. He was only a man, for goodness sakes.

The duke turned away from the door and began untying the belt of his dressing gown as he made his way to the bed. Bryans had followed the innkeeper downstairs to ensure he had no plans to return.

"I think I migh' have somefin' better to offer...to 'elp you unwind, Your Grace."

Stonebridge paused in the act of removing his dressing gown. The muscles in his shoulders and back tensed at the suggestive feminine voice behind him.

Will I never get some rest this eve?

He couldn't begin to imagine how the chit had managed to slip past the innkeeper and his valet in order to enter his room unbidden—not to mention that he was usually keenly aware of his surroundings. *What the deuce was in that drink anyway?* He tamped down the bulk of his ire and turned about to face the woman who had spoken. He braced his hands on his hips in the world-recognized sign of annoyance.

The barmaid, Annie, leaned casually back against the door to his room, half-dressed and posed to entice. She audibly sucked in her breath the moment he faced her fully. Probably because he was mostly unclothed, his dressing gown untied and gaping open as it was. Still, he made his anger plain with his eyes and by his stance, yet she seemed determined to ignore it. He took in the sight of her in return. He was irritated, but that didn't mean he couldn't take a moment to appreciate her charms before he sent her on her way.

She was comely and curvaceous, and too young to be missing her teeth or for the toll of hard living to be obvious in the skin of her face and hands. Her top was loosely tied, displaying more than a hint of her overly large breasts, and her leg was raised, her foot resting against the door, baring her leg to his view in an attempt to entice. It wouldn't take a lot of effort to bed her—in fact his cock stirred with interest at the sight she presented—but he was too smart to tempt disease and a bastard for a single night's pleasure.

After one more quick perusal of her voluptuous form, he drew in a swift breath but moved no closer; his patience tonight was finally at an end.

"Get. Out."

That was all he needed to say for her to turn and bolt out the door. He knew how to use his size and commanding voice to coerce when necessary, and he was tired of being bothered today; he had no more patience to be the gentleman and offer kind words to spare another's feelings.

"A bit harsh there, wasn't it?"

Stonebridge shook his head at the sound of yet another voice coming from the opposite corner of the room. He looked up and beseeched the ceiling. "What will it take to get some peace around here? I feel like a display at the British Museum with the number of people coming through the door."

"That's all right then. I didn't use the door."

The duke relaxed, marginally, and chuckled at the quip as he turned to face his best friend, Clifford Ross, the Marquess of Dansbury, who was sitting in a chair near the soon-to-be-dead foliage in the corner. Cliff was a broad man with golden hair and tranquil brown eyes, deceptive eyes. The man always looked relaxed; he epitomized the state, but in reality, Cliff was always watching, always calculating, always remembering.

But he was the only person with whom Stonebridge felt at all comfortable letting down his guard.

Stonebridge wasn't really angry at his friend for the intrusion—the information he might impart was too important—and it didn't strike him at all odd that his friend mightn't have used the door. The man was astonishingly stealthy for his size. Cliff was pushing six and a half feet and was equally as broad of shoulder, yet he could get in and out of anywhere completely undetected. If he didn't want you to see him, you didn't. If he didn't want you to hear him, you wouldn't. It was part of the job. Their real job. They were both agents for the Crown, and at the moment they were investigating the murder of the previous Duke of Stonebridge, his father.

Yes. His father's death was no accident. Stonebridge had always known—even as a newly orphaned boy he had known, and his conviction was validated three months ago when he received an anonymous note through the mail. The author suggested they had proof his father had indeed been slain and that it was all related to a little known assassination attempt on Prime Minister Pitt, which had occurred at about the same time.

The rest of the world still thought the worst about his father—that he'd been out 'carrying on' with another man—that it was all a tragic yet deserving accident. Now the proof he needed was within reach and Stonebridge was all too eager for answers.

"What do you have?" Stonebridge decided to get to the point. His friend wasn't just stopping by to share the latest *on dit*.

"You mean, besides the fact that this plant smells intoxicated?" Cliff laughed. "Unfortunately, not a lot, yet…Kelly and MacLeod arrived late last night with our man as planned. His name is Paddy Murphy. He's a former Irish assassin and mercenary with loose ties to the United Irishmen—or a known supporter, at any rate. He hasn't been officially seen or active since 1798, when he vanished in September of that year only to resurface last week in Belfast. We're positive he sent the note."

"I knew it," interrupted the duke as he slammed his fist against the nearby door frame. He could taste victory, and he wanted to shout 'I told you so' like a two-year-old. They were so close.

"Yes, it cannot be a coincidence. His disappearance coincides perfectly with your father's death. Murphy has been quite resistant to our methods of persuasion so far, but we'll get it. He's adamant he wants to speak to you and only you. He wants reassurances and safe passage to America."

"Ha! Not likely. And I find it difficult to believe he can resist persuasion with MacLeod around; that's one big Scot."

"We haven't used the Scot. Yet."

"This man might have murdered my father and you're going easy on him?"

"We don't yet know he's the one that pulled the trigger, so to speak. But I admit the evidence is damning. The problem is, well, the problem is the man is elderly and quite emaciated and somehow it just doesn't seem right to use physical force on someone in his pitiful condition. He's sharp, though, and strong willed. I'll give him that."

"You sound admiring, my friend. Has he indicated why he's been in hiding all these years? And why is he contacting me now? After all this time? And for that matter, who hired him to begin with?"

"No and no, and we don't know. We suspect he's been in hiding because he failed in his job to kill Prime Minister Pitt. We think he's coming out now due to the current conditions in Ireland—disease and famine is widespread there, as you well know. I think it's simply a matter of survival. He's gaunt and hunger is a powerful motivator. As far as who might have hired him, besides the United Irishmen? The only other group with the strongest motivation is the Secret Society for the Purification of England."

"Ah, yes. The aristocracy and their secret societies."

"Well, they certainly weren't in favor of the PM's politics seeing as how they wanted all immigrants out of England full stop. As far as I know, we still don't have a lot of concrete information about that group, only suspicions. Anyway, I've sent off a note to the Home Office asking our contact there to forward anything we have on Paddy Murphy and the assassination attempt on Pitt around that time. I've also asked him to send anything we have on the Society. I expect to hear something in the next day or two."

"Good thinking. Let me know what you find out. You are coming to Beckett House, aren't you?"

"Of course. I wouldn't miss seeing my best friend get engaged, even if..."

The duke merely lifted his brow. He didn't need words to remind Cliff that the topic was strictly off limits. And he was well aware of Cliff's thoughts regarding his fiancée and their engagement.

Cliff chuckled as he left, via the door this time.

* * * *

The next morning...
On the road to Beckett House...
Amberley, West Sussex...

Stonebridge leaned against the carriage window and perused the walking stick in his hand. The body was polished black with a silver handle and complementary tip, its handle fashioned in the shape of a lion's head. He held up the stick to the sunlight streaming in through the carriage window and rolled it back and forth in his hand, watching the light catch on the two emeralds that made up the lion's eyes. The emeralds were a bright, deep green, and the exact shade of his own eyes. It was the sole reason he had splurged on its purchase—a little vain perhaps, but he was, in a way, quite proud of his unique eye color because it represented a family trait that had been passed down through many generations of former dukes.

They had left behind the horrid inn at the first light of dawn. The innkeeper was less sycophantic, so perhaps the man had finally got the message that he was overdoing his subservience the night before. Stonebridge was relieved to be away, regardless.

Today, he would finish the last leg of his journey to a society house party in his honor being held at Beckett House in West Sussex. Everyone knew he was to announce his engagement there. He wasn't looking forward to it, which was probably one reason he had been more impatient than usual yesterday. He would much rather be discussing this year's wool production with his foreman than partaking of mindless flirtation with the latest crop of debutantes and their mothers. Hell, he'd rather watch the grass in the back garden grow. Then, there was the renewed hunt for his father's murderer. He was anxious to be doing something—anything—toward that end, not wasting time socializing with pompous nobility.

He really had no choice to attend, though; it was time he marry, and if he wanted to keep his good standing in society, he could not be a recluse. He needed his social contacts to keep his estates running efficiently, information flowing smoothly, and his political allies in line. Most importantly, though, if they were right, and the Secret Society for the Purification of England was behind his father's murder, he couldn't let on to anyone in the *haut ton* that the investigation was active again, and he certainly couldn't do anything that would hint at where his suspicions lay. Therefore, he had to do the pretty and practice good ton.

He laid his stick down to rest on the seat beside him and turned his gaze to the scenery passing by as his thoughts returned to the primary reason he was heading to Beckett House: to propose marriage to Lady Beatryce Beckett.

He tapped his fingers in a staccato rhythm atop his knee as his reflected on his soon-to-be betrothed. He had known Lady Beatryce and her family for many years; her father, the Earl of Swindon, had been a particular friend of his late father's. Though he had not kept in touch with the family until recently, Lady Beatryce was the first person he considered when he decided it was time for him to marry.

She had all the necessary background credentials: she had a traceable lineage that was appropriately matched to his own with no glaring scandals in its history. Her family's current standings, both financially and socially, were in good order. She was the classic English beauty with her pale blonde hair, light complexion, and deep blue eyes; together they would produce exceptional children…and the begetting of heirs would certainly be no hardship. Additionally, her family had unentailed property that bordered his favorite estate, Stonebridge Park, and was offered as part of her dowry. It would make a nice addition to his property there.

He had watched from afar Lady Beatryce's attendance at various society events in the little season, and he knew she was graceful and poised. She didn't appear to be silly and giggly as most debutantes could be. In fact, she appeared to be rather intelligent for the typical society woman. She had been schooled specifically to fill the role of duchess with ease; therefore, she was the perfect candidate to become his duchess in truth.

Thus, all things considered, he made the decision to marry with a logical mind, not a foolish heart as so many society misses and poets waxed on about. When one had doubts, even if rare, a man could always rely on the logic of facts to reaffirm the rightness of his decision.

Within days of reacquainting himself with Lady Beatryce and her family, he had spoken to her father, and as expected, the earl was enthusiastic in his acceptance of Stonebridge's request to court his daughter. Of course he was; Stonebridge was a duke with plenty of money in his coffers to keep him and his duchess comfortable for several lifetimes over. He was also young and handsome, with no prior marriages and no direct descendants in line for the title. In all, he was the catch of the season, and yet sometimes he actually despised that fact because he had no peace when going about in society. But such was his lot in life and he wouldn't really complain, for the benefits greatly outweighed the inconveniences.

And it wasn't completely by chance that he was considered quite the catch. It had taken years to re-establish the Stonebridge name following the scandal surrounding his father's death. Ever since that fateful fight at Eton when he was thirteen years old, the duke had been forced to lead an exemplary life — there had been zero room for error — in order to overcome public prejudice. And if they were successful in proving his father was murdered? Well, then the Stonebridge name would be completely and forever reinstated in the eyes of society.

Slowly, he let out the breath he hadn't realized he was holding. Now began the public ritual of courtship, and he was on track toward making the anticipated proposal. In fact, everyone was expecting one to be forthcoming this week; it was the reason for the house party, after all.

His silent musings were interrupted as he caught sight of two young boys playing at the side of the road. They were laughing and carrying on with sticks and a small, round ball. Both boys were in well-worn overalls, with numerous patches on the knees and the arms of their homespun shirts. Despite their obvious lack of wealth, the joy on their faces was easy to recognize and struck him poignantly as he realized how much time had passed since he had lived so carefree. How quickly life changed, and sometimes you didn't even recognize it had happened — the change — until you reflected back on a time long gone.

And it seemed a lifetime ago in which he'd felt so untroubled; certainly before his father's accident, and now, at thirty, with all he had seen and experienced, Stonebridge knew he would never be able to reclaim that blithe existence. Regardless, his memory of that time was still strong in his mind, and it was those memories that drove him to find his father's murderer.

His thoughts were jerked back to present day with the changing sound of the carriage wheels as his coach slowed to make the turn to Beckett House. The impulse to pull on his cravat was nearly overwhelming, but he refrained and forced his pulse to slow. He slammed his disturbing memories away in his mental box. He was nearly there, at Beckett House, and the time for inward reflection was at an end; his public face need be secured.

Damn, but he hated dealing with the sycophants he knew would be there, and house parties were the worst venue with so few opportunities to escape all the groveling. He knew he would do what he must, though, and on that thought, he grabbed his walking stick and hat as he prepared to exit the carriage, for it had just stopped on the cobbles in front of the house proper.

A footman jumped from his perch and opened the door for him to disembark. Stonebridge could clearly make out the earl and countess on the front steps, lying in wait to greet him. As he made his way to the door, he started at the image that flashed across his mind: that of a lion and lioness on the plains of Africa, lying in wait for some unknowing prey to pass within reach. And he felt like prey, despite his self-confidence.

He tamped down the stray thought, surprised it so easily interrupted his focus.

"Swindon, it is an honor to see you again."

He nodded his head as he approached and shook the earl's hand, who responded, "Your Grace, welcome to our home."

The duke turned to the countess. "Lady Swindon, you are as beautiful as ever. Thank you for graciously opening your home for my pleasure." He bowed and kissed the air above her hand.

"Your Grace, may I join my husband in offering you our most gracious welcome? Thank you for gifting us with your presence. We are honored and humbled by Your Grace. I do hope your stay is most comfortable and memorable, and if there is anything you need, please do not hesitate to inform us at once.

"Your Grace," she continued without taking a breath, "our butler is on hand to show you directly to your room so you can refresh. I do hope you find your accommodations satisfactory."

"Lady Swindon, thank you. I am sure the rooms will be agreeable. My valet, Bryans, is here to direct the unpacking of my carriage; however, before retiring, I should like to take a walk about your gardens to stretch my legs. If your butler would direct me there first, I would be grateful."

He desperately needed to stretch his legs after sitting for too long in the confined carriage. Even though the travelling coach was larger than his town conveyance, he felt cramped after so many hours inside, and with it still being before noon of the day, he thought the best time to take a turn about the garden would be now, when there was little chance of him encountering another guest.

Chapter 3

An Unfortunately Placed Mud Puddle in the rear gardens of Beckett House…

A knowledgeable lady understands that, typically, the best way to make a good first impression is not to fall bottom first into a puddle of mud. Alas, Grace Radclyffe, with her inclination towards unfortunate mishaps, found this knowledge to be generally useless in the reality of her everyday life.

Therefore, despite the uncomfortable feeling of wetness seeping through her gown and the faint-though-nearby sound of dripping mud, she did what any sensible lady of good upbringing would do in less than ideal circumstances. She cursed. With conviction.

"Bloody hell. Not again."

So maybe she didn't say *that*. But it was something she occasionally thought in her mind, though only in her mind.

In actuality, she chuckled lightheartedly (because it's always best to set yourself and any potential rescuers at ease in awkward situations) and graciously procured the proffered handkerchief dangling over her left shoulder. Then, after clearing the mud from her face so she could actually see and with cheeks tinged only slightly from embarrassment (because, really, that kerchief hadn't been dangling over her shoulder on its own), she peered up to thank her would-be rescuer and… Gasped. Out loud.

For staring down at her with one eyebrow lifted in question, were a pair of eyes — emerald green eyes, to be more precise. The most deeply penetrating emerald green eyes she had ever seen in all of her near twenty-one years.

No longer did she feel slightly tinged with embarrassment — of course not, that would be far too easy. No, now the heat from extreme humiliation spread up from her neck and behind her ears as she drank in the handsome sight of the dream — er, man — standing over her and witnessing what should have been her own private humiliation. Though why the sight of this man should make her more embarrassed than before was a mystery. It's not like she wasn't used to public embarrassment. Though admittedly it wasn't something one ever really got used to either.

So maybe gasping aloud was not the recommended method of laughing off an acutely embarrassing demonstration of inelegance either, but then it was not every day that one encounters eyes. Er, or green eyes. Or. Oh, this was definitely turning out to be one of her finer moments. She couldn't even talk to herself with any semblance of sanity.

She was so lost between her jumbled thoughts and the depth of those eyes, she didn't immediately realize those eyes, or more pointedly, the man attached to them, were verbally addressing her until the words "Ahem" finally (finally!) penetrated the fog in her brain — which, unfortunately, brought her attention to his mouth.

Two full lips registered in her mind — both slightly hitched to the side as if in a half-smile. The bottom lip just begging to be nibbled.

Nibbled? Ugh.

Now where had that ridiculous thought come from? Perhaps she should consider breaking her fast before taking a morning walk from now on? She hadn't felt hungry before…

Well, damn.

She closed her eyes and concentrated on breathing. Slowly and deeply. In and out. Out and in. She counted to ten. She needed to reign in her runaway mind so she could address the state of affairs at hand. She was not (mental foot stamp) a silly, scatterbrained chit. And that mouth most likely belonged to someone important to Aunt Mary.

Grace's eyes flew open with that realization. What would Aunt Mary do if she discovered…?

The thought was too alarming to complete. Grace now made a herculean effort to pull herself together (and not curse), confident she would be laughing off the memory. Later. Perhaps tomorrow. Or the next day.

"Excuse me, my lord? I am afraid the mud might be hardening and whilst I love gardens, I do not want to become a permanent fixture in this one."

There. This is good. My brain is functioning again, albeit a bit impertinently.

She let slip a light chuckle, hoping to further diffuse the awkwardness of the situation. Who doesn't appreciate a little self-deprecating humor to smooth over an uncomfortable state of affairs?

"Of course…May I ask? Does this sort of thing… happen… often?"

Apparently, not this man. His voice was harsh, and he had a stern countenance upon his face, and for just a teeny, tiny minute, she imagined sticking her tongue out at him whilst dumping a nice fat mud pie directly onto his head. She certainly had plenty to share. Of mud, that is. Really, did he think she plopped down in the mud on purpose?

So acutely was she staring at this man whilst contemplating some type of mischief to wipe away the scowl etched on his face, she only vaguely noticed he had pulled her up to stand. Without saying a word. Certainly, without any form of introduction. As was normal. And proper.

She shivered when his hands grazed the sides of her arms as he tested to see whether or not she was steady before letting go. Goose bumps broke out across both arms. Was she coming down with an ague?

She forced herself to return her attention to the conversation at hand.

"Why ever would you think that, er, my lord?"

She decided to stow away her thoughts of mischief and recall that she was (honest) a gentlewoman, despite the mud caked up the backside of her skirt. She didn't know who this man was, which, again, was rude, so she played it safe with a generic 'my lord'. The title would cover anything unless he was…

"Stonebridge." Mr. Green Eyes' eyes twinkled. She thought of emeralds.

"Of course, Stonebridge. Ah, Stonebridge. Er, Wait. Stonebridge, as in the Duke of?"

Please say no. Please, please say no.

He bowed stiffly, and she couldn't help but notice the tight pull of his morning jacket across his broad shoulders. Was that a hint of a smile on his face just before he tipped his head? Not likely. She shook off her wandering thoughts. Again.

"Indubitably."

"Excuse me?"

He sighed. "Yes, I am the Duke of Stonebridge. At your service."

"Your Grace! I am Miss Grace Radclyffe. Sir. Er, Your Grace," she exclaimed, breathlessly, as the reality of exactly WHO he was crashed through her scattered thoughts like a stampeding heard of wild wildebeests.

Wild wildebeests?

So, this was the Duke of Stonebridge and her cousin Beatryce's soon-to-be-almost betrothed? Well, certainly nobody bothered to inform her that His Grace had eyes.

Ugh. Note to brain: Re-engage, please.

Had her mother been in attendance, she would have been proud of the fluidity of Grace's curtsey despite the embarrassing circumstances and encrusted mud upon her

41

person. Perhaps it was the shock: it certainly wasn't her inability to remove her eyes from His Grace's bottom lip, but in her haste to greet her would-be rescuer as befitting his station, her flawlessly executed curtsey in reality only remained regal for approximately three seconds before her left foot slid right out from beneath her…

Oh, Hello mud. Nice to meet you again. We really need to stop meeting this way.

This encounter might possibly be her most embarrassing of all time.

Plop.

Was that mud dripping from His Grace's boots? Again?

Of course, and oh yes, to make things even better, mud was now splattered up the right leg of his tailored breeches… Fitted second-skin-painted-on tailored breaches encasing disconcertingly well-muscled thighs.

Hmm…Clearly, the duke does not believe in lying about all day doing nothing.

She shook away her wayward thoughts. For the umpteenth time. Without question, this event was more embarrassing than any of her previous mishaps. Ever. Probably.

"I think, perhaps, I have need of your assistance again. If you would be so kind, Your Grace?"

"Indeed. Mayhap we should dispense with further formalities of greeting and relocate to a more…stable…patch of earth, if such exists?"

"Yes. Certainly." She ignored the not-so-subtle quip.

Grace had barely completed her last thought when the duke bodily lifted her by the waist from her personal bed of mud. She closed her eyes to the experience. For the first time in her life, she felt feminine and delicate. She was not a short lady (in fact, she was quite tall at five feet, seven inches), yet her feet did not brush the ground as he carried her to safety. His hands held her aloft with ease, and in return, she gripped the sides of his upper arms with a surprising strength of her own.

The heat of his hands around her waist sent tingles of warmth out from her center and set her heart to racing. Before she knew it, his hands were sliding further around her waist as he pulled her closer until she was flattened against his chest. She told herself it probably made carrying her easier.

She kept her eyes tightly closed. She imagined this was a disconcerting (though shockingly real) dream. Perhaps, if she held her breath and opened her eyes gradually, she would find she was still in her room up at the house. And the heat she could feel all over her body would, in reality, be the result of a small house fire in the corner of her bedroom. One could dream, right?

Her fanciful thoughts were interrupted by a sound she could smell. Smell? And feel. And it wasn't an unpleasant sensation at'all.

"Ahem."

She reluctantly opened her eyes only to be lost in deep pools of green. She was at eye level with the duke, and so close, she could discern tiny golden flecks in his emerald irises. He pulled back from their tight embrace. Just the tiniest amount. Probably so he could look her in the eye when he spoke, but he continued to hold her aloft. He was so close, her peripheral vision was filled solely with his face and his black-as-pitch hair.

Nothing else existed in this world. Perhaps, this was a dream after all? She noticed his pupils were dilated and his eyes, in general, darkened by the minute. Odd, what with it being so unusually sunny today.

The man looking back at her now was a different man altogether. Gone was his cool and aloof manner from before. In its place was searing warmth tinged with a sense of caring that made her tremble. And he was staring at her mouth.

"Miss Radclyffe…"

She was so close she could feel his warm, minty breath mingling with her own. His voice sounded different. Almost gruff. Perhaps it was because she was so much closer now and could hear him better.

"Are you steady now?" His voice was a whisper, soft and decidedly unsteady.

No? "Yes."

Would she ever be steady again? Had she ever been steady in her life? Really. And would her brain ever function around this man? Ever? He probably thought her vocabulary singularly limited, and her brain filled with feathers to boot.

He released her. Slowly. Softly. Reluctantly. Or was it wishful thinking on her part? She slid down his body. Who knew it would feel so good?

He balanced her gently with his hands until she could remain upright under her own strength.

As soon as his hands left her person, he abruptly straightened, which was something considering he was already standing upright to begin with. However, it wasn't just his physical bearing that changed, it was his manner as well. The transformation was so quick as to be almost laughable. Once again, he was the aloof stranger. Gone was the dark, burning look in his eyes, as was the perceived gentleness with which he rescued her from her own awkwardness. Instead, his eyes held a cool detachment that made her wonder if she hadn't imagined the entire unfortunate event after all. Wishful thinking, that.

With all the excitement generated by her earthy encounter, her hair had begun to come unbound from its hastily applied chignon; several strands were flying about her face with the breeze. She raised her hand to brush away the loose strands. When she did, she felt the dried mud on her bare arms, thus disabusing her of the notion that it was all an incredible dream.

The duke jerked his eyes back to her face after watching her hands smooth her hair. Then he dipped his head in an almost imperceptible nod, and with a quick "Miss Radclyffe," turned on his heel and marched back to the house, leaving

Grace behind gaping at a curiously wet with mud, but nicely formed…

Chapter 4

Stonebridge virtually stormed his way back to the house. Several thoughts fought for prominence in his mind: what in the hell had come over him? How could one woman cause him to lose his composure so completely? And why did the name Radclyffe sound so bloody familiar?

He was a duke, thirty years old, at a society house party preparing to propose to Lady Beatryce Beckett, when suddenly a young miss he had only just met nearly had him grinning like a young, carefree…buffoon. He never behaved this way out in society. Especially not with near perfect strangers. It was too easy to stumble in the face of such scrutiny as with the watch dogs of propriety. Too easy to make a small slip and invite unwanted attention. His mask of calm indifference in any situation was one of his biggest defenses against the vultures of the ton. And some slip of a girl had unerringly flung it in the mud.

He threw open the French doors at the back of the house and marched inside, pulling at his neck cloth as he went as if it were a noose choking off the air to his lungs. He was heedless of anyone else about, his actions completely out of character. He was proud of his reputation for having a level head. He suffered no fools, and though people of society might find him cold and even boring at times, he knew nothing he ever said or did in the last fifteen years had suggested even a hint of scandal, and he wouldn't start now. And on top of all that, in the face of his self-directed anger, he was repeating himself. Dammit.

Abruptly, he let loose his grip on his cravat lest he embarrass himself by stripping it off in front of any guests who happened to be wandering about; never mind the state of his soiled clothes and the frightening scowl upon his face. At the very least, he would carry on to his assigned room with his dignity intact.

He reached the front stairs, and as efficiently as expected, the Becketts' butler was there waiting for him. At his nod and without a word to the state of his dress, the man guided him up the stairs to his temporary accommodations.

Immediately, his thoughts returned to the Incident. Fortunately, his many years' experience as a duke had provided him with the control he needed to keep from revealing any cracks in his perfectly cultivated bearing to his beautiful tormentor. It had been a long time since he had felt so carefree; therefore, it came as quite a shock to his peace of mind that some strange, silly woman, and a new acquaintance at that, could draw forth such a feeling so effortlessly. In point of fact, she wasn't even really an acquaintance, and yet it took quite an effort to reign in his sudden desire to chuckle lightheartedly and grin like a fool with her. She was utterly endearing to behold.

He worked his way up another flight of stairs, and his thoughts of Grace continued. Not only had he been feeling like the veritable green lad in her presence, but the warmth of her body against his had him imagining some very lewd and carnal scenes. As he carried her away from the slippery mud, he was overcome with the need to pull her closer into his embrace. And when her body had pressed so intimately against his, as if made for him, his desire to throw her back down into that bed of mud and have his way with her was nearly uncontrollable—despite having just met her and there being a house full of guests awaiting his attendance, not the least of whom was meant to be his future wife.

He knew his abrupt departure was rude and quite the conduct unbecoming a duke, but really, he had no choice. The chit was not just a danger to gardens everywhere; she threatened his peace of mind and his hard-won self-control.

Hell, she threatens my very sanity.

But damn me if she doesn't have the brightest eyes in a becoming shade of blue, more brilliant and brighter than the sky on a clear, spring morning.

And earthy brown hair that turned the color of caramel in the sunlight.

Her hair was definitely distracting. He wanted to touch it. Run his fingers through it.

And was that a kiss of sun across the bridge of her nose?

Damn, but it suited her near faultless face. Made her real. Human. Not the fairy she appeared to be otherwise.

And since when have I started cursing and talking to myself so frequently?

It must be the result of being agitated over such a minor incident, and the sleepless night in the boisterous inn the night before. And quite possibly nerves over his upcoming engagement. Who was he kidding? He was never nervous. Calm and self-assured, but never nervous.

He shook his head as if the action would clear his mind of unwanted thoughts and realized he was simply standing in front of the door to his rooms like a bedlamite. The butler was too well trained to comment on his odd behavior, but rather, stood stoically aside lest he have any further need of assistance.

Stonebridge jerked himself out of his silent stupor and threw open the door, fighting the urge to blush. Blush!

"Bryans!" he barked as he strode into the room. He didn't yell, of course. He definitely didn't yell. Dukes never raised their voices or lost their composure.

"Yes, Your Grace," replied Bryans, promptly as expected. Good. At least something was still working predictably.

The look of complete calm on his valet's countenance was expected—no, demanded—as it was of all his servants. At all times. Well, maybe he wasn't quite that tyrannical with his staff, but clearly, his own thoughts were out of character this morning. However, fortunately for his valet, the duke in his unreasonable agitation missed the slight upturn of the corner of his valet's lips.

Stonebridge marched off toward a nearby closed door, hoping it was an adjoining dressing room. He had never, not since he had become an adult at any rate, been in public in any state of dress that was less than orderly and precise. He certainly hadn't been this…disorderly…when he had alighted from the carriage this morning despite the many hours on the dusty road. And it was entirely her fault.

"Bryans, help me remove and dispose of these garments. And find me something appropriate and significantly less…soiled," he thundered from the adjoining dressing room, for he had indeed found the dressing room. He didn't normally care much about a bit of dirt, but he was too irritated and feeling out of sorts to stop and think about what he was saying. What was taking Bryans so long anyway?

"Yes, Your Grace," replied Bryans. Finally.

Stonebridge sat on a low bench and held up a booted leg. As Bryans bent to remove the offensive smelling boots, the duke's thoughts drifted back to his morning encounter with Miss Radclyffe, to the moment when she had looked up at him with those vividly shining eyes. At first, he saw humor in those rounded orbs before the shock of her embarrassing situation took hold.

When she had looked up at him that way, with humor and so completely at ease, time had stood still. And with her oval face, fair skin, and wide open eyes, she was so expressive he could read every thought that flittered across her mind. In real time. As if her every thought was written out visibly in bold, black ink. At the time, it had felt refreshing.

He shook his head of his wayward thoughts. She was decidedly not duchess material, to say the least.

Now, where in the hell had that thought come from? Duchess material?

"Pardon me, but did you say something, Your Grace?"

Stonebridge tried to cover up the fact that he had just snorted aloud. Never mind the mud and effusive bellowing. That he wasn't doing. Because Dukes didn't do that sort of thing.

"No, I most certainly did not. God, this jacket is irritatingly too snug. It's ridiculous that I should need assistance just to remove my damned jacket." He had stood after the removal of his boots and was now attempting to peel off his coat on his own. Bryans moved in to assist.

"Yes, Your Grace. Your Grace, if I may be so bold, is everything quite…"

"No, you may not be so bold," interrupted the duke. "She's…It's nothing. Everything will be resolved as soon as this damned house party is over and things return to normal."

A few moments passed without further comment as the duke, with the help of Bryans, removed his remaining clothes and stepped into his dressing gown to be worn until suitable replacement garments could be readied. Abruptly, Stonebridge spoke:

"Bryans, I want you to find out all you can about a woman here by the name of Miss Grace Radclyffe. I assume she's a guest." He wasn't sure what prompted his request; the words just seemed to burst out of his mouth of their own volition.

"No need, Your Grace. She's all anyone has talked about since we arrived. Apparently, she's the earl's niece through his first, now deceased, wife. All the servants are half in love with her, as she's quite friendly with the staff, knows everyone by their first name and all that. She's been living here about a year, since her parents died. Her father was a bookseller in Oxford, and probably why she doesn't put on airs with the staff. Shall I inquire further?"

"No, thank you. That will be all."

"Oh, and I almost forgot. It seems she has a peculiar tendency toward clumsiness."

"Don't I know it," murmured the duke.

"What was that, Your Grace?"

"Nothing. That will be all."

"Very good, Your Grace. I shall inquire further without betraying your interest."

The duke ignored the impudence and left without another word, slamming the door behind him.

Stonebridge reentered his bedchamber and walked over to the windows overlooking the west side gardens. Thankfully, he didn't have a view over the back lawn, though the formal and colorless style of the side garden wasn't much of an improvement.

He leaned his hands against the window frame, tapping his fingers in his habitual staccato rhythm, and stared out across the expanse of gardens, forcing his thoughts on to his soon-to-be betrothed. He was surprised she hadn't been in attendance when he arrived, though he had to admit he had probably arrived earlier than expected and he was glad for the respite.

He clasped his hands behind his back as he realized he was tapping the window with enough force to rattle the frame. He paced the floor instead and allowed his thoughts to wander where they would. They headed unerringly to Miss Radclyffe, of course.

He had never met her before today, despite knowing the Beckett family for many years.

I would have remembered her.

And she had not been living in the earl's house above a year ago.

Surely, I would have known of it.

Things had obviously changed in the last year, and when this house party came about, the situation must have forced Swindon's hand. He couldn't very well hide her from his guests, now could he?

He had no idea why Miss Radclyffe had not taken part in the little season with the rest of her family. She was respectable enough through her relationship to the earl to attend, and if she had attended, he would have known about it. They would have been introduced. In different circumstances. At a different time. At least he wasn't caught unawares *after* he had married Beatryce.

And why in the hell would it matter if I had met her after my marriage? It wouldn't change a damn thing.

He shut the door to further thoughts of the Mud Goddess and turned toward his dressing room. What was keeping his valet? "Bryans!" he bellowed.

* * * *

Grace's Room…
At the same time…

Phew.

Grace was familiar with all access points to her room, including the route through the servants' stairs, just in case a hasty retreat was required. More than once, she had been thankful for this knowledge and today was no exception. She made it back to her room without anyone bearing witness to her less than flawless attire.

While she took a moment to catch her breath, she noticed a change of clothes laid out on her bed. *Bessie. Ah, bless her.* And if she knew her maid, and she did, or rather if her maid knew her, and *she* did, then, there was also a copper bathing tub, filled with hot water, awaiting her behind the screen. Grace could smell the lavender oil already.

Someone scratched at the door. At Grace's "enter," Bessie, her lady's maid and pretty-much-second mother, entered the room. Bessie was round and petite and in her early fifties with a kind face and ginger hair. She had been with the Radclyffes as a helper, maid, child-minder, cook—everything and anything—for many, many years. Bessie was a real mothering sort, despite having no family of her own.

Grace and her mother (when she was living) had always helped Bessie with the daily chores. Their life had been too modest to require a full staff, as they danced on the edges of the gentry. Now, in this new life, Grace was closer to Bessie than anyone, in truth.

"How did you know?" queried Grace as Bessie hurried across the room to help her undress.

"Well, you took a wee bit longer than usual on your morning walk, and weel, based on past experience…weel, I just assumed…"

Bessie's gentle Scottish brogue trailed off. The maid looked pointedly down at her shoes, but not before Grace noticed the telltale blush that stole across her cheeks.

"Oh, no need for embarrassment, Bessie. I'm thankful you know me so well, and you never complain. I don't know what I'd do without you." Grace's voice trailed off as an unexpected wave of sadness crept over her when her mind touched on the changes in her life over the past year. Thankfully, Bessie spoke and put a halt to her wandering thoughts.

"Now, now dearest, there's no need to thank me, really. You're like the daughter I never had, and when your dear mother and father passed, bless their souls, I couldn't leave you. With no siblings and just your aunt? Oh dear, how I do rattle on. Let's get you situated in the tub and start setting you to rights. I've brought you a pot of hot chocolate and some toast since you'll likely miss breakfast before we're through."

"Thank you, Bessie, really. As always, you make everything just right." Grace, now undressed, relaxed into the steaming tub. "Oh, this water feels wonderful. It almost makes my trip to the mud bath worth it."

"My dear, what a lovely you are. You handle your incidents with such…well, grace. Now, you just relax whilst I run off to see what I can do for these clothes. I shall be back in a trice to help you dress and ready yourself for the afternoon. For now, simply relax and I'll be back before you know it."

And at that, Bessie left and Grace set herself to the task of washing away the souvenirs from her adventure in the garden.

After a thorough wash and final rinse of her hair, she calmed enough to relax in the soothing waters of her bath where her thoughts quickly returned to her encounter with the infamous Duke of Stonebridge, known stickler for propriety, noted for his impatience for anyone less than perfect, famous for his seriousness at all times, and well-known as the soon-to-be fiancé to her first cousin, Beatryce.

Though the duke and Beatryce had known each other since childhood, she never had the pleasure of meeting him before today, not directly anyway. She'd certainly heard plenty about him though. With his extreme wealth, title, and good looks, he was considered THE catch of the upper ten thousand even though everyone expected him to marry Beatryce.

Despite all of that knowledge, however, nothing prepared her for the reality of the *presence* of the Duke of Stonebridge. Just thinking about their encounter brought forth an alarming wave of heat across her body. Fortunately, it was quite easy to convince herself that these telltale signs were due to the warmth of her bath water. Not a result of thinking about him.

Of all the people to meet during one of my incidents. The duke himself. In the flesh. Beatryce's almost betrothed. Sigh.

Did she imagine the secret smile and the heat that seemed to flash in his eyes before he so abruptly left her in the garden? Nothing about their encounter fit with her mind's preconceived picture of the duke's personality. He was known for his seriousness and staid countenance. The gossip below-stairs had painted an all too vivid picture in her mind despite her best attempt not to prejudge someone she didn't know. Yet for a moment, she thought she had detected real warmth in his gaze, albeit briefly. Did she meet an imposter? Most likely this warmth was the result of her own overactive imagination. Or perhaps, wishful thinking that for once, her clumsiness could be overlooked by someone other than herself, the servants, and Bessie. Certainly, above all, she detected barely constrained power lurking behind his eyes. In her mind, that power equated to warmth and passion. So much for the cold, aloof man she had expected.

Ugh. And why should I care? Really. He is practically married. To Beatryce of all people.

And he was reputably too stuffy to warrant a turn of her head anyway. Just because he had heavenly eyes, didn't mean he...

Her thoughts were interrupted by a rapid knock on the door.

Chapter 5

"Aunt Mary! Beatryce!"

Grace knew them by the sounds they made as the barged into the room. Besides, who else would it be? Bessie had just left and wouldn't have knocked so soon after, nor so loudly.

"Please, just give me a quick minute and I shall be out…"

"Where have you been?" thundered her aunt, interrupting her. Grace barely had time to register her aunt's obvious anger before Aunt Mary peered around the bathing screen. Actually, glared would be more precise.

Aunt Mary looked like the veritable shrew of old. Her face contorted and wrinkled as it scrunched up with ire. Her eyes were lost beneath her plumped-up cheeks.

"Don't you know this is the most important week of Beatryce's life? And yet you decide to embarrass us before we've even had a chance to formalize her engagement to the duke? Do you wish to ruin your cousin's life with your selfishness?"

Obviously, the question was rhetorical. Aunt Mary's voice faded away as she paced about the room before she returned to peer at Grace behind the bathing screen. Grace stayed put in the cooling water. Duly chastened.

"To think that we have clothed you. Spent our time and money to give you a home when your mother and father died. And this is how you repay us for our generosity? I was sure your mother had raised you better than this." Aunt Mary attempted to portray sorrow and anguish over being treated so shabbily by her wayward niece, as if Grace's clumsiness was all performed on purpose.

"I do apologize, Aunt Mary. You see, I didn't see the mud and…"

"Mud???" Grace didn't realize her aunt's voice could trill quite that high. And the sudden purplish tint to her aunt's complexion was most alarming.

"What mud? Do you mean to say that you have already demonstrated the *common* blood running through your veins by behaving with your usual graceless comportment? I only knew that you had not bothered to join us at the breakfast table where you should have been on hand to meet Beatryce's future husband. Am I correct in saying that not only did you miss breakfast, but that you have further embarrassed this family with some sort of incident involving mud?"

Grace noticed Aunt Mary did not mention whether or not the duke had made it down to breakfast. Instead, Aunt Mary maintained her look of distaste and arrogance as Grace waited silently in the tub, trembling from the cooled water. Aunt Mary beheld Grace as if the mud were still present, tainting the room and the very air she breathed. Then, she proceeded to look about the room with determined eyes, as if additional mud might be lying in wait, ready to contaminate her when she least expected it.

Aunt Mary returned to the screen, refocused her gaze on Grace, and continued, "I can only be glad His Grace was not on hand to witness such unladylike behavior…"

Grace looked tellingly at the water, wishing she could hide beneath the surface. At Grace's betraying blush, her aunt cut her own words short with a gasp followed by, "No!"

Aunt Mary stopped talking, and for a moment, her mouth opened and closed like a fish out of water as she struggled with what to say. It was quite comical, actually, to witness this unusual occurrence. Aunt Mary always knew what to say and had plenty to say. The entire situation must be inconceivable to put Aunt Mary at such a loss for words; Grace could never have predicted this scenario.

Aunt Mary turned to leave the room, her tolerance at an end. She spoke to the room at large as she headed toward the door, "I don't think my constitution can handle any more abuse at the moment. Beatryce, my dear, I shall return to my room for a lie down until my nerves recover. Grace, you had better be back to rights and downstairs without a moment to spare or I shall not be responsible for my...*Aieeee!*"

Grace winced. Apparently a little patch of mud had managed to escape everyone's notice after all, and puddle in the perfect location just inside the door to Grace's room. As if lying in wait for Aunt Mary to attempt to exit.

Fortunately for everyone present, Aunt Mary caught herself in time on the door frame, but it was a near thing. Grace leapt out of the tub and threw on her dressing gown. Cautiously, she peered around the bathing screen.

Aunt Mary glared back from across the room, gripping the door frame for a moment longer before she turned on her heel with a "Humph" and stormed out. It took all of Grace's composure to keep from laughing aloud at the sight.

Throughout the entire ordeal, Beatryce had sat upon a low stool by Grace's vanity. She hadn't uttered a single word, nor had she attempted to help her mother. No, Beatryce remained poised on her stool, the picture of the composed debutante with an affected air of boredom about her as if she found the entire episode tedious. Beatryce sighed as if coming to some sort of important realization.

"Oh Grace, I really do not know how or why you manage to infuriate her so readily. You must know by now she is all that is delicate," commented Beatryce, breaking her silence.

Delicate? Ha!

It took all of Grace's self-control not to respond to that, though in her mind, she rolled her eyes. How could Beatryce say that with a straight face? If her career as a Duchess failed, she might find success treading the boards.

"Really, Grace, you look so unrefined standing there with that ridiculous grin on your face." Beatryce perused her nails as she spoke, belying the fact that she noticed anything outside of herself. "Yes, I've noticed you trying to hide your amusement, and I don't find it humorous in the least. You're lucky I don't tell Mother.

"But I'm warning you now—" Her voice hardened as she spoke. "—don't mess this up for me."

Beatryce stood and glared at Grace with that last statement. Then her face changed completely as if another, happier thought had suddenly come to mind, "By the by, I found this on top of your writing desk this morning..."

Grace grew alarmed when she saw the familiar sketch book held firmly in the grip of Beatryce's left hand. A lifetime of sketches representing all her ideas for clothing styles and designs, painstakingly drawn out in detail from her own imagination, filled the pages of that leather-bound book. Not to mention the encouraging notes from her father and mother tucked between the pages. The book and its contents represented a large part of her plans to secure her livelihood after her twenty-first birthday, and there it was. In the hands of her spiteful cousin. Grace knew she hadn't left it out for Beatryce to find; she wasn't stupid, for she knew what Beatryce would say if she came upon it, as she apparently had.

"I must say my mother would find the contents of this book very...interesting." Beatryce paused dramatically before continuing, "I find it difficult to believe you would ruin your own family by following in your father's footsteps and going into trade, but you'll be happy to know I am here to prevent you from making a dreadful mistake that you'll one day regret. Honestly, it's for your own good and because I love you that I do this, you know."

Grace couldn't breathe. Her heart pounded in her chest over what she suspected was about to happen. Her heartbeat reverberated in her ears, drowning out the sound of Beatryce making her way across the room. Everything about the situation felt unreal, as if the events unfolding were happening to someone else, and she was simply there as witness. Grace was wholly unable to believe what she assumed her cousin was about to do. Absolutely, there was no love between them, despite Beatryce's words to the contrary, but this?

Grace watched as Beatryce approached the fire burning in the fireplace, too stunned with disbelief to move and put a halt to what was about to happen. She simply couldn't fathom anyone being so deliberately cruel, even though she knew. Oh, God, she knew.

Beatryce looked over her shoulder, back at Grace, and offered a small, regretful smile. The look in her eyes suggested she was aware of how painful this would be, yet it mattered not, for she just as quickly faced forward again and unerringly tossed Grace's journal into the fire.

Grace closed her eyes and fought back her tears. Her eyes burned. It always seemed to make Beatryce happy to see Grace cry, especially when Beatryce was the cause of her tears. Grace battled to deny Beatryce that one, simple pleasure.

Once the tightness in her face began to ease and she was confident she held her emotions in check for now, Grace opened her eyes and sought out Beatryce, who studied her from across the room. Probably hoping to see the revealing signs of moisture trailing down her cheeks and brightening her eyes.

Beatryce would be out of luck today.

Suddenly, Beatryce's innocuous grin returned as if she hadn't just been viciously cruel. "If you need anything, Grace, please let me know. I am perfectly willing to lend you some of my old things if you have need of them. In fact, just tell your maid to find mine, and she will be happy to help yours out in any way necessary." Beatryce said it all with a look that suggested nothing whatsoever could help, and with that thought left hanging in the air, she glided out of the room with a mostly concealed smirk. Her words were ironic in light of this morning's theatrics over the dancing slippers.

Grace wrapped her robe tightly about her as she slid to the floor; her knees finally giving away their strength. She was stunned and horrified over what had just happened. Why, oh why had she not leaped to action and prevented Beatryce from throwing her beloved journal in the fire? Or at the very least said something, anything, in some attempt to redirect Beatryce from her intent? She was used to Beatryce's mercurial mood changes, but she still couldn't understand them. *My God, the loss of my work…*It was still too unbelievable to fathom.

Grace cried in earnest now that she was alone. Her eyes were drawn to the fire, and her vision blurred from the moisture as she watched the pages with her sketches on them curl and burn. All her designs? Gone. All those dreams on paper, stemming all the way back to when she was a young girl dreaming of her future? Fuel for the fire. A lifetime lost in but a brief moment in time. Then there were the silly little notes from her parents: words of encouragement offered up when her doubts threatened to overwhelm her confidence.

The room was brighter now as the fire was bolstered from the added fuel. How curious it was to see the fire flare with brightness, when the added light was the result of destruction that might lead to dark times in Grace's future, should she not find a way to recover from her losses today.

Grace pulled herself together. She wiped her eyes on the edge of her robe as she thought about what to do. She was a woman of strong will and knew she couldn't allow this setback to defeat her, and as the light began to dim whilst the last of the pages turned to ash, she knew she would persevere because no one could forcibly take away her hope or determination to succeed.

* * * *

"Ambrose Philip Langtry, by my eyes," boomed Clifford Ross, the Marquess of Dansbury.

Stonebridge, who had been gazing out the windows of the private sitting room adjoining his bedroom, glanced over his shoulder. He obviously hadn't heard the door, engrossed as he was in his private thoughts.

Cliff sauntered across the room. The duke smiled at him, raised his brow in question, but didn't rise in greeting. And without saying a word, Ambrose turned back around and resumed his study of the view outside.

Cliff was not offended. They had been friends for far too long. He proceeded directly to a side board to procure them both a drink.

"Yes, I had a pleasant journey south, thanks for asking," he said with a devilish grin as he walked across the room. His smile was lost to Ambrose's back.

"Hmmm? Oh, yes, wonderful, wonderful," responded the duke, perfectly distracted.

Ambrose? Preoccupied? This was new. The duke was the most focused man in existence. Cliff abandoned his plans for a drink and approached his friend instead. He considered his friend's profile as he said, "Yes, ahem, well, my mother fell in a ditch, you see, and I thought perhaps I should finally just pay the Prince Regent to haul her away. Clap her in irons and place her in the Tower, I say. She is far too much trouble to be sure, what? Ten pounds ought to do it, I should think. What think you, Ambrose?" He tried valiantly to keep a straight face as he watched his friend for any sign of awareness. Not only had he spoken utter nonsense, but he had spoken like a complete dandy, which was uncharacteristic of him and Ambrose knew it.

"Hmmm? For certain, yes, excellent decision," replied the duke without a blink.

"Ambrose!"

That should get his attention.

"What?"

"You haven't heard a word I've said. What's going on? You seem distracted."

Ambrose pulled his fingers through his hair in agitation. "Nothing. Nothing at all. Everything will be just fine once this damned house party is over. That's all."

*Hmmm…*Ambrose Langtry, the Duke of Stonebridge, well known for his vocal eloquence and composed demeanor, was anything but calm at the moment. Curious. Cliff turned and headed to the bar after all.

"Here," he said to his friend as he handed over a snifter half-filled with brandy. "It sounds like you might need this."

"Indeed. Thanks," replied Ambrose, again with that distracted air, but he wasn't finished. "I'm not sure what has gotten into me, really. I think I just wish this party were through already, and I could continue on to my duties in town. I dislike jumping through these hoops to betroth myself to Beatryce. We've known each other for years and it is expected. Everyone knows. Why can't we just make it so and move on? Yes, that was rhetorical."

"Are you sure this betrothal is the right move for you just now?"

Ambrose stood and began to pace before the windows. "Of course I'm sure. I've known Lady Beatryce my entire life. She's composed, prepared, beautiful, intelligent, *graceful*… Really, she's the perfect duchess to stand by my side, host my parties, woo my political rivals…" Ambrose's voice trailed off.

Cliff couldn't help but notice the emphasis placed on the word graceful. But the duke wasn't finished. "And when this party is through, Lady Beatryce will head off to London with that cousin of hers and enjoy spreading the news of our impending nuptials, and that will be that."

That cousin of hers?

"Cousin?" asked Cliff out loud. He was a good agent and had known his friend a long, long time. He knew how to pick out the meaningful words in his friend's response.

"Yes. Cousin. One Miss Grace Radclyffe, daughter of Leanne and John Radclyffe, both deceased. Are you familiar with the name? For some unknown reason, I find myself wondering why I feel as if I should be familiar with that name."

"I don't recall anybody by that name."

"From what I understand, Leanne, the mother, is…was…sister to Swindon's first wife, Lady Florence Beckett, Lady Beatryce's real mother. I believe Mr. Radclyffe was a commoner in trade, a bookseller, somewhere in Oxford, I think? Most importantly, Miss Radclyffe is a walking hazard to sane peoples everywhere." Ambrose pointed his snifter as if warning of some dire threat. "This, I understand both through rumor and direct observation."

Cliff watched and waited as his friend paused to sip his drink. He clearly had more to say on the subject. "Of this, I can say for certain, I shall be relieved to depart this madness on Sunday."

Cliff chuckled. "Well, I, for one, cannot wait to meet this walking safety hazard. And it sounds like this week is going to be amusing, rather than the staid ton event I was expecting. In fact, I think I shall retire to my room to refresh myself posthaste. I wouldn't want to miss a moment of tonight's entertainment."

"Hold! Might I assume there's nothing new to report on the other matter?"

"Oh, you mean work? You actually want to discuss work? No. Nothing. I'll check on our friendly neighborhood assassin this evening. I plan to steal away after dinner."

"Excellent. Keep me posted."

And like that, Ambrose was preoccupied again, which was quite unusual to say the least.

Hmmm…This week might prove to be most interesting indeed.

Chapter 6

The Drawing Room, Beckett House…
That evening before dinner…

"So, Stonebridge, where is the infamous cousin I've been dying to meet?" asked Cliff, *sotto voce.*

"She's not here. Believe me, you'll know she's arrived when you hear the disturbance," replied Ambrose, not willing to admit that he, too, had been looking for her dark head from the moment he walked into the drawing room to mingle before dinner. Self-preservation should not be underrated.

As if summoned by their conversation, Miss Radclyffe appeared in the doorway and it was as if the room had brightened with the addition of a hundred more candles. Ambrose was speechless. The word that came to mind was: lovely. She was just that. Lovely. Her hair was simply arranged in a small bun atop her head with a few wisps pulled down to grace her neck and frame her face. Her dress was unadorned and blue to match her eyes. It was modestly cut and perhaps a little outdated and worn, but it fitted her lithe form to perfection. She was one of those women who would look lovely in rags, and she quite unexpectedly took his breath away.

Damn, but I really need to get a hold of myself.

She caught his eye and smiled, and if the earth had opened up and swallowed them whole, he would not have noticed as long as she did not break the connection. He was halfway across the room to her before he realized he had moved. He checked himself before he looked the complete fool, drawing on the self-control he had spent the last seventeen years perfecting.

So smoothly no one could possibly have noticed with the possible exception of Cliff, he readjusted his stride and approached Lady Beatryce who, fortunately, had entered the room behind Miss Radclyffe. He mentally winced when he realized he hadn't even noticed her arrival.

"Lady Beatryce, how beautiful you look this evening. I must say that color of green becomes you immensely." Perhaps he laid it on a little too strongly in some bizarre attempt to apologize for his cheating mind.

"Oh, Your Grace, how kind of you to say so," replied Beatryce with a small smile. She flashed a coquettish look through her lashes, one she probably practiced in front of a mirror on a daily basis. It likely brought lesser men to their knees. Unfortunately, he was unaffected by her wiles.

"Your Grace," inserted Lady Beatryce's mother, "I hope your stay has been comfortable and agreeable, thus far. Truly, it is an honor for you to grace us with your presence. Thank you so very much for attending our small but exclusive gathering."

"Indeed, the honor is all mine," he replied, in no way revealing his inner thoughts.

There was a slight, almost uncomfortable pause in conversation while he waited for the countess to introduce him to her niece as manners dictated. It took every ounce of his self-control to maintain an unconcerned air and pretend as if every cell in his body were not completely attuned to Grace's presence nearby.

"Oh, Your Grace, I almost forgot; pray excuse my lapse in manners. May I present my niece, Miss Grace Radclyffe?

Grace, may I introduce His Grace, the Duke of Stonebridge?"

"Miss Radclyffe, it is a pleasure to make your acquaintance."

He lifted her hand to his lips. If anything, his manners were impeccable. Inside, nothing existed but the two of them. The air was charged with an electric current reminding him of that feeling in the air just before a lightning strike. The charge blanked his mind completely, and he nearly forgot to let go of her hand. And she forgot to curtsey or even respond to his polite greeting at all. He might have been the only one to notice besides Grace. Beatryce and the countess were too focused on him to pay Grace any mind.

For an instant it seemed as if she, too, had noticed the charge in the air. He noticed her eyes flare with heat and untapped passion. He mentally shook himself and settled his mask of calm indifference firmly in place. He dropped her hand as if it would scald him. It certainly felt like it had.

A gong sounded, and for a minute, he wondered if it wasn't his heart drumming loudly in his ears. Fortunately, that was not the case, and the sound of the gong meant dinner was ready. Ah, blessed relief. He was saved from trying to make small talk with someone who arrested his mind too completely at the moment. He just didn't trust himself right now.

"Ladies, it has been a pleasure, but I believe as manners dictate, I must escort the Dowager Duchess of Lyme in to dinner. If you will excuse me?"

He didn't wait for any of the appropriate inane responses, but turned quickly on his heel to attend the dowager. He was loath to admit it, but he was inexplicably glad to be away from the countess's censure. He wouldn't admit he was too discomfited by Grace's nearness to keep his composure intact, but honestly, it was with welcome relief that he sought out the Dowager to escort into the dining room.

*

Grace looked about to see if anyone else was aware of the turbulent atmosphere. Her eye caught on a smiling, elderly woman sitting sideways on a settee across the room. She was a handsome, wiry woman and obviously petite because her legs dangled girlishly over the side of the settee without even brushing the floor. The mystery lady leaned forward on the cane she had perched in front of her as she thoroughly inspected Grace from head to toe. The woman was colorful in a bright blue dress with a tangerine orange crocheted shawl, which emphasized her faded ginger hair peeking out beneath a wreath of feathers encompassing her head. But what struck Grace the most was the fact that the lady seemed to have a decidedly mischievous look about her. Especially when she caught Grace's eye and winked. Grace blushed in return, unsure of how to respond.

As the guests lined up for the promenade into the dining room, Grace stood back to allow the nineteen other diners to line up ahead of her. Firstly, with her penchant for mishaps, it was best that she allow a room to clear before she attempted to cross it. Secondly, with her lowly status compared to the other guests, she would most likely be entering last anyway, and she had no idea who her escort was supposed to be. Thirdly, she wanted to remain as far away from the disturbing duke as possible.

As she watched the gentleman find their dinner partners amidst the crowd, she noticed a tall, blonde man with laughing brown eyes headed in her direction. Despite walking in the opposite direction from the majority of the crowd, he proceeded across the room with absolute ease. Everyone automatically made way for this man as if directed by an unseen hand. Oh, she was envious at how easily he maneuvered through the throng of guests. He had a friendly, open smile on his face, and for a moment, she had the silly thought that he might be making his way to her.

"Miss Radclyffe?" he queried as he neared.

She looked behind herself. She still couldn't believe this man was actually seeking her out, but of course, no one else was on her side of the room and he had used her name. She looked at him with a hesitant smile.

"Yes?"

"Please allow me to introduce myself. I am Clifford Ross, the Marquess of Dansbury, at your service."

"A pleasure, my lord," she replied with a gracious smile. Unlike the duke, this man's open and welcoming countenance put her immediately at ease, as if she had known him for years. Strange, but true.

"Would you do me the honor of allowing me to escort you to dinner?"

"Is that proper, my lord? I mean I am…" her voice trailed off, unsure of what to say, really, without sounding gauche.

"Oh, I've known Stonebridge too long to care what he thinks about my manners and I certainly couldn't care less about anyone else's here with the exception of my aunt, but then she's never been one to play by the rules herself and she knows me far too well. No. I am simply here to enjoy a week with my closest friend and it would be infinitely more enjoyable with the company of a beautiful lady, such as yourself, beside me at what is sure to be an otherwise tedious dinner. Besides, apart from my Aunt Harriett, the impish looking lady in the brightly colored shawl just rising from the settee over there, the remaining old biddies here can take a…"

She interrupted him with a laugh. She couldn't help it. He truly did not seem to care about the rules and his pleasant demeanor was just what she needed at the moment. Clearly, the colorful lady with the wink was this man's aunt, and they were obviously two of a kind.

"Not that my aunt is an old biddy," he added.

"Oh? And what would your call her then?"

He looked across the room at his aunt as she rose from the settee with her escort in hand—as if giving the matter serious thought before saying, "A dragon. A rascally, harmless, colorful dragon. But a dragon, nonetheless. Now, how about our walk into dinner? Shall we rattle the duke's cage and set the biddies' tongues to wagging?"

"I'm sure I'm supposed to walk in with…"

"Oh, I already spoke to your escort and assured him that Lady Beatryce would be delighted if he would escort her to dinner."

Grace nearly exploded with laughter. She could just imagine how Beatryce felt about that. And his mischievousness must be contagious for Grace surprised herself by saying, "Well, when you put it that way…why not, my lord?"

"Please, call me Dansbury. When you say 'my lord', I have the sudden urge to look over my shoulder for my father."

"Well, if you insist, my…er Dansbury," she answered with a wide grin.

"Right, now that we have that sorted, let us proceed to dinner, shall we? I suspect we're in for a marvelous time of it."

And as she put her hand on his arm, Grace thought that perhaps this week might not be so bad after all.

*

Grace was laughing at one of Dansbury's jokes as they entered into the dining room, her hand on his arm. She stopped laughing when she realized everyone in the room, save for the duke and Beatryce, were seated, and all were watching her as if she were some obscene picture on display. Or perhaps some foul offal one picked off from under one's shoe. No one uttered a word.

She dipped her head to hide her face from the curious stares and tried to ignore the tinge of heat she felt creeping up her neck and filling her cheeks. It wouldn't do to faint from embarrassment. Not that she had ever fainted in her life. It bothered her that she was so prone to blushing and hadn't mastered the skill of maintaining a calm, cool façade while under scrutiny. Papa had always said her blushing was a sign of innocence and a heart filled with love and passion. Besides her mother and Bessie, no one else ever appeared to return that sentiment.

Eventually, conversation resumed as the footman entered with the first course. Grace was delighted to find herself seated next to the marquess and far away from His Boorishness, the duke. Not that there was a chance in hell she would have been seated by him. In fact, the more she considered it, she realized it was odd that Dansbury was not nearer to his friend, or that he was even sitting by her at all.

She looked at Dansbury, noticed his amused grin, and gave him a questioning look.

"All right, I confess," he replied, "I convinced your escort to change seats with me at the table as well as in the lineup. Alas, Stonebridge expects nothing less out of me, and it wouldn't do for me to disappoint, right?"

"Besides," he continued, "I expect the conversation here will be infinitely more interesting than what I would have endured in my previously assigned seat. You wouldn't have wanted me to resort to drastic measures to break the monotony, would you?" He grinned a devilish grin as he unfolded his napkin and placed it in his lap.

"Perhaps not," she said, "though my father always said laughter was good for the soul."

"And, I thank you," she added with a twinkle in her eye. She couldn't believe the audacity of this man, but she was pleased with the results. Dinner was going to be a much more pleasant affair with the company of this charming man.

"Please, don't mention it. I must say, I am delighted to enjoy your company for dinner this eve." He said it with a wink and a smile. Such a charmer, that man.

Like a magnet seeking its other half, she looked down the table at the duke. He was watching Dansbury, and he looked both angry and confused.

*

The first course of dinner proceeded nicely, and with the excellent company of the marquess, who kept up a steady flow of interesting conversation, Grace began to relax and enjoy herself. Alas, all good things do eventually come to an end, and for her, that especially held true when it came to moving about with refinement.

It started when she dropped her napkin near the end of the first course. The napkin fell—nothing shocking in that—however, Grace, who was quite used to retrieving fallen napkins with none being the wiser, was not prepared for an overly efficient footman, who being assigned to watch over her in light of her general clumsiness, readily moved forward with a replacement, only to be halted with a jab in a most awkward location by her elbow as she bent to retrieve said fallen cloth. To the footman's credit, a slight sheen of perspiration across his forehead was the only outward indication of what had transpired.

She froze. What more could she do than that really? She glanced furtively about. As long as the others proceeded to talk and eat as usual, she could assume no one else had noticed, and then, she could focus on keeping the telling blush from stealing across her face. Not to mention actually eating her food.

She heard the duke choke down some water and couldn't help but look down the table at him.

Why do I keep looking at him? Did he see my mishap? It would be just my luck. Wait. Was he trying to mask a smile? Surely not. He'd be scowling at me if he had seen anything.

Right. Keep calm. Take a deep breath. This does not mean more accidents are destined to follow.

Sadly, her relief that the incident had passed unnoticed was short lived; as the second course was being delivered, she put her hand down to the table a little too forcefully such that her hand actually hit the tines of her fork…Just. So. How did it get turned around in that direction anyway?

However it happened, her fork flew up in the air. Fortunately, the fork was snatched, literally, from out of the air by her guardian footman and another embarrassing situation was narrowly averted.

I Must. Remain. Calm.

She took her advice and slowed her breathing to calm herself. In and out. In and out.

"Your fork, my lady," said a soft, friendly voice from behind.

She blew out a long breath as she accepted the proffered utensil.

"Thank you, Bertram," she said quietly. She didn't dare look up lest anyone take note of their exchange.

Unfortunately, her eyes were, again, drawn to the duke. He was focused on his plate, though it seemed as if his shoulders shuddered briefly.

Was he stifling a laugh? No, definitely not. All right. Relax. Focus. Breathe in and out.

It was hard to relax with 'His Perfection' seated down the table, but really, she could do this.

1, 2, 3...

She counted to ten in order to restore her equilibrium. Then, fork in hand, she pulled herself together and refocused on her plate: prawns. Still shelled. Her worst nightmare. But there was nothing for it. It would be rude to leave the little buggers untouched; therefore, she simply must persevere.

Deep breath in. Deep breath out.

Right. Think delicate gentility and the meat shall simply slide right out.

Ha! Success!

Grace looked around to see if anyone noticed her extraordinary glee over the success of such a simple task, and again, could not stop her eyes from straying to the duke near the head of the table. Had he looked away just as she looked up?

Ha! Not likely. Right. I can do this.

The next prawn was even larger than the first. Excellent. No problem then. Delicately hold the prawn steady, thus, and with gentle persuasion using the explicitly designed prawn fork, simply pull…

"Oh. My. Goodness."

Of course, she said it under her breath so as not to draw attention to herself, but she did say that out loud. She watched with horror as her little prawn soared through the air. She didn't dare move her head as her eyes followed its progression, which seemed to arc down the table in slow motion. Alas, there would be no rescue from her guardian footman this time.

And, oh dear, it was headed straight for Stonebridge. This could not end well.

*

Stonebridge, who had been conversing with the dowager Duchess of Lyme, froze in horrified amazement as he watched Miss Radclyffe's flying prawn make its way down the table. Miss Radclyffe truly was a walking disaster. It amazed him how he could continue to be shocked by anything he witnessed happening within her presence.

After commiserating with the poor footman's pain and watching the flying fork, he still could not believe how things could possibly continue to go so completely wrong for Miss Radclyffe. Now this.

Plop.

He returned his gaze to the lady seated next to him whilst drawing forth his napkin from his lap. The Dower Duchess of Lyme, who had been talking incessantly up until now, froze, her eyes widened in shock. The prawn had narrowly missed her great beak of a nose, and she didn't even know it. He, however, wasn't so lucky.

"You were saying, Your Grace?" he prompted. He refused to acknowledge the feel of prawn in red sauce sliding down the side of his face. He casually wiped his cheek with his napkin as he encouraged the dowager to continue whatever it was she had been saying.

"N-Nothing, Your Grace. I was q-quite finished." The dowager blinked once in quiet confusion before looking down and attending to her plate. She studied it as if she had never seen one before today.

Stonebridge calmly folded his napkin and placed it next to his plate. He glanced down and noticed prawn sauce splattered all over his cravat and waistcoat. He ground his teeth as he drew on every ounce of his self-control; then he looked up and bored into the eyes of Miss Radclyffe.

She grinned (grinned!) in return and wiggled her fingers as if in greeting. He couldn't believe her audacity. She'd just flung a prawn into the side of his face, from down the length of a dining room table no less, and now she sat there, without a hint of apology twinkling in her eye, laughing and waving merrily as if they were simply acquaintances passing by on the pavement outside.

No one but he, and now the dowager, seemed to be aware anything was amiss, thanks to her sentinel footman and pure, dumb luck. He noticed she had placed her napkin on the table, a sign that she was finished eating. Good. It would be better for her to risk being rude and not eat, or even pretend to eat for that matter, rather than continue to tempt the hand of fate with additional opportunities for victual mayhem.

* * * *

Stonebridge was on his way to his rooms to refresh and change his clothes as a result of the disastrous dinner when the butler approached with a note from the earl, summoning him to his study at his earliest convenience. It wasn't an unusual request; he was supposed to propose marriage to

Swindon's daughter after all, but it was unexpected nonetheless.

Swindon was a garrulous man, yet the note was succinct and therefore completely out of character. Fortunately, for everyone else's ears, he rarely left his home, or more specifically, his dining table. He expected people to come to him. On his terms. And this meant one seldom had to suffer through one of his lengthy monologues in public. Maybe he only saw people in his own home because it gave him a feeling of power over his guests while expressing his unsolicited opinion on every topic known to man, and he was certainly that — opinionated, to the point that he infrequently, if ever, considered someone else's point of view. Despite all this, his personality was rather weak, but this lack of character was unimportant in the grand scheme of things since he rarely ventured out in society anyway.

It was too early in the week for any kind of proposal, or lack thereof, to raise any sort of concern on Swindon's part, so the requested meeting should prove to be curiously interesting.

Chapter 7

The Earl of Swindon's study...

"Your Grace, come in, come in," beckoned the earl. "I presume the courtship is proceeding as expected?"

"Yes, of course," replied Stonebridge cautiously as he walked across the room. He said no more, though he was interested to see where this discussion was headed.

"Excellent. Excellent," continued Swindon, somewhat fretfully. The earl rubbed his hands on his trouser legs several times before he attempted to stand as manners dictated; the nervous action betrayed his discomfiture. It was sad, really, to watch the earl rock a few times in his chair before he could use the generated momentum to heft his bulk into a standing position. Needless to say, Swindon was a large man. And that was an understatement, if anything.

Ambrose was patient. He knew Swindon would not push for details regarding the courtship even if he had every right to do so. And so it was with patience and confidence that he took a seat in front of the earl's desk and waited serenely in silence. He used the disquiet to his advantage, silently prodding Swindon to get to the point of why he was summoned.

It worked. Only a few moments of awkward silence passed, while the earl poured both of them a drink, before he spoke. "I'm not quite sure how to broach this subject delicately; so, I'd like to be blunt…if I may…" His voice trailed off as he looked questioningly at Stonebridge, silently seeking permission to continue.

"Of course."

"I noticed you were introduced to my niece, Miss Radclyffe, this evening before dinner. She is, of course, not a blood relation of mine. She is the niece of my first wife and first cousin to Beatryce."

Stonebridge did not respond to the obvious pause to confirm or deny the statement, but he did sit forward, wary of the topic being introduced.

Swindon continued, still hesitant. "I'm sure you are curious as to why we have not mentioned her to you before now…not intentionally to deceive, mind you," he was quick to add, "but as you might be aware, we are cautious to whom and how we introduce her, for as I'm sure you know by now, she comes from trade, regrettably." The earl spoke slowly, choosing his words with care despite his request to speak pointedly.

Stonebridge acknowledged what was said and prodded Swindon to continue with a simple nod of his head.

"Not to mention she is a bit awkward; though quite friendly, I might add…" The earl's voice trailed off again.

Get to the point, man.

"I had hoped to give you time to become reacquainted with our family and see that we are upstanding members of society before we discussed the, um, situation with the Radclyffe girl, er, my niece…"

Another dramatic pause from the earl and Stonebridge was ready to beg him to spit it out.

"You see, her father owned a bookshop in Oxford — owned the entire shop and the apartments above outright, actually — and it was, all of it, bequeathed to Miss Radclyffe upon his death. Currently, the apartments have a tenant, and the shop is being leased to a former apprentice to her father, who continues to sell books there. At a healthy profit, I might add. I have been managing the estate on her behalf, of course, and as you might expect, it is all being held in trust to be given over to Miss Radclyffe upon her twenty-first birthday, which is in two months' time."

The earl hesitated again, nearly panting as if he was out of breath. As if he had run for miles and miles at top speed. After a minute or two and a mop of his brow with his handkerchief, he continued, "However, we fear she may be planning to take over the space and start her own business there after her birthday."

Finally. It was all out. The earl had spit the last bit out in a rush and was anxiously awaiting some sort of response. No wonder the man was so on edge. It must be killing him to have to announce his tie to someone in trade.

He must be afraid I am going withdraw my suit should I find out about Grace's plans.

All was quiet as both men considered the ramifications of Miss Radclyffe's potential actions. Stonebridge was relieved the topic wasn't about his encounter with Miss Radclyffe this morning. *This* scandal was easy, child's play, but he waited in silence still, knowing Swindon would continue to talk if only to fill the silence. He wasn't disappointed.

"We've tried talking with her and demand she give up her ridiculous notions. Ultimately, I think she will obey us on this; she really is a reasonable girl otherwise, but I-I just wanted to make you aware of the situation…just in case…you know…"

"I see." Stonebridge was relieved this was all the earl wanted. It was easy to promise to take care of things and much more difficult to explain his actions from this morning. "Not to worry, Swindon. This situation is easily remedied, should the need arise, of course. If Miss Radclyffe is as reasonable as you claim, she will see the folly of her ways, and it will not be an issue. And if not, she won't ignore a more substantial offer of compensation if it means providing her with a comfortable life in the country or in some other capacity, such as that of a companion to a lady of means."

The look of relief on Swindon's face was palpable. Clearly, the earl had worried he would call off the engagement over the threat of scandal and was relieved to know the duke was prepared to assist should the need arise. If that were his fear, Swindon really didn't know him at all, which, he admitted, was by design. He carefully kept his own council in public. In actuality, he couldn't care less whether or not Miss Radclyffe wanted to go into trade, so long as it was respectable, but now was not the time to delve into such broad social issues as class distinction. If keeping Miss Radclyffe out of trade was all that was required to keep Swindon happy, so be it. It mattered little to him either way.

* * * *

Much later that evening…

Grace cautiously opened her bedroom door. It was late, well after midnight, and most, if not all, of the guests were asleep. Or, at least, they should be at this late hour. Still, in an attempt towards secrecy, she did not light a candle. The only illumination for her to see by was the glow from the banked fire and what little moonlight filtered in through her bedroom window; thus it was in near darkness that she peered left and right down the hall, squinting into shadows and looking to see if anyone else was about.

Concluding that the hall was indeed empty of guests, she tip-toed out of her bedroom. She pulled her door closed, carefully, with both hands, until it shut with a soft click. She let out the breath she was holding on a soft sigh then squared her shoulders and made her way toward the servants' stairs with purpose—albeit as quietly as possible.

She had left her spectacles lying somewhere around the house and needed to retrieve them. Despite the late hour and her every intention of getting a good night's sleep, she found herself unable to settle her mind. She was too wound up from replaying the events of the day and altogether too worried about her future in light of her destroyed journal. She knew the best way to calm her fears was to throw herself into some work—something tangible that would help her resolve her worries. Then, the elusive sleep might come with blessed relief. To do that, she needed her glasses.

Unfortunately, she was inappropriately dressed for her furtive trip, for she had already dismissed her maid after Bessie had helped her disrobe. Therefore, she knew her foray was risky, but the chances of coming across another guest at this time of night were slim to none. Besides, she wasn't looking to dally about, but rather to quickly make her way out and back to her room in all haste with none the wiser. To that end, she took the servants' stairs, just in case. It wouldn't do to run into a guest along the way on the off chance someone else was still up and about so late.

* * * *

Stonebridge stared off into the fire as he sipped his brandy and thought over the day's events. Swindon had retired much earlier, but bade him to remain in the library for as long as he desired. What he desired, in truth, was freedom from thoughts of Miss Radclyffe which seemed to plague him persistently throughout the day.

To make matters worse, Cliff had enjoyed his dinner with Miss Radclyffe and couldn't stop singing her praises, the bastard. In his eyes, she was a paragon, with all her optimistic ideals, and apparently, she had a quick wit to boot. Too bad she was a wreck in every other way, or at least, every way that mattered.

Stonebridge was disturbed by how jealous he was over the ease with which she and his friend conversed over dinner. He was supposed to propose to Lady Beatryce this week and all he could think about was the walking disaster that was Grace

Radclyffe.

Damn…

He slammed his fist on the table before he took another swallow of his brandy. He almost didn't recognize himself; he was behaving so out of character today. He relished the burn as the brandy warmed him from within. He couldn't settle his thoughts long enough to even enjoy a quick read before retiring, as was his ritual for the past fifteen years. Not only was Miss Grace Radclyffe physically dangerous to be around in person, but she was wreaking havoc on his orderly existence even when she wasn't around.

If he were to be honest, just for a moment, mind, he might admit he was purposely avoiding Beatryce and her repeated attempts to speak to him today. And for what? So he could sit here alone and contemplate some clumsy chit who would never, ever be a suitable duchess? Surely not. He simply felt it unjust to woo his intended when he was suffering such inner turmoil. Honest.

Yes, she (Grace) was beautiful. Yes, according to Cliff, she was intelligent and compassionate, but really, any future with her was impossible. He had an obligation to the duchy and she was wholly unsuitable.

So why couldn't he force her from his mind? He had only just met her — this morning, in fact — and already she seemed destined to remain entrenched in his brain. To make matters worse, every conversation since dinner seemed to be centered on her. No matter who he was talking to. Cliff, Swindon. Even some of the other guests tittered about her behind her back. Nasty old crones.

Right. Enough of this nonsense. He would go up to bed posthaste and get a good night's sleep — the nightcap should help with that. Cliff would find him should there be anything critical to report, which was fine. In his line of work, he was used to interrupted sleep caused by agency business. Then, tomorrow, first thing, he would ask Lady Beatryce to go for a ride and propose to her in the old folly near the lake he had heard mention of over dinner. He smiled. His sense of self and purpose was restored.

He downed the last of his drink and placed the empty glass on the table beside his chair. He was confident now that he had a plan to put his focus back on track with this marriage business. After a few more thoughtful moments, during which he tried in vain to block thoughts of Miss Radclyffe, he slapped his hands on his knees and stood, grabbing the empty snifter as he did. He was prepared to carry out his plans — sleep, wake, propose — without delay. He could do this.

A soft, unexpected sound from behind him caused him to drop his glass. It landed on the rug with a soft clink. The hair standing up on his arms told him without looking who had just entered the room. Or was it simply wishful thinking?

He pulled upon the last thread of his control as he turned about and painstakingly absorbed every detail of the vision standing just inside the doorway. Even though he knew it was she before he saw her, he was unprepared for the sight of Grace standing there silently before him. She was wearing a virgin-white cotton nightgown with a floor length long-sleeved wool robe — the nightwear of choice for the discerning spinster. And yet, she couldn't have looked lovelier if he'd conjured her image up in his mind wearing the most provocative of lingerie. Her hair was down and loosely braided in a thick tail that hung over her shoulder to her waist. She was dressed for…bed.

Ah, hell.

He was entranced. Yet how could this be? He had seen his share of women in the most provoking nightwear, guaranteed to inflame a man's desire, and yet nothing he had seen before had ever had him wanting to simply drop to his knees and worship a woman with all the passion in his soul. His quixotic thoughts were interrupted by her sudden nervous chatter.

"Oh, I'm sorry to disturb you, Your Grace, but well, I couldn't sleep and thought to read, and thought the library would have a most excellent suggestion, I mean, selection, of books…er, something to read, so I thought I'd have a look again, and learned also, that my spectacles…were…" Her voice tapered off.

They stood staring at each other for what felt like an eternity before he finally broke the silence. "Miss Radclyffe. Do you always run about your home, when any number of guests might be up and about, wearing nothing but your night clothes?"

His sudden surge of anger actually caught him by surprise. The thought of her running into another guest while wearing nothing but her night clothes, even if she were more covered than most ball gowns, set his teeth on edge and he was furious at the thought. What if Cliff had still been about? Perhaps that was what she was hoping for, to catch Cliff unawares? It didn't escape his notice that they had had an awful lot to say to each other over dinner. He even noticed his friend touching her arm a few times, and he shamefully remembered wanting to jump down the table and punch his friend in the face at the time. He had been horrified over the impulse.

"You weren't, perhaps, planning a rendezvous in the library with a certain marquess by chance?" He knew his face was rigid.

"A…what?" She stuttered. "You think…I can't…"

*

Grace was so angry she was at a loss for words, quite the opposite of her earlier verbal explosion of run-on thoughts. She had been unable to function properly for thoughts of the duke plaguing her all day, and now he was accusing her of setting up an assignation with another man? Such designs had never even crossed her mind, and she was simply stunned his thoughts would run in that direction.

For a moment, all she could do was stand there and gape at him. Finally, she pulled her thoughts together and twirled on her heel intending to leave…immediately. He was too much the insufferable boor to even waste her breath with a witty retort. To think she even considered this ridiculous lout for a single moment. Ugh. Well, now that she saw what he was like, he was well and truly made for Beatryce.

"Grace! Wait!"

She had almost made it out the library door before strong hands gripped her arms and pulled her back inside. He spun her around and pressed her against the nearest bookcase. She wasn't more than a hairsbreadth away from his chest.

He held her trapped, and the intensity in his gaze was back, but no longer cold. He sounded breathless, and she could smell brandy as his breath caressed her face. Shivers ran up her arms at his close proximity and the purposeful look in his eye. She was suddenly feeling too hot, and she knew she was blushing. His hands gripped the shelves on either side of her head now, and his knuckles were white with his grip, creating the perfect cage to hold her in place.

"Grace, I'm sorry."

He paused and held her gaze. For a moment, Grace allowed herself to stand there, locked in his sights. Despite her anger over his earlier implications, she undeniably longed for things that could never be. She was attracted to this man on a basic, animal level. It didn't matter that society frowned at their differing classes. His head drew nearer, and for a fleeting moment, she was confident he would kiss her, and oh, how she wanted it. But she was consciously aware that it would be a mistake. He was nearly betrothed to her cousin, and though her cousin and she were not friends, Grace would never betray her family that way, especially with a man she barely knew. It was wrong.

So before their lips could meet, Grace ducked under his arm and darted out the library door.

*

Stonebridge remained completely still. He closed his eyes as he tried to hold on to her lingering scent and the image of her staring up at him with so much intensity—with desire in her eyes. Then, ever so slowly, he leaned his head against the books where only moments before she had stood within his arms, within his reach. His heart still beat erratically.

He had nearly kissed her. And what a mess that would have been. And yet, he was completely undone, for it wasn't he who had stopped it from happening. He was inexplicably drawn to her. He, a duke, and she, a woman who was completely unsuitable for him in so many ways. On so many levels.

He didn't really know her, but she made him feel, damn it. She made him nearly lose his head in public, something he swore after his ruinous fight at Eton so many years ago, he would never, ever do again. Then, there was the irrational flare of jealousy sparked by her behavior. It was beneath him. *Him*! He, who always maintained the utmost self-control, a character trait that was essential in his line of work. And lethal to more than just himself if lost.

He slammed his fist into the books on either side of his head before turning to look for his brandy glass. He forced her out of his head. He had to. But he needed another drink to calm the fire still raging inside. For once, he sought oblivion.

"I didn't like that translation of Homer either, but you needn't take it out on the book."

Stonebridge didn't miss a step as he headed toward his empty snifter still lying on the floor. He was not in the mood for Cliff's brand of humor, and he was irritated, damn irritated, that he was caught unaware by his friend's presence in the room. Again. It was unusual for him to be so distracted. And potentially deadly.

He pulled it together and proceeded without missing a beat. As if this meeting was planned all along. As if nothing else had happened, or almost happened, in this very room.

"What do we know?"

Cliff sighed in exasperation. And Stonebridge knew his friend had witnessed far more than he would have liked. Fortunately, his friend chose to ignore what he saw. Good. For Cliff.

"No change on the current status of our informant. However, I do have a lot of news to impart. First, I received the information I requested from the Home Office. It seems that in the two years prior to the Irish uprising of 1798, the United Irishmen were actively rallying support for their cause: an independent Ireland completely free of English rule. As a result, many skirmishes erupted as tensions escalated. In an attempt to subdue the rebels and prevent a full out Irish Revolution, England's agents captured many Irish insurgents, including our man, Murphy. We have clear documentation that Murphy was interrogated and held prisoner for at least a year, and then nothing. No record of him having been released, hung, drawn and quartered. Nothing."

"Who was responsible for his interrogation?"

"There were many names listed over the course of the year; though, as with his release records, many pieces of documentation appear to be missing, tampered with, or plain incomplete. The most notable name we have on record is Lord Middlebury, but his interrogation was early on in Murphy's captivity. October 1796."

Middlebury? Good God.

"Also, there is a dated but unsigned letter in the file claiming that Murphy was spotted just outside of Bristol about a month after the paper trail ends. Based on the time frame, I suspect he was unlawfully released and secretly sent to Bristol. It doesn't make sense for him to head in that direction. It's not on the way to Ireland. Unless someone sent him there for a purpose. The timeframe is right; the letter is dated July 1797."

Bristol? Near my own home?

"Regarding the assassination attempt on the Prime Minister, there was no official investigation into any threats over the course of 1797; however, I have a note here from my contact at the Home Office that states there was an attempt on the PM's life during a house party at the home of the 9th Duke Stonebridge. At Stonebridge Park. In August of 1797. So, the timing is right."

In my own damn home??? How could I have not been aware of that?

"I see the look on your face, Duke. You're wondering how we never knew about the attack at Stonebridge Park. Well, remember, the attack was never officially investigated. My understanding is that William Pitt the Younger had many attempts on his life, and he often brushed off such attempts as inconsequential. It's by pure luck that my contact at the Home Office knew about it."

"But how could someone not make the connection? Someone attacks the PM in my father's home, and my father turns up dead a month later?"

"I agree it's odd, but then I believe that's why the 'accident' was so elaborate—the point was to discredit your father's character so that no one cared to look into it too closely. Add to that the Society involvement? We're talking men with power here."

The duke's thoughts raced, reviewing, discounting, and revising all they knew about the case thus far. Would his father have taken it upon himself to investigate the assassination attempt on his own? Considering what he remembered of his father's character, absolutely. He was certainly tenacious enough. Might he have been killed for what he discovered? Without a doubt.

Most importantly, if his father had discovered something, would he have documented his findings? Absolutely. His father was also meticulous.

A month had passed between the assassination attempt and his father's murder. Knowing how powerful his father was, he was bound to have discovered something. Mightn't he have hidden what he knew at Stonebridge Park? If his father had been following someone in the area, it made sense he would keep his findings there. The Park had been searched, but they must have missed something.

"Do you realize what this m—" continued Cliff.

"Yes. Damn it." This new information had far reaching implications. Plus, murder and high treason? The sentence for a conviction of either charge meant death to the guilty party.

His mind whirled as he considered the culprit's possible identity based on this new information. There were only two families near Stonebridge Park who would have the connections necessary to have a prisoner released and the documentation tampered with: one was laughable, the lord too weak and lazy to be involved with something so daring and shrewd; and the other, well, the idea wasn't impossible—the family was well-known for their underhandedness, intolerance, and strong political ambitions—but the lord always seemed to be all hot air with no action and no real power to back him up. It was quite a stretch to believe he actually had the clout, connection, and confidence to pull off evidence tampering without getting caught.

"What about the Society itself? Any news there?"

"There's not a lot to add to what we already know. We only have three suspected members, but no concrete evidence: Lord Middlebury, Lord Nash, and Lord Marchant. Middlebury is the highest ranking known suspect, but the Lord Middlebury from that time period is deceased now, and there has been no evidence to suggest his son has followed in his father's footsteps, though it seems likely, given the family's reputation and Middlebury's individual personality. None of the three known suspects are believed to be the real power and money behind the group, though. Lords North and Fox were investigated, but were never officially considered. They would have been an obvious choice, of course, if one didn't know them well. They had always been quite vocal in opposition to Pitt, but they never supported the idea of secret societies, preferring instead to operate publicly so as to never jeopardize their political careers. There has never been even a hint of a suggestion as to who was or is the real power behind the group, and since the Society seems to have all but disappeared since Pitt left office, further investigation into their activities has all but ceased in the last five years. Honestly, I believe they are just biding their time, but that's my gut speaking. We need to find out who pulls the strings, then, I think, the pieces will fall into place."

"Right. Middlebury cannot be a coincidence. He may not have been the kingpin, but he does have an estate near the Park, and his culpability is obvious. Perhaps, if we find proof through that avenue, we'll discover the evidence we need to catch the rest of the men behind all this. Get the word out. Inform the rest of the team we'll be meeting at Stonebridge Park Monday next."

Bloody hell. My life just got a lot more complicated.

Chapter 8

The Back Gardens, Beckett House…
The Next Morning…

The morning mist still clung to the earth as Stonebridge raced his stallion, Abacus, across the parkland surrounding Beckett House. He had brought his horse with him on this trip, though normally, he wouldn't have done so. He had suspected he would need the distraction, and he was proved right.

He had intended to ask Lady Beatryce to join him and propose this morning, but an aching head put him in too foul a temper for romance. He was in no mood to offer forth an appropriate proposal, and it wasn't fair to Beatryce. That was all it was. Really.

Yes, he had thought long and hard about whether or not to delay his engagement pending his investigations into his father's murder, but he decided he had to proceed as intended. He didn't want to raise suspicions with a sudden change in his plans; therefore, caution was his best approach. He felt a tad guilty for his suspicious nature, but he was a logical man and good at what he did, and he would follow every lead no matter his personal feelings. This meant he had to see the house party to its conclusion, then head straight for Stonebridge Park after.

Despite the sore head and late night, he arose early as was his custom and headed out for a morning ride to clear the fuzz from his mind. He had drunk steadily last night. Drunk until he barely remembered crawling up the stairs to his bed. Excess drink was something in which he never indulged, and the drink didn't even perform its intended function. He dreamt of *her* last night: Grace.

And long after stumbling into his bed at some untold hour of the morning, he awoke hard and aching for her. He had been dreaming of her naked and writhing in his bed as he…

Oh, hell, not again.

He pulled Abacus to a halt and rubbed his hand down his face. He had to put a stop to his recall of last night's dream; it was becoming decidedly uncomfortable to ride his horse.

Since he was almost back to the house, he decided to walk Abacus the remainder of the way while he got himself under control. Dammit, he had a full hard-as-steel erection throbbing in his trousers. He dismounted, but held on to the reins in order to guide his horse on foot.

As he crested the last hill abutting the house's rear gardens, he unerringly looked to the section of garden where yesterday's muddy introduction to Grace Radclyffe had occurred. Was it only yesterday? He could still make out the exact location on a slight rise above a circular rose garden.

He jerked his gaze away before he started reliving the encounter. For the hundredth time. He focused instead on a circular path nearby. It was made up of four distinct rose beds with graveled paths between that led to a center circle with a statue of Venus in the middle. Around the edges of the center circle were four benches set at even intervals from which an observer could view either the statue or the surrounding roses.

His eyes locked on to one of those benches. As if pulled straight from his musings, there she sat, the unforgettable Miss Radclyffe, gazing silently up at the house. She had her back to him and did not know he was there. Watching.

Absorbing every detail.

All he could do was stand in place and stare, absentmindedly rubbing his horse's nose as he was captivated by the sight of her sitting quietly in repose. A break in the overcast sky allowed a single ray of sun to shine down on her, casting her hair in that caramel glow he couldn't seem to eliminate from his mind.

She stood, and it was then that he noticed she was no longer alone. He was staring at her so intently, he hadn't noticed Cliff walking up the path to her left until she stood in greeting. Shite. With his recent inattentiveness, he might as well hand in his resignation at the earliest opportunity. How would he continue to survive in his line of work?

An intense pang of jealousy startled him, and he nearly jumped on his horse and spurred Abacus to a gallop to interrupt the private moment he'd witnessed. She seemed completely at ease with Cliff by the way her shoulders visibly relaxed at the sight of him and then alternately shook with what could only be mirth—probably at some witty remark made by his friend. Cliff was really quite charming with the ladies and was well known for putting others at ease with his friendly manner.

The duke halted his quick stride before he made a complete fool of himself by charging in on their rendezvous. He knew she wasn't really Cliff's lover, but jealousy made a muck of his normally rational thoughts. Honestly, they would make a splendid couple, and he should not begrudge them their friendship. He wasn't interested in a match with her himself; he was going to marry Lady Beatryce, after all. Lady Beatryce, his intended, who was perfect for him and the man he needed to be as the Duke of Stonebridge.

* * * *

"Good morning, Miss Radclyffe."

Grace stood at the friendly greeting; it was Lord Dansbury.

"Good morning, Lord Dansbury. How are you this morning?"

"Excellent — most excellent."

"That's good to hear. Won't you please join me? The gardens and house are beautiful from this aspect." She gestured to the bench behind her. It was large enough to seat four comfortably. Two should be no problem even with a man as broad of shoulder as the marquess.

"I would love to, thank you."

They sat on the garden bench, and for a moment, an uncomfortable silence followed. But after a minute or two, the couple looked at each other at the same moment and laughed. It worked to break the tension built from their awkward silence.

They talked of books, the weather, and the theater — the usual social inanities. Grace was charmed and laughed often. It seemed Dansbury had a funny quip to share on every subject.

After a furiously quick fifteen minutes, he said, "So. Miss Radclyffe. I must admit I had another purpose in seeking you out this morning besides hoping to enjoy your charming company. If you are still free, my aunt, who is currently taking coffee on the back terrace, would like to meet you — if you are amenable, of course. Oh, and don't worry; she doesn't really bite or breathe dragon's fire. Often."

Grace laughed; he was quite the charmer to be sure. "Oh, I'm not afraid of a rascally dragon. I would be delighted to meet her, of course." She stood. "Lead on, my lord."

* * * *

The Back Terrace…

"It is about time you returned, you rogue. I was beginning to think you had turned coward on me."

"Auntie, you know me better than that." Dansbury leaned over to kiss his aunt on the cheek before turning to introduce Miss Radclyffe.

"Aunt Harriett, may I present Miss Grace Radclyffe. Miss Radclyffe, Lady Harriett Ross."

"It is a pleasure to meet you, my lady." Grace curtsied.

"My, my. You are quite beautiful, Miss Radclyffe. No wonder he likes you. Please, have a seat and join me. Dansbury," she added. She did not even appear to look at her nephew as she said it, "although it is surprisingly becoming on you, it is not like you to blush. Besides, there's no need; I wasn't referring to you. Now run along. You've had her for quite long enough. It's my turn to evaluate Miss Radclyffe's character and make sure she's suitable."

Grace, who had been trying desperately hard not to laugh, was startled: "Er…suitable?"

"Never you mind, dearie, never you mind. So, tell me, what sort of trade was your father involved in? Was it something exciting? Daring and risky? Do tell."

* * * *

The Gardens…
Later that day…

It was a perfect day for pall-mall. The dew on the ground had dried completely once the sun came out at half past ten. By two of the clock, the sun was still shining quite brightly with no breeze to be felt. With such mild temperatures this time of year, it was the perfect weather for being outside.

Though one would think that Grace ought to avoid the sport in light of her tendency toward chaos, she could not resist playing it whenever the opportunity arose. It was her favorite sport, after all, and often, her mishaps seemed to help her game more than hinder it, to the disgruntlement of others, of course.

So it was with great trepidation (from the other guests) that Grace, Stonebridge, Dansbury, Beatryce, Lady Prudence Bookworth (a neighbor), Miss Bookworth (her sister), and Lord Richard Middlebury decided to play a game of pall-mall in the back garden.

Lord Richard Middlebury, newly arrived to the festivities, was clearly an outright rake of the first order. It was immediately obvious in the way he perused the guests the minute he stepped out on the back lawn. He was dressed from head to toe in colorful attire and was, without a doubt, classically handsome—beautiful, actually—with his pale blonde hair, blue eyes, and slim physique—though there was a disconcerting coolness about his eyes that appeared whenever he wasn't actively charming the ladies, which unsettled Grace.

"Lord Middlebury, it has been an age," exclaimed Beatryce with undisguised delight.

"Ah, Lady Beatryce, you are a vision as always, my dearest." Lord Middlebury had overabundant charm.

"Oh, Richard, you are ever the Lothario. I do believe you know everyone here? Or perhaps you are not acquainted with my cousin, Miss Grace Radclyffe?"

"I have not had the pleasure, no." He perused her with a not so subtle inspection of her figure. She felt as though she were being stripped of her clothing and studied.

"Well then, Richard, may I present my dearest cousin, Miss Grace Radclyffe. Grace, Lord Richard Middlebury. Ambrose and I have known Richard for quite some time, haven't we, darling? Oh, the times we had and the youthful adventures we shared…" exclaimed Beatryce in a sweet and dreamy voice. A false voice.

The sudden tension apparent by the duke's clenched jaw belied that statement.

"Miss Radclyffe, the pleasure is all mine." Middlebury bent to kiss her hand.

"Thank you, Lord Middlebury." Grace curtseyed in return.

Lord Middlebury held her hand for an inordinately long time, but just as she was about to become uncomfortable with his attention, he dropped her hand as if burned.

Grace looked at him, startled, but he wasn't even looking at her. Instead, his eyes stared down the duke.

"Stonebridge."

"Middlebury.'

The two men eyed each other with matching frowns. Neither shook hands despite their vocal acknowledgement. It was obvious these two men shared a troubled past. Each man radiated abundant fury; the surrounding air felt oppressed with it. The duke's infernal eyebrow shot up and his hands were clenched at his sides. She'd noticed he raised that brow an awful lot throughout the day, and she was disconcerted that she'd noticed that level of detail about him. It was painfully clear that a thousand words were exchanged between the two men, though neither uttered a word out loud.

The Bookworth sisters whispered furiously throughout the exchange, and Grace strained her ear to hear what they were saying. It was apparent the two women were discussing the two men.

"I never thought we'd be so lucky," whispered Lady Prudence.

"Don't I know it, Sissy. I've never seen them in the same room together. Have you?"

"No. But won't everybody in London be so jealous when we tell them. Ooooh, I wonder if they'll come to blows."

Goodness, I wish they'd say why. Why might they come to blows?

Grace should feel ashamed for her blatant eavesdropping, but she was too curious to care. She sidled closer, desperate to hear more.

"How dashing! Simply everyone would want to come to tea at our house if they did, just to hear all the juicy details. I wish they'd get on with it. And just think, we'll have front row seats."

Both girls giggled.

"Did you hear that Middlebury's father wrote to Eton's Head Master, and asked to be allowed to decide the duke's punishment after their big fight?"

Finally! Something worth hearing.

"No, I hadn't heard that part? How bad was it? I heard he nearly killed Middlebury. I bet the punishment was harsh."

"Yes, it was. And Stonebridge almost died from it. The Head Master was fired when it was over. And I heard it's why Dansbury and Stonebridge are so close. I heard Dansbury somehow saved the duke's life though they'd never met before then."

Both girls sighed together. They'd obviously romanticized the entire thing. Silly girls.

"Well, I heard the duke's father liked boys. Though I admit I'm not sure what that means. I heard the duke is just like his father that way."

"Ewww," they said in unison. Despite the fact that they had no idea what they were talking about.

Grace nearly snorted out loud. The idea that the current duke liked men, romantically, was obviously untrue based on what almost happened between them last night. As for his father, she didn't know, but it really didn't matter, did it? To each their own. But what it did say was that these two were degrading into fantastical rumors now, and so Grace ignored the rest of their questionable gossip.

During the entire whispered exchange, the two men continued to square off in silent fury. Neither was prepared to back down. And just when Grace thought they were actually going to throw down their mallets and begin brawling amidst the wickets, Middlebury relaxed his shoulders and readopted his rakish façade. It was a thin disguise.

"Well, let's get stared, shall we?" he said. And broke eye contact with the duke.

The crowd released their collective breath all at once. They all realized a more serious altercation had only just been circumvented. A few people continued to fidget with their mallets, their nerves stretched taut.

Grace shook off her anxiety and picked up her mallet, resting it against her left shoulder as she walked over to the starting wicket. She couldn't help but notice the others eye her with some hesitation.

Hmmm…Are they thinking to see the infamous 'Calamity Grace' in action, perhaps?

The secret imp in her couldn't help but come out then, and thus, with a subtle grin, she lifted the mallet high in the air and swung it about a few times before resting it back on her shoulder. She hadn't said a word and couldn't help her grin when the others all jumped or cringed, startled by her antics.

"Whatever is the matter? You look as if you've had a fright," she said to the crowd in general. "Let's get on with it then," she stated, with a cheeky grin. Humor was her strongest defense against her own personal anxieties.

She thought she heard a deep but quiet chuckle from behind, and with a surreptitious glance over her shoulder, saw the duke quickly look down, keenly inspecting his own mallet.

Did he actually just laugh at my jest? Doubtful. Mr. Stiffshirt.

She inexplicably desired to look back and stick her tongue out at him, but really, she was too much of a lady for such childish antics. Really.

As the game progressed all were surprised that although having been at it for almost an hour, everyone was still…intact. No one was more surprised than Grace. She had never made it this far in the game without some misfortune or other occurring. What a rarity. Her parents had owned a pall-mall set themselves, a rare splurge for sure, and they had played with people from the village on weekends or at village fairs.

Despite her success, she noticed that each time it was her turn to take a swing at her ball, the others seemed to hold their breath in anticipation, and throughout that time, the imp in her couldn't help but play on their unease by either physically accentuating her swings, attempting ridiculously odd shots, or orating verbal jests at her own potential for disaster.

Perhaps this was the key to success? She was enjoying herself and therefore she was completely relaxed; she quit worrying about any major incidents occurring in front of the others. So, perhaps she was a bit crass. Certainly for the high-sticklers of society to accept.

Everyone seemed to be more at ease as the afternoon progressed. Even the duke quit trying to hide his amusement, which seemed completely out of character. Normally, he was scowling at her. When he wasn't nearly kissing her, that is. The only person who didn't appear to be enjoying herself was Beatryce, though even her glowering looks could not prevent Grace's fun.

Grace shrugged her shoulders and proceeded to take her next shot. It wasn't a difficult one, and she relaxed as she took her aim. She was just about to take her swing when she heard Beatryce quip, "Ambrose, darling, I'd love to take a walk with you after the game."

Grace choked and ended up hitting her ball a bit too forcefully, sending it crashing off into the shrubbery. Gracious.

There was no doubt Beatryce spoke aloud for Grace's benefit.

Why does she think I even care? Why do I care for that matter?

Grace couldn't deny that her heart was beating in double time just thinking about Beatryce and Stonebridge taking a walk. Alone. And she was edgy and irritable because of it.

Didn't he try to kiss me in the library? Just last night?

Grace growled in frustration to mask the hurt that threatened her composure. It would do no good to revisit what happened — or didn't — in the library. Hadn't she already spent the entire night reliving the experience anyway? Over-analyzing every moment? Wondering what might have happened had she stayed?

Last night, she couldn't seem to stop herself from dreaming of something more with the duke. The hero out of her old dream, the one about the handsome stranger who rescued her for her life, now had a defined face (with green eyes, imagine that), yet she knew it would only ever be that — a dream.

So why did the duke's flirtation with Beatryce bother her? She didn't really know this man. She was attracted to him — absolutely — but this shouldn't matter. Likely, she was just tired of her family's attempts to make her feel less, simply because of the taint of trade surrounding her. And his actions fell right in line with making her feel as if she wasn't good enough, which was ridiculous, of course. Grace clenched her fists and firmed her resolve. She would not let them ruin her day.

With a newfound sense of confidence, she marched off through the hedge in search of her ball. She might be awhile at it, for hers was a natural sort of green, making it doubly hard to spot, so she bade the others to continue on without her rather than wait.

She had been searching for several minutes to no avail, when she thought she heard a rustling nearby. She looked about for a moment, but nothing appeared suspicious. She waited a few seconds more, then shrugged and carried on in her search. It must have been a squirrel.

A few moments later, she was focused on the ground beneath her, not watching where she was going, when her ball landed at her feet with a thump.

"I found it near the hedge; you must have just missed it," he said softly. He sounded odd. Hesitant.

Of course, she knew immediately who it was; his voice was etched too firmly in her mind already.

"Thank you. It's quite an unfortunate shade of green." She spoke without looking up, as if talking to her ball and not him, Stonebridge. She was too surprised and discomfited by his presence to confidently manage his direct gaze.

"It's easy to miss, for sure; I almost did myself." There was an awkward silence before he blurted out, "Do you know why I'm here?"

She was so surprised at his outburst; her gaze jerked up to meet his. She wasn't sure which he meant: here with her in the woods or here at Beckett House. She decided to play it safe and answer assuming the latter. "Of course. You're here to propose marriage to my cousin, Lady Beatryce."

He chuckled before responding, "Yes, I am, and I will; I must." He was quite serious when he spoke again. "I also wanted to apologize for last night. I behaved...badly, and I wanted to reassure you that it won't happen again."

She nodded her acceptance of his apology. At the moment, she didn't trust herself to speak. It was what she needed to hear, but the truth hurt. Which was ludicrous. Hadn't she just had this talk with herself? And yet when he asked her if she knew why he was here, she envisioned an entirely different response, one that involved heated kisses and...

She broke the chain of her thoughts, her face alight with flame. She knew the rules of life, and they said no handsome duke would be in her future no matter how much she wanted it otherwise. She pulled herself together and said, "We should return before we're missed. And, thank you."

Then, she picked up her ball and walked off, leaving the duke behind.

*

She didn't use his title, and she didn't clarify what she was thanking him for, but there wasn't anything else to say, and it was fine. He was glad she didn't use his title; it made him feel more human around her, and he liked that. Just a man. Not a duke.

He watched her walk back to the others, her head held high. He couldn't help but watch the way she moved with poise, despite her acknowledged clumsiness. He tamped down his desire, which always flared when she was around. They both knew the rules of society to which they were bound, but it didn't stop his lust from reminding him he was only human.

Chapter 9

The duke's dressing room...
The next morning...

"Your grace, if it pleases you, I would like to have a quick glance over your jacket in the brighter light, and one last chance to see your coat in perfect order before you brave the wilds of the back garden," said Bryans, with mock solemnity.

Stonebridge ignored his valet's dry humor—he was not in the mood—and stepped into the wash of light from the sun shining through the window, eager to look outside. He preferred the outdoors to being inside, regardless of the weather. Today, it was sunny and brisk. Perfect. He noted the various pathways lined by hedgerows filled with roses while Bryans brushed at his coat. Despite the almost stark formality of the gardens, he anticipated being out there, breathing in the fresh, crisp air. A vision in blue on the garden path beneath his window caught his attention. He faltered and his heart skipped at least two beats. Even from his great height above, he knew her.

"Er, Bryans, if you're finished, I'm off to take a turn about the gardens." He hadn't exercised Abacus this morning, yet a walk suddenly seemed just the thing.

"Certainly, Your Grace. May I ask? Will you be meeting Miss Radclyffe, perchance?" Bryans carried on with a few last swipes of his brush, pretending earnestness despite the knowing grin on his face. The servants knew everything. Or thought they did.

"No."

"As I suspected. I shall speak to the housekeeper at once and see what sort of supplies she has on hand. The old lawn shirt might do in a pinch. I'm glad I thought to bring it. And a bath along with a change of clothes will be necessary."

His valet walked away, mumbling to himself and making what appeared to be a mental list.

Stonebridge watched and listened. He could just make out the words: medical, herbs, bandages. When he could take no more, he asked, "Bryans, what on earth are you on about?"

"It never hurts to be prepared."

"Prepared for what?"

"An encounter with Miss Radclyffe."

"And what does seeing Miss Radclyffe have to do with my old lawn shirt?"

"One never knows. The housekeeper might be low on supplies. As such, it would make for fine bandages in a squeeze. Just in case, mind."

"Bryans, amusing you are not. Don't resign your duties for the stage." And he left with haste, directly for the back gardens.

Clearly, he was a glutton for punishment. He just needed to explore why: why he thought of her night and day. Why he physically reacted to her presence. Why he wanted to throw away his future just to embrace her. Why she affected him so profoundly.

* * * *

"Shhhh…" warned Beatryce. "You don't want Grace to hear us and spoil our plans, do you?"

Beatryce and Middlebury squatted indelicately behind a large rose bush as they watched Grace make her way along a garden path. Beatryce tried desperately to keep her morning gown away from the thorny branches while remaining out of sight.

She hated getting up this early, really, but she was desperate. Yesterday, it had become clear additional tactics were necessary to turn Stonebridge's wandering gaze away from her cousin. Fortunately, Beatryce was clever, daring, and willing to do anything to get what she wanted. She had no choice.

"Just what am I doing out here in the garden at such an ungodly hour of the morning? I didn't get a lot of sleep last night, you know," replied Middlebury, with a mischievous grin.

"Shhhh," warned Beatryce again. She raised her head above the shrubs to mark Grace's progress then ducked down again. As soon as Grace made it to the first bend headed into the copse of trees, she and Middlebury would move on and follow at a discreet distance.

Beatryce's knees creaked as she adjusted her position. She was uncomfortable and cold. Her back, thighs and neck ached from squatting down for so long. The dew dampened her gloves as she used the ground for balance.

Grace, thankfully, was wearing her blue cloak this morning. It wasn't a surprise, for it was the only cloak she owned. Beatryce had one exactly like it, but with a hood, which played perfectly into her plans.

Several guests were taking a tour about the gardens, and Stonebridge always did. Beatryce knew he was an outdoor lover, so it was just a matter of luck. And she was prepared for the opportune moment to present itself.

"How do you know Stonebridge will follow?"

"You must be joking? Have you seen how he looks at her whenever she's around? He wants her, and I know how easily men are led by their...impulses...if not guided properly by their women. If I thought it would do any good, even I'd suggest he bed her and get her out of his system, but

Stonebridge is too moral. He's just as likely to think he has to marry her, and that just won't do. So, no, I have no doubt he will follow if the opportunity presents. We just need to set the stage to our advantage. Believe me; if he thinks she's 'free' with her favors to just anyone — no offense, dear — he'll lose interest."

"None taken, darling. No need to say more; this, I can handle, but it's a good thing he doesn't know…"

Oomph.

Middlebury winced when she elbowed him in the gut.

"For your own health, and since I am still in need of your help, I am going to forget what you intended to say."

"Say what? Besides, you would miss me terribly if I weren't around to keep things interesting," replied Richard with a devilish grin.

At Beatryce's obvious scowl, he quickly continued, "Oh, don't go getting yourself worked up in a snit. Don't forget, we've got a play to enact, right? So, lead on, fair maiden, for our quarry has just rounded the corner. I shall follow your direction, mistress."

He said the last under his breath in a suggestive manner, and Beatryce forced herself to smile back at him over her shoulder before she crawled out onto the path.

Mistress, indeed.

* * * *

What the hell am I doing following this chit?

Stonebridge wasn't really paying a lot of attention to the beauty surrounding him; he was too caught up in his thoughts. His eyes caught a shimmer of blue up ahead in the distance. What he saw remarkably resembled the blue cloak he'd seen Grace wearing as she walked beneath his window.

He peered ahead and unconsciously increased his stride when he made out the cut and color of her cloak through the trees and determined she was not alone. As the lovers intimately embraced, fire raced through his veins, and his temper boiled.

To think she played the innocent and I fell for it. God, I am such a fool.

A moment passed before he realized he had picked up his pace to the point that he was running. Running? He slowed his speed to a normal, albeit brisk, walk.

God, I have surely lost my mind.

He glanced down and realized he was clenching his hands. In fact, he clenched them so tightly into fists, he was drawing blood. He forcibly relaxed and looked up in time to see Middlebury (Grace's lover!) approaching on the path ahead. *Was he adjusting his clothes and tucking in his damn shirt?*

He reigned in his instinct to attack—barely. Why should he bother? What man wouldn't take what was offered so freely from such a comely wench? No, he knew where to direct his anger, and she was clearly staying on up ahead.

As he passed Middlebury, he scarcely managed a curt "Middlebury" in passing. That would have to do—else he would throttle the man.

* * * *

Grace sighed as she looked out over the lake behind Beckett House. Such beauty was a sight to behold. It was her favorite place to be. This time, she was sitting on a bench built into the dock since, realistically, there were too many guests about for her to risk dipping her toes in the water as was her wont. Today, the air was crisp and tinged with the fresh scent of water. How refreshing for the soul, and how lucky she was to be able to enjoy such natural beauty.

"Well, well, well. If it isn't little Miss Innocence? What? Your lover had to leave you already? If I had known your favors were so freely given, our library encounter could have ended quite differently, to our mutual benefit," scorned a voice from behind.

Goosebumps traveled up and down her arms at the ice in his voice. How could a man that large approach so silently? The breeze had been blowing gently, enough to mask the footsteps of the approaching storm that was the Duke of Stonebridge. She had been so content in the tranquility of her surroundings, she had unconsciously attributed his footsteps to the water lapping below, gently rocking the floating dock on which she sat. Thus, she had been blissfully unaware of the impending fury until he spoke.

She continued to stare out over the water a moment longer. She would not react rashly to his provoking words, even though her first instinct was to retort with offended fury. She had thought they were past all this after his apology yesterday. Apparently not. He was determined to distrust her. She braced herself for a confrontation as she stood and turned to face the man who seemed determined to haunt her every thought.

And she decided at that moment to fight fire with overt friendliness. "And a good morning to you, Your Grace. It seems we're back to where we started, again. And what, pray tell, did I do this time? Meeting a lover, was it?" Well, perhaps friendliness with a wee bit of sarcasm thrown in for good measure. She always did wear sarcasm well.

"As if you didn't know? This time I *saw you!*" he bellowed. *My, such feeling.*

"You must be mistaken," she responded with poise. "I haven't seen a soul since I left the house this morning until you…to my everlasting regret."

She said the last just above a whisper. She was proud her voice remained steady when she was dying a little on the inside. She was not guilty of whatever he was accusing her of, but it didn't stop his anger from making her feel small.

"And a liar to boot," he continued to roar. "How can you face your looking glass in the morning when your lips drip with lies and deceit? You flirt with every man here, including me."

Now her anger flared to life. "You have got to be joking? Flirting? With you? Ha! And I told you; I have been alone. If you saw two people embracing, it wasn't me."

Scratch that, she was outright furious. How dare he accuse her of such heinous behavior?

"Like hell it wasn't. I saw you and Middlebury kissing. Christ, he was still tucking in his shirt as he walked away from your little rendezvous. You may have had your hood up, but that cloak, with its patterning and blue color, is unmistakable. You're still wearing it, for God's sake."

She laughed wildly. It was just too unbelievable, or perhaps not. Good ole Beatryce. Grace had no doubt that the mistake was deliberate. And he was going to marry that woman? Ooooh, they deserved each other. Grace wished she could witness the moment when he realized just what he had married.

She stepped toe to toe with the duke as she smugly revealed what she could so easily prove, "My. Cloak. Doesn't. Have. A. Hood. You. Miserable..."

Grace punctuated each word with a punch to his chest, and he just stood there, taking it all, as she did. She was crying now, for what she didn't know, but she threw her last punch with all the strength she could muster. Unfortunately, it was with too much force, and he, as large and muscular as he was, was too big to be moved. Which meant she moved, backwards, and head over heels into the water.

*

"Grace! Grace! Oh, God, Grace!" yelled the duke. Terror made his heart hammer inside his chest. It had all happened in slow motion: her sudden and obvious anger. The fire he witnessed in her eyes. His realization that he was mistaken. His surprise that she would actually hit him. Her fall...And through it all, he was stunned and slow to react, but only for a tick.

He snapped to with the realization that even if she could swim, her skirts and women's trappings would weigh her down. She would drown. He didn't hesitate then...*Oh, God, Grace.* He dove in.

The water was icy as it slid over his back, but bracing cold was what he needed. His adrenaline was in high gear as he searched for her in the darkness. If felt like an eternity had passed before he spotted her sinking beneath him. Fortunately, her coat was lightly colored, otherwise...He shut off that train of thought before anxiety got the best of him and dove down, reaching out toward the blue fading away below him.

His heart raced and his lungs were near to bursting as he broke the surface. He gasped beloved air into his starved lungs then looked down at the woman he grasped tightly in his arms. She was too still and he needed to make the shore, quickly. He hadn't gone far when he realized he had to remove her cloak. It was too heavy and slowed him down. He ripped it off, releasing it to fall to the depths of the lake.

He scrambled up the bank. She wasn't breathing. God, she wasn't breathing! He lifted her up, popped the upper buttons on her dress, and slit the laces to her corset with the knife he kept hidden in his boot.

"Grace, you will live, damn it! Come back to me!" he roared between breaths.

He alternately blew in her mouth and pressed on her chest to try to get the air moving and her heart pumping. His hands were shaking; he was terrified.

Water dripped from his hair and into his eyes, but he didn't care. He was too panicked to bother brushing it out of his face. He saw nothing but a dull world without her in it, even if he couldn't be an intimate part of her world. She was funny, in her own way, and nice. Too nice. Her antics made him laugh—for the first time in many years he felt light hearted despite the weight of responsibility resting on his shoulders.

Why didn't he think about that *before* he confronted her with his accusations? Because he didn't think. He saw the 'evidence' and reacted without forethought. He was enraged by the thought of another man, any other man, touching her goodness. But especially a scoundrel like Middlebury. He should have known something wasn't right.

She reared up suddenly and began to vomit water. He held her as she bent forward and continued coughing and gasping for air.

His relief was palpable. She'd almost died. It was his fault. All because he let emotions rule his actions. After Eton, he had sworn to never do so again. Would he ever learn his lesson?

After a few moments, her coughing subsided. As it did, she relaxed in his arms. He sat on the ground with her legs across his and held her sideways to his chest. He could not resist the impulse to brush back a few wet strands of hair off her face.

At his touch, she looked up, slowly, and as she squinted up at him, she weakly punched his chest with her fist and said, "Bastard…"

He laughed. He couldn't help it. After all that, the minx was determined to finish her tirade. He was simply relieved she was going to be all right. His soul felt light and he could finally breathe again.

After a few moments, they stood, a bit unsteadily, to be sure. He chuckled like a candidate for Bedlam as he worked off his coat. Grace grabbed him by the lapels of his ruined jacket before he had made any reasonable progress and said, "Are you laughing at me? I almost died, you big oaf. Oh, God, I almost died! And you saved me!" she shouted with obvious glee.

And then she was kissing him.

What started out as frantic pecks all over his face took a serious turn as she stopped and pulled back to look at him. He stood frozen; so still.

She searched his eyes. He didn't know what she sought. He saw her pulse beating furiously in her neck. And he could imagine why. Nearly drowning. Being alive. Being near him. Well, possibly the last. She was soaked and a mess and still clinging to his jacket. They both should have been shivering, but instead heat flared, arching between them as she dove into his eyes. Embedded herself into his soul.

He stared at her lips. And he wanted. Yearned. Ached. For her. Only her. And before he could stop himself, he reached out, grabbed her, and kissed her.

He angled his head left, then right as he sought the perfect angle. He tugged on her chin and whispered, "Open up for me, sweetheart."

She did, and he plunged inside with his tongue. His entire body burned. He was flooded with sensory input: her taste…of mint from the kitchen garden. Her smell…of lavender fresh linens hanging in the breeze to dry. Her sound…soft moans coming from deep within her chest. Then, there was nothing but heat burning throughout his body. The dukedom, the lake, Beatryce…the world…ceased to exist. Everyone and everything fled from his memories but this woman, Grace, whom he had only met a few days ago.

And he was quickly losing all control. Never had a kiss been filled with such all-consuming fire. Before, kissing other women, even Beatryce, had just been, well, wet.

This kiss, on the other hand, was explosive, hot, emotional. *Oh, God, why her? Why now?*

Abruptly, he pulled back and struggled to bank his desire. No matter what his wishes, this could not be. He knew when he became the 10th Duke of Stonebridge he would have to put the estate above his personal desires, but he never thought he'd have such difficulty in doing so. Never had there been such temptation, temptation that made him want to risk everything to slake his own personal cravings.

He was a cad; he knew that now. He was wrong about her, again, and he acted the jealous fool. He knew without the evidence of that blasted cloak that she had been telling the truth. But none of it mattered. His destiny was set.

He shivered with cold. They needed to get back to the house before they became sick from their sodden clothes and before they were discovered in such *dishabille*.

Why did that suddenly seem like a good thing?

He glanced at Grace. Her eyes were just now opening. He knew he shouldn't look, or he'd be lost again, so he looked away, everywhere but at her as he asked, "Are you all right?"

"Hmmm?"

He chuckled softly; he couldn't help it. She was still dazed from their kiss. It was probably her first, and he felt like a king.

"I asked, are you all right?"

"Oh, if you count almost dying, then flying to the moon, all right, then, yes. Yes, I am."

He still didn't look at her, but he could picture her sheepish grin in his mind's eye.

"Excellent. We must make haste, Miss Radclyffe, before we catch a chill."

"Shouldn't you call me Grace? I mean, it seems that formality at this point is a bit silly."

"No," he interrupted, cutting off whatever else she might have said.

How quickly her innocent statement made him realize, with absolute clarity, the full impact of his error. He knew he shouldn't have allowed himself to lose control, but in the moment, he had been helpless. The flood of feelings inside from the anger at seeing what he thought was her kiss with another man and the fright at her near drowning, to the joy of knowing she was going to be all right was too much for him to bear. He was only a man after all. Human. Flawed.

Now that he was regaining control of his sanity, his resolve to do the right thing was back in place. He was amazed at the damage their kiss had done even though there were no witnesses to the mistake. He couldn't change from the path he was on no matter his personal desires. Fate was a cruel bitch.

And he was going to have to be a cold bastard. He had to completely dash her hopes before they took root. He needed to make her realize that any future between them was impossible, but the only way—the easiest way, perhaps—was to be quick and brutal. He would douse any dreams that may have just begun with a cold, hard dose of reality. It was the only way. Any other way and he might give away signs of his own inner turmoil, like the voice deep inside his head that whispered, "She's the one."

No. He couldn't take the risk. She had to know, without question, that he would not deviate from the course he meant to follow.

"I apologize, Miss Radclyffe, for the affectionate display. I was…overcome, but you must know, it changes nothing. I am going to marry Lady Beatryce, and this mistake won't happen again."

He stopped just short of adding "I mean it this time" lest she question his resolve.

God, why did it feel like he just ripped out his own heart? He couldn't help but look at her as he said the last, and to see the hurt in her eyes, it almost had him kissing her again and begging for forgiveness, to plead with her until she believed him when he said he didn't mean it. It was too much. By God, it even hurt to breathe.

He was a weak fool, taking the coward's way out by hurting her in this way, but he couldn't take the chance of allowing her false hope; it was best for everyone if she hated him.

He expected her anger then. He needed it to steel his resolve, but instead, in so soft a voice he almost didn't hear her, she said, "I understand, Your Grace. You can put me down now. I can manage on my own from here."

Oh God, her soft words unhinged him more than anger ever could. He wanted to shake her and tell her not to give up on him. He wanted her to cling to him and beg him to carry her away. He was going mad. He was so caught up in his inner hell he hadn't even realized he was still holding her. He laughed like a maniac in his mind. His behavior was a complete contradiction to the words spewing forth from his mouth.

Despite his warring emotions, he set her down with care. He stroked her cheek with the backs of his fingertips—he couldn't resist—and said, "I'm sorry. Really, I…" He cut off the last thought. He had said too much. Done too much.

"Miss Radclyffe" was all he could manage now, and with a quick bow, he turned on his heel and stormed off to the house. Yes, it was rude. Yes, he did it again. He had no choice. He was at the end of his self-control. Another word or another look and he would have thrown it all away and begged her for another kiss, and that was something he could not do.

He didn't look back as he walked away. Not once, even though the urge to do so was almost overwhelming. He could feel her eyes drilling into his back. He knew if he showed any hesitation, a faltered step, a shrug of his shoulders, or worse, stopped and looked back at her, he would be lost. He'd turn around and run back to her. Beg her. Worship her.

He felt like he was turning his back on his future rather than walking toward it. He gritted his teeth, clinched his fists tighter, and carried on without pause. He had ahold of self-discipline again and he buried himself in it. Marrying Lady Beatryce was what he was supposed to do. Had to do. It was the only way to move toward the future he'd so meticulously planned.

He pushed any remaining doubts from his mind. He had never questioned his decisions over the last ten years, and he would not start now.

Chapter 10

Several moments passed before Grace realized she had not moved from the spot where the duke had left her behind. She was still staring at the last place she had seen him before he entered the copse of woods leading back to the house. She was too astonished to move. The change in his demeanor was so complete and swift it was almost droll, but of course, it wasn't really. She was devastated, more devastated than she had ever been, which was shocking and unsettling. She had lost her parents, both of them. Surely that was more distressing? She lived with relatives who would rather chew off their own lips than offer her a smile. Shouldn't that be more painful?

And she didn't know this man—clearly. Not only had she just met him, but his mood swings were foreign to her. Up until the past year, her life and the people in it were reliable and steady. She was happy and privileged to live a normal life. An every-day-nothing-to-stir-the-pot ordinary kind of life. And she was always calm and steady because of it. Until today. First, there was her anger at his high-handedness over…well, she wasn't really sure why he thought he had the right to be so angry before, really. Then, there was her fright over her unplanned swim…

Why isn't that near-death experience playing the starring role in my thoughts?

Then, there was the happiness and peace found in his kiss—followed swiftly by blazing passion. Now, though, she felt lost. Hollow. Rejected.

She jerked as the reality of it all hit her. The muscles in her legs twitched from physical exertion. Goosebumps traversed her arms and neck. She glanced about to see if anyone else was around to witness her bleak moment. But only for a moment. Who would care? A soft but cool breeze blew a lock of drying hair into her eyes, and she absentmindedly brushed it aside. She started walking to the house. She knew she needed to get inside and change before she caught a chill—not to mention that her dress and corset were gaping from being cut. Both barely covered her chest but for the sleeves of her frock holding them up. She could only just manage to step one foot in front of the other. Her legs were weak and unsteady. Yet she was calm and that scared her more than any of her riotous feelings earlier.

She made it to her room without encountering anyone else along the way. A warm bath awaited, and she, again, marveled at Bessie's ability to anticipate her needs.

It wasn't long before Bessie was there with her, humming softly while undoing the remaining buttons of her morning gown. By unspoken agreement, they voiced no words. Grace was relieved. She allowed Bessie to pamper her and bathe her, simply going through the motions without conscious thought.

When she was dressed, Bessie broke the silence to ask of her plans. She shrugged and said, "I guess I'll head down to the first floor drawing room to see what activities are planned for the afternoon. Thanks, Bessie, for your help, as always."

"Och, I don't know why you always offer your thanks; it is my job, you know. And of course, I love being there for you. You just let me know if there's anything you need gettin' off your mind, and I'll be here with ready ears."

* * * *

Grace trudged down the long, curved main staircase. Her mind was blank, and her emotions nonexistent. Despite not thinking about anything, it took several moments to register the loud voices emanating from the drawing room below. The voices were tinged with heightened emotion, the air marked with expectancy. What could have put everyone in such a state? She had been in her room for the last hour, so there was no chance the uproar was caused by one of her unfortunate accidents, unless…

A door slammed above, followed be several more, followed by more than one pair of muffled footsteps. Something heavy was being dragged across the floor. Grace looked up as if she could see through the ceiling. Confused.

Horses whinnied and nickered, drawing her attention to a nearby window. She walked over and looked down to the courtyard below. Several carriages were lined up on the cobbles of the front drive. Footmen, valets, and maids scrambled in concentrated haste. Like well-organized bees.

Realizing that the best way to get any answers was to proceed to the boisterous drawing room below, she squared her shoulders and picked up her pace. As she neared the downstairs landing, she heard snippets of conversation; most of it nonsensical:

"Why now? What could be that important?" said one voice.

"I heard she's in a right tiff over it all," said another.

"How could he?" offered a third.

"I think something set him off—perhaps there won't be a wedding after all?"

That last statement caused her to stumble and almost miss the last few steps. Somehow she kept her balance as her curiosity reached heretofore unknown heights.

All conversation seemed to stop the moment she entered the tightly packed room. Most of the guests were there and dressed in their traveling clothes. Most stopped for several moments and stared rudely at her before looking away.

What have I done? No one could possibly know what happened this morning, could they?

"Grace," her aunt called to her over the din as everyone else, thankfully, resumed their conversations. She cringed at the shrillness of her aunt's voice, but dutifully sought her out among the crowd. It was obvious Aunt Mary was dismayed about something, but trying to pretend all was well in front of the other guests. At last, she was going to find out, one way or the other, for better or for worse, what had everyone in such a state.

"Grace, where have you been?" Aunt Mary spoke quickly and quietly now. Grace had to stare at her aunt's rapidly moving lips in order to hear her over the crowd.

"Actually, never mind that. Stonebridge was called away to his estate, Stonebridge Park, rather unexpectedly. You know how important he is, and sometimes these things happen, of course they do. The rest of the house party has been cancelled. The duke, er Stonebridge, wishes to see us in London in two weeks' time, so we're all packing, and that includes you. I know you've never been, and you don't have the wardrobe for it, but we'll simply have to make do. You only need to go to those events that are absolutely necessary, so we'll manage. I just wished he had got on with the betrothing beforehand, but no matter—he will. Of course he will. You had best be off to make sure your inept maid gets everything packed properly and quickly. Now, don't just stand there and dawdle. I want to be settled in at the first stop on the road to London before the vultures arrive. Hurry. Quickly now."

* * * *

Grace made her way out of the drawing room in a daze. It seemed coincidental that the duke was called away, but what did she know about the affairs of a duke? She couldn't help but fantasize that perhaps he was having second thoughts;

that perhaps he was as moved as she by their encounter, despite what he had said.

Her musings were interrupted when a strong hand grabbed her by the arm and pulled her into an alcove created by the curve of the stairs. She turned to face her detainer with her hands on her hips and fire in her eyes.

"You know, I'm not the most graceful woman at the best of times; therefore, you must certainly know that to…to…manhandle me like that is to invite disaster, Lord Middlebury. What is it?" She stamped her foot in exasperation. Good. At least some emotion had returned. Even if it was bad.

"Miss Radclyffe, I honestly didn't mean to startle you so completely. In the madness generated by Stonebridge's sudden removal, I felt compelled to see you before everyone departed and the opportunity was lost."

She was too stunned to speak, but didn't dare show it. She continued to stand there, tapping her foot, arms crossed in front of her. She knew if she bided her time he would eventually say what he wanted—it worked with children anyway. She didn't have to wait long.

"Miss Radclyffe." Middlebury leaned forward and inhaled her scent. She was reminded of a dog sniffing another. It was decidedly not sensual, as she supposed he meant it to be.

He continued quietly in her ear, "Aaah, Miss Radclyffe, you smell like summer and heather. If only we had had more time to get to know one another—" He pulled back and stared at her lips. "—better. Must I wait until the next society event to see you again, my pet? You must know that your beauty renders me near speechless, and I find myself compelled to further our acquaintance."

"Lord Middlebury." She paused; she wasn't sure what to say, really. For a moment she wasn't sure whether or not she should be flattered or appalled. No one had ever spoken to her so suggestively before. She decided to harness her ire.

"First of all, I am not your pet. Secondly, I do not find you even remotely appealing, especially after your aggressive manhandling of my person when we barely know one another…"

"So you wouldn't mind the manhandling if we knew each other better?" he interrupted. He grinned as her eyes widened in surprise. "If you'll recall, I have already expressed my desire to address your second point. It is my fondest wish to get to know you, much, much better. Perhaps we could start with an innocent little kiss?"

She was speechless. He was shockingly bold; it must be a combination of his good looks and overconfidence. His status as rake of the first order was probably well deserved. Yes, he was a complete rogue and probably not used to woman rejecting him, ever.

Well, he was in for a surprise because she was not so shallow as to be swayed by a pretty face and suggestive words, a duke's notwithstanding. But she knew she was in over her head with this one, and that it was futile to try to reason with him. Therefore, rather than try to match wits, she turned on her heel and stormed off just as he moved to make good on his threat. His kiss met nothing but air.

*

Middlebury chuckled to himself and smiled. He admired her shapely derrière as she marched away. He found himself amused, which he rarely did when dealing with the innocent. Hell, he rarely found amusement in anything these days, though most wouldn't know it—he was good at hiding his true thoughts and feelings.

His plan had worked at any rate. Several other guests had passed by the alcove during his conversation with Grace and none had tried to hide their curious looks as they noticed their little tête-à-tête going on in the recess. No doubt the rumors would be making their way to London faster than he could get there himself.

With her back to the foyer, Grace couldn't have seen the raised eyebrows and questioning looks coming from the other guests, and they couldn't see her unamused expression of distrust in return. All they could see were the smoldering looks he gave the little hellion and the intimate way he stood too close to her. It would be enough to satisfy the gossipmongers and Beatryce would be thrilled. He tamped down the inconvenient prodding of his conscience.

*

Grace turned blindly toward the stairs and was nearly to the first step when Bertram, the head footman, called out to her.

"Miss Radclyffe, Lord Swindon would like to see you in his study, directly."

"Yes, of course," she responded with alacrity. She wondered what her uncle could possibly want. He rarely spoke directly to her, and she would be lying if she said she wasn't concerned about what he had to say.

At once, she turned about and followed the footman into her uncle's dim study.

"You wanted to see me, my lord?"

Her uncle, the earl, was already standing behind his desk in anticipation of her arrival.

"Yes, Grace. Have a seat," he responded with a smile. It was a smile that sent shivers down her spine, for it was the kind that did not reach the eyes. She had seen it before and the results were usually unpleasant.

As she sat, he came around to the front of his desk and sat on the edge closest to her chair. The desk creaked in protest; he was no lightweight. She was seated near enough such that he crowded her with this move, and she had to crane her neck to face him. His was a move meant to intimidate.

"As I'm sure you are aware, the remainder of the house party has been cancelled, and all of the guests are returning to London, post haste. In fact, your aunt may have mentioned that you should prepare to depart directly."

"Yes, my lord,"

"However, what your aunt did not know was that I have spoken to Stonebridge at length regarding your behavior over the course of this week. He is concerned, as am I, as to how you would behave in polite company in Town, so he suggested, and I have agreed, that it would be in everyone's best interest if you remained behind.

"Further, I am appalled that after everything we have done for you, you would so obviously attempt to steal your cousin's beau for yourself and sabotage her engagement with your suggestive smiles and come-hither attitude."

"But…"

"DO NOT INTERRUPT!" His already florid face showed bright red with anger now.

She tried not to flinch as spittle rained from his mouth while he yelled his displeasure. "Need I remind you how badly it would go for *you*, if you were to destroy Beatryce's chances with the duke?"

"No, but…"

"Do you realize how aghast I was to have him approach me with concerns about your behavior toward his person? How embarrassed I was to realize that you made our esteemed guest uncomfortable in our home thus necessitating his early departure? Not to mention the damage control Mary and I must implement to squash the gossip as a direct result of your wanton behavior?"

"Yes, but…"

"Quite frankly, I am uninterested in your excuses or your apologies. You will remain behind. I have and will again apologize to the duke on your behalf. In addition, should anyone ask, you are going to visit a sick friend in the North, hence your absence in Town. You shall, however, remain here.

The staff are aware that you are not to receive callers; in fact, they have been told to tell any visitors, not that I suspect you will have any, that you are away should anyone come to call.

"That is all I expect to have to say on this subject. You are quite dismissed, and in the interest of peace, I do not care to see your person again ere I leave."

* * * *

Grace raced up the stairs completely unmindful of the other guests. She watched her steps to avoid any missteps, as was her habit, and had just reached the landing when she decided she would chance a look over her shoulder to see if Lord Middlebury or Uncle George were following. She ran into a solid wall at the top of the stairs.

Strong arms reached out to stop her from tumbling back down the way she had come.

Am I destined to be manhandled all day long?

With her hands up and pressed against the warm barrier in front of her, she looked up to see Dansbury grinning down at her. She was relieved it was him and not someone undesirable like His Grace. The wretched liar. Dansbury, by contrast, was the quintessential gentleman. He was also nice, funny, and witty. Why couldn't he make her feel the way the duke did?

"Lord Dansbury. Thank you. I was not paying attention and…" She stopped talking when she heard his low chuckle.

He had a lovely smile. There seemed to be an overabundance of handsome men about the place this week. If she had been looking for a husband, she might have had several candidates from which to choose. This one was friendly, and therefore, she felt completely safe in his presence. And since she was decidedly not looking for a duke — er, husband — she was pleased to see him.

"Miss Radclyffe, I am quite certain I asked you to call me Dansbury yesterday, and I believe you agreed." He paused briefly, "And I'm glad we ran into each other…"

She rolled her eyes at his attempt at humor.

"I am devastated we aren't going to be able to have our planned ride in the morning. I was looking forward to it."

She smiled at his pretended devastation; his grin, however, showed he was being playful.

"Yes, it is unfortunate, but I guess these things happen. His Grace certainly couldn't have expected he would have to depart his engagement party early for an emergency summons to his home."

Dansbury raised one brow. "Of course."

He had a rueful grin on his face then, and she wondered what he was thinking. Before she could foolishly inquire, they arrived at her door in time to meet Bessie on her way out.

"Grace, I've heard the news and was wondering if you would be back soon. We've much to pack, but don't you worry, I have everything in hand, and am just off to retrieve a few things below stairs," reported Bessie upon her surprise at seeing them as she was leaving.

*

Dansbury smiled at Bessie. Clearly, she was a friendly sort and he was suddenly glad Grace had Bessie in her life. He had noticed the cruel way in which Lady Swindon and Lady Beatryce treated Grace. Their rude comments were so perfectly subtle that most others never recognized the insults behind them. Ambrose certainly hadn't noticed, which perplexed him. Ambrose was clever. How could he not see the true nature of the woman he planned to marry? Perhaps he simply didn't 'see' Beatryce at all? Or didn't want to?

Dansbury genuinely liked Grace. She was beautiful, witty, and nice. His thoughts left him uneasy. Ambrose was his best friend and seemed to have some sort of…well, something…for Grace. She seemed to get under his skin at any rate. If so, he would never…Well, only time would tell.

"Grace, I must be off to pack my things. Thank you for walking me nearly to my room. Perhaps I may call on you in London?"

She laughed. Then bit her lip in consternation. It was an unconsciously sensual act. Dansbury kept a tight a rein on his thoughts, refusing to be distracted by the sight. And he was attuned to her posture, her tone of voice. His senses sharpened. She was preparing to lie.

"I'm afraid that's impossible, my lord, for you see, I've received a letter from a close friend who is sick...in the country...and rather than go to London I'm off to...Yorkshire instead...Indefinitely, I'm afraid."

Right.

He grabbed her hand and pulled her completely into her room. Once inside, he shut the door with a decisive click.

He looked at Grace consideringly for a moment before he smiled, bussed her cheek, and said, "Grace, my darling, don't ever change, but, really, you make a terrible liar. Now, out with it, and the truth this time, if you please."

Chapter 11

Near Stonebridge, West Sussex…
Two Days Later…

Stonebridge raced his horse, Abacus, the remaining ten miles to Stonebridge Park, seat of the Dukes of Stonebridge for the last four hundred years. The brisk wind made his eyes water as he sped across the acres of open field surrounding his home. The run had him breathing hard; the cool air burned his lungs as he inhaled, but it was a pleasant blaze — as if he were clearing out built-up congestion from being cramped in an enclosed carriage for too many hours. The exercise was invigorating, and he felt clearheaded for the first time in a week.

At the top of a small rise, he reined in his mount to catch his breath and take in the view of the house and immediate gardens spread out before him in the shallow valley below. The glass from the upper stories of the eastward facing façade sparkled in the early morning sun, though he was too far away to make out the leaded lines in the glass of some of the lower floors. The stone near the roof began to glow orange as the dawning light slowly crept down its side. The slate roof was a motley of color and still glistened from the early morning dew fall. Having spent the best years of his youth here, it truly was a heart-warming sight to behold. This view of the house and grounds, from the rear as he approached from across his land, was quite different from the view of a guest or rider approaching via the main drive. There, the tree canopy was thick and the inner courtyard before the house appeared suddenly, cozy and inviting, yet hiding the true depth and scale of the house. He had always loved that aspect of Stonebridge Park—it made visitors feel welcome because they weren't overwhelmed by the size of the estate all at once. Not that he had many opportunities to entertain as he kept his life here separate from London society. No, the guests he invited here were more along the line of friends, local villagers, and tenants to his estate. In his view, it was vastly more important for them to feel welcomed than any high-strung dandy or marriage-minded mama from Town—most of who would prefer the house to stand out in all its glory so as to impress the unimpressible.

As he continued to take in the view, he forced his breathing to slow by taking deep breaths through his nose—the cold air bit at his insides but felt crisp, not unlike the sensation one gets after smelling eucalyptus.

"Well, Abacus…It's good to be home, eh, old man?"

His horse whinnied and bobbed his head as if concurring with the sentiment. *If only people could be so enthusiastically honest.* He patted his mount's neck. "We'd best not dally, my friend. We have a lot to accomplish and a short amount of time."

After one final survey of the view before him, he picked his way home. He smiled serenely as a sense of peace and calm came over him; then he smiled more deliberately as he realized how little, comparatively, he'd thought about *her* since he'd left Beckett House. Obviously, he had made the right decision by leaving the house party early. Here he could think clearly upon his course of action without unwanted distraction and temptation influencing his thoughts. Oh, sure, Swindon was in a decided huff over his precipitous departure, but he had no doubt he'd be able to smooth things over with the man upon his return to Town.

He guided Abacus directly to the circular front drive. Normally, he would have taken the horse directly to the stables and rubbed him down himself, but time was of the essence, and his staff was fully capable of seeing to the horse's needs. So, after a quick nose rub of apology to his steed, he handed off the reins to a waiting footman and bounded up the stairs to the open door and his butler awaiting from within.

"Your Grace, may I offer felicitations on your recent engagement?" prompted his butler, Boneswaithe.

"Actually, Boneswaithe, you may not, my good man. For in truth, I am not yet betrothed as anticipated, but I thank you for being aware of and remembering the reason for my recent visit to Beckett House."

"I'm sorry to hear that, Your Grace."

"Oh, it's nothing to worry over, Boneswaithe, for it will happen soon enough to be sure. It was only that I was called away unexpectedly before I could accomplish the deed, is all, but again, I thank you for your concern."

"Of course, Your Grace. Welcome home, then. I have taken the liberty of having a bath prepared. Everything should be ready anon."

He laughed. "My good man, you amaze me with your wealth of knowledge and your understanding of my needs before even I am aware of them myself. I am only surprised you didn't know of my engagement status before even I became aware that it wouldn't happen this week as planned…"

And if the butler was aware his master behaved cheerfully out of character, he did not acknowledge it.

* * * *

"Remind me…oomph…again why I…oomph…agreed to accompany you on this ill…oomph…advised journey?" queried Grace as she, Dansbury's Aunt Harriett and Dansbury himself were violently jostled about as their carriage rolled over a particularly rough patch of road in West Sussex.

Dansbury laughed — between similar grunts of discomfort — at Grace and her feigned indignation over their possibly ill-advised trip to Stonebridge Park. Aunt Harriett, who was tucked into a corner sleeping soundly, continued to snore, blissfully unaware of the appalling state of the back country road.

He decided Grace's question was rhetorical, and since he was still unsure as to the advisability of the trip himself, kept silent. Besides, he was preoccupied thinking about the chaos he was stirring up.

First, there was the murderous harangue sure to be heard from Ambrose when he discovered his unexpected guests — particularly Grace. Then, there was Grace's ire when she found out he had deliberately misled her as to their intended destination. She thought they were travelling to Aunt Harriett's house in Bath, not Stonebridge Park.

Auntie wasn't aware of their true destination either, but she could be counted on to find the whole thing a great lark and watch eagerly for events to unfold. Still, he was glad that Stonebridge Park was near enough to Bath so as not to alert her to his scheme in advance of their arrival, though he strongly suspected his aunt was not fooled anyway. She was quite clever that way. In fact, he was positive he hadn't deceived her in the least, but for once, she was going along with him and not attempting to stir up trouble the likes of which she was quite capable — and often inclined. In any event, Harriett would be quite content to stay a few unforeseen days at the Park as long as she had her coffee — and perhaps a drop or two of whisky. For her pains, mind.

Then there were the possible repercussions from Grace's uncle, Swindon, for Dansbury had taken it upon himself to send a note to the earl informing him that Grace would be accompanying Aunt Harriett to London for the season, which would be the case if all went according to plan…eventually. It was sure to tweak the earl's nose at any rate. He had yet to broach that subject with Grace at all. He hadn't even hinted about it. But did she really have a choice? She was riding in his carriage, which was definitely headed to London after their visit to the Park.

Again, Harriett wasn't a concern, for she was sure to be overjoyed at the prospect of sponsoring Grace in London for the season. In fact, though she didn't yet know it, she'd conveyed as much to the earl in her own note, reinforcing Dansbury's decision to bring Grace to London. Had he mentioned he was a good forger?

As such, everything would be cleared up and perfectly respectable. Eventually.

Back at Beckett House, after hearing a full report of her uncle's tirade and knowing the suggestive (yet questionable) evidence against his character—not to mention knowing Ambrose well enough to know he would never have said the things her uncle implied—Cliff had decided it might be detrimental to Grace's well-being should she remain behind at Beckett House. He had no real evidence to which he could point as justification for his actions, only his gut—which had never led him astray...when it mattered. Thus, his plan to bring Grace and Aunt Harriett with him to Stonebridge Park had been hastily conceived.

He had been cautious with his words so that he purposely led Grace to draw her own conclusions about their intended destination without outright lying to her. Further, he had been vague in response to her numerous questions and had relied primarily on her trust in him to persuade her to make the journey. It hadn't been easy. She wasn't inclined to trust him so effortlessly, clever girl—they hadn't known each other but a few days after all—but in the end, he had been more persuasive than she was wary (one of the many reasons he excelled at his line of work). Besides, her maid, Bessie, liked him and Grace had been willing to forgo her own reservations on account of her faith in her maid's ability to accurately judge a person's measure. Thank God. And Aunt Harriett was a perfectly suitable chaperone making the entire trip respectable.

Obviously, he had given neither Grace nor his aunt the real reasons behind his hasty decision—nor had he imparted any information regarding his mission and the role he and Ambrose played for the Home Office.

That was three days ago. Now he was late for his meeting with the team at the Park, but they were almost there. It was a matter of minutes.

Time to pay the piper, as they say...

* * * *

Grace was relieved when the coach made a turn onto an obviously better maintained stretch of road. The road here was shaded by dense trees with a heavy canopy overhead. It was lovely to behold. She could easily imagine she was headed to a secret place and found herself daydreaming about who might be so fortunate as to live here. From what she could tell, they were on the property of this mysterious friend of Dansbury's, whose name, for some reason, he would not divulge, for the purposes of staying a night there before resuming their journey to Bath. She suspected Cliff was being evasive with his answers. In truth, she was sure Dansbury was being deliberately elusive, and she even wondered if he wasn't taking her to the duke's estate on the sly, but maybe that was merely wishful thinking. Besides, there was no help for it now. She had made her decision to leave with him and there was no point dwelling on the wisdom of her choice when it was too late to do anything about it.

For three days, they had travelled the countryside and in some respects her last morning at Beckett House seemed further away than so little time might suggest. She tried to come to terms with the way she and the duke had parted company. But ever since she learned he had not proposed to

Beatryce, her heart seemed to beat much faster than normal. She was fidgety and restless and couldn't understand why. Stonebridge had made it perfectly clear they had no future, and upon further reflection, it was obvious that becoming a duchess, or, more likely his mistress, would be disastrous. Not that she would seriously consider becoming either.

Then why am I so edgy and excited?

That man, Stonebridge, was a cold fish and a—a nincompoop. Yes, a cold nincompoop. She nodded her head in satisfaction at her ability to recognize that behind the handsome exterior, he was nothing to be admired. He was moody, cold, authoritative, hot, passionate…

She should just face it, when he wasn't cold, authoritative, and moody, he was…he was splendid. He made her insides quiver, and when she was with him…well, he was marvelous. Sometimes.

Then there was her uncle's explosive tirade followed by Dansbury's surprising suggestion (and her astonishing agreement) that she disregard her uncle's orders and venture forth with him, Dansbury, to Bath.

So who was this adventurous and reckless person? She felt outside herself. She wasn't worried about word getting back to her uncle. The servants at Beckett House were loyal to her and desired her happiness. Her uncle would never know she wasn't sitting quietly at Beckett House awaiting the family's return—whenever that might be.

Her musings were interrupted by a change in the scenery as the coach pulled out of the tree canopy and into the quaint little courtyard in front of a welcoming Tudor-styled country home. The front façade and entry was framed by towering trees and shrubs, replete with a flowering garden and myriad pathways darting off from the main courtyard, which encircled a small but impressive two-tiered fountain. The house did not seem imposing or overtly massive, but she suspected there was more here than met the eye judging by the length and careful maintenance of the main drive.

The coach had barely pulled to a stop before Dansbury leaped from the carriage with a sudden burst of energy. For the past few minutes, he had seemed tense, yet calm and thoughtful. Not his usual, easygoing, charming self.

He scanned the door and front windows before barking out a "Wait here." Then purposefully, with long-legged strides, he made his way to the front door.

How curious!

Dansbury had just put his foot on the first step leading up to the entry, when the door opened, but it was no butler waiting to see him inside.

"It's about bloody time you arrived. What the hell took you so long?"

Stonebridge, dressed casually sans cravat, waistcoat, and jacket, barked out his question but followed it with a quick smile and a slap on Dansbury's back, welcoming. That is, until he spotted her.

From across the small courtyard, she could see his demeanor change from friendly and relaxed to forced and stiff. Dansbury didn't even turn around. The liar.

The duke whispered something brief in the deceiver's ear before jogging down the steps with a confidence she envied. Dansbury just walked inside, leaving her to the mercy of the duke.

She warily watched his approach. To say she was surprised to see him would be an understatement, but she hid her shock and faced him with a confidence she didn't feel. Hopefully he would not cause a scene in front of Lady Harriett.

"Miss Radclyffe, welcome to Stonebridge Park. I trust your journey was uneventful."

So that was how he was going to play it? Calm and polite? Never mind that the last time he had stormed off in anger, putting her firmly in her place beforehand. Never mind that he had betrayed her trust when speaking with her uncle, telling him a load of falsehoods. These men were two of a kind — liars the both of them.

She decided to respond in kind: polite, disinterested responses that encouraged no search for truth nor invited deeper discussion. "Why, yes, Your Grace, we had quite a pleasant drive to your home. Thank you for asking."

After that, they simply stared at each other, at a loss for further words. A voice from within the carriage broke the awkward silence.

"Oh, Duke, quit flexing your muscles at the lady and help this old girl out of the carriage. I don't trust your footman to stop me from missing that last step."

* * * *

Surprised, Stonebridge turned to greet and assist Aunt Harriet. She wasn't really his aunt, but he was close enough to her that he called her that out of affection. He tried in vain to suppress inappropriate feelings of joy. Grace was here, and more importantly, Cliff and Grace had been well chaperoned and not travelling alone for…Three. Whole. Days.

Once inside the house, he waited in the foyer and watched Grace glide elegantly up the stairs behind his butler until she was out of sight. His mind was disordered. It was odd to see her so composed, and he didn't like it. He missed the fiery, impish, often awkward woman he'd glimpsed at Beckett House. Her newfound cool formality annoyed him. Further, he was dismayed, knowing her change was likely his fault. And then there was the uncomfortable flare of envy knowing she and Cliff had travelled days together to get here. Even if they were appropriately escorted. He trusted his friend implicitly, yet regardless of that trust, he stormed off in search of his so-called friend, proving the point that too much emotion can wreak havoc on a logical mind.

He found his quarry in the library with the rest of their assembled team; yet regardless of their audience, he grabbed Cliff, who was still standing just inside the door, by the lapels of his jacket and slammed him against the nearest wall.

"What the hell were you thinking bringing her here—especially at a time like this? Did it somehow escape your attention that the entire team would be here and that our identities are meant to be secret, not to mention our activities? No. Don't answer that. You were the one responsible for sending out the missive gathering everyone here. Good God, Cliff…" He let go of his friend and stalked away. Cliff just smiled, but said nothing.

In reality, he was frustrated more at himself than at his friend. He had lost confidence in his ability to think logically with Grace anywhere in his vicinity. He was close friends with Cliff and had worked with him long enough to know that he would not have brought Grace here if he didn't think it was important. Cliff was well aware of the inherent danger of their mission.

He tossed back a finger of brandy and asked without turning around, "What the hell happened?"

"Are the rest of the team up to date?"

"Yes, I briefed them yesterday while we waited for you. We saved the rest of our reports for your arrival."

Two leather armchairs and a leather camel-back sofa were arranged around a small table. The grouping stood before a large pedestal desk upon which numerous papers were scattered haphazardly about. Two agents, MacLeod and Kelly, sat together on the sofa facing Cliff and the open doorway beyond.

Cliff closed the library door and made his way to one of the chairs opposite the sofa.

"Right. As you know our latest intelligence has placed a questionable, yet damning light on certain people and their possible involvement in the events that occurred seventeen years ago. As I was preparing to depart the earl's home, I ran into a distraught Miss Grace Radclyffe. After the usual pleasantries, I inquired about catching up with Miss Radclyffe in London in a few weeks' time."

Ambrose unhinged his clenched jaw and made his way over to the remaining empty chair. He was sure he wasn't going to like this.

Cliff continued, "Miss Radclyffe tried to pass off an obviously phony excuse about her need to visit a sick friend in Yorkshire. I was unimpressed with her ability to lie convincingly, so I pressed her further and discovered that her uncle, the earl, had forbade her to journey to London with the family due to a supposed conversation he had with you regarding her conduct toward your person over the week. Swindon claimed you approached him about certain untoward advances. Obviously, I knew this wasn't true, so, in light of recent events and dare I say it, my gut instinct, I convinced her to leave with me under the guise of travelling with Aunt Harriett to Bath. It wasn't easy, mind you, to gain her acceptance, but clearly, in the end, she agreed to go."

Unbelievably, the duke's first instinct was to inquire as to whether or not Cliff had defended him to Grace. Did Cliff tell her he was not the sort to go running to the earl telling tales — whether true or not? Clearly, that was not the important point of this tale. Swindon's actions were plainly suspicious. Besides, he was all too sure he'd find out what Miss Radclyffe thought of his character soon enough.

Cliff carried on, "I cannot fathom what his motivations are in preventing her from journeying to London, save that he sees her as a possible threat to your engagement with Lady Beatryce. Regardless of whether or not his actions are so simple or more sinister, I felt it imprudent to put Miss Radclyffe under our protection...for now."

"Indeed. And we will discuss what to do about Miss Radclyffe after we debrief. In light of her arrival, it is prudent we conclude our business swiftly so the rest of you can return to your assignments."

"Let me guess...we're ta leave afore settin' eyes on the floozy," said Ciarán Kelly with a lazy grin, in his thick, Irish brogue. Kelly was the team's Irish contact who could charm the secrets out of anyone, young or old, male or female, despite being bastard born. It was a testament to his skill that so many — especially the ladies — could overlook that fact and spill their secrets so readily. It didn't hurt that he was handsome as sin, with midnight hair and bright blue eyes.

"Just because you're a bastard doesn't give you the right to be crude, Kelly. Miss Radclyffe is a fine lady and I suggest you refrain from making suggestive or disparaging remarks against her character," said Cliff in his affable way, all the while eyeing the duke and his clenched fists rather than the Irishman. Yes. Ambrose was ready to take Kelly's head.

"In my experience, all women are floozies given the right incentive. Take my word for it, or you might as well put a leash on your cock and hand the lead to the next woman you see, eh Alaistair?" replied Ciarán as he elbowed the hulking Scot sitting next to him in the side — good-naturedly, of course.

"Och, haud yer wheesht. I doona give a damn," responded said Scot, Lord Alaistair MacLeod. MacLeod was a man of few words, with little patience for small talk. He was just as good at ferreting out secrets as Kelly, though he used his massive strength more than any practiced charm. He wasn't violent per se, but he knew how to use his immense size to intimidate, quite often without resorting to any violence at all — not many were so stupid as to take the risk of having to dodge his mighty fists. He also listened more than he spoke, which made him good at separating the lies from truth. Despite being bitter toward his estranged family in Scotland, he was dependable and honest. Though he was gruff and said little, when he did speak, he was worth listening to, as his thoughts were keen and well organized, if impatient and borderline rude when his patience was stretched thin, which was often. In all, he was a man of contradictions and very private. The team, save perhaps the duke, knew little about MacLeod's background and the real man behind the red, bushy beard.

"Figures…grumpy as ever. Seen your da recently, then?" taunted Kelly.

Alaistair glared at Ciarán, but didn't respond.

"Enough," interrupted Stonebridge. "Ciarán, you are correct in that it is best if Grace doesn't see the rest of you."

"Grace?" interrupted Ciarán, brow raised at his familiar use of Miss Radclyffe's given name.

He ignored Ciarán. "I'll lead off. Two days ago, I met with my butler, Boneswaithe, regarding the night of the attack on the Prime Minister. He was butler here at the time and was able to recall much about the ongoing house party as the attempted assassination created quite an uproar. It seems that an assassin attempted to enter the Prime Minister's room late in the evening on the first night. Fortunately for the Prime Minister, a snuff servant, a young Irish boy by the name of Seamus O'Brien, happened by at the exact moment our would-be assassin attempted to enter the Prime Minister's room. A struggle ensued and the boy, being the weaker of the two, barely managed to escape by slicing his attacker in the cheek with his snuffer."

"Guid, aye? Our man Murphy has a right nasty scar on his right cheek just there." MacLeod pointed to his cheek, the approximate location of their captive's scar.

"Undeniably. Of course, at that point, the assassin runs off as the household is beginning to stir what with all the racket from the fight. He gets away and the boy raises the alarm, but by the time a search party is organized, the man has all but disappeared."

"He couldna made it far with a bleedin' gash in his cheek without someone making note of it," said MacLeod.

"Aye. Someone was bound to notice that," agreed Kelly.

"Nevertheless, he seemingly vanished without a trace."

"That suggests help—and nearby—especially if the assassin arrived the first night of the Prime Minister's stay and knew which room to enter. Are we sure the Prime Minister was the intended target? Who else was at the party?" queried Cliff.

"Of course, Boneswaithe can only base his knowledge on what he witnessed, but certainly they were all convinced the Prime Minister was the intended mark. As we presumed, the Prime Minister was reluctant to put too much effort into the hunt, but my father was furious that someone would attack a guest in his home, putting his family and people at risk. Incidentally, the servant boy, thankfully, was unharmed. He also remains in the area and might be able to identify the assassin. He was only ten at the time; he's a young man now."

"Our captive assassin might be difficult to recognize. He's quite gaunt and has aged significantly from his suffering over the last seventeen years, yet somehow I don't think he will be denying his involvement, so the point may be moot," added Kelly.

"One can hope. As far as the attendees at the party, they are as follows: The Prime Minister, of course—and his army of assistants, advisors, and secretaries; Viscount Branbury; the Earl of Swindon; Lord Fox; Lord North; Lord Middlebury; Mr. Randall Smythe; and the Honourable Henry Roxburgh of Bury."

"Och, quite the eclectic mix of powerful men, then. Pitt's entourage muddles things up a wee bit—any one o' them coulda been involved, ye ken, but Fox and North?"

"Indeed. They are the most obvious suspects considering their intense opposition to Pitt's policies."

Stonebridge paused to let everyone digest the possibilities before continuing, "Boneswaithe confirmed that my father focused exclusively on finding the would-be assassin in the month between the house party and his death. Secretly, the household thought the two were related. That's pretty much it. Boneswaithe will let me know if he recalls anything else no matter how insignificant. Also, he will retrieve the housekeeper's records for that party so that we can have a full account of all the guests, including the aides, valets, etc. I've asked him to send the books to you, Cliff. I intend to interview the rest of the staff and continue searching my father's papers for any notes he might have left behind. I have to imagine he was on to something, hence his unexpected demise." He paused at the tightening in his chest. After taking a deep breath, he continued, "Ciarán, what have you to report?"

"We have our friend from Ireland securely tucked away nearby."

"How nearby?"

"Very," Kelly gave him a meaningful look before continuing. "He still insists upon speaking only to you. I recommend we arrange that straightaway."

"I'll talk to him tomorrow night, then. Alaistair, anything to add?"

"Nae."

"Right. Ciarán, speak to Seamus O'Brien. He's at the Duck and Anvil in Bristol. MacLeod, arrange my meeting with Murphy for tomorrow night. Cliff, I want to know more about the aristos in attendance—their allies, political leanings, and solvency, especially Middlebury, North and Fox. Also, check out the housekeeper's records."

"What about Swindon?" asked Cliff.

"Leave that one to me."

"Aye and what about our lovely lady friend?" asked Kelly with a meaningful smirk.

"Whit's this? Can ye no think with yer head instead of yer cock, ye bastard?" MacLeod rolled his eyes with a look of contempt. Stonebridge sympathized.

Ciarán snorted, but his retort was interrupted when the library door clicked open. MacLeod, who was still seated with Kelly on the sofa, stood abruptly and sharpened his gaze, while Kelly remained seated and raised his brow in both question and surprise. His ever-present rakish grin widened further, if possible.

Shite. She's here.

Stonebridge and Dansbury (both of whom had been sitting on one of the two chairs facing the sofa, thereby with their backs to the door) stood and spun about to find Miss Grace

Radclyffe, having clearly just stumbled into the now open doorway, grinning sheepishly.

Bloody hell, someone would be let go for this.

* * * *

"Miss Radclyffe, please sit…"

Stonebridge gestured toward the chair he had been sitting in previously as it was the furthest away from, yet still angled toward, the nearby pedestal desk upon which lay a mess of scattered papers—made up of written reports from his team and other evidence pertaining to the ongoing investigation. With anyone else, he might have sat on the chair next to her, or on the sofa across from her, but then Miss Radclyffe was proving particularly unpredictable. Instead, he proceeded to his chair behind the desk in order to surreptitiously clear it in the event she proved impulsive by not remaining seated.

After the appropriate introductions were reluctantly made, his other 'guests' made their excuses to return to their rooms so he could interrogate—er, talk to—her about her suspicious wanderings.

He got right to the point.

"Miss Radclyffe, do you often wander aimlessly through other people's homes, and more specifically, enter into rooms with closed doors other than the bedroom to which you were assigned, without first knocking and being bade enter?"

He glared at Grace while she clearly sought to formulate a proper response. He covertly stacked some of the papers directly in front him—rude but necessary.

"Not generally, no."

He jerked his head at the abrupt response. Imagine that. She wasn't going to even try to offer up an excuse.

"I see."

Right, so that's how she is going to play it? Well, two can play at that game.

He waited in silence, grabbed the nearest stack of papers, including his father's contact journal, and placed them in his top right desk drawer. He tried to make his movements casual while inside, his heart beat a little faster — as seemed to always be the case whenever she was around.

A small, loose paper slid out from the stack he was arranging and fluttered to the floor at his feet. He bent to retrieve it, and after a quick glance, tossed it haphazardly into the drawer with the others. Then, almost immediately, he reached wildly back in to reclaim said paper as its contents registered in his mind. On it, written clearly in his father's penmanship, was:

John Radclyffe

We cannot enter into alliances until we are acquainted with the designs of our neighbors.

That was all. No other direction or personal information about Mr. Radclyffe, Grace's father, was written. After a moment, he read the quotation aloud, but did not mention Mr. Radclyffe by name; this was a test.

"It is from the *Art of War* by Sun Tzu," said Grace automatically.

He stared at her, but she was calm and composed — confident even.

Eventually, he stood and made his way to a shelf on the far side of the library to retrieve his copy of the famous book. As he began to flip through the pages, something fluttered to the floor. It was a piece of parchment, torn and quite old. It was blank on one side, but on the other, he discovered two seals affixed upon it. The first was a seal he would recognize anywhere: Middlebury. It was a symbol that had come to represent so much pain in this life, and his gut clenched at the sight of it. The second was completely unfamiliar to him. The letters looked like a swirly P and an E entwined together making up the branches of an oak tree.

Hmmm…Curious.

He returned his attention to the book itself and quickly found the page containing the quote. A folded piece of paper was tucked tightly between the pages. He pulled it free, opened it, and discovered the complete contact information for Grace's father written in his own father's hand.

Startled, he looked across the room at Grace, but her back was to him. She was not even watching; she appeared to be gazing out the window behind his desk. He pulled himself together and walked back to the desk, his curiosity piqued. The evidence was damning to say the least. He had been stymied over why her name seemed so familiar. He must have come across it in his father's papers before, but had not made the connection. Now, more questions than answers arose.

As he returned to his seat, his gaze remained trained on Grace and her air of innocence. Doubts began to creep up in his mind, but he ruthlessly suppressed any thoughts that would lead him to jump to conclusions, even though all her past actions—including her easy capitulation to travel with Cliff—were suspicious and tried to fight their way to the forefront of his thoughts.

"What did you find?" she asked before he had even resumed his seat.

Interesting.

He didn't answer, but instead asked, "Did your father know my father?"

"Not that I am aware of. Why?"

Again, he ignored her question and asked one of his own, "Is it possible that he did?"

"I suppose. He often traveled away. He was a well-known authority on ancient and obscure texts. Oftentimes a client would invite him to travel to their homes or businesses to evaluate an old manuscript or book. He also travelled in search of rare items to add to his inventory. Most of the time, we did not travel with him. Certainly, never to your father's home."

"Why do you say that…certainly?"

"Mainly, because my father would never want to impose on his clients' hospitality. He would have felt obligated to focus entirely on the job at hand and leave promptly upon completion of his work. He strove to be efficient, unimposing, and discreet. Oh, he'd often talk about the rare texts he saw, but never about the owners themselves. You must understand, he was in trade, and his business was built on his reputation. He would never risk jeopardizing his livelihood by involving himself with a client in any personal way. He drew a clear line, and he never crossed it."

"Are you quite sure about that?"

"Quite."

"Did your father perchance attend university at Oxford?"

"Yes…yes, he did."

"I see." His father had attended there as well.

"I see as well, and I don't think I like your tone of voice, Your Grace. In fact, I know I don't like it and the obvious doubt in your mind." She rose from her seat on the chair. "I believe I shall retire for the evening, Your Grace. It's been a tiring day. Good evening."

"Grace…I apologize. I only ask because the quotation I read to you earlier was written on a paper I found with your father's name on it. Your father is John Radclyffe, I presume?"

"Yes." Grace looked less confident. She plopped back down in her chair; she appeared pale and nervous. Guilt?

"In addition in the book, I found the full contact information for your father's direction in Oxford tucked inside."

Her eyes widened further, but only briefly.

"Well that makes sense. If your father had need of my father's services…"

"Indeed," he interrupted. "But then why hide his direction in a book?"

Chapter 12

Tap, tap, tap…

Scratching on the bedroom door startled grace out of her silent reverie. She had been staring out her window, at nothing really, ever since she had entered her room after fleeing the duke's library over an hour ago.

"Come in," she answered, confident it was Bessie.

"Och, there now, lass. I've come with a spot of tea and some cakes." Bessie nudged her way in the room — arms laden with a large tray of tea and scones.

"Oh, Bessie. Thank you. I'm sure I've asked you before, but really, how is it you always seem to know just what I need?" said Grace with a grin.

"Well, dearest, normally, I would say that it's just me job to know, but honestly, today, I must admit I had a wee bit of help. That nice young lad, the Marquess of Dansbury, suggested it. Mind you, I don't know how he knew, but he has such a sincerity about him, I didn't think to question him."

Already, the smell of tea and warm raspberry scones spiced the air in the room. The aroma and the sight of her maid's friendly countenance helped Grace relax a notch.

"Well, in this instance, he was certainly correct. Thank you. Honestly, I've been sat here for the last hour thinking about my father."

"Och, aye, and such a fortunate man he was, to have such a good family and a comfortable life…not too excessive, mind, but just right."

"Bessie, do you know whether or not Papa knew the late Duke of Stonebridge…the current duke's father?" She stirred the sugar in her tea.

"Och, now why would I know a thing like that?" asked Bessie with a bit of cheek. "I'm sorry dearie, but no, I do not know. Perhaps they knew each other whilst attending Oxford, or maybe he was one of your father's clients? Certainly, I don't recall ever serving him in your parents' home. I guess you could check your father's personal papers to be sure."

"Papers?"

"Well, I donna know much about what's up there, but I know your father kept papers in the loft at the house in Oxford, as sometimes I would see him up there when I cleaned, or when I was coming or going from my room…"

"Oh, of course. Gracious, why didn't I think about that?"

"Well, dearest, your family, bless them, kept you pretty sheltered from the mundane, and with the whirlwind of your father's death and near immediate removal to your uncle's house, you probably never gave it another thought. Why would you?"

"You're right, as usual. Hmmm. What we need is a way to get to Oxford and find out for sure."

"Oxford? Isn't that quite a ways from here? If you don't mind my asking, why is it so imperative to know for sure? It seems the point is moot seeing as how both men have passed, forgive me."

"I can't say for certain, Bessie, but I just think it is important. So important, that I think I need to prevail upon our friend, the marquess, and find out for certain."

* * * *

The next morning…
The pool room…

Crack…

The six ball rattled the corner pocket before it sunk convincingly; the sound echoed throughout the room. The room was designed for the sole purpose of playing pool; its only furnishings were the racks built specifically for storing cue sticks and balls and a ledge for holding drinks. The walls were paneled mahogany and a fireplace and large window overlooking a private side garden added warmth, atmosphere, and light. With only a few paintings and one rug, the sound of the balls, colliding and rounding the pockets, reverberated satisfyingly about the room.

"Careful, Ambrose, or you may end up needing the felt refitted before the end of our match."

Ambrose tossed Cliff a brief glare before lining up his cue for another shot.

Playing pool was an excellent way to relieve tension. Specifically, slamming a ball hard enough into a pocket such that it rattled around the sides before it sunk was satisfying in a definite way. They all knew it. Needless to say, this room was used quite frequently. "I take it your conversation with Miss Radclyffe didn't go as well as you'd like?"

"Four ball, side pocket." Ambrose called out his next shot.

Crack…

"Don't pretend you didn't hear every word of that conversation. I know you, remember?" Ambrose chalked up for this third shot.

Cliff chuckled. Ambrose knew him better than anyone. And his eavesdropping wasn't really an invasion of privacy; he was well aware Ambrose had wanted him to hear the conversation firsthand so they could discuss it later. At least, that's what he told himself, anyway.

"So do you really suspect her father of…Well, hello, Miss Radclyffe. What a pleasant surprise?"

Thunk…

Dansbury chuckled at the sound of Ambrose's miscue.

"Good afternoon, Lord Dansbury," replied Grace. She didn't even acknowledge Ambrose.

Ambrose slammed his stick down onto the table. "We can talk in the library."

"Oh, but I'm not here to speak to you, Your Grace. I would like to speak with Lord Dansbury. In private, if possible."

It was difficult for Cliff to keep a straight face. Miss Radclyffe, putting Ambrose squarely in his place; what a sight. She must be truly angry, even though she appeared composed and serene.

"Why, absolutely, Miss Radclyffe. It would be my pleasure. How about a stroll about the garden? The weather appears ideal for it."

"That sounds marvelous, thank you."

As he put away his cue on the nearby rack, Cliff tried to remain serious despite the shock on his friend's face. But as he walked by his speechless friend, he couldn't resist taunting, "I presume we'll finish our game later, Your Grace."

* * * *

Cliff escorted Grace down the back patio steps. He got his first good look at her in the bright afternoon sunlight. It was immediately apparent that her serene expression was just a façade. She hid it well, but Cliff's powers of observation were such that he could see the tell-tale signs of strain around her eyes. She was worried. He decided to get right to the point:

"Darling, what is the matter?"

She didn't waste time, either. "Last night I spent over an hour being interrogated by the duke over something I know absolutely nothing about."

"I see."

"Let me finish, please. I am well aware that you probably already know about this, so please do not insult my intelligence by placating me." She held up her hand to forestall any further interruptions.

Aaah. Welcome back my little spitfire, welcome back.

"You played an awful trick on me—bringing me here without telling me the truth about where we were going. And your aunt, was she in on it too? Never mind. Don't answer that as it is entirely irrelevant. The point is, the way I see it—you owe me."

He was stunned and said nothing.

She took a deep breath before dropping her bomb. "I want you to take me to Oxford."

Chapter 13

An abandoned tenant hut, Stonebridge Park...
Midnight...

Stonebridge and Alaistair MacLeod arrived at the abandoned tenant's hut by horseback a few strokes after midnight. The place would have looked convincingly abandoned were it not for the telltale sign of smoke drifting up through the chimney.

The front door was there, but held in place by crude wooden bars stretching across the width of the door frame, the hinges having been removed long ago. The duke guessed the bars were improvised by MacLeod to keep their prisoner secured within. As they approached, he couldn't resist looking over at the Scot, his brow raised in question at the makeshift lock.

"Och, weel what else was I ta do?"

Stonebridge chuckled at that.

MacLeod lifted the bars away and hefted the door out of the opening—setting it neatly against the wall to his left. The Scot was a big man. Two more bars remained on the inside of the opening, in place to keep the loose door from falling into the room when closed.

He laughed some more and regarded his friend.

"I'll juist wait oot here an keep an eye oot," said MacLeod as he dusted off his hands without looking at Ambrose.

"Right."

He walked into the ramshackle hut, not quite sure what to expect. The place was clearly in decay, most of the furniture broken or long gone. The inside was dark, dusty, and cold despite the fire blazing in the hearth. The blaze made the air smoky and smelly as the chimney was clearly in need of repair, and the meager warmth from its flames battled valiantly but futilely against the cold air drafting in through cracks in the walls and gaping holes in the moldy, thatched roof.

He took in the remaining furniture: two wooden rocking chairs. One was occupied by their reluctant guest.

Despite prior words to the contrary, he imagined a strong and wily brute of a man—one who clearly looked like he might have had a chance of taking down the mighty Duke of Stonebridge.

What he saw was an old man, bent and gaunt, with stringy, unkempt white hair, but with a keen look about the eyes and the firm line of his lips. It was difficult to match the sight before him with the image in his mind's eye of the man who might have murdered his father. Yet, those eyes undoubtedly held secrets. Yes, this man could have done it, despite his current physical frailty.

"Aye, it is ye. Ain't it? Ye have yer faither's look about ye," grumbled the old man. His voice held strength despite his weak physical form.

Stonebridge took a moment more to take in the appearance of this man who might know the truth about his father's death—who might have been the man to do the deed. The flickering light from the fire danced across the side of the assassin's face, making his scar appear to writhe on his cheek. The duke suppressed a shudder.

"Yes, I am Stonebridge."

"I know ye want ta know about yer faither's murder. Who can blame ye, aye? Well, I can tell ye that the two events, yer faither's accident, which weren't an accident, and the attempt on yer prime minister were related—the same men were behind it."

"Go on."

"Have ye any knowledge of a man named Mr. John Radclyffe? Oh, aye, I see that ye do."

The man was peculiarly sharp, to be able to determine that in the low light.

"Yes, I know, but I don't believe he would have worked alone, if you are indeed implying his involvement. Something like this would have required men with money, men with power. You must know more."

"Oh aye, I know more, a lot more. But I'm needing reassurances, aren't I?"

"What do you want?"

"Don't play games with me, boy. Ye be knowing what it is I am wanting. I've made that plain from the beginning—I want passage to America, money to start a life there and reassurances that I won't have the law breathin' down me neck every time I take a piss. What I want is yer word that ye'll make it happen, or I'll take me bleeding secrets to me grave."

"Let me ask you something, Murphy. Do you have proof— hard evidence—that what you tell me is the truth?"

"I might at that."

Abruptly, Murphy tossed something at the duke's head. The duke caught the object, reflexively, and looked down to behold a silver stamp, old and grand. The duke, who was still standing just inside the doorway, walked over to the fire and leaned in to get a better look. The seal was used for stamping an insignia in wax when sealing or witnessing documents. The insignia, worn but clearly visible, was that of a swirled P and an E making up the branches of an English Oak. Chills chased up his spine. He jerked his gaze to the old man watching him.

"I'm listening."

"Aye, I thought that might get yer attention. Now, have ye ever heard of the Secret Society for the Purification of England?"

* * * *

Oxford, High Street…
2 days later…

Grace could barely contain her excitement as she and Dansbury made their way to her father's shop on High Street. The current tenants had moved in a month after she left for West Sussex last year. Their occupancy was temporary. They would run the book store on her behalf until she reached her majority, with the assistance of her solicitors and Uncle Beckett, of course, at which time, she could decide how she would like to proceed moving forward. As such, she was anxiously anticipating seeing her father's legacy in continued action.

After checking into the main hotel in Oxford yesterday, she had wanted to walk over to the shop straight away, but Dansbury and Aunt Harriett had talked her out of it. Both had suggested she rest and clean up so as to arrive fresh on the morrow. She hadn't wanted to agree, but she had been admittedly tired, so after a little debate, she relented.

What were a few more hours' delay? Besides, she might be there awhile, looking through her father's papers, and would work more efficiently if well rested.

Today, she was glad she had waited, albeit impatiently, as she now felt restored and ready. To help matters, the morning weather was unusually fine—bright and sunny, whereas yesterday it had been damp and clouded over. Now, with only one more bend in the road before they reached their destination, she was nigh giddy with excitement on Dansbury's arm. Her eagerness must have been obvious because every so often, he would look down at her and just smile.

Well, what did he expect? It had been over a year since she had last stepped foot in her father's shop, and she was anxious to reacquaint herself with the place. Would it be the same as she remembered? Would the purple primrose still be alive in its pot on the counter? She was flooded with memories reminding her of the sights and comforting smells inside — the scent of paper, coffee & tea, tobacco, and leather all combining to make up the unique odor of a book store and lounge.

As they made the last turn before her father's shop, she was surprised to see five carts, heavily laden, lined up at the edge of the pavement nearby their destination. Her spine tingled inexplicably at the sight, and she unconsciously increased her stride.

Dansbury, however, seemed to do the opposite. He slowed his pace to the point that she began to drag him along.

"Grace, darling, let us slow down, shall we?"

She would have none of it. "Cliff, we're nearly there, and I cannot help it. Something isn't right."

"Grace." Dansbury halted their walk and pulled her to the side of the walkway nearest the buildings, his hands resting gently on her shoulders. "Listen to me. When we get there, I want you to keep quiet and let me do the talking. Understand?"

"But..." she began, but Dansbury interrupted her with one raised hand. She was nauseous, and the child in her wanted to turn back to the hotel and hide beneath the covers. She wrapped her arms around her stomach.

"Grace, I am serious. Just go along with whatever I say, no interruptions. Grace, look at me." Dansbury caught her eye as she tried to look to the ground at her feet, "Please, trust me," he said gently.

"All right."

Dansbury searched her expression a moment longer, and a slight warning crossed his eyes before he added, "Good. Let's go."

They began to walk on at a frustrating, leisurely pace. Dansbury looked ready to begin whistling a tune, while Grace, who was beyond nervous now, began to tremble on his arm. The air no longer felt warm. In fact, she felt chilled to the bone despite the sun shining brightly above. Up ahead, it was plain that men were regularly filing in and out of her father's shop, their arms overloaded with packages that were being placed on the carts out front.

Nothing was being brought inside.

As they approached the first window of her father's shop, she searched past the glass. The place was empty. The familiar display of books to entice customers into the shop, all of it, was gone.

Her breathing quickened and her legs wobbled. She felt like she walked through mud and her surroundings became both sharp and blurred at the same time, if that were possible. If it weren't for the strength of Dansbury's arm beneath her hand, she might have collapsed in a heap on the pavement while she covered her eyes to block out the reality of what she could see before her.

Dansbury briefly covered her hand with his, for she hadn't collapsed after all, before leading them inside. The door was already open, propped wide by a large chunk of wood. She realized then that she was squeezing the life out of Dansbury's arm, but couldn't care. She stumbled over the threshold as she walked inside.

And stopped. And sucked in a breath. And beheld: Nothing.

All of it: the freestanding shelves, the actual counter itself behind which her father had always stood and wrapped up purchases, the grouping of leather chairs where men sat to review a book before purchasing it and partake of cigars or coffee or tea, the little primrose her father kept at one end of the counter. All of it. Gone. Gone. Gone.

All one could see now were empty walls and dusty, dirty flooring—scuffed and scarred. On the floor near the shop window to their right, more packages waited to be picked up by the workmen now skirting around them. Grace and Dansbury stood frozen just inside the doorway, shocked at the sight. There wasn't even a curtain over the entrance to the back of the shop where the kitchens and the stairs leading up to her home were located.

Her knees buckled just as Dansbury stepped forward. His grasp on her hand tightened—conveying strength—as he literally held her up and propelled her forward toward the back of the shop. She stumbled before her legs caught up with their forward momentum. She was dimly aware of a voice angrily shouting at someone in the back rooms. But all of her strength could not stop the tears from flowing freely down her cheeks.

"This place was supposed to be entirely cleared as of yesterday. Why are you still here? My client needs the place cleaned and ready before the auction two days hence; we are out of time," came a disembodied voice, raised in anger, from the back of the building.

"I'm sorry, sir, but we have everything out from upstairs now. I just completed one last walk-through and was leaving," came a softer, slightly nervous voice.

Grace followed Dansbury through the emptied doorway leading to the back rooms. Anger replaced shock and grief like a veil. Her tears continued, but they were of a different source now. She held her head up, refusing to acknowledge the tears, her gaze direct and fierce.

"Good morning. I am Clifford Ross, 7th Marquess of Dansbury." Cliff, who preceded Grace into the back rooms, squeezed Grace's hand in warning, reminding her to hold her tongue, as she followed behind through the narrow entryway.

A short and rather round gentleman with thick, gray hair and sideburns, spun around at the newcomers' arrival. He was dressed in quality clothing although he was unkempt. His cravat was mussed and stained, and his buttons and boots were not polished. He had been standing with his back to the door talking, or more like yelling, to a kindly looking gentleman of about forty years of age, clutching his hat in dismay.

"My lord, Mr. Edward Banks, Esquire at your service," spoke the rotund man, a solicitor, who mopped his wide forehead with a kerchief before stuffing it in his pocket and proceeding toward Dansbury, his hand outstretched in greeting and a wide, greedy smile on his face. His expression turned solemn as he waddled his way across the room, hand still outstretched. His somberness did not reach his eyes, which still held the fires of greed.

"I am the solicitor representing the owners of this property, and I truly regret to inform you that the premises are closed to prospective buyers until the auction on Friday next."

The solicitor tried to look surreptitiously at Grace around Dansbury's shoulder as he spoke (for she had not been introduced), infernal hand still outstretched, but neither she nor Dansbury acknowledged nor soothed his curiosity.

Dansbury, who was generally considered an affable man by one and all, looked down his nose at the solicitor's hand before ignoring it, and brushed past to face the unacknowledged gentleman with the crumpled hat, his brow raised in question. Clearly, Dansbury knew how to issue the cut direct—quite convincingly.

The other man, clearly a gentleman though a little rough around the edges, smiled in return. He had dark-brown hair peppered with gray and kindly, brown eyes—a father's eyes. He was dressed in a plain, brown jacket, a dark green waistcoat and brown trousers. The buttons were brass and one might detect a little fraying at the edges of his cuffs; nevertheless he appeared tidier than the solicitor. He seemed respectable, if a little haggard today. In light of what they had overheard before entering the room, it was understandable.

"My lord, Mr. Marcus Smythe at your service," he answered at the implied question, most respectfully.

"I'm pleased to make your acquaintance," answered Dansbury in turn. "I understand you were managing the bookstore before it closed." At the gentleman's nod, Dansbury continued, "Did I correctly overhear that you were previously living in the rooms above until recently?"

"Yes, my lord, for the past year until we received notice last week that the owners were not renewing our lease. We were given a few days to remove our belongings and no time to notify our customers of the shop's impending closure," Mr. Smythe added with an angry look over Dansbury's shoulder in the solicitor's direction.

"Now, see here. The renewal of the lease was never a guarantee, as you are well aware," blurted out the solicitor. He looked worried and afraid. He had to be aware that he risked angering a high-ranking member of the peerage with his behavior. Not to mention that both Grace and Dansbury were well aware of who the solicitor worked for.

Dansbury looked over his shoulder at the solicitor's interjection. "You're still here?"

The solicitor paled before gathering his courage—or stupidity. "My lord, I appreciate that you might see this situation as highly irregular, but I assure you that our actions are completely necessary and in accord with the owners' consent. As such, I must insist that I remain present until I can be assured that Mr. Smythe has indeed vacated the premises and has left no other possessions behind; my client expects no less."

"All is clear save for this key we found under a rug as the men came to clear away the last of the furnishings this morning. It is not ours," replied Mr. Smythe, his voice fretful again. Mr. Banks glared at him as if he were a thief attempting some crime. Mr. Smythe pulled out a small key from his waistcoat pocket and handed it over to the solicitor.

Dansbury was silent as he watched all this. He no longer seemed to care about the fact that the solicitor hadn't left. He watched Mr. Smythe hand over the key.

Then he spoke. "Well, Mr. Smythe, it has been a pleasure to meet you. What is your direction should I need to contact you in future?" His affable façade returned.

"My lord, we will be staying with my sister and her family for a few days until we find new accommodation, #4 St. Clement's Street, Oxford. It would be our pleasure to speak with you again."

"Excellent. I'll be in touch."

Dansbury turned to the solicitor. "Mr. Banks, forgive me for not shaking your hand earlier; I apologize for the misunderstanding." He held out his hand and clapped the solicitor on the shoulder as if they were men of the world, bosom friends, who knew a thing or two about life. Grace seethed, but said nothing.

"Perfectly understandable, my lord. I understand this was unexpected," replied the solicitor promptly and with no small amount of relief.

Dansbury turned to offer his arm to Grace, yet he looked over at Mr. Smythe one last time. Mr. Smythe smiled knowingly before nodding at Dansbury and quitting the room.

Dansbury winked in return.

"Let us be off, Miss Radclyffe," he added for the solicitor's benefit.

To the solicitor, who stood out of sight behind them, he added, "We'll be in touch."

* * * *

As soon as Grace stepped out into the brilliant sunshine, she whirled on Dansbury, ready to give him a piece of her mind, but he forestalled her tirade with a lift of one finger.

"Grace, we're outside. Wait until we're in private."

"But we didn't even go upstairs."

"Trust me; there's nothing left, darling."

"But…"

"Grace, trust me. I have something better. Now, let's go."

He led her back to her room at a dizzying pace—quite a contrast to their stroll earlier that morning.

Grace wound her way through the lobby of their hotel, headed in the direction of Aunt Harriett, who was seated on a sofa near the fire, but Dansbury redirected her to the stairs and on to her room. Once inside, he shut the door and locked it. Grace whirled around to tell him exactly what she thought about his behavior at the bookstore, but forgot her point at the sight of him standing there holding out a small brass key.

"Is that the key Mr. Smythe gave to Mr. Banks?"

"It might be."

"But, why?"

"Think about it, Grace. The key obviously didn't belong to Mr. Smythe, or he wouldn't have tried to pass it on to the solicitor. It clearly isn't a key to the property or anything in the bookstore, or he would have known what it was for and said so. I strongly suspect this key belonged to your father, and I have a pretty good idea what it goes to." She crossed her arms across her chest as she waited for him to continue. "I believe it belongs to a safety deposit box—in a bank—in London."

She paced the floor, her thoughts awhirl. "I see, and how do you know this?"

"The engravings on the key. The letters identify the bank and the numbers identify the box number. I have one like it myself."

"How did you do it? Take the key, that is. Especially without him knowing about it? And won't he notice and realize you took it?"

"Grace, I answer can't your first question, and honestly, it was quite easy. My summation of the solicitor's character is such that by the time he notices, he'll think he lost it—if he even remembers."

"But why would you do this? Effectively steal, for me?"

"Grace, I suspect whatever is in the box this key goes to is important, and I suspect that had I allowed the solicitor to pass it on to the earl, you would never know what secrets it holds."

She stopped pacing and plopped onto the bed, too emotionally drained to stand any longer as a whirlwind of feelings spun around in her mind: grief over her father's emptied shop; all his possessions gone. Despair over the possible loss of the shop and her future prospects. Anger over the machinations of her uncle. Frustration at her inability to stop events that seemed so completely out of her control. Fear over all the secrecy and implications about her father, the old duke, the earl…She looked up at Dansbury in a silent plea, the weight of it all almost unbearable.

He knelt at her feet and took both her hands in his.

"Grace, try not to worry, darling, though I know it's difficult."

She nodded in silence, conceding his point. Meanwhile, her tears were back and sliding down her reddened cheeks.

"Listen to me. Here's what I want to do. I want you to stay with Aunt Harriett. Travel with her to London tomorrow as we planned. And no matter what happens, I want you to stay with her. Do not go to your uncle, even if summoned by him. Do you understand? This is important."

"I understand. What are you going to do?"

"I'm leaving for London. Now. I think we need to see what's inside that box, and with your permission, I would like to go ahead of you. I can get there faster on horseback and retrieve the box on your behalf. I think it's safe to say that time is of the essence."

She nodded her agreement. "What about the auction? Friday is only a few days away."

"I'll do my best, Grace. You'll have to trust me."

"I seem to be doing an awful lot of that today," she added with a chuckle at the end. She wiped at her eyes, her nerves calmed with a plan.

"You'll be all right, Miss Grace Radclyffe."

She nodded. "I know. And, thank you."

She reached out to hug Dansbury, who was still on his knees before her, but as she pulled back, he had a strange look about him. And before she knew it, he kissed her.

Chapter 14

A Posting Inn on the way to London…
Later that afternoon…

Stonebridge swirled his drink as he warmed his feet by the fire. He was in a private parlor at a posting inn en route to London. His long legs were stretched out before him and resting on the bars of the iron fender. He was only stopping for a short rest and food while his coachmen exchanged the tired carriage horses for fresh stock.

He was travelling to his London residence, having exhausted his interviews and his search of Stonebridge Park. And he was trying hard not to think of Grace and Cliff traveling to Oxford and then on to London together…quite unsuccessfully. Frustrating that.

He set down his glass in defeat and picked up the book he had started. He refused to allow his thoughts to go there. Again. He needed something to do, something to engage his mind.

He had just reread the same paragraph for the fifth time, and he still didn't know what it said, when someone knocked on the parlor door. He placed his mark in the book and called out, "Enter."

A messenger, clearly road-weary and dusty, burst into the room. "Your Grace, I have a message for you from Lord

Dansbury."

He was relieved for the distraction and wasted no time accepting the missive. He tore it open:

Ambrose,

> *Store and residence closed and swept. Property to be auctioned Friday next via Mr. Edward Banks, Esq; Oxford. Our mutual friend is distraught.*

> *Found key to unknown Lockbox in L. Off to L to retrieve contents. Miss R to follow with Aunt H.*

Cliff

He stared off into space and remained that way for an awkward minute before he acknowledged the waiting footman.

"That will be all, thank you."

"Yes, Your Grace."

He tossed the missive into the fire, his thoughts awhirl. This was an unexpected maneuver for Swindon: not surprising, per se, just bold. He knew his next logical move was to make for London with all due haste, but Oxford wasn't too terribly far away. Especially on horseback, was it?

Yes. It was. Particularly since he was needed in London. The contents of this lockbox could well hold the key to solving everything. He repeated that mantra over and over again in his mind as he sought out his valet, Bryans, outside.

"Bryans, gather everyone and send them on ahead to London."

"Very good, Your Grace. But where are you going?"

"I am going to Oxford. Follow when you can. I'll take rooms at the Oxford Arms." Aaah…To hell with logic.

* * * *

Oxford…
The next morning…

Grace walked along High Street and peered into every shop front along the way. Not that she needed to buy anything, mind, and she was certainly staying away from the end where her father's shop had been. No, the window shopping was all a ploy, really, to distract herself from herself—or her chaotic thoughts at any rate. It wasn't working. She looked in the storefront windows and tried to focus on the items on display, but they didn't really register in her mind. Other thoughts obsessed her.

Could my life turn any further upside down?

Two years ago, she had been blissfully happy, having never been touched by trauma. Even a month ago, though having suffered heartache with the death of her parents, she had settled into her new life with some semblance of normalcy and some measure of contentment. It hadn't been blissful by any stretch of the imagination, but there had always been a future to look forward to, and it had sustained her through the rough times.

But today? Not only was her future uncertain, but her emotions were all a jumble over men—of all things. Curious creatures that they were. Who would have guessed it? A month ago, no men danced around her in her mind. Now, she was bombarded by thoughts of two.

First, she was inappropriately consumed at all hours of the day (or at least it seemed that way at times) by a handsome, wildly attractive duke: Stonebridge and all his brooding glory. And now, as if she needed any further complications in her life, there was Dansbury. And his sweet kisses.

Dansbury was handsome and steady, a fine man, and she enjoyed her time with him. He made her laugh. He was safe. He was perfect. And she should be shouting with glee over his obvious interest; though realistically, as with the duke, he was way too high for her, socially.

She had never before considered Dansbury in any sort of romantic light, though. He just didn't consume her thoughts like Stonebridge. She didn't tingle all over with just a look. She didn't feel like throwing her reputation and her life away should he even hint…Well, it was frightening to even think about it, really, how much she might risk should she forget herself with the duke.

Stonebridge was moody and a little bit cruel. To her anyway. And he was altogether too unpredictable. Definitely not the stoic man everyone else portrayed him to be, at least in her experience. Yet he constantly occupied her thoughts. It was pitiful. By all accounts, she should rejoice in Dansbury, not yearn for a fickle duke.

And it wasn't that Dansbury was unattractive, for he was undeniably handsome, and she was attracted to him in a general sort of way. As any woman with eyes would be.

And yesterday, when she realized Dansbury was about to kiss her, she didn't stop him as she ought. She was curious. She had never kissed a man, romantically, before the duke, and she had wondered if the experience would be the same, or at least similar.

It wasn't. Oh, Dansbury's kiss hadn't been bad or unpleasant at all. In fact, she had responded to it. She wasn't dead, and it had been awfully naughty of them to engage in such behavior. It hadn't been a kiss of fire or thunder, like with the duke, but more gentle, like a soothing rain. She hadn't slapped him as she probably should have done, either, and her heartbeat had quickened, for she had felt nervous; after all, what they were doing was all taboo. But at the same time, her thoughts had been actively cataloguing sensations throughout it all.

Unlike with the duke and his kiss.

With him, her thoughts scattered like the wind. She was on fire with passion, and the world about them fell away into oblivion. And afterwards, she relived the kiss over and over and over. For days. And nights. In her dreams. Where she awoke overwhelmed with sensation and touching herself…

She stopped, her cheeks flushed with embarrassment. She looked about. Oh, it really was a good thing one's thoughts were one's own. Goodness. If the people walking by had even an inkling of what she was thinking, they'd be mortified and expire on the spot. She laughed at the thought. It was odd what things she found funny these days.

But her chuckles died in her throat as she caught sight of the very man who occupied her mind day after day: Stonebridge.

Her hand rose to her chest as if she could physically steady her racing heart. He was so mind numbingly handsome and her heart literally ached with the knowledge that he would never be hers. It was so ridiculously unfair.

She watched as he entered a nearby building. He hadn't seen her amidst the crowd, of course. Once out of sight, she was able to walk again. She strode forward hesitantly. Honestly, she should flee to the safety of the hotel, not loiter outside, dying with curiosity and the desire for just another, quick glimpse, but alas, she couldn't make herself leave.

She passed the building he had entered and tried hard not to be so obvious as to ogle the door, but she did look and made note of the sign identifying the place as the offices of Tolley and Brinks, Esquire.

She passed a few more shop fronts, then turned. Her face was warm with embarrassment.

What am I doing?

She walked past the solicitors' office again and passed a few more shops before shaking her head, resigned.

"Extra! Extra! Read all about it! Prince Regent plans Grand Jubilee in London!" called out a young boy, hawking broadsheets nearby. She heard him above the general din of horses, carriage wheels and people bustling about their business as she maneuvered her way through the throng of carriages to the opposite side of the street.

Once there, she purchased a paper, then made her way to a nearby bench which happened to be situated directly across the street from the duke's solicitors' office.

Convenient, that. She sat, only for a moment, mind. To read the paper. Honestly.

Oh, who am I trying to fool?

For half an hour, her heart missed a beat every time the door to the solicitors' office opened. Really, what was she planning to do once he did come out? Dash into his arms? Call his name from across the thoroughfare? Run away and hide? She asked herself these questions, over and over again, the entire time; she certainly was no more aware of the latest news than from before she'd bought her paper.

Finally, at long last, he came out of the building, and he saw her instantly. She stood on reflex and looked back. For an eternity but only a minute, they stared at each other across the avenue, and her heart thundered faster than ever. Before reality intruded. This wasn't wise and just as she recognized the truth of that, she saw his expression change from surprise to murderous.

Right. Time to go.

She tried to go around the bench at the same he stepped out onto the street.

Zounds! He was coming.

But in her haste to leave, she rounded the bench too carelessly, only to have her reticule catch on the bench's arm, jerking her to a stop. Unfortunately, her nerves, along with the bench, conspired against her, and she stumbled to her knees.

The hand holding her bag came down hard onto the bench seat, over the arm rest. She'd have a bruise under her arm tomorrow from that. The straps of her reticule, still caught, pulled tight on her wrist, turning her skin white, then red and puffy. Her other hand, which had whipped out reflexively, hit the ground. It just stopped her from cracking her chin on the bench.

Why, oh why, did I even get out of bed this morning?

She closed her eyes in humiliation. All around her, people fell silent; even the boy no longer peddled his papers. She could make out the occasional horse and carriage, but even the whinnying of a nearby horse sounded like laughter to ears colored with embarrassment. She could hear the sound of running feet, boots striking on cobbles, and she knew that Stonebridge was dashing across the street—coming to rescue her.

He arrived a moment later, slightly out of breath, and she smiled at the thought that he'd run all that way…in public. For her.

"Grace, are you all right? Here, let me assist you, please."

How ridiculous that all things considered, her heart leapt over the fact that he had used her given name rather than Miss Radclyffe, as was proper.

"I'll be fine, thank you, Your Grace."

After he helped her up, he worked to untangle her bag whilst she evaluated the state of her dress. It was dirty, of course, so she made to brush off the loose gravel and dirt as best she could. She could feel her knees burning as her movements made her stockings rub against the scrapes. They were bruised as well; she could feel it every time her hand brushed one. In addition, her left hand was throbbing from where she scratched it on the pavement as she attempted to catch her fall. Even the fabric of her dress hurt her as it caught on her wounds, but the pain was good in that it distracted her from the imposing man beside her.

He untangled her reticule, and handed it to her before taking her right hand, and placing it firmly on his arm. She could see his emotions warring between concern and anger. Dansbury had warned her to stay with Aunt Harriett, and of course she had disobeyed.

Stonebridge, surprisingly, kept his counsel the entire way back to her hotel. No inane pleasantries. No inquiries into her health, the weather, Napoleon, the state of the kingdom. And she didn't bother to question how he knew where she was staying. He nodded politely at the people who attempted to waylay them, but made it clear he was not prepared to stop for a chat.

Once inside her hotel, he guided her to the main staircase and simply said, "To your room."

Succinct and abrupt as usual.

At least he hadn't already known which room was hers. When they arrived, Bessie was there, packing away their belongings for the return trip to London.

"Madam, Miss Radclyffe is injured. Please go downstairs and bring back whatever suitable liniments they have to treat minor scrapes and bruises."

"Yes, Your Grace."

After Bessie left, Grace sat on a chair, and watched, bemused, as he patrolled the floor. After a minute, he turned to face her, and as usual, got right to the point.

"Why were you out on the streets alone? I'm quite sure Dansbury told you to stay with Aunt Harriett…er, Lady Ross."

He was mad; she could see that. Not only did he speak with an angry tone, but his hands opened and closed as if he only just stopped himself from shaking her. She was surprised by the contradictory look in his eyes — which showed concern, worry, possibly desire if she were not mistaken, and ire. That thought of his desiring her thrilled her as much as the sight of him surprised her earlier. A dangerous feeling to say the least.

She smiled wryly, which only served to intensify the look of desire part about him before saying, "Well, good morning, to you, Duke. What brings you to Oxford?"

"Don't try to change the subject, Grace. Don't you realize? Actually, forget that. I see you're packing for London. Good." He continued to pace the floor and as he did, ran his hands through his hair in agitation. She was pleased.

No one said anything further before Bessie arrived with the requested supplies. He relieved her maid of it all and without pause or even asking permission, bent to the task of tending to her hands.

Grace was astounded. What was he doing tending her wounds? It simply wasn't done, but she was too astonished and pleased to stop him, either. His touch was surprisingly gentle, yet sure, and she was taken aback. She just couldn't believe he was there, on his knees before her and unaware of the shocked expression she wore. Grace looked over at Bessie. Her maid didn't appear surprised in the least; she simply stood there, smiling serenely, as if his behavior weren't odd at all.

Grace hissed in a breath as he swiped over a particularly deep scrape. She refocused on the man knelt before her. He hesitated, and his shoulders tensed briefly at the sound of her indrawn breath before he relaxed and resumed his task.

She could see him clearly for he was so close, and the room was bright with morning light streaming in through the window. And she relished being able to study him uninhibitedly. This close, she could make out the tiny things. Like the shape of his ear: she had the sudden, inappropriate urge to kiss the shell. She saw the beginnings of fine lines around his eyes; he looked tired, yet intent on his task. She saw the shape of his brows and the direction of which the small hairs lay shaping his eyes. She saw his eyelashes, inky and black and far too long for a man.

He had a small, round scar on his temple, and she had yet another craving to kiss it…weird. It was odd the details you noticed in an intimate setting such as this, the minutiae you didn't see on a quick glance and the proper distance between you. And she saw him then, on a human level, as a man, real and alive. It shook her to the marrow of her bones.

Unexpectedly, he stood, startling her out of her silent study. He had finished cleaning and applying the liniment to her hand. It was not appropriate for him to see to her knees to tend to them, and they both knew it. He would leave that task to Bessie. Though she wished he wouldn't.

She stared at him standing there proud and confused. Happy and angry. Frustration surging out of every pore. Finally, he simply turned and headed for the door. "Grace, I've got to go; I'll see you in an hour. Be prepared to depart for London at that time."

Chapter 15

The Stonebridge Mansion in Mayfair, London…
The Next Evening…

Stonebridge entered his home in Mayfair, tired and dusty from his frantic ride to London from Oxford. He had not ridden to Town with Grace and Aunt Harriett despite every cell in his body desiring he do so. He knew he had to travel on ahead, at a faster pace, so he could meet with Cliff before Grace arrived in Town as she would expect delivery of the lockbox's contents upon her arrival, assuming the box did indeed belong to her father. He expected Cliff to be waiting for him; he was not disappointed.

"Your Grace, Lord Dansbury awaits you in your study," stated his butler before he had even removed his great coat.

"Thank you, Ledbetter."

"Your Grace."

He entered his office to find Cliff relaxed on one of the leather sofas, his booted feet propped on a low table before him. One arm was spread across the back of the sofa; his other rested on the arm. He held a glass of brandy in his hand. The table underfoot was scattered with papers.

He barely glanced at his seated friend before loosening his cravat and taking the chair opposite the sofa. He didn't beat around the bush.

"What did you find?"

Cliff laughed. "What? No 'How was your trip, Cliff?' 'Did you run into any trouble along the way, Cliff?'" in typical Dansbury style.

The duke just looked at Cliff, who shook his head, set his drink on the side table, and fortunately got on with it.

"Right. So what would you like to hear about first, Duke? The will naming Mr. Smythe as Miss Radclyffe's guardian—you know, the man Miss Radclyffe didn't acknowledge she knew when she and I met him in Oxford just last week? Or how about a partial copy of a formal Writ of Execution for the life of one Prime Minister Pitt the Younger from the Society for the Purification of England? The idiots. Oh, I know, how about your father's personal notes from his hunt for the would-be assassin?" Cliff smirked, his entire manner dripping with sarcasm, as he picked up a small leather-bound journal from the table before him and shook it in the air before replacing it back amidst the scattered papers.

"Damn…"

"Indeed."

"Did you read my father's journal?"

"Yes." Cliff passed him the journal. "I've marked the most interesting pages. He mentions the Society and the usual suspects involved there, but with the addition of one new name we haven't heard in connection with them before: Swindon."

"Swindon? I'll admit he holds similar views as that of the Society, but *Swindon*? He barely leaves the comfort of his own sofa. I cannot imagine a person less likely to involve himself in secret society meetings."

"All true. He's a right lazy bastard, to be sure, or a cunning one. Just consider the possibility, and he does have an estate near Stonebridge Park. Also, your father mentions our would-be assassin, Murphy, in his notes. Are we still holding him, by the by?"

"Yes, MacLeod has him. He's pretending to befriend him in order to get him to open up more."

"Good. I don't know how your father found out about Murphy; he just identifies him as the assassin. And he suspected Murphy had headed straight for Swindon's estate to convalesce from his injury."

"Well, it all fits, but it's difficult to look past Swindon's character and picture him in a role of power like this. And he would have to be in a position of power for no one to have suspected him of being involved in the Society before now."

Stonebridge relaxed down into his chair and banged his head on the back as he stared up at the coffered ceiling and tried to make sense of a world where a lazy coward could be responsible for murder.

"Yet a difficult theory to swallow, to be sure," added Dansbury.

"And this writ of execution? I suppose Swindon's signature isn't conveniently printed there amongst the others?"

"Of course not. The document appears to have been partially burned, such that at least two signatures might be missing." Cliff started laughing, though he tried to control it. "Oh, I can't help it. I'm trying very hard not to laugh at these clowns for writing up a formal document spelling out their intent to murder the prime minister. What arrogant bastards. It's a solicitor's dream come true to be sure. I'd give anything to know who the scribe was. I wonder how much they paid him off to keep quiet. Look at the detail in the stationary heading…" Cliff leaned forward to hand over the document. "It's meticulous and gold leafed on top of that."

Stonebridge didn't bother to take it, but continued staring at the ceiling. "Good. It should make it easy to track down the scribe then. An expert will be able to come up with a list of people who have the skills and not many will have that kind of talent. Not to mention that they each have their own signature style. It works to our advantage."

"I really hate to mention this, but Radclyffe was known for having this talent. It was one of the many things I learned from our Grace…Miss Radclyffe…while on our journey to Stonebridge Park."

The duke lifted his head and looked over at his friend at his mention of Grace by name. He wanted to shout: *"Yes, and what else did you discover about our Grace over the thousands of miles you traveled with her, practically alone?"* But that would have shed too much light on his inner turmoil. As it was, Cliff looked pointedly at his clenched hands. Bad enough he gave away subtle signs at every turn. And Cliff was far too observant to miss them.

Stonebridge relaxed his hands and laid his head back to ponder the ceiling again. Huh. There was a crack in the plaster and a missing piece of dental molding. After a moment while each man sat in silence, considering their own inner thoughts, he said, "I'll find out if there is someone who can verify this as Radclyffe's work while you're in Oxford."

"Oxford?"

"Yes, to speak with Mr. Smythe. You're better than I at persuading people to talk. We need to find out why he was named Miss Radclyffe's guardian and why she went to live with Swindon instead."

"Fine. It just so happens I have Mr. Smythe's direction and had promised to connect with him in future. He's moved in with his sister for now. I'll leave tomorrow afternoon."

"Smythe is not with his sister."

"He's not?"

"No. I've reinstalled him in the quarters above the bookstore for now." Stonebridge knew Cliff would question his motivation for taking care of the situation in Oxford personally. His friend didn't disappoint.

"I see. Ah, Ambrose? What are your intentions toward Miss Radclyffe? Do you care for her?"

Stonebridge sat up from his reclined position and leaned forward, elbows on his knees. He looked his friend in the eye.

"Cliff, we've been friends for a lifetime, and for all that you know better than to ask me a question you know I have no intention of answering. And—" The duke took a breath and looked down to his feet for a moment before he looked back up at Cliff with renewed conviction. "—you know how important it is that I do my duty to the dukedom. Nothing is more important. Nothing."

The duke stood and made his way to the far side of the library to pour himself a glass of brandy. There was nothing else Cliff could say to that.

Cliff did not track his movements, but rather, picked up his own drink from the table before speaking, his back to the duke. "There was another interesting item in the lockbox I have yet to mention."

Stonebridge practically dropped the decanter onto the bar. He set down the crystal stopper and waited. The crystal rolled in a semicircle until it tapped the side of the vessel with a clink.

"There was a sealed letter to Miss Radclyffe from her father."

"Go on."

"In it, Radclyffe urges her to go to Smythe and to stay away from the earl. I believe Radclyffe was frightened for her welfare, and I think Smythe might know more than we realize. It's even possible, depending on whose side we find he was on, Radcliffe was murdered for what he knew. I've never asked Grace about the circumstances surrounding her father's death."

The room was quiet for a full minute before Stonebridge resumed pouring his drink. When he could speak, he said, "Nor I. Right, then. All the more reason to make haste. Oh, and make sure you don't cross paths with Miss Radclyffe and Aunt Harriett on your way. I'll hold onto these documents until your return."

"And what am I to say to Miss Radclyffe when I do see her? She'll be expecting these items upon her arrival to Town."

"I'll leave the explanations up to you—you're the charismatic one, remember? I'm sure you'll think of something. But for now, officially, the lockbox turned out to be empty."

* * * *

The seated man shuffled his feet beneath his desk and squirmed, red faced, as he tried to suppress a cough. A cloud of smoke billowed over his shoulder and swirled about his head, making his eyes water and his lungs burn. The cloaked man standing behind him took another long draw of his cigar. The cloaked man would kill him without hesitation should he demand the man cease smoking or even suggest discomfort because of the smoke.

"We understand that Miss Radclyffe arrived at the bookstore…unexpectedly," came the gruff voice from behind him.

The seated man looked straight ahead and spoke to the emptiness before him, for he was not allowed to look upon the man standing behind.

"I-It was unexpected to be sure. B-but my man said there was nothing left for her to find; the place had been cleared of everything by the time she arrived."

"Good. However, Himself is not pleased. There are too many loose ends about for our comfort. Your job was simple: keep Miss Radclyffe in hand and under guard."

"And I am. I shall. She is here by invitation of Lady Ross, who is powerful in her own right…"

"Silence! I did not ask for excuses. Do what you must to bring her back under your control."

"O-Of course." The seated man released a sigh of relief. For a moment, he had been worried his life would end here…tonight.

"Secondly, Himself is concerned that you have not secured the duke's loyalty. I trust we will be hearing news of an engagement in the near future?"

"Absolutely, without a doubt."

"Further, to prove your loyalty, we have a new task for you, a new...problem...that needs to be resolved. Dansbury. His appearance in Oxford was most distressing to Himself. We want you to take care of it."

The seated man's relief at being spared was short lived, as a document, landed on the desk before him. The fancy lettering of the heading stood out clearly despite his watering eyes — brought on by the smoke still encircling his head, not fear, of course:

Writ of Execution

The seated man paled. Dansbury would not be an easy man to kill.

Chapter 16

London, Bond Street...
Two Days Later...

Grace exited Lady Harriett's carriage at the start of Bond Street and drank in the scene before her. As far as the eye could see, flags and bunting hung over the street—attached from the second floors of shop buildings on the left side and across to their counterpart on the right. And it wasn't just the English flags dancing about in the breeze. Flags representing all of the allied forces who fought on the continent and helped bring about the defeat of Napoleon Bonaparte just a few short weeks ago hung there as well. The flags, along with colorful lanterns, brightened the street and gave it a festive air. It was a vibrant sight to behold. Also, in the air was a sense of joy and expectancy as people anticipated the return of British troops from Toulouse and elsewhere in Europe.

Her eyes watered with pride at her fellow Englishmen and their support of their troops. And she was proud of the British troops who'd proven capable and brave.

"Did you really sell the pearls?" inquired Bessie, her chaperone for today's outing. Lady Harriett was tired from their journey and needed to rest.

"I most certainly did. They were Beatryce's, and they were fake. You know that's the only reason they gave them to me in the first place. Besides, I needed the money to purchase a new journal to replace the one Beatryce threw in the fire, so it seemed especially fitting."

They had arrived in London yesterday. Grace had sold the pearls that same day, for she had no sentimental attachment to them whatsoever. Even if she had held a fondness for the pearls, they did her no good hanging out amongst her unmentionables when she had very little money to her name. Therefore, she sold them without a second thought.

Being in London was a true stroke of good fortune. It provided her a golden opportunity to further her plans for her future, and she intended to make use of every moment of her time here doing just that. Despite the setback of her father's store being auctioned off, she put her faith in Dansbury and trusted that he would take care of everything as promised.

The Becketts were vehemently against the idea of her setting up her own fashion house, but they couldn't force her to abandon her plans, either. Besides, Oxford was far enough away to minimize the risk of scandal, but not so far away as to be too remote to earn a living dressing society's fashionable set. The Becketts just needed to get over their pretensions.

She only had a month until her birthday, and her time here was limited. She had no desire to ever be dependent upon her aunt and uncle again. Thus, over the next month, she needed to establish contacts, seek out commissions, research reputable suppliers, and eye the competition. It was a lot to do in such a short amount of time, and she had to do it all without raising suspicions. It helped that she was staying at Lady Harriett's house instead of with the Becketts.

There was little time to waste, but still, it was difficult not to stop and ogle every shop they passed. It was amazing what one could find to buy in London. Anything one might imagine could be found here. And each and every store had elaborate window displays designed to entice shoppers to enter and browse the various wares.

Bessie and Grace walked past at least ten different shops before they came upon their first clothier.

"All right, Bessie. You know the plan. Keep a vigilant eye out for Beatryce, the duke, or Aunt Mary while I question the staff. After witnessing the lengths to which Beatryce will go to stop me, we cannot be too careful. I don't want to find out just how far the Becketts are willing to go, yet I do not intend to live under their thumb for the rest of my life, either."

"Yes, miss."

* * * *

"Bessie, one more stop and we can go home. I'm that exhausted," sighed Grace as they approached Madam Beaumont's House of Fashion.

They had visited numerous shops throughout the day with little time to rest. Now, her head was swimming with facts and ideas. She was surprised they hadn't run into Beatryce at all today, for she was aware via Lady Harriett that the duke had planned to take Beatryce about Town for the day.

She forced thoughts of him from her mind. She damn well refused to be hurt by the thought of him and Beatryce together and having fun. She had accomplished too many of her goals on this outing to ruin it now by thinking of him.

Her anxiety increased as the day wore on, though; she anticipated running into Beatryce at every stop, and it was the thought of an unpleasant altercation with Beatryce that set her nerves on edge. Not the thought of running into him, of course.

As they entered the last shop, she was immediately impressed by the atmosphere. The furniture and displays were situated such that one felt compelled to browse. Yet the colors were soothing, inviting one to relax and be at ease. Even the gentleman's waiting area, though more masculine than the rest of the shop, fit in with the décor and appealed to her senses with its leather chairs and dark, wood tables, at least the parts she could see from the door.

Grace walked through the shop taking her time and noting every little detail along the way. She passed the gentlemen's waiting area without looking too closely. She was focused on the accessory display at the moment, though she'd come back to furtively look over the other on her way back through.

She was just making notes in her journal when she heard a well-known voice speak above the background sounds of the shop.

"No, I don't think you understand. I must have this dress ready by tomorrow."

Whoever responded did so quietly, so as not to draw further attention from others in the shop.

Oh, God, Beatryce is here.

Thankfully, Beatryce was in another room being measured for a new gown and couldn't know Grace was there as well.

She needed to leave. Immediately. Knowing Beatryce's behavior when she was displeased, Beatryce could suddenly step out of the dressing area at any moment just to make a scene, and if she did, she would spot Grace straight away. Then, Beatryce's suspicions would be instantly aroused, for she knew Grace had no money with which to purchase anything.

Grace backed up, afraid to take her eyes off the curtains separating her from where Beatryce was being fitted in a dressing room. She didn't want to be caught unaware in case Beatryce decided to come out.

She had only taken a few steps when she was stopped by a warm, solid barrier at her back. She shivered as a voice spoke softly in her ear.

"Grace…"

Oh God, it was him. Of course. She had forgotten he was meant to be escorting Beatryce today. Her heart pounded in her chest. She always reacted that way to his presence, and she hated it. His breath tickled her ear as he spoke her name, sending shivers down her spine. She didn't want to see him, yet at the same time, she yearned to stretch her ear a little closer to his mouth and feel the gentle press of his lips there.

God, I am going mad.

Grace whirled around before she succumbed to temptation, Beatryce momentarily forgotten. He lifted his hand, to do what she didn't know, but she didn't intend to find out.

"Don't," was all she said. She held up a finger to accentuate her warning and held his gaze so he could have no doubt she wanted him to stay away.

"Grace. What are you doing here?" He looked pointedly at the open journal in her hand as he asked the question.

She closed her journal and shoved it haphazardly in her reticule before responding, "Research."

She lifted her chin daring him to criticize her for her choices. "Dansbury has assured me he is going to take care of the problem with my shop, and I trust him completely." She had angered him with her admission. That much was obvious.

"Well, well, well, what do we have here?"

Grace cringed. Ugh. Despite all her preparations, the thing she wanted most to avoid had come to pass. Beatryce had spotted her. How could she have forgotten the true threat lurking nearby? Grace turned around to face Beatryce. She needed to keep her biggest threat in front, and for some reason, despite everything, the feel of Stonebridge at her back reassured her, like he was there to protect her from the monster she now faced rather than being the monster himself.

"Beatryce." She inclined her head in acknowledgement, but said no more. Let Beatryce be the instigator. Grace would not be the one to cause a public scene.

"What could you possibly be doing in here? Have your circumstances changed so completely since this morning?" It was a spiteful barb.

"Beatryce…" Stonebridge spoke, the warning clear in his tone.

Grace surreptitiously reached behind her and squeezed the duke's arm in a shockingly bold move. He couldn't interfere. She appreciated his defense, though she didn't know why he had done it, but she needed to face Beatryce herself, and she didn't need him risking his own reputation coming to her defense (a commoner) over his own (soon-to-be) fiancée.

Clearly, he wasn't thinking at the moment, but fortunately, he took her hint and said no more, though he still remained at her back, unconsciously demonstrating his support. She slid her hand down his arm intending to release him, but at the last minute, he grasped her hand with his. They were standing too close for anyone to see. For truth, anyone paying attention should find it odd for him to stand behind her that way, but Grace liked the feel and strength of him there too much to move away. She was emboldened further when she felt him squeeze her hand in reassurance.

"Oh, Ambrose, it's fine, dear. Grace knows I speak only out of concern. Grace, what do you have there in your bag?" Beatryce nodded her head pointedly at Grace's reticule.

Grace tried to hide her sharp intake of breath. Beatryce had noticed her new journal and was suspicious.

"Oh, it's nothing, really. Just a gift. For a friend, actually. One of the servants at Beckett house, that's all." She had to add the last even though it would give Beatryce more ammunition to belittle her. Beatryce knew she didn't have any friends other than the servants and wouldn't have believed her had she implied otherwise. Beatryce didn't disappoint.

"How provincial, friends with the servants? You certainly enjoy living on the edge of scandal, don't you, Grace?"

Grace simply stared at Beatryce. There was nothing tasteful she could think of to say to that, and she had no desire to further prod Beatryce's wrath or to stoop to her level. She just wanted to get out of there with her dignity, and her journal, intact.

Beatryce stared at Grace in return, a definite smirk curved about her lips. Beatryce was still distrustful, but then out of nowhere, her face brightened and she said, "Ambrose, dear, I think we should be off. The clientele here is particularly undesirable. Madame Beaumont, I'm cancelling my order. In the future, I suggest you take more care in who you allow to patronize your shop."

Beatryce said it all without breaking eye contact with Grace. Her look threatened further action later in private. The suddenness and ease with which Beatryce left disturbed Grace more than anything else. Beatryce had let her off easy, which could only be bad.

Beatryce took the duke's arm and made her way gracefully out the shop. Grace was relieved she was not staying at Beckett House in London now, and yet she thought frantically about where to stash her journal for a few days where Beatryce could not find it if she chose to 'visit' Grace at Lady Harriett's. Just in case.

* * * *

"I'm ready."

Stonebridge mentally (he hoped) cringed at the sound of Beatryce's voice. They were sitting in his curricle; she was impatiently waiting for him to drive on. The sound of her voice was starting to grate on his nerves. She had done nothing but complain and gossip throughout the entire day. She had nothing meaningful to say, ever, and he was at the end of his patience.

Where in the hell had the intelligent woman I witnessed back in February gone?

Perhaps that was why he had approached Grace in the shop: his control had been weakened throughout the day as he put up with Beatryce's constant haranguing, and thus, was practically nonexistent when he and Grace had crossed paths.

Well, I'm still good at making up excuses anyway.

He admitted he was jealous over Grace's trust in Cliff. She thought it was Cliff who had saved her shop and her home.

But it was I who saved your precious home, your father's shop! Me! Not him.

He had screamed the truth in his mind as he stared at Grace, willing her to hear what he couldn't say aloud. He desperately wanted to know what it felt like to be trusted by her so completely, and his jealousy over her faith in Cliff made him want to punch something. Like a child. He had wanted to tell her everything then. But hadn't. No, it was for the best she not know it was all him.

Then, there was the confrontation itself — in a public shop, no less. Beatryce, he was quickly discovering, could be a vicious piece of work, and he was supposed to marry her? When had she become the veritable shrew? He couldn't have missed that when he saw her during the little season as he was making his decision to court her, could he? He was seriously starting to question himself. Hadn't he chosen her based on facts and how perfectly suited they would be based on those facts? Were his facts wrong?

Grace, on the other hand, had acted the perfect lady, proving one couldn't breed proper behavior.

Now, he was starting to have genuine questions about the wisdom of his choice in wife — not even considering Swindon's possible involvement in the Society for the Purification of England and all the implications that came with it. Unfortunately, he wasn't really in a position to back out now, though no one would fault him if her father turned out to be a murderer and a traitor.

For now he was committed, even though he had yet to officially propose. Everyone knew, and he was beginning to think that was why Beatryce felt so comfortable revealing her true self to him now, when he had no way of gracefully backing out of his commitment without compromising his own reputation.

"Yes, quite so," he finally responded. It was all he could manage.

* * * *

Grace returned to Lady Harriett's home exhausted — mentally and physically. At the same time, she was relieved. She felt safe here.

As she walked in the front door, the butler directed her to a silver salver on a side table in the hall where a letter for her awaited. She shivered with apprehension. It wasn't likely to be Dansbury, as he had already left her a note explaining he had to leave town for a few days and would see her when he returned. That left the Becketts because she didn't know anyone else and there was no way it would be the duke. Therefore, whatever was written in that letter was likely to be unpleasant. Her anxiety increased with her every step toward the plate.

She hated being right.

Dearest Grace, my niece,

It has come to my attention that you are in London despite my express wishes forbidding it, you ungrateful child. We always knew you would be incapable of grasping the simplest concepts such as obedience and respect for your elders… especially toward those who provide for you. It has been my experience that women with common blood do not have the mental aptitude required for understanding these things — therefore, I shall strive to remember that and not punish you too harshly for what you cannot help.

With that in mind, I expect you to remove yourself from Lady Harriett's home post haste and come directly to Beckett House in London before you have further opportunity to embarrass our good family name with your disobedience and objectionable ways.

What the Duke Wants

As such, I shall expect you within an hour of receipt of this letter. Do not further disappoint me on this or the consequences will be unpleasant for you and your friends working for the Beckett Family.

Sincerely and Affectionately, Your Uncle by Law,

Lord George Beckett, Earl of Swindon

She choked back a sob, choosing instead to harness her anger and inner strength. The nerve of that judgmental, fat bastard. She ran into the library looking for paper to send off a quick note of her own. Dansbury had warned her that if she had any contact from her uncle, to notify him immediately — and if he wasn't here, to notify Stonebridge. Well, she may not want to notify His Grace, but she trusted Dansbury. And until he arrived, she would repeatedly remind herself that her racing heart was caused by anxiety over the note from her uncle and not due to anticipation of seeing the duke again.

Chapter 17

Grace was pacing the library floor, her nerves on edge, when Stonebridge arrived per her summons. She furtively wiped her clammy hands on her dress as the butler stepped aside to admit him. He looked handsome as always and was dressed to perfection—not overdone, but simple, pressed, and well-tailored. He was clearly concerned, though, and he did not hesitate; he strode across the room with long strides, and grasped her hands in his.

"Grace, I came straightaway. What has happened?"

"Dansbury said I should contact you if he wasn't here."

At his nod of agreement, she released his hands, walked over to the large library table in the center of the room, and picked up the letter from her uncle. She turned and handed it to the duke, who had followed in her wake.

"It's easier if you just read it," she said and stepped back, hands clasped behind her, as he began.

She watched him, taking advantage of his distraction to study the beauty of his face and the concern etched clearly on his brow. She watched his lips, so full and seductive, move as he mouthed the words as he read. She longed to reach up and kiss the corner of his mouth. She was overcome with awareness but chased the thought away.

When he finished, he looked up at her and searched her eyes a moment before he smiled. He was trying to reassure her with that smile, but also, she detected a hint of pride in it.

He was proud of her? She smiled in return to let him know she was fine.

"Grace, do not worry. I shall speak to your uncle today. You must remain here at Lady Harriett's house."

"But, why? Not that I'm anxious to return to Beckett House or anything. I just can't help but think something is going on. What is going on, Duke? And what of my friends in Beckett House? Are they in some sort of danger? Does this have anything to do with my father knowing your father?"

"Why would you say that?"

She chose not to answer, saying instead, "Are you forever going to be suspicious of me and of my father? I keep thinking we're moving past that, yet it seems like you are never truly letting go of your doubts."

"Grace, until I have the answers, and proof to support them, I will always be suspicious. It's why I'm good at what I do. I refuse to let my desires and feelings rule my head."

"But I want you to trust me." She shook her fist at him in frustration.

"And I want you to trust me like you do Dansbury."

She snatched back her letter, walked over to the fireplace on the far wall, and tossed the letter in. She turned back to face him—brushing her hands together as if ridding them of something foul. Again, he had followed in her wake.

"To earn trust, you first have to be trustworthy and demonstrate trust in the other person in return. Do you trust me, Duke?"

"Yes. I want to."

She heard the unspoken 'but' in that statement and wanted to stamp her foot in aggravation. Stupid, stupid man.

He stepped closer, close enough for her skirts to brush his leg.

"Don't you ever just go on instinct, Your Grace?"

He took another step, and this time she had to tilt her head back to see his face.

"Yes. In fact, my instinct, right now, is screaming for me to kiss you. Tell me, Grace, would you welcome my kiss?"

He looked at her and desire flared to life in their eyes. Their craving was mutual, and a dangerous, forbidden thing.

*

Grace nodded in answer to his question, though he would have missed it if he weren't studying her so keenly. Relief warred with warning bells in his brain. He touched her face, rubbed his thumb across the smooth satin of her cheek—he was amazed at the softness. She leaned into his hand, and that was all it took for the dam to break. He slid his hand around the back of her neck and pulled her to him as his lips swooped down and captured hers—at long last.

Their kiss was voracious at first, the culmination of desire thwarted for much too long. He arms slid down and encircled her, pulled her close—body to body. Toe to toe.

Mine.

After his initial ravenous fill, he slowed the kiss—to savor her. To know her. He kissed the corners of her mouth, one and then the other, as he had wanted to do on far too many occasions in the past. He kissed the center of her bottom lip, and lightly bit at it, and she laughed at his playfulness. That laugh, so seductive and womanly, jolted him to his boots, and he knew he could hear that laugh every single day for the rest of his life and never, ever tire of hearing it.

He touched his forehead to hers, content to stand there and be near her for the moment—pretending for a while that they were different people in a different place. A place where they could be together. Yet all too soon reality, in the form of Lady Harriett, intruded upon their idyll.

"I say, with all the carryings on in here, there's no need for the fire; might save us a bit with the coal man if you two keep that up." Lady Harriett chuckled with amusement as she barged into the library. "Now, step away from the gel, Duke, before I have to order a maid mop you up off of the floor, heh, heh. We'll have none of that going on under my roof, mind, unless you're willing to do the smart thing and put a ring on that gel's finger."

He lifted his head, but held on a moment longer. He didn't want to let go. And the thought of marrying her despite the scandal sounded much too good right now.

I really needed to get my head out of the clouds. Marriage? To Grace? Impossible. Wonderful.

Grace, having similar ideas, though probably stemming more from embarrassment, pressed her forehead to his chest for a moment more before stepping back and out of his arms. He regretted the loss. And the fullness of her skirts there to hide the evidence of his desire.

"Well come on then, Duke. Pull yourself together. Think about shoveling snow or mucking out stalls for a minute, then, when you're able, come around and give this ole gel a hug. You should have sent word you were coming by, I would have laid out coffee. I have half a mind to toss you out on your ear, boy, for not warning me. I'll make a note of it for future."

He turned fifty shades of red and did, indeed, think about mucking out filthy stalls before he was able to turn around. He didn't easily embarrass, but this was Auntie Harriett, and her good opinion meant the world to him, though he suspected she was far from disappointed. In fact, judging from the gleam twinkling in her eye, he was sure she was altogether delighted over the idea that he was in here kissing her temporary ward.

He walked over to where Aunt Harriett was standing just inside the door.

"Aunt Harriett, it's a pleasure to see you as always."

"Oh stuff it, Duke. While I know you are glad to see me, you needn't sound so formal about it. Are you planning to stay for a visit?"

He had barely opened his mouth to respond before she answered for him. "No, of course not. I know you're a busy man, but one of these days you're going to need to slow down and learn to appreciate some of the simpler things in life…mark my words. And, yes, I can anticipate your next question before you even ask it. And no, you know me better than that. I am not going to chastise Grace for kissing you in my library. She's the innocent here; you, however? Not so much."

He smiled at the woman he loved like a mother. She was one of a kind to be sure, and as much as he wanted to prove her wrong, he knew she was right. He had an earl to see. Especially now that he knew Swindon expected Grace's arrival within the next few minutes. And time was slipping away. So without much further discussion, he said his good byes and took his leave.

*

As soon as he left the room, Lady Harriett homed in on Grace, who was trying desperately to blend in with the curtains on the opposite wall. It was so easy to be overlooked at the Becketts' house — here, not so much (to use Lady Harriett's favorite turn of phrase).

Lady Harriett smiled, a mischievous look on her countenance, and said, "Now, come over here, gel, and tell me all about how you're going to snare that handsome duke for your own."

* * * *

Beckett House, London…
Later that same morning…

"I have just one more item to mention, my lord. The property in Oxford, your niece's bookshop and apartment on the High Street, has been purchased by an anonymous buyer for £1775," said Mr. Clerkson, Swindon's secretary.

"Excellent, most excellent," replied the earl, salivating over the vast sum as he rubbed his hands together in greedy anticipation of adding to his own coffers. A knock at the door prompted his secretary to rise and make ready to leave; their meeting was at an end anyway.

"Come in."

The butler opened the door at his summons and announced, "The Duke of Stonebridge, my lord," and stepped aside to allow the duke to enter. There was no question as to whether or not he was 'at home' to the duke.

"Your Grace, what a pleasant surprise. Come in, come in. Brandy? Cigar?"

"No, thank you, Swindon."

"Fine. Fine. To what do I owe this honor, Your Grace?"

"I'm here to discuss Miss Radclyffe and one final detail regarding Beatryce's settlements."

Swindon's eyes bulged out of his head.

"Your Grace." He had stood upon the duke's arrival. Now he plopped back into his chair, shaking his head in forced dismay. "I am dreadfully sorry about her. We've tried our best; honest, we have. I think it's her common blood..."

"Pray stop before you say something you will regret, Swindon. Miss Radclyffe has been a most agreeable companion to my dear friend, Lady Harriett; nevertheless, I am concerned. Lady Harriett seemed particularly distressed this morning over the idea that Miss Radclyffe was planning to remove herself from Dansbury House and spend the rest of her time in London, here—at Beckett House."

"Of course, you see, Your Grace..."

"Naturally, since I am fond of Lady Harriett—you realize she's like a mother to me—I assured her that I would handle the situation as I find the thought of her in distress most distasteful."

"Certainly, I understand, Your..."

"Further, I assured Miss Radclyffe, though she vehemently denies it was anything but her own decision to leave so abruptly, that I would see to it she could stay with Lady Harriett for the remainder of the season—with your full blessing, of course."

Damn. Stonebridge had him cornered. He could only agree to allow Grace to stay with Lady Harriett. Shite.

"Certainly, Your Grace. While I do miss my niece, she can stay with Lady Harriett for as long as she likes…with my full blessing, of course."

Stonebridge smiled and nodded his head in acknowledgement of the earl's graciousness.

"I am most pleased to hear that. I am sure both ladies will be relieved knowing you feel this way. Now, about Beatryce's dowry, I believe we have come to a general agreement over the terms; however, I have one—trifling—change I would like to see. An addition to the total cash amount. It's a negligible sum, really, but important for a project I am undertaking for a…special friend. Specifically, I would like to increase the cash portion of the dowry by…let me see, I have the figure written here. Ah, yes…£1775."

Stonebridge looked up from his notes.

Damn, damn, and damn. He knows.

His 'adjustment' was the exact amount of the purchase price of Radclyffe's shop.

And Stonebridge was no longer smiling. Shite.

"I see, Your Grace."

"Clearly, I hope."

"Well," the earl choked out after wiping at his sweating forehead with a cloth, "I shall have my solicitor draw up the final papers then, if that is all."

"Indeed, that is all. For now."

Chapter 18

Oxford...
Grace's Store...

Dansbury walked into Grace's bookstore and stopped, surprised by the work in progress. A counter was being constructed at the back of the room, and there, amidst the dust and commotion was his quarry, Mr. Smythe.

Mr. Smythe, attentive to his surroundings, noticed him immediately.

"Lord Dansbury, what a pleasant surprise. Welcome back," Smythe said with a smile as he approached Dansbury, hand outstretched for a shake. He was a much more jovial and relaxed man than the one Dansbury met with Grace in this very room not three weeks before. He had a twinkle in his eye and a wide friendly grin. Even his clothes were less ragged, though still simple and tidy.

"Mr. Smythe, it's a pleasure to see you looking so well. I admit my friend said you would be here, but I am quite surprised to find all of this—" Dansbury gestured toward the room at large. "—going on. What is going on, by the by?"

"Ah, you see, the d...er, new owner and I met briefly the last time he was here, and we discussed recreating this counter here; like it was before...for...well, before. So that's what I'm doing, making it ready, as much as it is possible, for her. I mean, the new owner's return."

"I see." And indeed, Dansbury did see. He also noticed that Mr. Smythe did not mention Miss Radclyffe nor Stonebridge by name and had looked about him quite thoroughly before speaking of it at all. Smythe was being careful.

"Yes, the new owner appears to be a generous man. Why don't we go upstairs where we can find a cup of tea and speak in private?" Mr. Smythe gestured toward the doorway at the back of the shop.

"By all means. After you," Dansbury said with a smile.

Once upstairs, Mr. Smythe directed him to a comfortable chair in a cozy drawing room. The man brought out a tray of tea and a plate filled with bread and cheese. Mrs. Smythe was not at home, so it was just the two of them.

"I apologize for the mess. We've only just taken up residence within the last week, you see. Most of the pieces here belong to Miss Radclyffe. When the earl tossed us out, I had them all stored in a barn just outside of town until I could figure out what to do with it all. Lucky for me, His Grace swooped in and sought to restore everything for Miss Radclyffe."

"I noticed, before, that you did not refer to Miss Radclyffe or Stonebridge by name when we spoke downstairs. Why not? And why are you speaking so openly of them now?"

Mr. Smythe assessed him for a moment until he seemed to come to some sort of decision.

"The duke said you might be by here, and that I can trust you. Miss Radclyffe also seemed to trust you when we met before, which carries the most weight in my book. So I'll try to be frank and hope that I am as good a judge of character as I think I am. The earl is monstrous, and there is no doubt in my mind that he has people watching this place all of the time—he has done for years."

"Did you happen to mention this to the duke?"

"No, I did not. The subject never came up. As I said before, we met only briefly and the entire discussion centered on restoring this place, better than it was before, for Miss Radclyffe."

Dansbury measured the man before him and decided to trust him. He decided that the best way to approach the man was with upfront honesty.

"Mr. Smythe, the duke and I are part of a team of agents working for the crown. We're attempting to determine the members of a secret society of Englishmen who are determined to purge England of all immigrants. They call themselves—"

"The Society for the Purification of England."

"You've heard of them."

"Yes—sanctimonious bastards that they are, I know of them. Sorry, you were saying?"

"Precisely. Hmmm, we'll come back to how you know of them in a moment. As I was saying, we believe they are responsible for attempting to murder Prime Minister Pitt the Younger in '78 and for successfully murdering the previous Duke of Stonebridge the month after. We discovered a "Writ of Execution" calling for the assassination of the Prime Minister, though it is not intact with some of the names burned away. We suspect Swindon's involvement, possibly in some capacity of power."

"That doesn't surprise me, though I have no evidence to support it."

"Yes. Well, we also know that the former duke knew John Radclyffe. I must admit, we are attempting to discern Mr. Radclyffe's involvement in all of this. We want to determine the truth and hold the men responsible accountable for their actions. So I'll ask you straight out, was Mr. Radclyffe a traitor?"

"First, I can tell you, my lord, that despite suggestions to the contrary, Mr. Radclyffe, John, was sympathetic to the Irish. I know you do not hear it in me now, but I was born in Ireland myself. Through the years I have worked to refine my accent; despite it, John took me on as his apprentice and the decision to work out my Irish accent was one I made on my own. John would never be involved in any nefarious scheme to kill anyone — for any reason. John was the kindest man I knew; the kindest man I know."

Mr. Smythe paused to take a sip of his tea. Dansbury waited patiently for him to continue, pleased that his assessment of Mr. Smythe was spot on.

Mr. Smythe continued, "I can confirm that the previous duke and John were friends. They knew each other at Oxford. And they maintained contact with each other through the years. I actually have some of their correspondence, and I feel comfortable passing that on to you before you leave today. But you must pass them on to the duke."

"Why haven't you sent them on before now?"

"Well, that, my friend, harkens back to the problem of the earl. John warned me to be overly cautious where the earl is concerned. He warned me to put Miss Radclyffe's safety first, as I'm sure you understand. And when the earl took Miss Radclyffe, against John's express wishes, I knew that as long as she was under his control, I would be risking her life if I made a wrong move. And, like I said before, this place was being watched all the time."

"But why didn't you give the duke the letters when he was here?"

"As I said, there wasn't much time, and I didn't have them in my possession at the time. They were in the barn with the rest of John's things. I have them now, though."

"So you were aware that Grace was to be under your guardianship, then?"

"Of course I knew. John and I discussed it at length before his death. Unfortunately, the earl holds a lot of power and has wealth to back it up. I know it sounds unbelievable. The man is a coward and a pig. But he's paid everyone off — it's hard to know who to trust anymore."

"So I assume when I was here before, you did not acknowledge Miss Radclyffe due to the fact that the earl's solicitor was present?"

"Exactly. I was afraid for her safety, and felt it wise to remain silent."

"Indeed, it was the right thing to do. In the past, Miss Radclyffe indicated that her father acted in the capacity of a scribe outside of his work with books—a man of some renown in these parts."

"Aahh…I know what you're getting at—you want to know if he might have scribed the Writ of Executions?"

Dansbury did not answer, but Mr. Smythe was too astute to misinterpret his line of questioning.

"No, John did not scribe them. They were the work of another man—incidentally, a previous apprentice of John's."

"And you know all this, how, exactly?"

"Because I saw both Writs. The one for the Prime Minister and the old duke."

"What?" Dansbury jumped to his feet at this admission. He was incredulous. After all his years of sleuthing and interrogations, he never expected this. He returned to his seat and waited for Mr. Smythe to continue.

"They weren't signed copies, of course. The scribe, Mr. Will Jenkins, made copies of his work—and can you blame him? I don't mean to sound like I admire the man because up until a year and a half ago, he took a bribe to keep quiet about it all. That is straight up treason, through and through. But the nature of his assignment was worrisome—who wouldn't be, right? You've been asked to put something like this in writing? I don't think Mr. Jenkins realized it would make him paranoid for the rest of his life…but that's what happened. He became fearful and unreasonable and in his attempt to protect himself, he confessed everything to John—who had been a mentor. Immediately, John changed his will and brought me in on everything. Not a month later both Mr. Jenkins and John were killed—I believe by the earl's request."

Silence followed this admission. For a few moments all one could hear was the clock ticking on the mantel and the occasional burst of noise from the work ongoing downstairs. A shiver of unease swept through Dansbury. To think of Grace being under the earl's guard…he let the thought pass. He couldn't dwell on that now. Besides, she would be safe with Ambrose in London. He needed to finish up here and get back as soon as possible.

"Do you know where the copies are now?"

"I do. We hid them, immediately. We were both too frightened to have them anywhere near at hand. I'll take you to them before you leave—they're not here, of course. I do have other paperwork of John's that may or may not have information that might help you, besides his correspondence with the duke, of course."

"Thank you, Mr. Smythe, for being so forthcoming. You have been most helpful."

* * * *

Beckett House, London…

"You wished to see me, Father."

Beatryce stood attentively just inside the door of her father's study. To say she was nervous would be an understatement. Her mouth was so dry that when she smiled, her lips caught on her teeth, making her feel awkward and embarrassed; she hated feeling that way, humiliated.

"Come in, Beatryce. Have a seat, daughter."

Her father stood while she dragged her feet across the room like a convict being led to the gallows. She kept her smile pasted on, literally, for it was impossible not to with such a dry mouth, yet she feared it looked more like a grimace to her father. She kept her hands clasped firmly behind her back—to steady them—and pressed on, confident her nerves would not betray her. She tried her damnedest to appear confident.

As she neared, she could see that while he had a smug expression on his face, her father's hair was standing on end — or what was left of it anyway — from repeatedly pulling at it or running his hands through it as he was wont to do. In addition, his neck cloth was loosened and slightly askew. He wore no coat or waistcoat — she could see both flung haphazardly across the back of his desk chair — and he stood with his arms folded above his ever-widening stomach with a riding crop tucked under his left arm. Dark circles on his shirt under both arms bore further evidence of his agitation, though excessive sweating was common for him even at the best of times. If possible, her anxiety increased ten-fold.

She sat gingerly in a club chair before his desk — desperate to look anywhere else, but too sensible to take her eyes off her father.

Her father eyed her in return with an open look of disgust upon his face, and she knew without a doubt that this interview would be unpleasant. But perhaps this time, it wouldn't turn to physical punishment.

She waited patiently for him to speak, his face growing redder by the second. Was it too much to ask for a convenient apoplexy to take his life?

"Daughter, I ask you this. Have I not raised you and given you every comfort? Every opportunity? Your every desire?"

"Yes, Papa." She knew better than to disagree, and she did have many fine things.

"Then why do you not show more gratitude by obeying me when I ask something of you? Do you not owe me? Do you not feel obliged to please me for providing for you? For giving you food and shelter and clothing?"

She knew better than to answer. No matter her response, it would be the wrong thing to say, so she sat still and attempted to look contrite yet sure, while she waited impatiently for him to continue. He would prey on her fear if he saw it.

"I've explained the facts of life to you many, many times before, yet for some inexplicable reason, you seem unable to remember these simple truths as I have illuminated them to you. If I didn't know any better, I would question whether or not you are mine. It's too late for that now, though; the world believes you are and that makes it real. So, I will remind you one more time—you are either with me, or you are against me. Period. There is no middle ground."

He began to walk around his desk. Her eyes widened with alarm. She couldn't help that as her fear escalated.

"So with that lesson fresh in your mind, do you recall what one specific task I asked of you this year?"

"Yes, Papa."

"Let me hear you repeat it, daughter." He was directly in front of her now, looking down upon her seated self. He leaned back against the desk—he was too lazy to remain standing for long—and he involuntarily grunted as the air was forced from his lungs when he did. The desk groaned ominously beneath the added load. He was breathless simply from talking and walking the short distance around his desk, so little did he get out of the house. Yet still, he was a strong man, despite the excess weight, and she was right to be scared.

Her voice was barely a whisper as she said, "I am to bring the Duke of Stonebridge u-up to scratch." She hated that her voice caught as she spoke. She wanted desperately to stand up to this man she despised, her own father, and she hated herself for being intimidated by him.

He smiled, though it came across as a grimace as if he had just stepped on a bug or in a pile of shite—certainly no joy was reflected in his beady, piggy eyes.

"Indeed. Perhaps there is hope for you yet. Your mind might not be as unstable as I have feared. At least you are listening, at any rate. However," and here he unfolded his arms and grabbed ahold of the riding crop with his hand. She was well and truly afraid now. "You have yet to bring

Stonebridge up to scratch and that leads me to believe that rather than working with me, you are working against me. I realize you are not a beauty, and anyone who tells you otherwise is outright lying to your face; however, I do not expect that to stop you from achieving our goals. Need I remind you what is at stake should you fail?"

He raised the riding crop as he said those last words, and she screamed in terror.

"Papa! No! Please don't hurt me!"

Her mind raced as she grasped for a way to break through to him. He had a manic look now; his anger was so fierce.

"You mustn't strike me. It will cause unnecessarily delays. I must be seen with the duke…to further our plans. If I am injured…" She choked on her last words, too frightened to speak further. She cowered in fear in her chair and attempted to make herself small. To offer him less of a target for his fury.

However, her father simply lowered his riding crop; sense seemed to penetrate his haze of anger.

"True. Too true. Yes, you are correct, daughter, this once. I shall let you off easy then, this time, but I'm warning you. Do whatever you must to bring about the duke's proposal, or you will dislike the consequences. For if you fail, I will have to find some other way to proceed, and you will then become completely unnecessary to me. To this family."

He threw the riding crop across the room, knocking over a vase in the corner. It shattered when it hit the floor. Her relief at having reached through to her father was short-lived. She flinched, expecting her father's wrath to return so he could blame her for the loss of the vase, but instead he looked at her, the smile on his face proving, as always, that he was completely unpredictable…or insane.

"You may be excused, daughter, but first, how about a kiss and a hug for your father?"

She stood and reached out to hug the man she loathed with every fiber of her being.

He was so large that her hands were unable to reach fully around his wide girth. He smelled sour, of onions and rotten turnips, and she struggled not to gag. She bussed him, reluctantly, on the cheek and tried again not to gag; then she pulled back to look up at him.

She masked her revulsion and drew on every ounce of inner strength. She forced a smile and appeared every inch the dutiful daughter as she said with conviction, "I shall make you proud, Papa."

She would do anything to bring the duke up to scratch. And confident her father was temporarily appeased, she turned and slowly quit the room, almost regally, yet all the while, her lip quivered with suppressed emotion.

*

The earl watched his daughter leave, satisfied she would do what was necessary to secure his future. He began to whistle, a jovial tune, as he made his way back around to his comfy chair. His whistling didn't last long, for he was already out of breath again with the effort…And he knew that, too, was somehow Beatryce's fault.

Chapter 19

Hyde Park…
The Next Day…

Dansbury returned from his 'business' trip in Oxford early the next morning, and immediately sent Grace a note asking her to accompany him on a drive about Hyde Park at the fashionable hour of five o'clock.

Now Grace was restless with anticipation as she sat on the window seat of the first floor drawing room and eagerly watched for him to arrive. She was fair bubbling over with excitement over her chance to ride in a curricle for the very first time.

He pulled up in front of Lady Harriett's house precisely during the first chime of the hour in a sleek black curricle with a pair of matching midnight horses, though one horse had a white sock on his foreleg just to be different.

And a few minutes later, as she descended the wide, marble steps of Lady Harriett's home on his arm, she discovered that though the curricle's body was completely black, it bore a contrasting white bonnet which a footman was raising into place to protect her from the sun during their drive; the effect of the opposing colors was stunning.

Dansbury, who was dressed in black and white with the exception of his waistcoat and the band about his tall hat, which were both dark blue, appeared every inch the London gentleman. She was impressed.

Initially, they drove along in silence, content to look at the scenery passing by. Grace finally broke the silence as they finished their first circuit of Hyde Park.

"Thank you for taking me on a drive today. The park is quite lovely this afternoon." It was a fine day, and she was happy to be outside enjoying it with Dansbury.

"No need to thank me, Grace, for the honor is all mine. I should probably say something like 'The Park is made lovelier by your very presence', but that just sounds a touch too cliché for me, doesn't it? Though you are lovely, by the by." He looked at her as he said this and winked. The rogue.

She smiled in return, thrilled with the compliment. "Thank you, my lord."

"Aaah...so we're back to 'my lord' now, are we?" He chuckled good-naturedly. "I shall never leave Town again if the result is that we return to the formalities whenever I do."

Grace sighed in resignation. She did try to recognize the proprieties, but today, even she was ready to set them aside. She was anxious to hear about her father's lockbox, and she was growing impatient with Dansbury for his unwillingness to introduce the subject.

Well, if he wants informal, I'll give him familiar with a side dish of bold.

"All right, Cliff, where is my father's lockbox?"

He regarded her thoughtfully for a moment—like he was taking her measure—before he faced forward again and said, "Officially? There was nothing in your father's lockbox."

He didn't look at her as he said that. Rather, he pretended to pay attention to the brake, then his driving; though his hands were loose with the ribbons and his arms were relaxed and resting on his knees. He acted as if he hadn't a care in the world—as if he didn't realize the implication behind his statement or the impact it would have on Grace.

Of course she was clever; she knew his wording was deliberate and his posture too forced.

Right, I'll play his game.

"So what, pray tell, did you *not* find in my lockbox, then, Cliff?"

Who does he think he is? The contents of that box belong to me. ME!

Cliff laughed. "Before I answer your question, I have a question of my own. How do you know Mr. Smythe? And don't pretend you don't know who I'm talking about. I didn't say anything at the time, but when we met him in Oxford, it was clear you already knew each other." He watched her for her reaction as he spoke.

She smiled. "My, you are the observant one, aren't you? Yes, it's true. I've known Mr. Smythe my entire life. He was an apprentice with my father. He's family to me."

"So why didn't you tell me at the time?"

"You asked me not to say anything, remember?"

"And after we left the bookstore?"

"I think it is safe to say that I had a few more pressing things on my mind at that point—such as…oh, I don't know…my future, or the uncertain lack thereof?" She said this not without a little bit of sarcasm.

"Sure, sure."

"Enough, Cliff. I've answered your questions. It's your turn."

"I'm thinking."

"About what?"

"About what I can or should tell you."

"Do you mean you may decide to lie?"

"If the occasion calls for it, yes. But I prefer to call it being 'judicious with the truth'. It's for your own protection, Grace. There is much more going on here than you can possibly imagine." His usually affable demeanor turned serious.

"My, you are serious. Who are you? I thought I was speaking with my friend Dansbury?"

He laughed at that, per his usual self, and the world righted. Apparently, he decided to be more forthcoming, somewhat.

"I am part of a team of agents who work for the crown. I am more than the gentleman of leisure I portray myself to be."

"And you work with the duke, I presume?"

He tipped his head in acknowledgement. "He's in charge, in fact."

"Then, perhaps it is he I should be talking to. I presume it was his decision to 'judiciously hide the truth' from me? About my lockbox, I mean?" Her curiosity was being replaced with frustration. Men and their managing ways.

"Certainly, it was his decision, as you say, but not for the reasons you might think. I can honestly say he only has your best interest at heart."

Humph. She leaned back in the curricle, arms crossed, and more than a little frustrated. She tried to calm herself, but she was a roaring mix of conflicting emotions: a little angry, a little fearful, a little intrigued…Well, perhaps, more than a little intrigued. She decided to practice patience and allow Dansbury to make whatever decision he needed to make about what to tell her.

He pulled to the side of the carriageway to allow others to go around them. She toyed with a ribbon on her reticule while she waited for him to decide what to tell her. Even the horses pranced a little in their harnesses as they awaited his next command.

At long last, he stared at her for an uncomfortable moment more before sighing in resignation and saying, "Inside your lockbox was a copy of your father's last will as well as some notes from an investigation the previous Duke of Stonebridge was working on at the time of his death."

She struggled to take her next breath. For a moment, she knew true fear. Then, she was angry. She sputtered, very ladylike. "My father…"

He held up a hand in the universal sign of "Shut up and listen a moment."

"Grace, no one suspects your father had anything to do with the duke's death."

She, having sat forward in her outrage, leaned back in her seat and crossed her arms again. "The current duke most certainly does. Do you not recall his inquisition at Stonebridge Park? The one where he all but made the same such accusations against my father?"

"I do recall, and in his defense, he had to ask the hard questions—it's his job. Do you honestly think he enjoyed it?"

"It certainly seemed that way at the time, yes."

"Trust me. I doubt he found any delight in it at all. Now, let's get back to the point, shall we? We have since confirmed that your father and the old duke were friends and had been since their time together at Oxford."

"So, the information in my lockbox, the duke's research notes, has some bearing on a case you both are involved in now?"

At his affirmative nod, she continued, "And has the information proven useful?"

"The evidence does not paint the full picture, no, and most of it is conjecture, but it does give us some direction. It's a starting point."

It all sounded quite ominous.

"So what is your motive in telling me all this? Why not just lie and say the lockbox was empty like Stonebridge commanded you to do? I would have believed you, you know. Probably."

That thought was unnerving. She certainly had an awful lot of faith in him. Was it misplaced?

"I know. I can be quite convincing even when I am being judicious with the truth." They both laughed at that. "And I had hoped that, assuming your responses to my tale were responsible and reasonable, one day in the future, should it be necessary, we might prevail upon you to assist us with our investigation."

She was quite surprised by that.

"As in…spy for you?"

"If it is required, then, perhaps."

"How…em, why me? I'm not sure I see how I could even begin to help you."

"That's because I haven't told you anything. Generally speaking, there's not a lot I can tell you at the moment; however, I will say that our inquiry centers on your uncle."

She broke eye contact and looked down at the ribbon in her hand, which had started to fray due to her fidgeting. Her hands were shaking. She feared her uncle.

But she strengthened her resolve and looked up at Dansbury; the shredded ribbon dropped to her lap, all but forgotten.

"What would you have me do?"

"Good girl," he said with respect. "For now, just be you, beautiful you. I'll let you know if or when we need your help. But in the meantime, you must steer clear of the earl."

"Done and done. Now, about my bookstore…"

"Ahhh, yes. I'm working on it; however, I can say with supreme confidence that it will be back in your possession soon enough."

She sighed dramatically before smiling and saying, "Liar."

"Grace, I mean it; you'll have your place back."

"Oh, that I don't doubt. I mean the other bit. The part about you working on it? You were lying: I could tell, but it doesn't signify. I believe the rest of it, and that's what matters, doesn't it?"

"Undoubtedly." He checked the road behind him and clucked to the horses. Their carriage moved forward with a jerk.

"Well, since we've exhausted those unpleasant subjects for the time being, why don't we continue on our ride and enjoy the rest of our afternoon? How about another pass through the park, shall we?"

"Lead on, sir."

* * * *

As Dansbury and Grace drove on, the couple failed to notice Stonebridge, across the way, watching them. Grace chattered on animatedly, while Dansbury drove, markedly enchanted by Grace's zest for life.

The duke's envy flared hot and bright. He wanted desperately to run across the street, heedless of the scandal, and carry her away. From his best friend, who he knew was an honorable man. Obviously, he restrained himself from behaving so brashly, but deep inside, his jealousy burned, making him want to scream aloud at the injustice of it all.

"Darling."

He tried not to recoil at the grating sound of Beatryce's voice as she attempted to reclaim his attention.

"Look over there. It's Dansbury and Grace out for their drive. They invited me to go, of course, to chaperone, but you know I didn't want to feel like an interloper. I think we might have a budding romance in the works—at least if Grace has anything to say about it—and I promised her I would give her a chance, if the opportunity arose, for some private time with Lord Dansbury—if you know what I mean?" She said the last with a hearty measure of innuendo.

He hoped her question was rhetorical, for he was too astounded to reply. He had always suspected something might be developing between them, but to hear it confirmed? It made him feel…lost. Bleak. He would give anything at that moment to be somewhere else, some*one* else. Never had he ever wanted to be someone else until he had met Grace Radclyffe.

Further, he had never before been envious of his best friend, but now his resentment was intense. Fortunately, Beatryce wasn't expecting a response, and she carried on talking without caring or considering whether or not he was attending. Which was fine because he couldn't respond rationally just now.

He focused on his inner turmoil and failed to notice the smug smile on Beatryce's face as she spoke. Nor did he take time to consider that after yesterday's scene in the dress shop, Grace and Beatryce were not likely to be speaking to each other, much less going on an outing together. Envy had a bad habit of polluting one's thoughts.

However, his jealousy fizzled out as quickly as it started as he homed in on a shady character standing at the narrow opening of a nearby alleyway. The man was clearly out of place and trying to be inconspicuous, but failing miserably. He was dressed like a gentleman, though his demeanor was rough, more like a hired thug than a man about Town.

The stranger looked to be haggling with a dirty street urchin, a young boy of about seven or eight, while occasionally marking the carriages as they passed. At one point, the man nodded to the boy, and they appeared to come to some sort of understanding.

The gentleman-cum-thug flashed a coin, and the boy nodded his agreement just as the older man looked up and froze, his gaze trained on something in the distance. He tilted his head toward the road as he said something to the boy, who also turned to look.

The duke followed their gaze, his intuition screaming to life as he recognized Cliff's curricle drawing near. He didn't hesitate; he leapt from his curricle and ran, ignoring Beatryce's gasp of outrage and the sounds of shock from nearby pedestrians.

He ran harder than he'd ever run in his life, his hands knifing the air as he pumped his legs faster and faster. The sound of his boot heels striking the cement throbbed in his head with each step. The guttersnipe was on the move ahead of him, running directly for the road and Cliff's oncoming curricle.

This was going to be close.

He sidestepped pedestrians and walking sticks as he sprinted down the walk. He lost his hat at his first dodge of a twirling parasol. He leapt over a trash can, a gift from a dog and one awkwardly placed park bench in his haste. He was little more than a few steps behind his quarry now, but it felt like a thousand feet and a million inanimate objects separated them.

He managed to grab ahold of the boy mere moments before he would have stepped off the pavement in front of Grace's carriage; the boy's intention had been to spook the horses.

He spun himself and the boy, putting their backs to the carriageway. It was quite easy, for the boy weighed next to nothing. He set the squirming, smelling, foul-mouthed child down, though he kept a hold on the boy's filthy shirt.

"What is your name, boy?"

The urchin stopped squirming, probably due to surprise, and answered, "John Paul Smith, milord." Then his eyes widened in fear. It was obvious he had told the truth out of habit.

He expected the boy to struggle and pull away in an attempt to escape. What he didn't expect was the boy to rush him and kick him in the shin instead. He let go in surprise.

Damn, but that kid has some nerve. I just saved his life.

It was sad, really, what the hungry would attempt for very little coin.

Stonebridge chose not to give chase. Instead, he bent over at the waist and attempted to catch his breath. He rubbed his abused shins while he felt the muscles in his thighs twitch from his exertions. It took only a moment for him to recover—he was physically fit after all—and when he could breathe normally again, he straightened, turned around, and looked up to see Cliff and Grace looking down from their ride. Grace was on her feet showing more than a little concern.

Of course, he only had eyes for Grace.

She stood above him like an ethereal fairy amidst mere mortals. Tendrils of escaped hair blew gently in the breeze, and her eyes were wide pools of blue as she gazed at him in relief and obvious thanks. She recognized the danger they had been in and his herculean efforts to see her safe. He wanted to shout with unrestrained joy to see her look upon him so favorably. He was an animal, with heightened senses and excitement pulsing through his blood.

He barely noticed the men nearby who patted him on the back in support of his heroism. At the moment, he only cared about Grace and what thoughts possessed her mind.

All too soon reality intruded. Hell, he had left Beatryce spitting mad in his own curricle a few hundred yards back, and he had completely forgotten her. It was worth her wrath, of course, and he would do it all over again even if given the chance to think about it ahead of time, but alas, he had to return to her at once.

He bowed to Grace, never once uttering a word aloud, then looked to Cliff, who as expected, kept his horses under tight control. Their silent exchange said they would discuss this later. Tonight.

Crisis momentarily adverted, he returned to his own carriage and the dragon seething within.

Chapter 20

The Russell Ball…
One week later…

Grace tried—with little success—to keep from fidgeting. Her dress was already wrinkled from her fiddling hands. It was the night of the Russell Ball—the first ball of the season and her first ball ever—and she was nervous with anticipation. She tried to turn her anxiety into enthusiasm, for these events with Lady Harriett would be her only chance to experience this side of life, and it would be a relatively short experience—over all too soon. A month from now, she would be home, in Oxford, and her time here would be but a distant memory.

This evening, she was attired in a simple yet elegant ivory dress she'd designed and made herself with the help of Bessie. She was especially thrilled to wear it as the material was of the finest quality silk she had ever beheld, much less owned. The fabric was a gift from Lady Harriett and purchased right here in London on Bond Street. She had never before owned anything so fine.

Her long tresses were drawn up into a particularly nice coif by a maid of Lady Harriett's who was skilled at dressing hair. The maid had woven a strand of pearls and sapphires into her coiffure—the jewels borrowed from Lady Harriett's vast collection of gems.

Grace also wore sapphire earrings and a matching necklace — likewise on loan from Lady Harriett — and the blue hue of the gems coordinated perfectly with the simple, blue velvet ribbon tied beneath her breasts, all of which brought out the color of her eyes. A length of ivory tatted lace from Bessie adorned the short sleeves and neckline, completing the ensemble.

She felt like Cinderella on her way to the prince's ball, and she couldn't help but imagine what Stonebridge would do when he saw her. Would he seek her out across the crowded ball room and ask her to dance? Would he compliment her on her dress, her beauty? So, perhaps she was being vain, but she couldn't help it. A part of her soul was desperate to bewitch the duke even though her head knew it was a pointless endeavor.

Dansbury arrived to escort her and Lady Harriett to the ball, promptly on time as usual, and she was satisfied by the dumbfounded look on his face when he saw her. She felt like the proverbial cat who got the cream, and her nerves relaxed in response. Now, if only the duke would be similarly awestruck.

She was a little ashamed of her prideful vanity, but she wanted badly to impress the duke, and knowing she looked fine greatly boosted her confidence and enthusiasm. It also helped ease some of her tension.

The carriage ride from Lady Harriett's house on Belgrave Square to the Russell mansion on Grosvenor Square was relatively short, and Grace wondered about their early departure. However, as they turned the corner and Grosvenor Square came into view, she saw the reason for it. The carriage line around the square was extensive. Carriages were lined horse to rear wheels on both sides of the street and around all four sides of the square. The sound of horses whinnying, horseshoes striking cobbles, drivers and footman calling out to each other, and guests gossiping as they made their way up the pavement created a cacophony of noise that echoed oddly through the square. This ball was going to be a veritable crush, and her eagerness for attending it made the wait interminable.

She peered out her window and looked about in awe at all the people, especially the ladies with their ostentatious dresses. She was not unfamiliar with the latest fashions, of course, for she was going to be a dressmaker herself, but she only ever really saw the latest evening wear by looking at fashion plates from magazines and her own charcoal drawings. Certainly, she was familiar with the limited society about Oxford, but this was London. Seeing the ladies, the crème de la crème of the ton, in all their glorious colors and sparkling gems, was an altogether different experience from the guild teas and afternoon assemblies in Oxford.

For a moment, she thought she spied a familiar face in the crowd, but then the lady turned, and it was not someone she knew. However, the incident reminded her of the possibility of encountering the Becketts at this ball, and a little of her nervousness returned. She honestly didn't know how she would react if she were to see them here. The letter from her uncle and her limited knowledge of Dansbury and Stonebridge's investigation made her edgy about what to expect. In her mind, she imagined all sorts of different scenarios: her quivering in fear from a verbal set-down by the earl to her triumphantly giving them all the cut direct before being swept away into a scandalous waltz with the duke. That particularly pleasant dream currently occupied her thoughts, but was interrupted when the carriage door was opened in front of the Russell mansion by an attending footman. All too soon Dansbury, who had stepped out first, was reaching back in to assist her.

She was surprised to see that the pavement from the street to the door was covered with a red carpet, and that a dozen torches were lined up on either side. There was a slight warm breeze that blew the little tendrils of hair about her neck and carried with it the smell of perfumed water and burning torches. It wasn't an unpleasant smell, and with the light from the numerous torches casting wavering shadows and sparkling lights from the myriad of ladies' gems, the air had a magical quality to it—which filled her with a hopeful sense of anticipation.

Once inside the main doors, her breath was stolen by the beauty and opulence of the main foyer. A glistening chandelier with hundreds of sparkling crystals and five tiers of candles hung in the two-story room that was larger than her drawing room in Oxford.

Beneath the chandelier was a large and round mahogany table upon which sat a magnificent ice sculpture of two swans intertwined and what seemed like a thousand red candles. The candles were scattered haphazardly about the table's surface. The entire foyer was black and white marble and paneled mahogany. Expensive and grandiose.

Two grand curved staircases, one on either side of the foyer, were covered with more of the same red carpeting from outside, and at the top was a long balcony that opened to the foyer below. She could see three sets of double doors, all ajar, along the back wall of the balcony that led to the ballroom. She could just make out the occasional swirl of a lady's dress through the openings. Near the middle set of doors, the hosts for tonight's fete greeted guests.

Grace could not conceive of what it must be like, living day to day with this sort of luxury, and though it was all brow-raising impressive, it also seemed like such a waste, really. So many people had so little, and yet these people seemed to have so much more than they could ever need in ten lifetimes. It left her feeling thoughtful.

The sounds above and around her were quite loud and distracting, thoroughly halting her inward reflection. Yet above the murmur of voices, she could just make out the sweet sound of a violin, and she could not stop herself from tapping her toes to the music as she waited in the receiving line that was so long it trailed down the stairs to the ground floor. She touched her hand to the brass railing, smooth and warm from the hands of so many guests, as her party made their way up the stairs. She looked everywhere, trying to take it all in while telling herself she was not looking for a certain dark-haired duke.

Twenty minutes later, Grace, Dansbury and Lady Harriett stood just over the threshold of the ballroom, taking in the scene. Several hundred people filled the room. Groups of guests stood clustered amidst dozens and dozens of potted plants around the perimeter of the room, while roughly a third danced in its center. The room was rectangular in size, with Grace and her party standing in the middle of one of the long sides. The opposite side held three sets of French doors leading to the back gardens, all of which were open to allow much needed fresh air into the room. Three chandeliers, double in size to the one in the foyer, hung from a three-storied ceiling painted with cherubs and angels. The walls were paneled, like the foyer, but this time they were painted white with gilded trim.

On the left wall of the room were more double doors leading to what promised to be a sizable buffet. Grace could scarcely take it all in.

"Dansbury, I see the Dowager Duchess of Lyme in the far corner. Take me there and then you may dance with Grace," said Lady Harriett.

As Dansbury guided them around the room, Grace was amazed at the scene about her, and yet though she looked the part, she couldn't help but feel separate—as if she didn't quite belong. This was Stonebridge and Dansbury's world, and suddenly she felt more apart from the duke than ever.

Their party reached the Dowager and her court of attendants at last.

"Eugenie," said Lady Harriett as they approached.

"Harry," said the Dowager, affectionately yet primly, "How are you?"

"I am well. Eugenie, do you recall Miss Grace Radclyffe of the Beckett Family?"

"Indeed, how could I forget?" said the Dowager as she raised her lorgnette and looked Grace over, somewhat suspiciously. She had been a front row witness to the dining disaster at Beckett House last month.

Lady Harriett, having heard about it and guessing the cause of her concern, laughed and said, "Not to worry, Eugenie, Grace does not have any prawns on her person today. Do you, my dear?"

Grace could do nothing but smile and go along with it. "Certainly not. I only toss prawns on Saturdays, Your Grace."

Lady Harriett laughed good-naturedly, though the Dowager hardly looked satisfied. Further introductions were made, and after, while Dansbury and Lady Harriett talked of the Dansbury estate in Cornwall, Grace removed herself from the conversation and turned to watch the dancing.

"Grace."

Her heart skipped a beat at the intimacy of the male voice behind her. She was relieved to turn and acknowledge Dansbury standing there with an affable grin on his face. She had known it wasn't the duke before she turned, but her nerves were stretched thin, and therefore, everything seemed manufactured to make her heart jump.

"Lord Dansbury."

"Will you honor me with your hand for this dance?"

"Of course. I would like that very much, thank you." Grace smiled. She was genuinely happy to dance with him, and without another word, she and Dansbury lined up for the cotillion.

After a while, she realized she was not plagued with her usual clumsiness, and it felt good; no, better than that—it felt great. She realized, then, that she was content, and she let her face shine.

Neither noticed the duke's jealous scowl as he watched from an alcove nearby.

* * * *

During a break in the dancing, Lady Beatryce glanced about her court of admirers and smiled behind her fan. There were a dozen young dandies vying for her attention, all of them worse gossips than any woman she knew.

One particularly young buck leaned near. "The lady dancing the cotillion with Dansbury earlier, I understand she is your cousin?"

Beatryce smiled to herself. This was going to be all too easy. She assumed a somber look before replying, "Yes, I'm afraid so."

The young fop, noticing her subdued countenance, responded all too predictably, "Is that a bad thing?"

Beatryce sighed dramatically. "No, for we love her dearly and have opened our hearts to her despite her b…" Beatryce blushed convincingly. "Well, I shouldn't say."

"Oh please, Lady Beatryce, do tell, we shan't tell a soul nor hold it against you. Your generosity is well known," said the love-sick, and lying, fool. They hung on her every word in the hopes of acquiring new gossip.

"Please see that you do then, as many would frown upon what I'm about to tell you…But, well, you see, her family was in trade." A collective gasp sounded from her circle of admirers. "And I'm afraid she has had little instruction in the art of being a lady. Now, I see you are surprised by this, yet despite how most of the ton feels about people in trade, we have opened our home to her, inviting her in when she was orphaned last year."

The dandies panted—trade? Oh, the scandal. The horror. They tried to mask their fervor for gossip by nodding solemnly at the Beckett family's obvious benevolence; however, eager eyes gave them away. Beatryce smiled and continued, "And though we've tried to give her some rudimentary instruction in proper decorum, I'm afraid she doesn't seem to understand that there are certain…things…a lady must never, ever do in order to safeguard her reputation."

The men around her salivated and leaned forward on their toes as Beatryce lowered her voice scandalously. They couldn't afford to miss a word. Their faces well-nigh shouted at her to be more specific.

One particularly bold peacock said, "For instance…" his voice trailing off for Beatryce to fill in the blank.

Beatryce wanted to thank him and kiss his feet for the lead-in. "Well, I'm sure it's because she is so kind and loving, but we cannot seem to make her realize that she cannot go off unescorted with certain…people…Men. Who are not relations, you see."

The men's eyes widened at the news, and Beatryce could practically read their wicked thoughts as they wondered who Grace was running off with unescorted, and more to the point, who they should relate the news to first.

Beatryce sighed with feigned exasperation as she looked pointedly across the room.

Right on cue, Middlebury.

"And there she goes again," she said with a nod toward the potted palms across the way. "Excuse me, while I attempt to save my cousin from herself." And before Beatryce could take another breath, the young swains scattered like cockroaches at dawn, gossip ready to slide off their wagging tongues.

Beatryce headed to the ladies' retiring room rather than make her way across the dance floor. As if she had any intention of saving her cousin. Ha!

* * * *

After her dance with Dansbury, Grace was happy to take a break and simply walk about the public rooms with him. She had yet to see any sign of Stonebridge, and by now, she was no longer looking for him through every break in the crowd.

She began to relax. This ball demonstrated a side of life she had not been a part of growing up, and she was glad to be able to experience it before her return home.

They walked into a side room where a large buffet table held every sort of delicacy imaginable, including fresh fruit imported especially for the ball. Judging from the few guests inside, it appeared that much of the food would remain untouched and probably thrown away at the end of the night. She thought of the orphans and the poor back home, and it made her somewhat ashamed to enjoy the lavishness even for a moment.

They toured the gallery before returning to the ballroom.

The extravagances on display that evening were extreme — and it was both fascinating and nauseating to witness. It disgusted her, but neither could she look away. One particular woman wore diamond rings on every finger, in her hair, around her neck, and dangling from her ears. She even had diamonds on her fan and sewn into her dress. Grace thought she likely had them sewn into her drawers as well and chuckled to herself as she thought about how uncomfortable it must be for the woman to sit.

She had barely finished that thought when two women walked by with elaborate head pieces. One appeared to have peacock feathers in her hair, enough to rival a full-grown male, while the other appeared to have an entire garden of rare orchids draping her head. She hoped the lady was not allergic to bees.

Despite her earlier eagerness to attend this ball, Grace suspected this life wasn't for her. She didn't belong. She didn't suit this life.

An hour later, she was alone watching dance after dance from a little alcove created by judiciously placed potted plants. She was content to simply watch from afar rather than participate. She had met numerous people through Lady Harriett before she managed to sneak away to her little private haven amidst the masses. Growing up in Oxford, she had never had trouble talking with customers in her father's shop or at artist guilds and teas, but here she found it difficult to think of what to say. Her brain seemed to freeze. Probably because she had little in common with these people. It might be her own insecurities, but she just couldn't relax and converse easily, which left her feeling awkward and lonely.

It wasn't a surprise she didn't 'take', and she was fine with that. She didn't want it, and besides, the ball was so much more enjoyable while observing it from her own private niche. She watched people cut each other and smile out both sides of their mouths. Without being in the midst, she could laugh at the irony and cruelty of it all without her own feelings engaged. Yet with her prospective business in designing custom clothes for women, she couldn't afford to mar her reputation either, so she did her best to steer clear of the gossip, even if she did look on with envy at the numerous couples performing the waltz, which she had not gained permission to dance.

Her musings were interrupted by a familiar voice:

"Grace, my love, what a pleasant surprise."

Lord Middlebury. Ugh. Grace cringed as she recalled their last conversation at Beckett House. How could such an innocuous statement make her feel so dirty? Unfortunately, she couldn't go so far as to publically embarrass Lady Harriett by being rude to him, so she turned with a forced smile to greet his lordship.

"Lord Middlebury, how nice to see you again." What a lie.

"The pleasure is all mine. What a waste. Hiding amongst the plants? You simply must join me for a turn about the dance floor. I've been holding this waltz open in hopes that you will favor me with your company."

Do people actually fall for that drivel?

"Excuse me?"

Zounds! Did I say that out loud?

"I said, absolutely…without…er…quibble…It means I'd be delighted, I'm sure; however, as you must know, I've not been granted permission to dance the waltz by the Almack's patronesses; therefore, I must respectfully decline." God, now she was relieved to be denied that pleasure.

Middlebury grabbed her hand and hooked it through his arm. He would not be deterred.

"Well, then, Miss Radclyffe, I am in desperate need of a breath of fresh air; it's ridiculously stuffy in here with the crush. Allow me to escort you outside as I'm sure you could do with a bit of fresh air as well. For sure, you cannot visit Russell House without viewing their extraordinary gardens."

Before she could even contemplate the wisdom of going outside with this man, he swept her out the balcony doors and onto the darkened terrace.

"Lord Middlebury, I don't think we should."

"Oh, stuff," he interrupted. "It's perfectly respectable out here. Do you see the lights scattered along the paths? Lord and Lady Russell wouldn't have bothered if they didn't want their guests to take the opportunity to explore their beautiful gardens."

He moved swiftly as he spoke, gripping her hand. She became alarmed. Despite the presence of numerous torches dotted along the garden paths, no one else appeared to be outside taking the air. She couldn't pull away without causing a scene, but what else was she supposed to do? She was unprepared for this situation. No one had told her what to do.

Lord Middlebury turned a corner and pulled her down to sit beside him on a low garden bench. He clearly knew what he was about in this garden.

"Grace, my dear, it has been my fondest desire to find a moment alone with you so we could speak privately. I can't help but remember our connection at Beckett House, and I find myself thinking of you constantly."

What in the world was he talking about? His statement seemed suggestive, as if their previous encounters had been more than what they were. She grew alarmed; she needed to put a stop to this. Now.

"Lord Middlebury."

"Oh, darling, I knew you felt the same, oh let me show you…"

His ridiculous speech was cut short as he pawed at her and kissed her. Dear Lord, this man was known as a disreputable rake, yet to her, he seemed to be acting out the scene from a bad play. Were women in London actually flattered by this nonsense? Did they actually like his advances? Ugh.

She fought him in earnest now, creating a scene be damned. And despite her alarm, she was aware enough to realize that perhaps there was a reason he seemed to be acting for an audience. She could not afford this sort of scandal.

She fought harder, with no more success. The man had eight arms and ten legs. But then suddenly, he was gone. There was nothing but air where previously there had been an over-amorous Lord Middlebury.

She blinked as she made sense of the scene before her.

Lord Middlebury was sprawled across the ground, moaning. His hand squeezed his bleeding nose. And over him stood one thoroughly enraged duke.

"I will, this once, assume you were too overcome by the lady's beauty to realize your attentions were unwelcome. I am letting you go only because I wish to keep her name from being attached to any scandal should I call you out. However, if you ever attempt any such attack on her person again, I will not hesitate to kill you where you stand."

And without waiting for a response, Stonebridge turned on his heel, lifted Grace by her elbow, and pulled her off along another path with a gruff, "Come on."

He was furious, though she didn't think it was directed at her, so she followed along, confident he wouldn't actually harm her. She was relieved and knew not to look a gift horse in the mouth.

He walked swiftly and silently, and she kept pace without attempting to converse.

They approached the rear terrace at a different direction from which she left previously. He stopped and turned to look at her.

"Grace—I…" He paused and regarded her intently. For a moment, she thought he meant to kiss her, and she would willingly accept his kiss. But instead, he shook his head and didn't kiss her.

"I went this way in case there were others along the path. I suspect…Well, never mind. You might want to make your way to the ladies' retiring room. If you make your way through these doors, you'll see a set of stairs. At the next floor, you should come out in the hall near where you want to be without having to pass through the ballroom. I'll head back up to the balcony and reenter that way. Grace…I…It will be all right."

He touched her cheek briefly before turning to head up the balcony stairs. She thanked him, but she knew he hadn't heard. Silently, she turned and made her way to the retiring room without mishap as he suggested.

* * * *

Stonebridge took a moment to straighten himself and cool his ire before reentering the ballroom. The sight of Grace in Middlebury's arms had pushed his temper to the breaking point. He was furious and needed to regain his composure. He couldn't believe he had threatened Middlebury with his life. After a few minutes, he went inside and found his friend.

"Cliff."

"Ambrose, where have you been? I've just been regaled with the most ridiculous rumors about Grace and Middlebury. It was laughable really, and I set what gossip mongers straight that I could, but well, we know how fast these things spread and we both know who is at the source of these rumors. Don't we?"

"Beatryce," he grumbled.

"Frankly, I am appalled she would do as such to her own cousin. And you're going to marry this girl? Ambrose, you and I both know these rumors aren't the least bit true. What are you going to do about it? Lady Beatryce is your fiancée."

Suddenly, he was angry. At everyone. At everything. At life. And he spoke with anger, words he really didn't believe, but he said them anyway.

"Don't I? I could easily think otherwise based on what I just witnessed in the garden, and Beatryce is not my fiancée, yet."

"If you weren't my best friend, I'd call you out right now. How can you even suggest such a thing? I really thought...never mind."

"Are you thinking? You escorted her here; therefore, it is your responsibility to keep an eye out for her welfare. She's lucky I spotted her leaving the ballroom with Middlebury."

Cliff shook his head. "Ambrose, are you doing the right thing and do you even know what that is anymore?"

He chuckled sarcastically. There were so many shades of right in this world. "What I truly believe is irrelevant. Grace is common, and I highly doubt she's the innocent she pretends. Thus, I would never marry her. I'd take her as my mistress before I'd grace her with my name. It's the way of our life and you had better get used to it. You're titled as well, or have you forgotten?"

Cliff turned at the gasp both men couldn't help but hear. Stonebridge didn't look. He couldn't. He was ashamed. As he should be. He knew Grace had heard what he said, and it galled him to realize how pathetic and cruel he had sounded. Deep down, he knew she was innocent.

And he had done it after all, shamed the Stonebridge name. And through his own actions no less. Wouldn't a true gentlemen always defend a lady? Regardless of whether or not she deserved it? His father would say yes. His father would be disappointed, but damn, these were the decisions a man had to make in his life. He couldn't marry Grace and that was that. It was a fact of life, whether it was right or not. Whether he agreed with it or not. Whether he liked it or not.

Of course, that didn't mean he had to be a jackass about it. Hell. Any man would be lucky to have her for a wife, and he knew it. But he was not any man, and the deed was done. He had said the words, and there was nothing he could do about it. He just couldn't do right by her, and it was all his own stupidity that kept fucking it up. Bloody hell.

Cliff looked at him as if he saw a stranger. "You're despicable, and right now, I'm ashamed to call you my friend." And with a look of contempt, he turned on his heel and stormed off after Grace, leaving Stonebridge with only his guilt for company.

* * * *

The Earl of Swinton entered his study long after the end of the Russell Ball, seething in frustration. His daughter was a complete failure, and he was disgusted with her. Her inability to bring Stonebridge up to scratch infuriated him. That bitch! Shite. He was going to have to force the issue.

Now that the duke was obviously suspicious, he had no qualms about using less savory tactics to push the betrothal through. The next ball would do.

He glanced down at his desk and realized with alarm that a note was attached to the desktop with a knife through the middle—driven right through his papers and into the inlaid leather top. It read:

Swindon,

Your attempt to see to the issue of Lord Dansbury was an appalling failure. You have three days.

Tick. Tock.

His fury at Beatryce was forgotten as he wet himself in fear.

Chapter 21

Arnold Polyweather's Apothecary…
Portland Place…
The next morning…

Grace stood on the pavement outside Arnold Polyweather's Apothecary on Portland Place. It was at the north end of the road and slightly out of the way from the main shopping district. This was definitely the place recommended to her by Lady Harriett's maid, as it was the right address and the correct name was written in gilt letters above the shop window. She looked at the shop's large bay, bemused by the signs plastered to the glass:

HEALING TONICS AND EXOTIC ELIXIRS — FOR ALL
MANNER OF MALIGNANT HUMOURS.

And:

WE SELL DR. HYDE'S VITAL ELIXIR — CURES BILIOUS
HEADACHES, IMPURE BLOOD, GIDDINESS, MENTAL
DEPRESSION, SKIN ERUPTIONS, PIMPLES ON THE FACE,
AND TUMOURS IN THE LEGS.

Grace laughed and walked on to the door located to the right of the window. The door was primarily glass and posted the following sign:

ARNOLD POLYWEATHER, DEALER IN TONICS, HERBS, AND PERFUMERY. PARTICULAR ATTENTION GIVEN TO THE DISPENSING OF FAMILY MEDICINES AND REPLENISHING OF MEDICINE CHESTS.

Perfect. Bessie, who was under the weather, had sent her out with explicit instructions for Mr. Polyweather on how to mix her special healing tonic.

A bell above the door jingled cheerfully as Grace entered the shop. From the counter at the back, a jolly, middle-aged fellow with brown greying hair and a thick mustache looked up from a journal and called out a good morning, presumably Mr. Polyweather.

"Good morning," she answered in reply.

The aisle from the door led directly to the back counter, and she walked down it, taking time to look about at all the miscellaneous items for sale. To her left and dividing the middle of the room were open shelves with various jars and tools for mixing compounds. Along the outer walls were shelves lined with premixed concoctions. Below the wall shelves were cabinets with hundreds of small drawers, each labeled with the various names of plants, berries, herbs and oils contained within. But the most interesting aspect of the shop were the plants and herbs hanging from the ceiling to dry, which lent the shop a strong, herbal smell. Grace breathed in deeply and detected the scents of rosemary, peppermint and lemon.

"How can I help you today, my lady?" queried Mr. Polyweather as she reached the counter.

"Oh, I'm Miss Radclyffe…just a Miss. My maid is feeling poorly and is in need of a tonic for her cough. She sent me with her special recipe in hopes that we can have the tonic made up here this morning."

"It should be no problem. Let's see what we have here, shall we?" The proprietor held out his hand for Bessie's notes.

He took the paper and perused the written instructions. His review was punctuated with the occasional "Hmmm…" and "I see…" followed lastly by "Interesting…very clever."

Mr. Polyweather looked up at her with a friendly smile.

"This should be no problem, miss, no problem at all, and I have all the ingredients on hand; it shouldn't be but a moment to put it together. Will you be waiting here or returning later?"

"I'll wait here, if you don't mind."

"No problem at all, miss. Please feel free to look around while you wait. Excuse me." He rose from his stool and began to pull out items from beneath the counter as he set to work making the tonic.

Grace wandered to the far side of the shop around the other side of open shelves, drawn by a glass display case along the far wall which appeared to hold all sorts of elaborately shaped bottles for holding perfume. She was trying desperately to determine whether or not she preferred the teal swan with gold lettering or a golden griffin with red lettering, when the bell over the door chimed announcing the arrival of another customer.

"Good morning, Your…er, my friend. Come to check on Mrs. Polyweather and the little runt, did you?"

There was a brief chuckle before the man responded, "I did indeed. I have here a soup, bread, and cheese that Cook says will put your lady to rights in no time at all."

Grace spun around, dropping her reticule as she did. It slid across the aisle until it hit another set of shelves. She knew that voice.

The duke was here? In Polyweather's Apothecary?

She edged toward the free-standing shelves dividing the room and tried to peep between the glass bottles sitting there.

"Why, thank you, Your…Sorry. Habit and all. Philomena will be pleased, very pleased."

Grace could only make out the vague shape of a tall, dark gentleman through her distorted view. Slowly and very, very carefully, she pushed bottles aside to create an opening through which she could better see the gentleman at the counter.

"How is she?"

"She is on the mend and should be back to her duties, ordering you about in no time, Your..." Mr. Polyweather cleared his throat.

Grace could see the back of the gentleman more clearly now, but his clothing did not seem to fit with what she was used to seeing Stonebridge wear. This man's clothing was loosely cut and worn. The colors were muted, brown. His boots were rough and dull, and on the counter he had set a simple woolen cap and gloves. Perhaps she was mistaken. She needed a better look to be sure. He certainly sounded like the man who invaded her dreams, but his clothing was all wrong.

"So how about the boy, John Paul? How is he working out?"

Grace was confused. If this man was Stonebridge, had Polyweather just implied that he had found the boy who tried to run out in front of Dansbury's carriage the other day? And brought him here?

"He's doing fine, fine. He's right eager to please—and smart, very smart. He'll make a fine apprentice. Right now, he's out back tending to the herbs I have growing there." Grace leaned over as far as she dared to try to peek around the shelves.

"Well, I'm glad to see he's working out. It was disheartening to see a child so desperately hungry that he'd risk his life for so little coin. I'm pleased we were able to find him and give him a chance, and I'm pleased he's smart enough to recognize the opportunity. I had a feeling about him."

"Aye...'tis sad, fer sure. If only you could save them all— eh, Duke?"

Crash...

The men turned toward the sound of shattering bottles. One of the free-standing shelves had collapsed at one end, the bottles sliding off and onto the floor. The duke walked around to the head of the aisle to see what might have caused the accident.

"Miss Radclyffe."

Her heart raced. She could see his boots out the corner of her eye as she stared down at the floor. She gathered her courage and looked up to see Stonebridge shaking his head and frowning down at her. He looked exasperated. He wasn't the only one. Well, she was overdue for an accident, after all, but why, oh, why, did it always have to be in front of this man?

She looked back down at her hands. Maybe the floor would swallow her whole so she could avoid facing him? She cringed at the sound of crushed glass as he walked across the littered floor toward her.

He squatted down and lifted her chin. "Grace, please, let me help you." He offered his hand in assistance.

She took it.

And couldn't help but stare at his bare hand as it tightened around hers. He had such large, strong, capable hands. She didn't often see them as usually they were gloved, and it surprised her how tanned they were, considering. His nails were perfectly manicured and in her mind she saw this image of him sitting, smoking a pipe (she didn't even know if he smoked) while his valet clipped his nails for him, wearing a purple paisley dressing gown. The image struck her as unbelievably funny, and she giggled. And giggled. Until she laughed so hard her stomach ached.

"What do you find so amusing, Miss Radclyffe?"

At the innocently worded question, she laughed that much harder. She couldn't stop. Tears streamed down her eyes, and still she laughed. He smiled as one does when watching another laugh with such abandon and without understanding the cause.

He helped her over the broken glass and to the back counter where Arnold Polyweather waited with a bemused smile. Her laughter was infectious.

"Do you know Miss Radclyffe, then, Your...er...Mr. Langtry?"

"I do, indeed. I will see her home Mr. Polyweather. She clearly needs a breath of fresh air, and please, send me the bill for the damages."

"What about Miss Radclyffe's order? Shall I forward it on to you?"

"No!" she blurted out between lingering chuckles.

The duke considered her a moment, then said, "I'll leave one of my men behind and he'll see to delivering it per Miss Radclyffe's instructions."

"Right. Well, good day then to you, Mr. Langtry. Miss Radclyffe, it's been a pleasure to meet you. And thank you, again, Ambrose, for the basket for my wife."

Grace stepped outside Mr. Polyweather's shop. She had finally managed, just, to stifle her mirth. She didn't see the duke's carriage; the only vehicle nearby was a nondescript one parked at the curb. It was completely black and without a crest upon its door, and both the driver and footman wore simple clothes, certainly not the duke's livery of green and silver.

Now that her sanity had, somewhat, returned, her instinct screamed for her to run—though she was torn as to whether or not her instinct wanted her to run away or into his arms.

Stonebridge must have noticed for he said, "Please, don't go. I need to talk to you."

Was she that obvious?

He looked so contrite, and even though she despised him, for surely she did, she considered hearing him out.

"Do you have time to take a ride with me?" he pressed.

"Not really. I must get back to my maid. She is ill; hence my visit to the apothecary." She gestured behind her at the shop they had just exited.

"Ah. I'll send my footman to Lady Harriett's with the tonic as soon as it is ready."

"Are these your footman? They're not wearing your standard livery."

"I'm not advertising my presence; it's…it's complicated."

Realization dawned. The ton would collectively frown if they knew he was helping out orphans the way he did. He was actually *involved*. Sure, aristos contributed vast funds to charity works and held gay balls to raise money for their pet projects. But actually seeking out an orphan who had tried to commit a crime? And then finding him meaningful employment on top of that? Never. Then, there was the fact that he went out of his way to check on a sick employee. Absolutely unheard of among his set. She wanted to admonish him for hiding this side of himself from the world—damn the consequences. Ah, but his world was ever more complex than hers, and she understood. Or tried to.

"I think it's serendipitous we met this way, Grace. I need to talk to you—to apologize—and this way," he gestured to his attire and his unmarked carriage, "I can talk to you freely without interruption, without straining our conversation as we attempt to ignore curious onlookers. If I rode about as the duke right now, we would be watched by everyone passing. All the time. I don't think either of us wants to invite their scrutiny."

It sounded so reasonable put that way, though she couldn't help but feel he might also be somewhat ashamed to be seen with her. Or perhaps not ashamed per se, but he certainly he didn't want to advertise her presence and jeopardize his plans…for marrying Beatryce.

Her reproving thoughts increased her confidence. She didn't want a man who couldn't face public scrutiny if what he wanted wasn't 'acceptable' by people who shouldn't matter anyway. Then again, if she heard him correctly earlier, he had rescued an orphan boy and gave him an opportunity to get off the streets rather than haul him to the magistrate for his attempted crime. Argh! But this man was complicated. Fine. She would hear him out. Let him say what he wanted; it wouldn't affect her future. She wouldn't let it.

"Fine." She brushed past him, nose in the air, and stopped before the carriage door.

He smiled ruefully as she settled in his carriage. She ignored it. And as he left to charge his footman with the task of delivering Bessie's tonic, she sat calmly in the carriage awaiting his return. She didn't feel nervous anymore, even though they would be alone. Righteousness was on her side, and it gave her the confidence she previously lacked. She knew where she stood with him; he had made that perfectly clear in the past.

She even thought she knew what he was going to say, but she would hear him out anyway even though he didn't really deserve it.

A moment later, he climbed inside, interrupting her sanctimonious thoughts. His presence dominated the small space and her heartbeat increased its pace, unsettling her newfound composure.

Many called her a 'Long Meg' due to her above average height, but now, she felt tiny and feminine next to his larger frame. After a few moments of adjustment, he settled in the seat across from her; then he tapped on the roof, and the carriage took off.

For a while, neither of them said a word. She looked out the window to enjoy the sights of London, but all the time, she was aware of his regard. After a few moments, he relaxed. He stretched his legs across the space between the seats and crossed his booted feet at the ankles. He folded his arms behind his head as he reclined against the back of his seat. He looked thoughtful now. She knew this because she was watching him from the corner of her eye, and it made her less confident of what to expect from him after all. Her nervousness increased as time passed, and still, he did not speak. Then finally, after what seemed an eternity, he said, "I like you, Grace, and you like me, too—despite what I've said and done in the past." He held up his hand to forestall her interruption, preventing her from unleashing her fury upon his head. "I apologize for my boorish behavior—all of it. I've been ungentlemanly." That was an understatement.

"I won't offer excuses for my behavior, though many come to mind. My actions are inexcusable. You are intelligent and know as well as I we can't be more than friends; perhaps not even that. It's the way of our world whether we like it or not. However, I find I cannot bear being at odds with you and I do enjoy your company. So, I am hoping that today, we can simply enjoy the day together as I attempt to make reparations—perhaps we could even cease being the commoner and the duke and simply be Grace and Ambrose. Just a man and a woman."

She nodded in understanding as he spoke, and when he finished, she remained outwardly calm, though inside her mind raced. He spoke truthfully. She did understand the way of the world, though she was saddened by its reality. And a small part of her wished he would defy convention and stand proudly beside her and declare her his. But he had been right earlier; the public scrutiny would mar this beautiful day and undermine what could be a wonderful time together. Perhaps their only time together.

She knew what her future held. She would become a shop owner, and probably before that, a seamstress until she could save the money to start her business. Her life would not be easy, but she would be happy and free to chart her own course.

One day she might even find a nice man in the country to marry and have children with, though she would not make her plans with that possibility in mind. However, she also knew that what she could experience with the duke was a once in a lifetime opportunity that would never come her way again.

He desired her, that much was plain, and she desired him in return. So, even though it would only be temporary and he didn't really deserve her consideration, she agreed to a truce — if only to suspend reality for a single day.

She looked him squarely in the eye now that she was certain. He smiled in return.

"What would you like to do today, Grace? Have you seen London from the Thames?"

* * * *

Grace gripped her seat as the carriage turned onto Oxford Street. She bounced with elation. For the first time ever, she was headed to Drury Lane to attend the theater, and she could barely contain her excitement.

The entire day had been filled with wonder. She and Ambrose (she could no longer think of him as the duke or Stonebridge) had spent the entire day touring London, and what an adventure it had been: from taking a boat up the River Thames all the way to Covent Garden, to viewing the annual exhibition at the Royal Academy of Art.

She mused over every detail, for it had been perfect. Her thoughts were scattered in her excitement, flitting about from one remembered event to another at random: Ambrose picking a flower for her in St. James Garden, Ambrose helping out a little boy set upon by bullies, sharing an ice from Gunter's Tea Shop on Berkeley Square (from within the carriage of course)…And all the while, they laughed and enjoyed just being in each other's company — as friends of a sort — content to enjoy life and disregard reality if only for a moment. During their time together, she saw a side of him he allowed few to witness, and it felt good. Wonderfully, beautifully good.

Now, she was dressed plainly in anticipation of attending

the Theatre Royal. They planned to forgo his box, and to continue their charade, were dressed as commoners. Their carriage slowed as it made its way to Russell Street (only a peer could enter via the main entrance on Catherine).

"Ready?" he asked.

"Definitely."

* * * *

Inside the theater, they took their seats on a bench at the back of the ground floor viewing area. Grace's eyes were wide with wonder as she took in the gas-lit chandeliers and three floors of box seats filled with members of the ton — watching and being seen. Her fingers gripped the bench beneath her; she fairly hummed with excitement.

Stonebridge had been here many times before, though never from this vantage point. Regardless, all he could do was watch her as she took in everything around her. He was content to simply see her eyes alight with delight at all she saw. She was marvelous, witty, and kind, and he had enjoyed every minute of their day together. He was smitten. And in trouble. But he refused to consider that their time together was almost at an end. The night wasn't over... yet.

The gaslights dimmed in signal for the play to begin, all but wreathing them in total darkness. The cacophony of sounds from the crowd dulled to a low murmur as the players took to the boards. The orchestra ceased tuning their instruments. Occasionally, the quiet was punctuated by shuffling feet as people sought vacant seats.

The intimacy of their situation became palpable despite the crowd — or perhaps because of it. They were forced close together now, to make room for others on the narrow benches... forced to touch... to feel...

Before long, the sounds of *The Tempest* portrayed with such feeling on stage added an element of passion to the air. They were sitting so close, such that every movement, no matter how small, was felt acutely by the other.

The brush of her arm became a caress…

Her whispered comment became a kiss…

By intermission, his blood burned in his veins.

His cock hardened painfully in his breeches as her leg pressed snugly alongside his. He shifted to try to lessen his discomfort, to no avail. Every move she made became another touch of seduction. He could no longer stand it. He gripped her hand, and leaned across to whisper in her ear.

"Grace, this is too much. I'm very nearly unmanned here."

He pulled back to look in her eyes. Despite the dimness of their surroundings, he could see her eyes were as dark and as filled with passion as his. She, too, had noticed the charge in the air.

"Ambrose…We can leave, if you'd like," she responded, breathlessly, to his implied query. He felt her eyes devour his lips.

"I wouldn't like for you to miss your first play," he responded like the idiot he was. Like a man whose blood no longer flowed to his brain. Was he trying to convince her not to leave?

She pressed her fingers to his lips. "I-I want to go, Ambrose," she whispered.

She was serious! Yes! Without wasting another moment, he pulled her to a stand and guided her down the aisle and out the door.

* * * *

Once outside, they stood within the colonnade on Russell Street as they awaited a hired hack. They were hidden in a corner, the gaslights not quite able to pierce the darkness there. She was drawn to the warmth of his body and leaned back against him as they waited. She could feel his warmth through her cloak, inviting her to relax. She still felt chilled in front, though, and the opposing sensations made her edgy as her senses heightened with expectancy.

She felt him shift at her back before he leaned over and blew gently in her ear.

What was he doing?

He placed a gentle kiss there, and she shivered at his tender touch. Oh, that.

He chuckled softly before he proceeded to trail gentle kisses down the side of her neck and along the top of her shoulder. She laid her head on her other shoulder to allow him better access while his hands slid around her waist to pull her further into his embrace. They had a few minutes to kill before their conveyance arrived.

* * * *

They rode in unnerved silence. The atmosphere was charged and heated despite the chill night air. The sounds of the carriage wheels and the horses clopping over the cobbles punctuated by the occasional outburst from the London nightlife seemed surreal — part of another world outside their own. Inside, his senses were heightened with expectation. He was jittery with anticipation, his passion having built to a fevered pitch starting from the moment they first met.

They didn't touch, despite his intense desire to do so. The ride would be too short and the carriage was too cramped. Besides, he relished how the interminable wait sharpened his desire.

However, after a few more turns along various side streets, the hush became too much for either to bear, and he turned to her just as she turned to him:

"Ambrose…"

"Grace…"

They chuckled at their simultaneous words, and as their laughter died, searched each other's face to read the signs of desire.

Through recent experience, he had gained enough sense to

refrain from speaking further, thereby spoiling the moment. Instead, he raised his hand to touch her face. He was gentle. She was warm and oh, so soft. He cupped her cheek, and she leaned into his palm in return. She closed her eyes as he slid his hand down to caress her neck. He studied the progression, and her involuntary response. She moaned softly, and he was completely and utterly in awe. He looked up and searched her eyes, which had opened and rejoiced when he saw her desire so plainly apparent. And then the dam broke.

Chapter 22

Grace returned his kiss with all the passion in her soul. She was exposed and vulnerable to him now. A full day of stimulation and laughter had worn down her defenses. She was honest, though, and admitted that she had left her propriety at home from the beginning. From the moment she stepped inside his carriage this morning, she knew where this day would lead. She had gone along anyway, knowing it was futile to resist her last chance to be with Ambrose. Perhaps that was the real reason for her excitement earlier? Not the chance to attend the theater, but her chance to be with him intimately.

Their carriage slowed to a stop, but she was blissfully unaware of that fact. After a few minutes, though, the carriage rocked as a footman climbed down from his perch. John Coachman knocked on the carriage door, bringing her back down to earth.

They touched their heads together as they sought to reign in their emotions. As her breathing slowed, Grace pulled back to look at Ambrose. His desire for her was writ plainly across his handsome face, and she reveled in it.

"Grace, this is my home—well, one of my homes. It's just a small place I use occasionally when I need to get away from the dukedom and all it entails. We would have complete privacy here…"

She cut off what was sure to be a long-winded explanation. He was nervous, poor man. She pressed her lips to his, and smiled at the sweetness driving his sudden discomfort. She knew he struggled for the right words. She put him out of his misery. "It's all right, Ambrose. I would love to go inside."

Inside, she stared at Ambrose, relieved to finally be able to look him over at her leisure. Unguarded. Thoroughly. He was beautiful in his plain clothes with no fancy togs to distract the eye. Her desire climbed a step higher. He had already removed his boots and coat, and it made him appear more virile, more obviously male, now that she could see the hardness of his body clearly defined in the light and without the extra layers of clothes to hide what lay beneath.

She closed the distance between them as her curiosity compelled her to move. She wanted to initiate first contact to prove her acceptance of what they would do. She didn't want to approach this night as a victim, vulnerable to his desires. She wanted him to see and remember her as an equal this night—equal in desire, equally capable to take what she wanted. What she needed.

He reached out at her approach, but she forestalled him with a raised hand.

"Don't. Move."

The order in her demand was unquestionable.

She ran her hands up his chest and steadfastly unbuttoned his shirt, relieved he wore no cravat with which to inhibit the unveiling of his chest.

She saw that her boldness set fire to his desire. Hers had been ratcheting up in unhurried degrees. She wanted to take it slow, but his eyes blazed with passion and she lost a little bit of her own control.

He fisted his hands as he fought for command, but she was determined to take the lead.

*

Grace finished unmooring the last button of his shirt letting it gape open, naturally, to his sides. Then, she slid her fingertips up his abdominal wall, trailing her thumbs though the arrow of hair that ran from his navel and disappeared into his trousers. His muscles hardened at her contact. Each of her fingers sent a bolt of lightning through his body everywhere they touched making his heart thunder in his chest.

Breathe.

She flattened her hands on his chest and pushed up toward his shoulders. When her hands rubbed over his nipples, they beaded in response. He had never known them to react thus, and he gritted his teeth that much harder. It would kill him, but he would stand still and let her do this. It was important he let her do this.

She placed a gentle kiss on one distended peak.

And his control nearly snapped.

Breathe.

She pushed his shirt off his shoulders, and it fell, but stopped short of the floor as the sleeves caught on his hands. She walked around him, slowly, looking over every inch of his body as she did. He had never been more aroused in his damn life. One of her hands remained in contact with his skin the entire time, trailing about his waist as she moved. She paused behind him, then yanked his shirt the rest of the way free, discarding it where it landed. The buttons at his wrists were ripped from the fabric and bounced a few times before settling on the floor. He wasn't going to survive this unscathed.

Breathe.

She ignored the orphaned buttons as she continued her circular path. Her questing hand still followed, dipping dangerously close to his buttocks before reaching his side. Every one of his muscles tensed in anticipation of her touch as she circled back around to his front.

She paused only a moment before she knelt and began to unbutton the placket of his breeches.

Ah, sweet Mary, mother of God.

He was harder than stone and wanted to beg for relief. His cock was so swollen it pushed against the front of his trousers, making it difficult to undo the buttons.

But they came loose anyway for she was determined, his sweet, indomitable Grace.

And finally, as the last button was unfettered, his cock sprang free with welcome respite.

Aaahhh, sweet, blessed relief.

*

His prick bobbed a few times, and her eyes widened at the sight. She gripped his thighs to steady herself. His shaft was long, hard and dark, with a prominent vein running its length. The bulbous head flared like a mushroom cap, and it looked soft and shiny in the firelight. She wanted to touch it. She needed to touch it.

She ran her finger over the smoothness of the head before circling the hole at the tip and was surprised to find the pearly wetness there. She felt the softness of the flared edge, before continuing down the shaft — tracing the vein as she went.

Ambrose sucked in a sharp breath, and she was distracted by the sound. She looked up, gauging his response. His hands were fisted so tightly his knuckles were white, and his eyes were squeezed closed. A muscle in his jaw twitched from the pressure of him clenching his teeth. She didn't think he was in pain — her touch had been too soft — so she determined he was possessed of a desire so strong he almost couldn't control it.

She grinned with satisfaction, then, returned to her perusal of his manhood. She patted his hip in understanding. He would be fine.

She gripped his shaft, her fingers barely meeting around its circumference, and was surprised at the feel of steel beneath the velvety skin, such a contradiction in texture. She gripped firmly and slid her hand down to the base, drawing forth a low moan from her man.

"God, Grace, I am about to explode. Unless you want a close-up view of my seed, you had best stop."

He actually looked at the ceiling as he spoke. And she smiled and almost laughed out loud at the sight. The thought of witnessing his 'seed' pricked her curiosity, but she could see he was struggling with his control, and she knew there was more to experience first. Maybe she could see it later.

She felt powerful. A goddess in control of this man.

She inhaled and caught a whiff of his unique, male musk. Without thinking about what she was doing, she leaned forward and pressed a kiss in the wiry hair next to his shaft. Her nose buried, she inhaled deeply his unique scent, and felt a curious splurge of wetness between her legs in response.

She leaned back, looked up, and was distracted by the sight of him standing there— his chest bared and his legs spread wide, his cock jutting out from the opening of his trousers and surrounded by his dark, male hair. He looked magnificent. Commanding. All man. And for the moment, he was all hers.

He finally looked down at her after perusing the ceiling again. What was he thinking when he beseeched the heavens? His eyes were ablaze; his stare intense. *Ah.* She knew. He was at the end of his rope, and she smiled as she recognized her effect on his self-control.

"It's my turn." His voice was gruff and shook with emotion.

He knelt before her and pulled her hands from his thighs. Then he pushed her to the floor and straddled her legs. His hard shaft lay across her still-clothed belly. She could just feel the kiss of its erotic caress. The thought of it inflamed her, and she reached down to touch him again, but he caught her hands. He leaned forward and pushed them over her head, holding them to the floor. Cheek to cheek, now. Breast to breast. She liked the feel of it. She was his prisoner. Out of control, now, herself.

"Grace, let down your hair." His voice was soft, his breath warm in her ear. Her skin tingled all over in response, but he just freed her hands.

*

She pulled at her pins, those that remained anyway, as he unbuttoned her dress. His hands caressed every inch of her skin as it was revealed to his sight. She was dressed plainly, thus, the buttons were in front and he could see her body being exposed to him in stages, as each fastener left its mooring. One button. Two. Now, three and four. Pale, smooth skin was exposed one button at a time.

She wore a corset and no chemise. And a drop of liquid leaked from his cock at the sight. The corset was simple, white, and unadorned, and the most tantalizing thing he had ever seen. Her breasts were pushed high and he wanted nothing more than to bury his face and worship them. Maybe thrust his aching shaft between them. He groaned at the thought and his cock twitched in agreement.

He was relieved to see the corset tied in front, rather than with laces at the back. He would be able to bare her completely without leaving his enjoyable position on the floor.

As soon as he reached the last button at her waist, he tackled the ties on her corset. Her breasts spread outward as they were relieved of their tight confines. He reached up and pulled them completely free of their cage, enjoying the sight of her nipples—swollen and distended, their rosy color begging for his touch. He touched.

One hand kneaded her left breast as his lips sought out the hardened nipple of the other. He held her breast in position for his tongue as he licked her everywhere but her nipple. She moaned and twisted in torment. Finally, unhurriedly he sucked the tip into his mouth.

Grace bucked off the floor, and he smiled at her responsiveness, her passion, her fire. And after paying sufficient homage to both breasts, he blew on each nipple to ensure their continued stand. He returned to the ties of her corset. Her nipples remained tight and peaked. Taunting him as he worked to unwrap her body.

Once he bared her completely, he paused to take in the sight. She took his breath away. And at that moment, he was the most fortunate man on earth.

Breathe.

He moved down her body and planted tender kisses along the way, and he could tell she had to stifle the urge to giggle. Good. He was delighted at her ticklish response to his touch. He kissed her hip and delighted when her flesh prickled in response.

He stuttered to a halt when he reached her woman's mound. She had removed her underthings before they went out as if she knew where this night would lead. He was humbled and honored with her gift. Her plan. He wouldn't waste it. He leaned in and inhaled, taking in her sweet, feminine smell. And he nearly lost control. Again. It was as if her scent was created for him alone. It fired his blood. Embedded itself in his brain, destined to remain for eternity. Tied to his soul.

He could smell her arousal, and he simply had to taste.

He slid his shoulders under her so she straddled his head, his face centered at her feminine core. He didn't take a light taste. No. He dove right in and licked the petals of her sex before plunging his tongue into her tight channel.

She screamed her pleasure.

She tasted of honey and cream, and heaven and everything he had ever wanted in his whole damn life. He sought more. He found the pearl of her clitoris and began alternately tonguing and sucking it with furious intent while his fingers claimed her wetness below.

Ah, hell. Who had time to breathe?

*

Grace squirmed and clamped her knees to either side of his head, the sensation of his tongue and swirling fingers overwhelming. She tried to relax, but gave up that quest as futile. Instead, she reached forward and gripped his head making it clear he stopped upon pain of death.

He was so quickly there, his face buried between her legs; she didn't have time to process his intentions before she was shaking with pleasure. She could never have imagined this scenario before, and she had no time to consider if it was proper now. She didn't care. It felt too good, and before she knew it, every muscle in her body tensed with restrained energy. On instinct, she sought the sensation. It hovered out of reach, something she knew to reach for. Heat gathered in her feet and hands, like they were dipped in molten fire. Then, the dam burst and her body exploded, all the built-up energy shooting out from her center.

She screamed again as she thrashed in uncontained frenzy. Her channel contracting. Her cream gushing. Ambrose suckled her bud until her tremors subsided and her screams and moans turned to little whimpers of pleasure.

Goodness gracious. What was that? And why wasn't everyone doing this all the time?

He sat back and she looked up at him through eyes she could barely open. She was languid and relaxed. But he didn't stay still for long. He all but tore his trousers from his body. Then, returned in a rush and centered himself over her, ready to join with her without delay.

He put his weight on one arm and reached down to position his iron cock at her entrance. He guided the tip. She shook both with anticipation and the aftershocks of her release. But he stopped and instead reached down to pinch the base of his penis; his face contorted in pain. His eyes squeezed shut.

"Are you all right? Ambrose?"

"Yes, sweet, I'm fine. I just need. A moment. Or it will be over before I begin."

A moment more passed as she waited expectantly. Yes. It wasn't over. His cock was still turgid and long. Dark purple and swollen. A mighty tool designed for her pleasure. She could tell by the look on his face that he was unsatisfied and needing more.

He opened his eyes and unerringly sought out her own. His own softened for just a moment. "This might hurt, darling. But I will endeavor to be gentle."

He caressed her face. Soothed her. And she nodded her head in acceptance. He kissed her once on the tip of her nose, then he reached down, grabbed his cock with his hand, and pushed in to her still pulsing sheath. He pushed on and on and on. Until he was entirely seated, thick and full in her.

She stiffened for just a moment at the intrusion. The pain wasn't bad, only a light pinch. She looked at Ambrose. He was laboriously still, his eyes clinched and she wondered at his pause.

"Are we finished?"

Ambrose let loose a burst of laughter. "Oh God, Grace, hardly. I was just giving you…and me…a moment to adjust."

She laughed in return, though with undisguised relief, before leaning up to whisper in his ear, "If you don't move now, I will not be responsible for my actions."

That was all it took. He pulled back and thrust forward, deep. She watched his cock moving in and out, the sight erogenous to behold. Then, she could hold herself up no longer, and she fell back to the rug with a moan.

He grabbed her hips and pounded into her. He gave her everything he had. She took it all.

"Grace. Oh, hell, Grace!" He roared her name. Thrusting. Thrusting. Thrusting. She felt his shaft harden even further as he pistoned in and out. Out and in. On and on and on.

She gripped his waist with her legs and held on, powerless to do anything else but let him ride. The pleasure was intense, and she felt that energy building inside again, but now, she knew what was coming and she reached for it. It was upon her without warning, and the pause just before release seemed to last an eternity before she detonated and cried out in ecstasy.

Ambrose stiffened above her, and with one final thrust, the head of his cock brushed her womb as his seed exploded from his cock.

"Grace, I'm coming. Oh, God, I'm coming. Grace." He roared her name again and again as he pumped on while he bathed her insides with his seed. She felt the heat of it scorch her. Brand her. Claim her. She held on and cherished his gift.

Later, he rested his head against hers, as she wrapped her arms around his. They were both slick with perspiration, and for the moment, content in each other's arms.

They might have dozed. Who knew? It was Grace who finally broke the silence. "That was wonderful. Tha…"

He interrupted her when he stood and carefully lifted her from the floor. His face was intent upon his course. He set her down and turned her toward the foot of the bed. She followed his unspoken lead, trusting him completely.

He pushed down on her back and bent her forward at the waist before he leaned over and whispered, "Grace, my sweet. You speak too soon. I'm not nearly finished with you, love."

He placed both her hands on the foot board and squeezed them to indicate she retain her grip before he slid his hands down her arms, down her sides, and gripped her hips.

"Now, love, you had better hold on." And he plowed into her from behind.

Chapter 23

Grace burrowed deep into her covers. She was in her room at Lady Harriett's. Ambrose had driven her home before dawn. She grinned from ear to ear as she remembered how they had lingered at the rear garden gate for several minutes, groping and kissing playfully, each loath to part.

Now, the sun was shining brightly through the plain cotton curtains in her room, beckoning her to awaken from her dreams…and such delicious dreams they were, too. She grinned widely, eyes still closed, as she recalled one or two touching memories from last night. She wasn't quite ready to awaken and let them go.

Beatryce had always referred to Ambrose as somewhat aloof, stuffy, and boring—Ha! Ambrose had loved her thoroughly all night long. He was a wild, virile man beneath his polished exterior—someone, she realized, few people had ever been privileged to meet.

Sometimes, their bodies came together furiously with heated passion, while at others, they met hesitantly, lovingly, slowly…By the end of the night, Ambrose had called her many precious names: love, sweeting, darling…and it was clear from the many times she looked into his eyes, that he cared for her on some deeper level than either of them had previously thought possible. He had even suggested, quite clearly to her mind, that he had never before experienced passion such as they had shared.

Grace stretched in her bed, her arms extended above her head, her feet pointed toward the footboard. She arched her back—she felt like a woman, strong and powerful. Finally, she relaxed her stretch and opened her eyes. She had to get up and face the new day.

Today was her 21st birthday, and it felt like a positive beginning of a new chapter in life. She had much to do, a meeting with her solicitor being the priority. She had told Ambrose she was not going to attend the Lyndhurst Ball tonight with Lady Harriett, and it was the truth, though secretly, she hoped to make it in the end. It depended greatly on getting her affairs in order today, therefore, there was no hope to it—she must get going and save her remembrances for later.

An hour later, Grace bounced merrily down the stairs feeling more carefree than she had in over a year. As she reached the last several stairs, she was surprised to see Dansbury in the foyer handing his hat, gloves, and overcoat to the butler.

"Ah, Grace," he said upon noticing her on the stairs, "you're just the woman I was coming to see. How are you?"

Dansbury approached, his arms outstretched in greeting, and she blushed with guilt. It was unexpected and irrational, yet she couldn't help but fear that Dansbury would be able to guess immediately what had happened last night, as if the word "wanton" was branded across her forehead as clearly as the nose on her face. And she remembered that he held some small amount of affection for her. She felt like she had betrayed him, though they had no understanding.

She shook off the sensation, for it was absurd.

"I am fine, Cliff. How are you?"

"Excellent—now. Might I have a word?" And he gestured with his arm toward the ground floor drawing room where they might have a few words in private.

She preceded him into the well lit room—for it had a grand bay window facing the street, and the curtains were pulled fully back to allow in the maximum amount of sunlight.

They crossed the room and sat together on a settee facing the window. He took her hands in his.

"I've come to ask an important favor of you."

"Of course, go on."

"Remember our conversation a week and a half ago, about your uncle?"

"Of course."

"Well, I have it on good authority that the family will be out for the morning at Lady Jersey's garden party and breakfast. I also understand that one of your friends on the staff, Janet, traveled here with the Becketts from Sussex."

"Probably."

"Good. I was wondering if you would like to visit Janet, and see how she is doing—perhaps have her introduce you to the staff."

"I see. And where will you be while all this is going on?"

He just looked at her, baffled, as if she had said something utterly nonsensical.

"So what you are really saying, is that you want me to distract the staff while you search the house."

Dansbury's, surprisingly, looked chagrined, but only for a moment.

"You must understand, Grace. I realize this is highly irregular, but the situation is grave and time is of the essence."

He was serious. All traces of his normal good humor vanished. His face was grim, and she became nervous in response. She knew he was keeping something from her, but she didn't know what. All she knew was that this was important—perhaps, though it seemed crazy to think so, important to her own future. "Of course, I'll do it. Anything to help."

Dansbury relaxed, relief evident upon his face. "Excellent. We leave now."

* * * *

The Earl of Swindon's Study…
Earlier that morning…

"Your Grace, welcome to my home. Thank you for attending so promptly."

Stonebridge studied him from the doorway for a moment before he strode across the room. Confident and sure.

"Swindon."

Swindon was about to offer the duke a drink, but stopped short as he took note of the duke's concentrated demeanor.

Stonebridge took a seat in a chair facing his desk, not bothering to wait for the standard courtesies or an invitation to do so. He crossed his legs and rested both his arms on the sides of the chair. Clearly, he was ready to get on with it. Fine. All right. Sure.

Stonebridge did not look relaxed by any means, but rather, he appeared forcibly composed. Yet beneath the surface, Swindon could sense the duke humming with a fierce, predatory energy.

Swindon knew he had to proceed with caution, but at the same time, he had to be firm, for his life was in danger. Fortunately, society and the law were on his side. He mopped his brow with his handkerchief, cleared his throat, clasped his hands behind his back to hide their shaking, and began to pace behind his desk.

"With all due respect, Your Grace, I must be frank this afternoon. It has been four months since you requested permission to court my daughter."

He paused and peeked at the duke to determine if there was any change in his demeanor at the audacity of his words. Stonebridge had his jaw clenched, judging by the muscle ticking in his cheek, and his hands were balled into fists over the arms of the chair, but his gaze was focused on one of the windows behind the desk, and he uttered not a word in response. Concluding it was still safe to continue…

"We…" He paused to mop his head again. His gaze caught on the sliced leather of his desktop left from the knife embedded there previously. He mopped his profusely sweating brow again; fear for his life emboldened him to continue.

"We have reached a mutual agreement as to the terms and both our solicitors have approved the stipulations of the contract. Further, society is aware of and has tacitly approved the match."

Again, he paused to gauge the duke's reaction and to catch his breath. This time he waited a few more minutes. Stonebridge tore his gaze from the window and looked directly at him, but did nothing more than raise one brow, encouraging him to get to the point.

His point came out in a rush. "So, in light of that, I asked you here to tell you I expect an announcement at the Lyndhurst Ball tonight."

*

Bold move, Swindon.

"Indeed," was all he said out loud.

Stonebridge returned his attention to the window; he watched as droplets of water pelted the glass then joined seemingly random trails of water running down the panes. He was caught for the moment, in his own watery trail, of his own making no less, unable to do anything but go along with the flow. For the moment.

"Excellent. I've already taken the liberty of sending the betrothal announcement to the papers; it shall appear in the morning edition. I presume you would like to see Beatryce now?"

* * * *

Beckett House…
Later…

Grace sat in the drawing room of the Becketts' town house and calmly drank her tea. It was all a façade. In reality, she was a nervous wreck. Every carriage that sounded on the street outside made her jump, thinking the family had returned. She half expected her uncle to barge into the room at any minute and accuse her of some crime. Of which she was guilty.

Janet seemed to be aware of the situation…or something. Hence the unusual sight of the staff chatting it up in the drawing room. Grace had fully expected to greet everyone in the kitchen, but Janet had insisted they do it here. Two footmen stood on either side of the window—each taking turns to glance outside—probably watching for the Becketts' return.

She wondered what Dansbury was doing now. Searching the library? The study? She wondered if he had planned to search the drawing room—for what she wasn't sure, but that would be impossible now with the staff gathered here. Perhaps she could do it, look for anything out of place.

Junk littered every available surface—knickknacks and the like. It was quite surprisingly cluttered—probably an attempt to show off their wealth. She set her tea cup down on the low coffee table and looked about.

Hmmm…Where to start?

She was exhilarated to be helping Dansbury and Stonebridge.

Just thinking the duke's name heated her cheeks as memories from their evening together threatened to flood her mind. She shook off her recollections and forced herself to look carefully about the room—choosing to begin with a curio cabinet on the far wall.

She maneuvered her way across the room and laughed when she realized that apart from meeting everyone initially, the staff were content to talk excitedly amongst themselves. No one paid her any mind. Having a break from their duties by tacit approval from a relative — at least that's what Janet had told them — seemed to raise their spirits, and they were happy to take advantage of the break.

Twenty minutes later, Grace reseated herself on the settee. She was frustrated. She had found nothing suggesting even a hint of scandal — not a single clue. Not that she really expected to find anything, but for a moment, she daydreamt of finding the key that solved the investigation for her duke. Oh — how exciting that would be.

Alas, it was not meant to be. She hoped Dansbury was having more success. Grace rested her arm on the settee — determined to relax as she gave up on her quest — when she inadvertently knocked her hand against a carved wooden box on the side table next to her. She picked it up, curious now, and looked it over, for it didn't move far when she hit it, suggesting it was much heavier than it appeared.

She brushed her fingers along the carvings and turned the box in the light coming from the windows in order to get a better look at the carvings all around it. It was while looking over the box's top that she noticed that the center medallion on the lid had been burned with a symbol — one she had seen somewhere before, she just couldn't place it.

It might be nothing; it might be everything. To be sure, she looked about the room, then hastily stuffed the box in her reticule. She would give it to Dansbury later.

* * * *

The Lyndhurst Ball…
That evening…

The path to his future had never looked so bleak.

265

Stonebridge leaned casually against a column on the balcony overlooking the ballroom; his calm demeanor was only a disguise, for inside, his mind was churning. He watched the dancing couples below; the swirling colors of the ladies' gowns seemed too fantastic to be real. He shook his head, but it was no use. He had felt outside himself since his meeting with Swindon this morning. He was still no further in uncovering the truth of the earl's involvement in his father's murder, and the clock was ticking. Tick. Tock.

He needed to resolve the case before he married Beatryce. Or at least, absolve Swindon if he was innocent—which seemed less and less likely every day.

Then, there was the marriage itself. He didn't want to marry Beatryce any longer; she wasn't a particularly nice person, and he was quickly finding out that a person's character was more valuable than one's blood lines or betrothal property. How could he have overlooked something so obvious? And what could he even do to change his course now? If he broke his betrothal without just cause, his honor and reputation would be compromised—hell, his entire livelihood would be compromised and many people depended upon his livelihood. His tenants at the Park; his staff.

And what if Swindon was found guilty? Sure, the ton would consider that just cause to break the betrothal, but was it honorable to abandon Beatryce in her time of need? Sure, she did seem to be somewhat conniving, but he was quite positive she was innocent of her father's wrongdoings. Should she suffer for her father's actions? Should Adelaide, Lady Swindon, and the others? And they would suffer. They would lose everything, possibly even end up in a work house if he dropped Beatryce once the scandal hit.

So no matter how he looked at it, marrying Beatryce was the only decent thing for him to do. But wouldn't marrying Grace be noble too? Oh, what torment to see two rights, two paths, yet knowing that choosing one over the other would always be wrong, regardless of which path he chose.

Aaaah, Grace.

He had stopped by to see her after his meeting with Swindon, but she was out. After that, he tried to catch up with Cliff—to no avail either, though later in the day, his friend sent over a vague note about a box and the suggestion that he was being followed. That piece of news had thrown some recent accidents involving Cliff in a more sinister light. He was concerned for his friend, who said he'd fill him in later, yet still all he really wanted to do was gather Grace in his arms and take her away. Far away. Where society and liars and murderous earls couldn't touch her. Or him.

Damn. His future was out of control and his time was out.

Swindon had been shockingly bold this afternoon, pushing the limits of rudeness and disrespect. He had allowed the man to get away with it. Perhaps it was his own feelings of guilt that stayed his tongue.

For the past month, he felt he hadn't been able to do anything right; everything he did, every decision he made or action he took, seemed destined to make a muck of his plans and his life. Of course, it never appeared so at the time.

And then there was Grace…

Ah—hell, he couldn't go there. Not tonight of all nights. He couldn't allow his memories of his time with her to be tainted by the reality happening today. And he couldn't let her go. Thank God she wasn't going to be here. He had had no chance to talk with her about anything…to prepare her…to explain why things must continue on the path laid before them—at least for now, possibly forever. What he wanted seemed to be irrelevant.

* * * *

Grace entered the brightly colored ball room floating on a cloud of air. She was blissfully happy. The day had gone perfectly—better than she had expected, in fact. Dansbury was pleased with the box she found; he said it was significant. Plus, she learnt from her solicitors that she had her shop back, returned to her — and one hundred percent completely hers — by some anonymous benefactor who she suspected was Dansbury, though she had no proof. She had more money available than she had anticipated, set aside in a secret account the solicitors had managed to keep hidden from her uncle, and they had reinvested the funds wisely. The money produced enough of a return that she could open her shop sooner than she had thought possible.

Then, there was Ambrose, the prominent reason for her happiness.

Oh, her future looked bright. In fact, she was so excited, she managed to stop by a ready-made clothing shop and find a suitable and stunning gown to wear to tonight's ball.

It had required minimal alterations to fit her to perfection. It was serendipitous.

Ding...Ding...Ding...Ding...Ding...

Someone chimed a glass in the distance; it was an attempt by the host to get everyone's attention.

"Ladies and gentleman, may I have your attention, please?"

Grace looked to the balcony above the ballroom to see Lord Lyndhurst speaking to the crowd, but her eye was drawn to and held captive by Ambrose, standing to his right.

Goodness. He was a sight to behold. So handsome. So fine. He was all she could see. All she wanted to see.

Lord Lyndhurst continued, "My dear friend the Duke of Stonebridge has an announcement to make, and my wife has probably fainted with excitement that he chose her ball with which to do it."

The crowd laughed at Lord Lyndhurst's witticism. He stepped back so Ambrose could take his place.

A prickle of unease crept up her spine. Butterflies fluttered about in her stomach, making her feel queasy and ill. Her heart began to race and her senses became acute. The noise in the room hurt her ears. She tried to tune it out so she could hear what he had to say.

He stepped to the edge of the balcony, and that was when she noticed Beatryce, her arm through his, standing and smiling by his side.

Oh, God, no!

Her heart beat louder, almost drowning out the sound of his voice. Her hands became clammy, and she rubbed them on her gown to dry them.

"Friends and acquaintances, it pleases me for you to be the first to know Lady Beatryce Beckett has graciously agreed to become my wife. Behold. The future Duchess of Stonebridge."

He raised both hands toward Beatryce to direct every eye toward his betrothed and then clapped along with the crowd, a false smile on his face. A liar's smile. His actions seemed peculiarly demonstrative for his aloof nature. But then who really knew what was in his black heart?

The sounds of cheers and riotous clapping commenced amongst the multitude of people. She shut it all out. All she could do was stare at the man she loved as the room and everything about her faded to gray. She imagined this was what it would feel like to be shot, for her heart, which had been racing furiously before, seemed to have stopped beating altogether. She didn't even notice the tears streaming down her face; she was overcome with shock.

Abruptly, he faced forward again and looked directly at her, and the previous suspension of reality ceased, and with a quick flip of a switch, life returned to normal. Though not. Everything became loud and confusing. Here was an alternate reality she did not want to live in. His gaze pierced the gloom around her and jolted her heart. For a brief moment, pain seemed to flash across his eyes. He was a liar and a cold-hearted bastard. And she was a lovesick fool. The noise from the crowd reached a crescendo, and she was compelled to flee its torturous cacophony.

*

Oh God, Grace is here…

If he could have leapt over the balcony and survived to chase after her, he would have done so, though he didn't know what he could possibly say. Despite the rudeness of the action, he pushed through the crowd of well-wishers to chase after her anyway. Many patted his back as he ran, and he was indeed running, but he ignored them all; he was determined to catch her.

He gambled she had headed toward the rear garden; it was the closest escape route available to her based on where she was standing when he first noticed her there. He wasn't sure what he would say; it seemed ridiculous to even try; perhaps, even better that way. It didn't matter; he was compelled to seek her out.

He raced across the crowded ballroom floor and out the back doors. He randomly chose a garden footpath and headed down it, his boots crunching on the gravel beneath his feet. He hoped he had chosen the right path.

He caught up with her just as she was about to exit a rear garden gate.

"Grace. Stop!"

She froze at the sound of his voice. For some unknown reason, she stayed. She turned to face him, her chin held high, and he was proud of her fortitude.

He could see she was crying; she didn't try to hide it. She had every right to be angry and upset, but his fury at the unfairness of life seized control of his thoughts and shredded what remained of sound reasoning. He was cruel when he finally spoke. He spoke from pain, not sense. Logic had long since flown the coop.

"How did you think this was going to end, Grace? With a ring on your finger and a wedding at St. George's?"

She squared her shoulders and stood up to his cruel words. God, she was beautiful. A goddess. A light in his world of darkness.

"Contrary to what you might think, Your Grace, I had no expectations of how this would end, at all. However, I was under the mistaken impression that you were not a coward. You, with all your power and privilege, could have anything you want. At the very least, you could have found a way to speak to me today. After last night, yes, I admit, I had thought there might be a possibility…" She stopped and shook her head. She laughed to herself, a self-deprecating laugh he hated to hear at the moment. She said something else instead. "I had thought you were a real man." She looked him up and down. "I see I was mistaken." Then she turned to leave.

Cliff stood behind her, and it was clear that he was beyond furious. He gave her a brief, reassuring smile, though, before confronting him.

"Name your seconds."

"Cliff, no," interrupted Grace, "I know he deserves it, but I won't allow this."

"He's not worth your concern."

"Then, relax with the knowledge that it's not him I'm concerned about. I don't want to be embroiled in the scandal. I don't want my name linked with his in any way. At all. Don't you see? I have a future planned. I am on my own. And my future would be threatened by this humiliation."

She had become a good little liar. They could all see the truth on her face. She was miserable.

"All right, but wait for me, will you? I shall see you safely home."

"Yes. I'll wait."

He winked at her. To him, Cliff continued, "I am going to abide by the lady's wishes, for now, but I don't want to see you approach her — ever — again."

Cliff turned to leave but stopped and looked back once more. "And we are no longer friends. You disgust me."

He had lost. Despair had embedded her talons deep into his very soul.

Chapter 24

Grace cried herself to sleep last night. She cried until exhaustion claimed her. Then she bawled all over again in the morning the minute reality intruded on her mind. Like a thief it stole her happiness. She was hopeless. Lost.

Bessie brought a full pot of chocolate to her bed, knowing she was too upset to face Lady Harriett in the breakfast room. But even chocolate could not soothe her wounded soul.

Once she was all cried out again, she dressed and headed out to the gardens. She hoped the fresh air would help. She had no more tears to give.

She sat alone on a bench out back, hiding amidst the roses. Her thoughts were too troubled to be calmed by the beauty surrounding her, for in addition to overwhelming grief, she was ashamed. Her aunt and uncle, Beatryce even, had not been terribly pleasant over the past year, but they had given her a place to live, even though they didn't have to. And what had she done in return? She'd had amorous congress with Beatryce's fiancé.

What kind of person did that make her? Shameless? Untrustworthy? Yes and yes. Certainly she had behaved no better than her spiteful relatives. She had no excuse. Even though she was in love with him.

God, I love him! And it hurts. Oh, God, it hurts.

The pain squeezed her heart. It pierced her with every beat. She cried all over again, deep, gasping sobs. Her muscles ached from the involuntary contractions involved in sobbing so hard.

She was quieter now, though her breath was still shaky. And the back of her throat ached from her silent screams. She was starting to get a hold of herself and was finally coming to terms with the fact that life moved on regardless of how she felt. She thought on the unfairness of that universal truth.

In fact, she was too caught up in her distressed thoughts to note the light tread on the path behind her.

Lady Beatryce had come to call.

"Well, I'm glad he scratched his itch before we married. It wouldn't have done to have him pining over you and wondering how good it might have been *after* we married."

Grace could hardly credit the malicious tone and hurtful words spewing from Beatryce's mouth. She couldn't imagine speaking so to a perfect stranger, much less her own family. Despite what they might have done. Did she deserve it? Perhaps. She had betrayed Beatryce, after all. Tears silently fell as she acknowledged her guilt in all this, but she did not turn to look at her cousin.

Then, another more disconcerting thought entered her mind. *How could she possibly know?*

"I am sure you're wondering how I could possibly know." Beatryce let out an exasperated sigh, as if she were speaking to an ignorant child. "Dear, dear, Grace. How easily you forget. Ambrose is going to be my husband. We've known each other for many years, Ambrose and I, and we wouldn't be getting married if we weren't close. If we didn't share confidences. He tells me everything, you know."

Grace was mortified. How could she have been blind to the true character of the man to whom she gave her innocence? How could she have been so completely fooled by his devilish smile? She felt gullible and used.

"I should hate you for what you've done. Have you no shame? He is my betrothed."

She couldn't fault Beatryce for the sentiment. It had bothered her before, and somehow, God, she didn't know how, but somehow, she had managed to block that out of her mind in the end.

She was completely humiliated, yet Beatryce continued.

"But Grace, dear, I love you despite all that, and for that reason, I am prepared to forgive you your betrayal. However, I expect as a gesture of apology on your part that you seek immediately to dispel any further thoughts of opening your shop in Oxford, lest I make it known your disgrace."

Now that was something she could not do. In her shame, she had yet to face Beatryce; she had her back to Beatryce, in fact. But she squared her shoulders in defense. She would still do what she must despite her cousin's threats. She had to; she had no other choice.

Beatryce must have noticed the hardening of her shoulders and spine for she laughed, an insincere, patronizing laugh, before continuing. "You think I didn't know? You think I actually believed the falsehoods you handed me in the dress shop? You've been scheming to embarrass us again, and I have to ask what we've done that you would seek to destroy our family's standing in society so completely?"

Grace bristled in indignation. She stood and turned, having gathered the shattered pieces of her self-esteem enough to face Beatryce. "You must be incredibly self-centered to think my plans have anything to do with you. This is my life I'm planning. My only hope for a future, and despite what you think you know about my actions and despite your ridiculous threats, I intend to follow through with my plans."

Clap…Clap…Clap…Clap…

Grace whirled around to the welcome sight of Dansbury walking up the garden path.

"Bravo, my dear Grace, bravo. It's so good to hear you stand up to that bitch at long last."

He reached her side and bussed her gently on the cheek before redirecting his attention to Beatryce.

"Run along now, Beatryce, you've spewed enough hate for today." And with a dismissive wave directed at Beatryce, returned his interest to Grace.

Beatryce was speechless. That much was clear, but she didn't gainsay the marquess. Instead, she turned on her heel without so much as a word and marched back to the house, her head held high.

"Grace, darling, let's sit, shall we?"

Cliff was all kindness and smiles now that they were alone. He guided her to her vacated seat on the garden bench. She was relieved to have him by her side. He was strength, while her swinging emotions left her weary.

"Are you all right?" he inquired, obvious concern writ plainly across his face.

"I'll be fine, thank you, Dansbury."

And she would be fine. Eventually. It would be a lie to say she was fine now, though she was better with his timely arrival.

"Well, at least we haven't reverted back to the formalities."

She laughed in spite of it all, happy he was trying to cheer her up with his humor.

"Grace, I hate to bring up anything unpleasant, but I couldn't help overhearing Beatryce. She wasn't exactly subtle or quiet. You must know, despite Stonebridge's ungentlemanly actions of late, he would never have spoken to Beatryce of you. They aren't as close as she would have you believe."

"But how does she know?"

"I'm sure she followed you out of the ballroom, as I did. You and Ambrose weren't exactly inconspicuous in the Lyndhurst Gardens."

"You're probably right, I know, and thanks."

She didn't know, not really, but if he believed it, then perhaps she should consider that he might know better, though it was much easier to believe Beatryce's hateful words.

"Grace, you have nothing...nothing...of which to be ashamed. And yes, I realize, fully, what has happened between you and Ambrose. And no, he never spoke to me about it either. He wouldn't, even if I hadn't told him I was no longer his friend. He's much too private a person to reveal himself that way. I know him."

"Cliff," she interrupted with a light grasp to his arm, "I know you mean well, but please don't patronize me. I did do wrong, and I am ashamed. Regardless of how you or I feel about Beatryce, I knew she was nearly engaged to him, and therefore, it was a betrayal, regardless of the kind of person she is."

She looked at her hands, twisting nervously now in her lap as she sought to regain some little bit of composure.

Cliff reached beneath her chin and tilted her face.

"I'm not sure what's left to say then except that I truly don't believe you have a dishonorable bone in your beautiful body, and I hope you come to terms with what's happened without being too hard on yourself."

He turned to face her more squarely now and reached down to grasp both of her hands before continuing, "Grace. I honestly didn't come here to speak about Ambrose, and I'm sorry to have been witness, again, to your private conversation. I promise not to speak of it again. I hope you know that I have enjoyed our time together, and over our brief acquaintance, I've come to care for you."

She was surprised by the sudden turn in their conversation. It almost sounded as if he had wanted to add "as a friend" at the end of that statement, but had intentionally left it off. She was nervous now and somewhat fearful of what he was going to say. Her abused emotions could not handle anything else.

"Grace, I believe we suit each other well, and I know, God, I know, the timing is not ideal. However, I suspect you'll be leaving soon and so time is against me at the moment, but I was wondering…" He smoothly slid off the bench and knelt beside her. "Will you do me the honor of becoming my wife?"

Goodness. His proposal was completely unexpected. She was not horrified, for she knew Cliff well enough to realize he was asking out of affection and not pity. He was right, though; the timing was poor and they were out of it. Time, that is.

"Cliff, please do get up, you'll ruin your trousers," she admonished, but with a gracious grin.

As he resumed his seat, a forthcoming smile on his face, she continued, "Oh, Cliff, your timing is atrocious. You are one of my dearest friends, and I have so very few to my name. However, I think of you like a brother, and even if I did not, I am not a fickle woman. Despite the horrible things Ambrose has done, I can't simply shut off my feelings like a switch. I— oh, God, I love him. And I hate the fact that I do. And I wouldn't have him even if he changed his mind, but I do love him, and it will be quite a while before I will be able to move past that and consider another suit. I hope you're not too terribly disappointed. I would rather not hurt you after you have been so good to me."

"Love, it's fine, and I understand. I do. I'm saddened, but I shall recover, and I, too, know you more for a friend than for some undying love. I thought perhaps it, love, if you will, could grow in time, and we are well suited. Please promise me this, though: should an unfortunate event occur as a result of your time with Ambrose, you won't hesitate to contact me, will you? I would be there for you, Grace, and my offer would still stand."

A child? She hadn't even considered the possibility since their falling out. She shoved it aside to worry about later.

"I know, and I thank you, truly. Oh, how I wish I could be in love with you, Cliff. How much easier it would be."

He chuckled at that. She knew he wasn't devastated by her rejection.

"Grace, if you need anything, anything at all…"

"Anything?"

"At all," he confirmed.

"Well, then, might I borrow your traveling carriage?"

* * * *

An hour later…

Stonebridge spurred his horse through town on his way to Belgrave Square. He desperately needed to see Grace—to talk to her—despite her justifiable anger and Cliff's warnings against him doing so. He travelled through the mews directly to Lady Harriett's private stables rather than to the front door.

As he walked up the alley beside Lady Harriett's house, he picked up his pace. The need to make haste intensified in his gut and spurred him on.

He turned the corner of the house in time to see Cliff's travelling carriage leave the front of the house—with Grace inside. He darted forward with a shout. She looked back in his direction, obviously spied him coming, but did not acknowledge him. Instead, she waved one last time to Cliff, who stood on the pavement in front of Lady Harriett's house, then faced forward and out of his life.

He ran right into the street, heedless of the traffic and hollered, "Look at me! Grace, look back at me!" beseeching her to look back through the rear carriage window. He heard Cliff approaching with anger in every step, but he refused to break eye contact with her carriage. Had she looked back, even once, he would have found his horse and raced after her.

"Grace, dammit, don't give up on me!"

Unbelievably, he was crying as he shouted after her. She never looked back.

An explosive ring sounded in his head. The pain of her leaving without acknowledging him felt like a shot to the heart, and then he looked down and noticed the blood spreading across his shirt, surprised to realize that he had, in actuality, been shot.

Literally shot in the middle of the street.

He looked at Cliff with disbelief in his eyes. "I think that was meant for you."

Chapter 25

"She's gone."

Stonebridge was about to take a sip of his whisky when he heard those words. He froze, his whisky glass elevated just out of reach of his lips. He was in his bed, convalescing. Still. And he stayed that way, frozen with his glass raised, long enough to tamp down the desperate flash of pain caused by those words. He looked up to stare down his ex-best friend, Clifford Ross, who bore that painful news. There was no need to ask who she was.

He took a moment more to glare at the man standing before him before tossing back the contents of his glass in one swallow. Of course, he knew she was gone. He was there, dammit. He saw her leave with his own disbelieving eyes.

"You look like hell, Duke."

He set down his glass and ran his good hand through his bed-mussed hair and then down his face. He felt the scratch of two-day-old stubble on his chin. He knew he looked like shite; no words were required to acknowledge it.

"What day is it?" he choked out. His voice was hoarse and scratchy, probably from loudly cursing Grace and himself to Hades—primarily himself—numerous times over the last couple of days.

"Thursday. I understand you haven't been sober since you woke up last week. You're one lucky bastard, you know. I hear the shot went clean through. Though your shoulder might give you trouble the next time you take up fencing."

"Checking up on me, old man? It appears I have a butler to fire. And I thought we were no longer friends."

"We're not, but old habits die hard. And we still have a job to do, if you'll remember. I care for her too, you know."

"I know."

"She's a remarkable woman."

"I know."

"You're a right jackass."

"I know."

"Well, I'm glad we got that straight."

A few uncomfortable moments passed as each man grappled with their emotions—anger being the predominate mood. Stonebridge finally broke the silence.

"So, are you going to tell me more, or did you just stop by to give me hell for old time's sake?"

"She left with her maid, Bessie, and everything she owned, with no intention of returning. Ever. She stood up to your fiancée, quite admirably I must say. Then she graciously thanked Lady Harriett for inviting her to London and left without looking back. That part you know."

"Good for her."

Another uncomfortable silence passed as he considered everything Cliff said. Then Cliff dropped the news guaranteed to get a much stronger reaction out of him:

"I asked her to marry me."

He threw his glass into the fireplace, shattering it. Grace and Cliff wedded. Just a hint in that direction brought forth pure rage. His heart thundered in his chest, the sound so loud in his ears he was fearful he might not hear Cliff's next words. He needed to hear them. He needed to know. He was impatient to know.

"Spit it out, man."

"What?"

"Did. She. Accept?" He could barely contain his anger as he spat out the words between clenched teeth. What else could he possibly want to know? Cliff could be damned obtuse at times. His glass was gone; he would be after Cliff's neck next. And he was angry enough to overcome the twinge in his shoulder to do it.

"Of course not. Would I be here if she had? You need to get a hold of yourself and use your brain for a change, Ambrose."

He couldn't help but feel relieved, even though it was ridiculous, considering the circumstances.

"Oh, and another thing. Beatryce threatened Grace. I heard it all. I suggest you keep a tight leash on your fiancée. She's a vindictive bitch, and I don't trust her not to make Grace's life hell."

It said a lot that he didn't care in the slightest about the slur to Beatryce's name. In fact, he even nodded in agreement as Cliff spoke. Even he knew, now, that Beatryce was all Cliff claimed and more. The knowledge that he had no way to separate his future from hers left him bitter. Though she wouldn't know it, he would protect Grace for the rest of his life.

"You may depend upon it," was all he said.

"Good. And I'll have you know, I will hold you personally responsible if Beatryce ruins Grace in any way," threatened Cliff.

"Damn, you must really care for her."

"I may not love her, but I do care for her, and I would joyfully marry her and spend my life trying to make her happy if she would have me, but her heart is otherwise engaged—though she hates the man and genuinely hopes to never see his sorry hide again. I can't say I blame her for the sentiment."

He thought the sun had peaked out and shone on him and him alone.

She loves me?

Just touching the edge of that thought made the room seem brighter, his future look promising. And horses could fly and pigs could sing.

Grace would be happy in her new life. She would probably marry a nice man and have children of her own one day, while he would live the rest of his life in misery with the spiteful witch, Beatryce. The reality of his future burned like acid in his chest and he rubbed at it with his hand.

It was then that he realized the full extent of all he'd lost, and how deeply Cliff's words sliced his soul. He knew she was forever out of his reach, and he knew how much he had lost because of it. Life with Grace would have been filled with joy and peace. She was smart, witty, and compassionate. His future was bleak.

"We've got another problem."

He looked at his friend, bleary eyed and weary.

"Did you happen to read your betrothal announcement? It was in this morning's paper."

"No. Why would I want to read that rubbish?"

"You should have. It is quite informative. It seems you are to be married in one week's time."

He spat out a curse. "A week? Is he mad?"

Cliff would normally have laughed at this point, but he didn't. Evidence that he, too, was still quite angry. "I did some investigating and it seems that your wonderful future father-in-law and your kindly fiancée are spreading some interesting rumors about. They suggest you have reason to marry in haste, if you catch my meaning."

"Good, God! I never."

"Oh, I'm sure." Cliff laughed, some of his usual good humor returned.

Stonebridge pulled at the ends of his tousled hair. "Damn, but I have to do something. We've got to have a break in this case soon. I'm convinced the investigation is what is prompting Swindon to be so bold. We must be on to something."

"Well, there is the box that Grace found."

"What do you mean, the box that Grace found?"

Cliff told him about his search of Beckett House the day of the ball, initially leaving out Grace's involvement.

"And how did you manage this search, during the day, with the servants wandering about?" he asked, anger dripping from every syllable.

"Grace."

Cliff never saw it coming. Stonebridge exploded from his bed and tackled him to the floor.

"How *dare* you put Grace's life in danger that way! Do you know they are watching that house every minute of every day?" he roared.

Cliff pushed Stonebridge aside; it was easy to do since he had not yet recovered from his wounds.

Cliff stood, brushed himself off, but left his friend on the floor.

"Who are you? I don't believe I know this emotional, rash man on the floor before me. What happened to the calm, logical leader I know? You've not been the same since…" Cliff stopped and shook his head.

"Go on. Spit. It. Out. I've not been the same since…?"

Cliff tried again. "There's the man society knows; there's the man I know, and there's the man you've become since you met Grace. Do you know what I think? I think Grace has made you aware that the man you are and the man you think you need to be are not the same person. And the truth is ugly. She's turned you inside out and you don't know what to do with yourself."

"Nonsense."

Cliff ignored him. "You want her, desperately; she fits the man you are, but you think you cannot have her."

"What would you have me do? I'm trying my damnedest to be honorable, yet every move I make—every decision I make—results in someone getting hurt. I try, but despite my noble intentions, everything turns out wrong."

"And you'll continue to suffer with that problem until you embrace the man you are. Until you choose to create the life you want. Take hold of it with both hands. You've only got one life to live, friend."

"I don't know how to be both. My private self is none of the ton's business. Society expects…"

"Who the hell cares what society expects? Hang society. Why do you care what those people think anyway? You don't have to live with them day in and day out for the rest of your life. Like a wife. Don't you realize the power you've amassed over the years and the influence you have because of it? Do you think your father cared what society thinks?"

He looked at his friend as he thought over Cliff's advice. Hope floated filled his chest. Peace beckoned in the distance. Could he do it? Could he tell society to piss off?

Possibly.

"Since when did you become a philosopher, old man?"

"I'm relieved you find that amusing. I'm through. I've said my peace. But we don't have time for me to continue blowing sunshine up your arse. We have a case to solve and we're wasting time here over something that is over and done with, for now. There's nothing you can do about it anyway, not until that shoulder's healed."

Cliff helped him from the floor, and he crawled back into bed, wincing as the wound in his shoulder throbbed with his movements.

Cliff carried on. "Now, we have this box that Grace found at Beckett House. It has the symbol for the Society engraved on the lid, but it's empty."

"Circumstantial evidence. It wouldn't put Swindon away or hang him for his crimes."

"I know, but while you were incapacitated, we got a note from MacLeod. Our friendly neighborhood assassin has confessed. Everything. He even told MacLeod where Swindon keeps his Society papers hidden at his place near the Park. They need me to retrieve them; I'm headed there now."

"Good. I hope to God you find something. Go then, I grow tired."

As Cliff turned to leave, the door opened, admitting none other than Aunt Harriett.

The duke scrambled to cover himself with his bed clothes.

"Aunt Harriett?" he said on a surprised gasp.

Aunt Harriett paid Ambrose no mind. She simply marched over—a fierce and determined look in her eye—and bashed him over the head with her umbrella. Then, she turned on a huff and walked out the door. Without uttering a word.

"Ouch!"

He heard Cliff laughing all the way down the stairs, while he sat in his bed now nursing a sore head in addition to his sore shoulder. Women.

* * * *

Swindon entered his study to find another note impaled on his desk, the same as before:

Writ of Execution

The Earl of Swindon

Tick. Tock.

He paled. And needed to change his trousers. Again.

* * * *

Oxford…

Grace stood in the middle of her father's shop. Her shop now. She still couldn't believe the transformation. Many of the details she recalled from her old life here had been recreated with obvious care.

She inhaled a deep breath and drowned herself in the atmosphere, the memories. She was glad to be rid of London and its smell. And the people, or most of them. This store was her future, and she was miserable. She had left part of her heart behind, and it would be a while before she was whole again.

She knew she should be thrilled at how perfectly her plans were working out. She had inherited this place and her childhood home above it. Dansbury had seen to that. She had enough capital to open her shop within in the next three months — and still be able to make ends meet — just — until her business took off. It all seemed perfect.

However, despite her good fortune, she was miserable with grief. True, Ambrose had been cruel — a real cad — but oh, how she loved him anyway, and her heart broke all over again. She should have looked forward to getting over her despair, but right now, it didn't seem possible.

She refused to dwell on his upcoming nuptials or she would lose her barely controlled composure completely. As it was, she was constantly on the verge of hysterics, and she held on to her sanity by a thread. Her emotional state was chaotic from bouts of near happiness, to grief, to heart-racing anxiety over what they had done.

What if I am with child?

Reflexively, she placed her hand to her stomach and imagined the child that could well be growing in her womb. She would love his child, and a small part of her hoped she was indeed *enceinte*.

For the most part, however, she felt uneasy over the possibility — she was somewhat afraid to face the prospect of the birthing and subsequent child rearing — alone. Of course, she had Bessie, but it wasn't the same as a husband — a lover.

She wouldn't call on Cliff as he asked; she couldn't pass off her child as his. He had his own life to live — his own love to find — and she wouldn't burden him with her mistakes. Of course, she certainly couldn't call on Ambrose.

She sighed, depressed over her maudlin thoughts. She knew she would be all right in the end, that she would survive, but the prospect was still frightening to contemplate if she found she were increasing.

"Have you thought about your story—what you plan to tell everyone should…you…you know…?" Bessie asked, with a pointed look at Grace's hand on her belly.

She jerked her hand away even though it was obvious Bessie had been watching and guessed at the direction of her thoughts.

"I hadn't, not yet, but I guess I should plan for the possibility, just in case."

"May I make a suggestion, dear?"

"Of course."

"I suggest you change your last name. You don't need to change your entire background—too many people will recognize you, having been gone only a year anyway, but perhaps just a small white lie is in order? I suggest you choose a new last name and pretend to be married…possibly a soldier's wife?"

"Yes, that does sound like the wisest course of action. He could be abroad…"

She shuddered. "Eventually, he'd have to meet with an untimely demise, but after the business is up and running smoothly, of course. When I could better afford to deal with my mourning?"

She felt mercenary—even if her 'spouse' was just a fictional character. She hated that she had to do this, live a lie, but it would be far worse should she find herself increasing sans husband. Her business would suffer then.

Why didn't I consider the consequences before?

The reality was she knew she wouldn't have done anything different even given all the time in the world to reconsider her actions. Sure, it hurt now. Her emotions were still volatile and frayed. The pain still simmered, constantly, just beneath the surface, but in the long run, she knew she would cherish the good things. She would remember her night with Ambrose fondly. She would move on, and it would no longer hurt, eventually.

Chapter 26

The night before the wedding…

Stonebridge paced his library floor, anxious for Cliff's return. Any minute now, Cliff would be back with whatever proof he had found at the earl's place near Stonebridge Park. Hopefully, he had found something. Anything. Otherwise…Well, he couldn't consider the alternative.

Stonebridge heard a horse racing up the street and ran out into the foyer just as his butler opened the front door to admit a messenger. He blasted forward and took the message directly from the courier, tearing it open while leaving Ledbetter to pay the young man.

Ambrose,

Nothing. Place cleared.

Cliff

Damn.

His heart sunk, but not for the obvious reasons. Not for caring about whether or not they had the proof they needed to bring charges against Swindon. Finally. After all these many years. No, he ached with despair born of loss.

He rubbed his chest as his thoughts crawled across his mind like snails attempting to traverse a pool of molasses, slow and tortured.

Time had run out; he was to be married in the morning. But did it really matter? He pictured a lifetime with Beatryce and her father, but his mind instinctively shied away from the thought.

Worse, he imagined a lifetime without Grace, and the agony was nigh unbearable. He doubled over, his stomach queasy and ready to review his last meal. His mouth watered in preparation of being sick, saliva dripping from his lips. The notion of never again seeing her smile, of never hearing her voice, of never touching her skin, was inconceivable and too painful to contemplate. He would never have the right to touch her again.

Was this love?

Is it love when she is the first thing you think of when you awaken and the last thing you think of until you fall asleep at night?

Is it love when you'd rather tear out your heart than never see her again?

It must be, for who would ever conceive of such a thing but one who is faced with the idea of never seeing, never holding, their dearest again?

The realization hit with force—a solid jab to the gut that brought him all the way to his knees.

I love her! I completely and utterly love her from the top of her head to the tips of her toes.

And though having no proof of Swindon's duplicity made everything infinitely more difficult, difficult was not impossible. And anything not impossible meant there was a chance.

I am a duke!

He held the highest and most powerful title in the aristocracy with more wealth than he knew what to do with, yet what use was having all of that power and position when he was powerless to control the direction of his life?

He sat back on his arse and leaned against the wall with a silly, stupid grin on his face. If any one of his staff saw him, they'd consider him a candidate for Bedlam.

He loved Grace Radclyffe. The more he said it, the happier he felt. And he refused to live without her. No, he was incapable of living without her. Society and their hypocritical judgments could go hang. He knew just what to do. He jumped off the floor with a newfound spring in his step. He had to get ready. He had to go get her.

* * * *

Dansbury House…
The next morning…

"Rise and shine…you lazy toff."

Ambrose smiled at the answering groan emanating from within the mound of blankets. The covers were rumpled and piled high in the middle of the large bed that dominated the bedroom. Somewhere within that nest of blankets lay his friend, Cliff.

Ambrose opened a second set of curtains and turned to see if the light was bright enough to highlight his sleeping friend; he'd already opened the bed hangings before shouting out his unconventional greeting.

He watched as Cliff opened one eye, searched the room, found him standing amidst the draperies, and glared with that one eye for what felt like a full minute. The sun interrupted his friend's stare by choosing to peek out from behind a cloud, bathing the room in more light. Cliff winced and squeezed both eyes shut.

Ambrose laughed at his friend's uncontrollable grimace. The bright light must've hurt, and it seemed to purposefully seek out his friend as always seemed to be the case when one was sporting a nasty hangover.

Ambrose resumed his duties—waking his friend and adding more light to the room—while whistling a jaunty tune and ignoring Cliff's discomfort. He jerked open another set of drapes; the curtain rings jingled as they rattled against their rod. "Why are you still abed?"

Cliff ignored him and all but growled, "What do you want? Just tell me, then go away."

"Don't you recall what day it is? It's my wedding day. Why aren't you up and dressed for it?" Ambrose pulled open the last set of drapes. Dust leapt into the air, dancing in the sunbeams. He fanned away the motes in front of his face and suppressed a cough.

Cliff moaned. "I don't like you right now, and I certainly don't like your fiancée, so of course, I'm not planning to attend your ill-fated nuptials. Remember? I told you an age ago..." Cliff's words tapered away as he dozed off again.

Well, Ambrose couldn't allow that, now, could he? He walked to the bed, bent over, and slapped his friend about the face, good-naturedly but with purpose, of course.

"Enough!" Cliff bellowed, swatting away Ambrose's hands. He rolled away and presented his back.

Ambrose really shouldn't take such joy in his friend's suffering, but he was walking too high in the clouds at the moment to care. He leaned in, undeterred by the outburst, and sniffed. "Damn, but you smell like a distillery, Cliff. Long night?"

"You could say that," Cliff murmured.

Ambrose plopped down on the edge of his friend's bed and leaned back against the footboard, causing Cliff to roll back toward him with the added weight. "Hmmm...sounds like an interesting story. I look forward to hearing about it...another time."

"Please. Hold your breath while you wait, but do it at your house. Your death would have me answering all sorts of inconvenient questions. Besides, disturbingly cheerful morning people make me ill. And since when did *you* become a disturbingly cheerful morning person, anyway?" Cliff burrowed into the bed clothes, his last words muffled by the thick quilt.

Ambrose had glimpsed Cliff's smile just before he disappeared beneath the covers. "Ha! I see you haven't lost your sense of humor with your head. Excellent. But seriously, I need you to get up." Ambrose nudged what he presumed was his friend's leg. "Now. I have a task for you."

Cliff poked his head out from under the covers. "Am I going to like this?"

"Oh, you're going to love it."

Cliff raised one brow in question, clearly unconvinced.

Ambrose laughed at the sight of Cliff's serious face, for the man sported rumpled hair and a thick crease down the side of his face from the press of sheets against his skin for too many consecutive hours; it was completely at odds with his thoughtful mien.

"Don't look at me like that. You will. You care too much about Grace to see her remain unhappy for the rest of her days, living and working without the man she loves. You'll relish this task. I promise."

"I'm almost afraid to ask, but, exactly, what are you planning?" Cliff's look suggested he didn't want to know the answer to that question.

Ambrose crossed his arms, all but daring his friend to disapprove. "I'm going to ask Grace to marry me."

Cliff lurched upright; the covers falling to his waist. "What? Are you crazy? Have you forgotten you're about to be married in...oh," he squinted over at the clock on the mantle, "about half an hour to someone else?"

"Of course, I haven't forgotten—could you?" Ambrose rubbed one hand down his face as he always did whenever he contemplated the fact that he'd almost married Beatryce. "Never mind. Don't answer that. I already know the answer. No, I'm simply not going to marry Lady Beatryce, and that's all there is to it."

Cliff cringed, then said, "Good God. It's about bloody time. But what about contractual obligations, your word, and all that other shite you've been spouting for the last month?"

Ambrose all but snorted. "Funnily enough, I never actually asked Lady Beatryce to marry me. We just announced our betrothal as if I had. And I never actually signed the betrothal contract either." Admitting it aloud made his heart feel lighter. It was amazing how freeing it felt to let go, despite breaking his implied word.

"Damn me, you're actually going to do this, aren't you?"

"You may depend upon it, and I need *you* to go to the church and inform Beatryce of the change of plans."

"Ha! Of course." Cliff fell back and threw his arm over his head. "But why don't *you* do it?"

"I don't have time. I don't want to waste another minute without my Grace. I need her like I need air, and I'm on my way to Oxford to tell her that, or something like it. I'm sure much begging and groveling will be involved."

Cliff laughed from beneath his arm, still hiding his eyes, but changed the subject. "What about our investigation? Did you get my note?"

Ambrose shook his head and stood. He understood his friend all too well. "I did. Don't worry about the place being cleared. I have a plan, but that's for later. Right now, you need to get up. You do want to make it to the church before all hell breaks loose, don't you?"

Cliff's grin, visible from below his armed sun block, was answer enough. Cliff loved setting the ton on its collective ear. "Well, I'd say good luck, then, but you don't believe in luck do you?"

"I've always thought of luck as a sentiment for the unprepared."

Cliff laughed. "So, you're prepared then?"

Ambrose's heartbeat fluttered at the thought of just how unprepared he was. "Perhaps not, but then, I met Grace, and I was wholly unprepared for her, yet she is the best thing that ever happened to me, so I might be willing to concede the possibility that not only does luck exist, but that I could use a bit of it from time to time. Especially now."

He could imagine Cliff's shocked expression at that sentiment. Yes, he'd been the all-too-level-headed, logical duke for far too long; it was time to relax his guard.

"And by the by," Ambrose added before stepping out the door, "I'll be paying you back for asking my woman to marry you...later."

And he laughed as he made his way down the hall and out the door to his future — to Grace.

* * * *

St. George's Church...
Hanover Square, London...
Forty-five minutes later...

"Where the hell is he?"

Dansbury leaned against the door frame, arms and legs crossed, as he watched Lady Beatryce pace the antechamber of St. George's Church. She had spoken out loud to herself, and she had yet to note his presence. He suppressed a stab of indignity over the fact that he was so easily overlooked.

The chamber was made up of marble and stone, and her footsteps and voice echoed loudly around the room. Since the groom had yet to arrive, her nervous wandering was understandable.

"Hello, Beatryce." His voice, tinged with sarcasm, added to the already heavy tension permeating the air.

Beatryce whirled around and faced him. Her eyes seemed to widen with fear before she snapped, "What are *you* doing here?"

"Let's just say I'm here to spread good tidings and cheer, and all that rot...though perhaps not for you."

She smirked, though her eyes betrayed her anxiety. "So are

you going to spread your good cheer or stand there staring at me all morning?"

He frowned at her unfortunate choice of words, but then forced a smile to his face. "Yes. Well. I am here to inform you that there has been a slight change of plans. Stonebridge, you see, has finally, shall we say, come to his senses? You see, he won't be joining us here today. He's headed to Oxford to marry Grace, his love."

Chapter 27

"Oh, God!" Beatryce screamed, her eyes unfocused in fright. She actually screamed.

Dansbury was stunned by the look of horror that flitted across her face as she cursed aloud. Her obvious fear threatened to undermine his resolve, but only for a moment. He only had to think of her last confrontation with Grace to harden his heart, but still, he watched her, wary. She was the consummate actress.

She rushed over, her eyes pleading. She grabbed him by the lapels of his jacket with both hands. "Please, Dansbury, please, you must take me with you. Please."

He was taken aback. Beatryce? Begging and fearful? When hell froze over! He checked the urge to look outside to see if it was snowing despite it being summer. He reminded himself that she was a gifted actress. She had nearly entrapped his best friend into marriage—a tremendous feat that—and he smiled at her knowingly. She was up to something. Though a part of his gut screamed at him that this wasn't an act—that she was genuinely frightened. It didn't matter. She had squashed any sympathy he felt for her through her actions towards Grace.

"I'm sorry, Lady Beatryce, but you're confusing me with someone who gives a damn."

He turned his back on her, prepared to leave.

"Wait."

Despite his better judgment, he stopped. It wasn't the force of her command that halted him, but the quiet, yet resigned confidence he detected in her voice. He turned to face her, his hands on his hip, brow raised in question.

"I can help you, if you help me. I can...I can lead you to what you need to know...to solve your investigation. I know where my father keeps his secret papers."

He was shocked. How the hell could she possibly know? He reached her in two long strides and grabbed her. He gripped her harshly, shaking her in his anger.

"Tell me what you know. Tell me now!" he yelled.

She held her hand up to shut him up. "Shhhh. Are you crazy? Lower your voice. First, get me out of here, safely and without being seen, and then I'll tell you what I know. Not before. And be quick about it."

He growled in frustration. She stood with her arms crossed, seemingly at ease and in command of the situation, but he noticed she kept looking at the door, fear flitting across her face with each glance.

Damn. He had no choice. He had to pursue any lead.

"Fine. Let's go."

He held out his hand. She took it without hesitation.

* * * *

Oxford...

He's likely married by now.

Grace wasn't sure exactly what time the festivities were to take place; she hadn't been invited, of course, but she knew it was today—and it nearly killed her, the pain was so powerful.

She hadn't bothered to get out of bed today—there was no way she would be able to see people with a smile on her face knowing that inside, her heart was breaking all over again.

Logic couldn't mend a broken heart, though it did stop her from making a fool of herself by flying back to London to beg him to take her back—not that it would have stopped the impending nuptials, but when you're heartbroken things rarely made sense.

She could just imagine how handsome he looked in his wedding finery. Perhaps he'd wear an emerald pin in his cravat to match his eyes. She rolled over and punched her fist into her pillow. How ridiculous was she to torment herself so by thinking such things?

She buried her face in her pillow to muffle her scream. Her bedroom door clicked open.

"Oh, B-Bessie, I'll be f-fine. I'll be d-down in a bit. Maybe. Eventually," came her muffled, sob-broken voice.

Male laughter made her jerk her head up in surprise. Had she finally lost her mind in her grief? It couldn't be him. He was probably on his way to his honeymoon by now.

"Actually, I'm not. And yes, I am really here."

Goodness, was she talking to herself? Out loud? She closed her eyes, but the tears fell regardless. She must be dreaming, but she didn't want to be.

"Yes, you are, and no, you're not dreaming, my love. I really am here."

She felt the bed dip as Ambrose sat beside her. She still hadn't looked away from her headboard—afraid to see an empty room and know for sure she was going mad. Now, with the undeniable evidence of the added weight to the side of the bed, she rolled over to her side and looked up at him.

There he was—looking down at her with love and tenderness in his eyes.

"Ambrose? How?"

She reached out to touch him, though still afraid she'd find he was a figment of her imagination.

"I'm not going to marry Beatryce, my sweet. In fact, I quite rudely left her standing at the altar…literally—well, hopefully Dansbury caught up with her and explained the way of things first; I didn't really have the time. I came here as fast as my horse could run."

"The way of things?"

Good God—it was like when they had first met in the garden so many months ago. Her brain was racing, unable to make sense of what was happening, unable to form coherent words, yet trying to process it all. "Silly woman. Don't you know? I love you." He slid off the bed and knelt beside it.

"Grace, I want to spend my life making you...us...our children...happy. I was cold and lonely—miserable—before I met you and you gave me a glimpse of how different—how much better—life was meant to be. I thought I knew what I wanted, but I was wrong. Now I know. All I want is you and the life we could have together. I never expected it to happen this way, but I can't bear to wait anymore. Will you make me the happiest of men? Will you marry me?"

She was stunned. There was no other way to describe it. She searched his eyes for the truth behind his words. His true desire. His words were more beautiful than she could have ever dreamt—words she had longed to hear so many times—including mere minutes ago. So why wasn't she throwing her arms around his neck and kissing him relentlessly between frantic screams of "yes"? It was what her instinct and her heart told her to do. It was what she wanted; yet still she hesitated.

"I'm not sure. Oh, how many times have I dreamt of hearing you say those words? And now that you've said them, I'm not sure. I don't know."

He lost the smile. She was sure he wasn't expecting her not to say yes.

"Grace, you love me. We love each other. I..."

"I know I do. I know you think you do. But is love enough? I need to know what kind of man you are. I thought I knew. The man I saw when I gave myself to you was the man of my dreams. But your actions after make me wonder if I only saw what I wanted to believe. Who are you, really, and do you even know?"

"I see."

"I don't see how—I'm sure I don't. I can't believe I'm saying this at all. I've been crying all night over the thought of you marrying Beatryce. I love you. But just like you thought you had to put aside your wants for the good of the estate, I find myself needing to make this decision with my head and my heart. My heart says yes, of course, yet you've been a certain type of man for most of your adult life. That day we spent together, when you pretended you were not the duke, I saw a man who was so much more. A man with compassion and strength. That is the man I need and who I want to be the father of my children. But is that man you?"

"Yes. I know it is. But let me show you. Come back to London with me. I'll prove it. I know it's inconvenient, but please, just believe in me."

Chapter 28

The Duke's London House, Stonebridge House…
Two days later, the afternoon…

Grace and Stonebridge arrived at the duke's London mansion two days later. On the way, he received a note from Cliff urging him to return to his London home post haste. Therefore, they went to Stonebridge House rather than to Aunt Harriett's house as planned.

He walked into the foyer and asked after Cliff.

"Lord Dansbury is in the green room with our guest," replied Ledbetter, his butler.

"Who is our guest, Ledbetter?"

"I couldn't say for sure, Your Grace, but she appears to be a lady."

"Interesting. Incidentally, do you have the morning paper on hand, Ledbetter?"

"Yes, of course, Your Grace."

"Good. Find the society pages and bring them to Miss Radclyffe. We'll be in the green room."

"Of course, Your Grace."

He and Grace climbed the two flights of stairs to the second floor which contained the guest rooms, including the green room, their curiosity piqued.

At the end of the hall, he could see Cliff pacing the floor outside a closed door. His friend was visibly agitated.

At their approach, Cliff looked up and acknowledged them with a nod, before he crossed his arms and leaned back against the door. As if he hadn't just been pacing the floor and mumbling to himself a few minutes ago.

He was surprised to see him so disturbed; he had never seen Cliff behave that way before.

Stonebridge, who hadn't stopped grinning since he decided not to marry Beatryce, spoke up. "I understand we have an unexpected guest."

"We do. She promised me concrete evidence. She all but guaranteed she could solve our investigation, but that was two days ago. If she tells us anything before I throttle her, it will be a bloody miracle."

He and Grace shared a curious glance. Right.

"May I?" he inquired, reaching for the door.

"By all means," said Cliff, whose face darkened with a scowl as he moved out of the way.

The door swung open to reveal Beatryce tied to a chair and gagged. Her eyes blazed with fury; her daggers sought out and aimed their threat at Cliff. She thrashed in anger and screamed through the cloth covering her mouth.

He wanted to fall to the floor, laughing, at the sight. Instead, he said, "I'm not surprised she hasn't told you anything." To Beatryce, he added, "Can I count on you to be civil if I remove this?" He pointed to the cravat being used as an effective muffler to her ire.

She offered one final scowl to Cliff before she looked back at him and nodded once.

"Excellent."

*

Stonebridge removed the cravat from Beatryce's mouth and stood back. She flexed her jaw and glared at Cliff as she poked her tongue into the corners of her sore mouth. His friend's scowl darkened in return.

Huh. His usually affable friend was acting deuced odd today.

Lady Beatryce turned away from Cliff and faced him. "I know you're investigating my father, and I know why. I can lead you to the evidence you need to put him away. Or better yet, hang him."

"Yes? And how did you come by all this information?"

"I notice e-v-e-r-y-t-h-i-n-g. I've seen the men watching my house; I've watched Dansbury searching my house." She shot Cliff a mocking brow as she said that. "And I know all about my father's involvement with the Society for the Purification of England. I know where he keeps his papers, including all of their silly, idiotic little Writs of Execution where they spell out who they intend to murder and why."

"I see." He stifled his excitement over the depth of her knowledge. "And what do you want in exchange for this information?" Finally, they would have proof!

She bit her lip for a moment, then visibly firmed her resolve. "Money."

"Hell—of course," Cliff interjected with a curse.

He held up his hand to forgo further outbursts from his friend.

Beatryce glared at Cliff and shouted, "Don't you *dare* judge me right now. I am putting my life on the line for your treasured Grace and your precious case."

She cleared her throat. She looked back at him and calmly continued, "And I want safe passage out of town; a quiet home to go to in the country; simple country clothes; and a new identity."

Cliff, who was back to leaning against the door, arms crossed, asked, "How do we know you aren't just as guilty as your father? I mean, it's clear you knew of his guilt and yet you've never said anything before now? Sounds highly suspicious to me."

She shot daggers at Cliff, again, before returning her attention to him. "Does he really need to be here?"

He barked out a laugh. "Probably not, but I'm just going to tell him everything anyway, so this saves time. Just answer the question: you must admit, your knowledge does cast you in a questionable light."

"I only discovered all of this recently—when I started to realize that my marriage plans were on shaky ground." She gave him a quick scowl over that. "I knew my father was behaving strangely…well, stranger than normal…and I had noticed peculiar men watching the house—so I set out to determine why. I broke into his office, found his hidden box, and picked the lock. Imagine my surprise at all I discovered, including that my father was behind the deaths of your father…and hers." She nodded at Grace.

Grace gasped.

"You didn't tell her, I see."

"Shut up!" yelled both men as Ambrose raced to comfort Grace.

"Grace, darling, we suspected the possibility, but we didn't know for sure."

Grace looked up at him with tears swimming in her eyes. He pulled her close and closed his arms around her. "Had I had proof…had I known for certain…Oh, Grace, I wouldn't have had you find out this way."

"I know…I know…Oh, poor Papa…" came her muffled reply.

He pulled back, looked down at her, and brushed away the tears that had fallen. "Do you want to leave? Maybe you shouldn't be here."

She looked over at Beatryce before saying, "Yes. Perhaps that would be best."

He started to leave with her, but she stopped him. "I'll be fine, Duke. You stay here. It's simply the shock coupled with the long journey. Not to mention everything else."

"All right, I'll ring for someone to escort you to a room where you can refresh and relax."

"That would be wonderful."

As Grace made to leave, she stopped in front of Beatryce and said, "Thank you for coming forth and telling us what you know."

Beatryce squirmed in her chair, clearly speechless and discomfited by Grace's kindness. He watched with pride swelling in his chest.

Well done, woman, well done.

Once she was gone, he turned to Beatryce and suppressed his anger at the callous way in which she imparted her knowledge. "All right, now, tell us what we need to know."

She raised her chin. "First, I have one more condition. Once the arrangements are made for my passage out of town, I want him to take me." She nodded at Dansbury.

"Like hell!" shouted Cliff.

Stonebridge gave his friend a speaking look for the unusual outburst. "Are you sure that's wise, Lady Beatryce?"

"No. But he's the only one I trust to keep me safe." She'd hesitated before uttering the word trust. "You must understand. My father is incredibly guilty and has done some horrid things, but I'm telling you someone else is out there pulling his strings. I don't know who—I've not an inkling, but think about it. My father can barely get out of his bed without assistance. He's out of breath just walking from the drawing room to the library. He's weak. I can't speak of the time when your father was killed, but any move he's made recently has been done out of fear and a touch of insanity. Someone else is behind all this."

"Done." He didn't hesitate.

"What?" shouted Cliff; the man looked at him as if he'd lost his mind. Perhaps he had.

He looked back at his friend. "I said done. You'll take her. You'll protect her. But until the arrangements are made, she'll stay here." He turned back to Beatryce. "Now, tell us what we want to know."

"Fine. But will you please untie me from this chair first? I cannot feel my arms anymore."

* * * *

After leaving the green room, Grace met a footman at the top of the stairs.

"The duke rang for someone to escort me to a guest room to rest."

"Certainly, Miss Radclyffe. This way."

Surprisingly, the footman led her up another flight of stairs where the rooms for family were located. He showed her to a feminine, floral room in blue and green. A fire was blazing in the hearth, and a maid was there laying out tea and cakes.

"Good afternoon, miss. I've laid out the paper you requested on the table here along with a tea tray."

"Thank you, Miss…?"

"Martha, miss. You may call me Martha. Your maid, Bessie, has put away your things, and is settling in upstairs at the moment. She said to ring if you need her."

"Thank you, Martha; I will. That will be all."

"Yes, miss."

After the maid closed the door on her way out, Grace walked over to the tea tray, her heart heavy with sorrow.

Oh Papa…

The tears fell as Grace collapsed into a chair before the table. She leaned forward, propped her elbows on the table, and sobbed quietly into her hands.

She wept for what felt like hours before her sobs began to subside. She sat up and took a look at the table. The tea was cold now, but she poured a cup anyway. As she was stirring her sugar, she noticed the society papers laid out before her — bits of the paper were smudged from her tears and she'd probably find newsprint on her face if she were to look. She laughed at the image.

She picked up the paper and began to read. Ambrose had obviously wanted her to read it for a reason. She scanned over various bits of gossip, including the biggest article of all, the Duke of Stonebridge not appearing at his own wedding, but she saw nothing of interest that he might want her to see. She looked again, and let out a squeak when she saw it. The notice was printed right in the center of the page in larger type with a box around it—she had read everything around the notice but the notice itself.

She put her hand over her mouth, and began to cry all over again as she read:

Ambrose Philip Langtry, 10th Duke of Stonebridge, announces his intention to ask Miss Grace Elizabeth Radclyffe, proprietress of the House of Grace fashion house in Oxford, for her hand in marriage…if she'll have him.

Twenty minutes later, Grace washed and composed herself before lying on the large tester bed. Someone knocked on the door.

"Come in."

She smiled as Ambrose, all disheveled and handsome as sin, walked in and looked around the room for her. He spotted her on the bed and smiled.

"Better?" he asked.

"Yes, better."

"Good. Do you want to talk about it?"

"Not about my father, but I do have questions. Did you find out what you needed to know from Beatryce?"

"We did."

"I'm glad." She chewed her lip.

"What else is on your mind, love?"

"Well, I was wondering. What will happen to Aunt Mary and the girls when this evidence becomes public? What will happen to my uncle?"

Ambrose rubbed the back of his neck. He clearly did not want to answer, but he did it anyway. "Honestly, Aunt Mary and her daughters will have to find a relative to take them in. But it will not be easy. These charges against your uncle? Murder, high treason? They are all quite serious. All his holdings will revert to the crown. As for Swindon, he will likely be executed. Grace, I realize he's your uncle, but these crimes, they are grave."

"I know. He is horrid. He killed our fathers. Though I pity him, I do, but I'm more worried about Aunt Mary and the girls. Especially the girls. They'll have difficulty, won't they? They certainly won't be accepted in society after this, will they?"

"No, I'm afraid they won't. Society is harsh and hypocritical. I'm afraid your cousins might even find it difficult for a relative to see past that and give them refuge. Life will certainly be very different for them."

She looked at her hands twisted together with worry. "I'm a relative," she whispered; then she peeked up at Ambrose. "Ambrose, we must do something. I cannot bear to think of little Adelaide homeless. I can't bear it at all."

Chapter 29

Beckett House London…
2 am…

The earl paused in the hall on his way to his study; he needed to catch his breath. He hadn't walked this fast in twenty years and he was hyperventilating, but he needed to make haste. He needed to arm himself. He needed to do something. That damn duke had stood him up, and now Beatryce was missing—the ridiculous cow.

He was going to vomit.

He pushed on. By the time he reached his study, his hands were shaking and he fumbled about as he tried to find the key to his locked study. He tried six different keys before he found the right one and his clammy, shaking hands made it difficult to fit the key to the lock.

At last, the door opened, and he stepped inside. It was dark, and what little light that was available came from the moon shining in the study windows. The fire was out, as were all the lamps. Good. He felt safer in the dark.

He moved into the room to the floor-standing globe on the far side of the rug. He struggled to slide it off—it was heavy—and he dropped the keys he was still holding as he did. The sound of keys landing on the hardwood echoed loudly in the dark room. He ignored them.

Once the globe was out of the way, he got on his knees and pulled up the now freed corner of the Aubusson rug. Argh. The weight on his knees was excruciating, but he had to ignore the pain. He found the trick release in the floor and pulled up several loosened boards that were normally hidden under the rug. He threw them haphazardly to the side as he worked, sweat dripping everywhere. The wood floor became slick.

When the hole he was making was wide enough, he reached in it for the box he had hidden there. He felt around in the dark and became panicked with worry, but alas, after a few minutes, he found it.

He pulled out the box, set it on the floor, and pushed it across the room as he crawled toward his desk. When he reached the chairs in front of his desk, he set the box on one and used the chair to pull himself up. It wasn't easy, and he hoped to God he never had to get on the floor again. He could barely stand.

But once he was, he placed the box on his desk and went to the book shelves on the far wall, looking for the secret book that was really a hidden compartment holding the key to his box. It was impossible to see in the dark, but he was too frightened to light a lamp. If someone were watching the house, he didn't want them to know he was in his study. Best for them to think he was in bed. Mary was there; maybe they'd mistake her for him.

He returned with the key and held the box up in the moonlight so he could find the keyhole—there.

He opened the box with haste, looked inside, and screamed for all he was worth, "Noooooooooo!"

It was empty. Immediately, the sound of steel striking flint sounded on both sides of the room, and before long, two lamps burned brightly, revealing the Marquess of Dansbury and the Duke of Stonebridge.

"Hello, Swindon. Looking for something?" asked the duke.

His eyes bugged out of his head with shock. He looked between the two men several times, as if he wasn't sure they were really there, before he moved. He spun around and glanced out the window before racing—or waddling—around his desk. He grabbed Stonebridge.

"Stonebridge, you must help me. Take me. I beg you. He'll kill me if you don't. Please. Please. Please. I'll tell you everything; I swear I will...just don't let him kill..." Those were the last words he ever uttered. The gun shot echoed loudly in the night. Swindon was dead before he hit the floor. Stonebridge and Dansbury looked up in time to see a cloaked figure race away from the window.

Chapter 30

The Duke's London House…
The next morning…

Grace scrunched her face. Something tickled the end of her nose. She opened her eyes. Above her, looking down, was Ambrose, who was tickling her with a feather from her pillow.

"Good morning," he said when she smiled.

"Hmmmm…morning," she responded in kind, then chuckled at the yawn that escaped her. "What time is it?"

"Almost ten."

"Almost ten? Goodness, I've slept for eleven hours."

She sat up and attempted to rub the sleep from her eyes. Ambrose reached over and picked up a cup from the table. He wafted it beneath her nose. The smell of hot chocolate titillated her senses.

"Hmmmm…chocolate in bed? A lady could get used to this." She took the cup from him. He blew on it before handing it over.

After a few sips, while Ambrose just sat there watching her, she placed the cup on her bedside table, folded her hands in her lap, and said, "Right. Tell me what happened."

Ambrose sat back against the footboard.

"I'm afraid I have some rather unpleasant news. Your uncle was murdered last night."

"Murdered? By who?"

"We don't know. A cloaked figure shot him through the window and ran off. Bow Street is looking into the matter."

"And Aunt Mary? How are the girls?"

"The girls were still sleeping when I left. Your Aunt Mary felt it best to wait and tell them in the morning. As for your Aunt Mary? Well, she seemed surprisingly glad, actually. She took to weeping at first, then began laughing hysterically. It was all rather odd and uncomfortable, to be honest."

"Really? Well, that is certainly unexpected. Laughing, you say?"

"Yes—in fits and giggles, then outright guffaws. A few of the runners had difficulty controlling their mirth, despite the grave circumstances. Apparently, it was catching."

"Strange. So what happens now? Does this mean Aunt Mary and the girls are safe or are they still at risk of losing everything once the evidence comes out?"

"Well, funny you should ask that. I mean, yes, if the evidence of your uncle's activities were to come to light, his property—the money, houses—would all be forfeit despite the fact that he is deceased, but it seems that in all the confusion last night, the evidence has disappeared."

"Disappeared?"

"Yes, disappeared…Unexpectedly, I might add."

"How could it just disappear?"

"I don't know. I gave the papers to Dansbury. He said he gave them to me. But we both looked, checked all our pockets…and…well…nothing."

She jumped up and threw her arms around him, her love.

"You would do this for me?"

"Darling, I have no idea what you are implying, but yes, I would do anything for you."

He kissed her. And it felt good. It felt wonderful.

He was just beginning to nuzzle and kiss her neck, when she pushed him away and asked, "What about Beatryce?"

"Beatryce and Dansbury are readying to leave town. She still might be in danger. It seems she was right in that someone else is involved, but none of the evidence we found in your uncle's study gives us a single clue. Everyone mentioned by name is already dead, so for now, she will remain in hiding; your aunt will be putting it about that she is visiting family on the continent. Beatryce will be safe with Dansbury — if they don't kill each other first."

They both laughed at the thought.

"Why aren't Aunt Mary and the girls in danger, too? If Beatryce is in trouble…"

"They clearly know nothing. I'm not worried. Now, enough about murder and mayhem. Where were we?"

"I believe, Your Grace, you were about to ask me to marry you."

Ambrose, who had been leaning in for another kiss, froze, his lips still puckered. He pulled back and cocked his head.

"What did you say?"

"I said, I believe, Your Grace, you were about to ask me to marry you."

He grabbed her hands and slid to his knees on the steps to the bed. "Well, we wouldn't want people to think I ever denied a lady anything, now would we?"

He cleared his throat. "Miss Grace Radclyffe, proprietress of fashion, voice for the less fortunate, and the love of my life, will you marry me?"

"Yes. Yes. YES!" she yelled and pulled him into her arms.

The door to her room burst open, and Bessie and Aunt Harriett practically fell into the room.

"Congratulations," they both shouted.

"It's about time; thought I was going to have to beat some sense into the both of you," added Aunt Harriett.

"My," Grace said, startled by the unexpected intrusion, "were you listening at the door?"

"No…" said Bessie.

"Of course," said Aunt Harriett at the same time. "What kind of guardian would I be if I allowed my ward and my nephew alone in her bedroom without putting my eye to the key hole to make sure no shenanigans were going on? Had you made any further advances on her, young man, I would have marched right in and boxed your ears, boy, and don't you doubt it for a moment."

"I would never doubt you for a moment, Auntie, I swear."

"Now," she continued, "since Grace is officially in mourning, and I know that neither of you want to wait, Bessie and I have seen to the packing of a small valise for the both of you so you can head off to Gretna immediately. No sense in wasting a moment, I say."

Ambrose laughed and looked at Grace. "What say you, love? Fancy throwing convention completely to the wind and running away with me? I'm willing if you are."

Grace's ensuing smile was brighter than the sun. "Why not? Let's start off as we mean to go on. Let's set the ton's tongues wagging."

And that's how Grace Radclyffe, fashion designer, dress maker and voice for the less fortunate, started her unconventional life as the 10th Duchess of Stonebridge.

Epilogue

Six years later…

What a beautiful morning. Grace walked along the garden path, her bonnet, shoes and stockings in hand, and looked at the beautiful land surrounding her. Stonebridge Park was her home now and she loved it here more than any other place in the world.

She smiled as she heard her daughter laughing and calling her name from somewhere behind the bushes.

"Mummy, Mummy…"

Five year old Mairi ran around the corner of a hedge, shoes in hand, her long hair streaming out behind her.

I wonder where she gets it from?

Mairi laughed gaily as she ran into Grace's open arms.

Almost immediately, Ambrose came running around the corner giving chase, laughing and, yelling, "I'm going to get you, love."

He halted at the sight of his wife tapping her foot, her arms folded across her chest. She looked down at him, one brow lifted questioningly. Mairi stood to the side, watching their interaction.

"Ahem…Is this the appropriate conduct becoming a duke and the example you set for our daughter of proper behavior and decorum?" Grace said in her most haughty voice. She sounded full of disapproval.

Ambrose grinned ridiculously. He was in his shirt sleeves—sans coat, waistcoat, and cravat—and his valet, Bryans, was probably having an apoplexy right now over the grass stains on his knees and elbows. She tried hard to look stern.

"Of course, not, dear. Now, this…this is the proper behavior of a peer of the realm…"

And Grace screamed delightfully as he tackled her to the ground. Of course, both of them laughed uproariously at his silly antics. Mairi, not wanting to miss out on all the fun, jumped on top the melee, laughing merrily as well. They were, at last, a happy family; full of peace and joy. Love and life. For ever and ever.

The End

Stay tuned for Clifford Ross, Marquess of Dansbury's story… What the Marquess Sees.

About Amy Quinton

Amy Quinton is an author, wife, and full time mom living in Summerville, SC. She enjoys writing (and reading!) sexy historical romances. In her spare time, she likes to go camping and canoeing. She also loves to sew, knit, and crochet (I ♥ Ravelry!). Amy graduated from the College of Charleston, a liberal arts college in beautiful Charleston, SC. She worked 10 years in the computer industry as a software designer before becoming a full time mom, and now, a full time novelist.

www.amyquinton.net

CPSIA information can be obtained
at www.ICGtesting.com
Printed in the USA
LVHW091811230819
628744LV00003B/347/P